Eve of Destruction

Rochelle Kaplan

Published by FastPencil Publishing

Eve of Destruction

First Edition

Print edition ISBN: 9781495831096

http://www.fastpencil.com

Printed in the United States of America

Table of Contents

Chapter 1 Saturday Night

Lisa Benton absentmindedly tapped her boot against the bar stool to the beat of a song coming out of the vintage jukebox, subliminally agreeing with Dwight Yoakam's musing about being a thousand miles from nowhere. Far from home herself, desiring to be in no place in particular, Lisa air-toasted the country singer, swigging her Heineken straight out of the bottle. How appropriate for someone in this dive bar to choose that song out of any number of tunes in the machine.

Sitting alone at the bar in some godforsaken Phoenix suburb, Lisa closed her eyes, feeling the alcohol slowly working its numbing effects on her central nervous system, wondering if the next song would be another suitable number to match her mood. She'd impulsively driven to Arizona following her unfortunate confrontation with Detective Derrick Miller and his lover and homicide partner, Sylvie Stevens atop the dead-end road in Fallbrook, California. Grateful for narrowly escaping death, having sustained only superficial injuries, Lisa had slipped away unnoticed when the cops arrived on the scene. God only knew if either Derrick or Sylvie was still alive, and at this relatively serene moment, Lisa couldn't have cared less.

Sensing someone's unwelcomed presence, she opened her eyes and turned to her left, spotting a man in a white cowboy hat at the far end of the bar smiling and tipping his beer bottle in her direction. Freezing, acting like she hadn't noticed him, Lisa diverted her gaze toward the jukebox, just as Dwight's song ended. Nonchalantly lifting her bottle of beer, eyeing its contents, she quickly downed the remaining dregs, then slammed it down on the counter.

On cue, the female bartender slid another Heineken in front of Lisa, offering her a sly smile.

"Oh, sorry," Lisa said sheepishly. "I didn't mean to, uh...I didn't want other beer. I was just–"

"No need to apologize," the bartender said evenly. "It's from the gentleman at the end, in the white cowboy hat."

Lisa quickly glanced at the man and shook her head, then matter-of-factly said, "That's very kind of him, but I can't accept it. I have to get going."

"Nonsense, sweetie. He's a regular and he'd be very insulted if you refused. Besides, he's harmless." The bartender waved her hand dismissively and offered another guileful smile. "He just likes pretty ladies."

Lisa swiveled in her seat, consciously turning away from the man. "Well, I have no intention of insulting anyone," Lisa said apologetically, "but all the same, I've had my fill. Can you cash me out please?"

"Absolutely, sweetie, though Jared will be hurt, and it may take his ego a while to heal." She placed the handwritten check near Lisa's empty beer bottle. "See you again?"

"Doubtful," Lisa said, slapping a ten-dollar bill on the counter. "Movin' on to greener pastures."

"You're not from around here, are you?" the bartender asked, grabbing the money, looking Lisa in the eye.

"No, I'm not. Is it that obvious?"

"Not really, it's just that–"

"Where're you off to, pretty lady?" Jared, the man in the white cowboy hat had suddenly appeared behind Lisa, his hands firmly planted on her shoulders.

"I've, uh, got to go," Lisa said, stiffening, turning to face him, her eyes narrowed, studying his face.

"But it's still early! And it's Saturday night for Pete's sake," he said, sliding his hands down her arms. "C'mon, sit yourself back down and let me buy you a drink. I promise I won't bite."

"I really do have to get going," Lisa said sternly, wriggling out of his grasp, grabbing her purse off the hook under the bar, and slinging it over her shoulder.

"What's up with you? Got a hot date or something?" Jared seemed offended, agitated, his eyes dark as agate.

"As a matter of fact, I do." Lisa gruffly brushed past him and hustled to the front door, not looking back at him.

"Well, fuck you, you *bitch!*" Jared shouted after her. "You probably have a hot date with your cat!"

CHAPTER 2 SATURDAY NIGHT

Chynna Leigh Lindley blinked away tears and clumsily shook her hair out of her eyes, staring at the dark, empty road in front of her. Her boyfriend, Axel, was at the wheel of his beat-up Mazda Miata, driving erratically toward town, anticipating a large cash payout later that night. The two lovebirds had been smoking meth before they got into the car, priming themselves for another night of street hustling. Having heard about a new, prolific spot on the corner of Baseline and Beck—frequented by transients looking for quick, cheap diversions—Axel could barely contain himself with excitement.

Axel couldn't have given a rat's ass what Chynna thought about their new destination. She had no say in the matter if she wanted to keep an ever-flowing supply of crank around. The bitch was at his mercy, having neither friends nor family members concerned with her welfare. Even though she was just 19, Chynna had burned all her bridges with everyone she'd ever known. And, if she were to die prematurely, no one would care, much less ask how she met her untimely demise.

Approaching the intersection of the thoroughfares, Axel searched for a driveway leading into the Candlewood Apartments, an overpriced haven for short-term renters, many of whom had just relocated to Phoenix and had not yet found a home or an apartment. Sliding into a parking spot a good distance from the rental office, Axel snorted loudly and ran his finger under his nose to wipe away snot. Glancing over at Chynna, he regarded her contemptuously, then slapped the left side of her face.

"Wake up, bitch! Time to get to work," said Axel, slapping her neck this time.

"Stop it, Axel, you're hurting me!"

"You want me to *really* hurt you?"

"No," Chynna whined, instinctively bringing her hands up to her face, cowering in fear.

"Then get the fuck out and get to work. We ain't making any money jus' sittin' here in the car." Axel shoved her left shoulder.

"Okay, okay. Just gimme a minute to freshen up."

Chynna reached into her backpack, pulled out a makeup bag and opened a small compact containing a mirror. Staring at her face, she cringed when she saw her reflection. Dabbing on foundation, she tried to cover up a new patch of breakout on her chin but was unhappy with the results. Sighing loudly, she shut the compact and threw the makeup bag into her backpack.

"No one's gonna notice your zits in the dark anyway," Axel said deridingly, "so don't be so damned concerned with it."

"I just wanna look presentable. What's wrong with that?" Chynna reached for the handle, but before she could pull it open, Axel yanked her long hair, jerking her back.

"Just get the fuck out and get to work," he said, shoving her hard against the door. "You better come back with some decent money this time or–"

"Or what?" Chynna asked, suddenly confident.

"Don't make me hurt you, bitch. Don't make me hurt you."

Chapter 3 Saturday Night

Elizabeth Canton flinched as she draped an ice pack around her neck, closing her eyes and leaning back comfortably onto two propped-up pillows on her bed. The unusually high humidity hitting Southern California the past two days had taken its toll on her, sapping her of her typically high energy, precluding her from participating in her favorite activity, target shooting. She'd been looking forward to a night session at the range tonight, but then her new instructor, DJ—for Daniel James—Denninger cancelled the last minute and the sticky weather pushed her over the edge.

Truth be told, she had a crush on her shooting instructor that for the life of her couldn't be qualified. While not homely, he was not particularly good looking, was definitely too young, and to top it off, he was a bit shorter than she was. Still, DJ exuded a seductive vibe that was irresistible to Elizabeth, and he smelled good, too. She'd met him by chance at a new range off Washington Boulevard when she'd sought a gunsmith to work on her .45 SIG Sauer, literally bumping into him as she turned around to leave. Offering him a wide smile and an apology, Elizabeth surprised herself by how turned-on she became in that brief encounter.

Had she not dodged another close call—this one a few weeks ago when Damian Jenkins, bodyguard to the now deceased pervert, Richard Van Heusen, tracked her whereabouts to a hospital where she'd been recovering from an auto accident—Elizabeth would have never met her new love interest. Recalling fondly her initial—albeit accidental introduction—to DJ, she shifted her position on the bed and reapplied the ice pack by turning it over. Inhaling deeply and shutting her eyes, she envisioned DJ hovering over her, waiting to plant soft, damp kisses on her face and neck. It was all she could stand just imagining it when her doorbell buzzed, interrupting her fantasy.

Tossing the icepack onto the bed, she shuffled lazily to the front door, grabbing her .22 off the dresser in her bedroom. Annoyed, not expecting anyone at this late hour, Elizabeth tightly gripped her pistol, keeping her finger away from the trigger as she eyed the person through the keyhole. Opening the door slowly, she slid the gun up the door jamb, stopping at eye level.

"State your name and business, mister, or I'll shoot."

"DJ Denninger, ma'am, at your service!"

"Be careful what you offer, sir," Elizabeth said, lowering the pistol. "I'm a very demanding customer."

With few streetlights illuminating the highway, Lisa drove cautiously, heading west, hoping to reach Los Angeles by morning with as few stops as possible. Why she ever thought to come to Arizona in the first place still mystified her. Except for the Grand Canyon and Sedona, Arizona as a whole and the greater Phoenix area in particular was soulless; one big, culture-less, boring desert inhabited by retirees, sunbirds and meth heads. Still, needing a place to heal for a few weeks after her skirmish with Derrick and Sylvie last month, she thought the dry air would be more suitable than a coastal climate.

Phoenix was nowhere she wanted to be for more than a few days, much less a few weeks, and not liking the vibe of the area, she didn't want to waste any more time. Jared, the cowboy in the white hat at the dive bar in Gilbert, turned out to be an omen: get the hell out of Dodge.

Glad to have nearly completed the Highway 202 Loop around Phoenix, Lisa was within a few miles of Interstate 10 when her low-fuel light illuminated on her dash, forcing her to seek a service station. Fortunately, she spotted one within a few blocks of exiting the freeway. After filling up her tank, Lisa breathed a sigh of relief when she saw the onramp to the interstate up ahead, to the left.

But her escape from Phoenix would be delayed when she heard a man and woman shouting, then noticed a scuffle on the other side of street. A large male was dragging a scantily clad woman by her hair through a parking lot in which a sleazy motel was situated. Unable to make out the words the woman screamed, Lisa knew she was distressed and demanding to be let go. Alarmed, unsure if she should meddle in something that didn't concern her, Lisa impulsively decided to drive to the lot to help the woman.

Screeching into the lot, her car's high beams blinding the man, Lisa watched the perpetrator suddenly switch directions, pulling the woman toward the motel. Sensing danger, Lisa floored the gas and nearly knocked the duo over as she sped to the motel's entrance. But before she could exit her car, someone else had pulled up next to her: a disheveled young man in an older model sedan with a large dent on the driver's side door.

Unsure of the relationship of this new person to the duo, Lisa debated inserting herself into a mess that could suddenly turn ominous. Still, the woman's screams had increased exponentially, and the massive man now had her in front of one of the motel room's doors. God only knew what he'd do to her once he had her inside. Quickly jumping out of her vehicle, Lisa ran smack into the disheveled guy, who'd positioned himself in her path. Stepping back, smelling a strange odor radiating from his clothing, Lisa glared at him, his pupil-less eyes glinting back at her in the dark.

"Get out of my way, dude," Lisa said, trying unsuccessfully to go around him.

"Who the fuck are you and where the fuck do you think you're going?" the tall, disheveled guy asked, jerking from side to side, blocking her movement.

"I said, get out of my way. I don't have time for chitchat." Lisa glared at him again, fearlessly boring her eyes into him.

"Tough chick, huh? Is that what you think you are?" he said, folding his arms over his chest, puffing up his scrawny body. "Let me tell you somethin' bitch. No one talks back to me. Especially bitches." He then scrunched up his face and poked two long fingers into Lisa's chest.

Stumbling back, Lisa quickly righted herself and before the disheveled guy knew what happened, she had her .45 jabbed into the left side of his ribs, her left hand clenched hard on his right wrist, twisting it backwards awkwardly.

"The fuck you doin' bitch?" he pleaded, moaning in pain, trying in vain to wriggle out of her grasp.

"Just a sample of what you can expect from a bitch like me when you piss me off."

"Let go of me, you cunt," he cried. "Do you know who I am?"

"Don't give a fuck who you are," Lisa said, twisting his wrist behind his back. "But I can assure you you'll be deader than a doornail if you don't get out of my way."

"Fuck you, bitch!" he said, spitting in her direction, but she ducked away in time.

"No, actually fuck you!" Lisa said, pushing him away, firing two rounds, purposely missing his right ear by millimeters. But it was enough to scare him off, running into the darkness.

CHAPTER 4 SATURDAY NIGHT, LATE

Tossing back her second Newcastle in fifteen minutes, Lonnie Dautremont slammed the bottle down on the bar, signaling the bartender for another. When the ale arrived, Lonnie thanked the female bartender, then asked for a shot of Wild Turkey.

"Are you sure?" the bleached-blonde bartender asked over the din.

"Of course, I'm sure. Why would you ask such a question of a customer?"

"Just wanna make sure. I mean, you seem to have had—"

"Had what, *enough*? Is that what you were gonna say?" Lonnie took a long swig of the brown ale. "Actually, I'm just getting started."

"Rough night?" the bartender asked before turning around to snag the bottle of Wild Turkey off the back shelf.

"Rough year. What else is new?" Lonnie watched her pour the bourbon.

"Here you go, hon. Hope things work out for ya."

"I doubt it, but I can always have hope, right?" Lonnie downed the bourbon before the bartender blinked.

"Another?"

"Sure, sweetie. If you insist." Lonnie winked at the young woman.

"You're funny," the blonde giggled. "I'm not insisting on any-thing."

"Well, you coulda fooled me," Lonnie washed the bourbon down with more ale. "I think you're flirting with me."

"Now that would be against the club's rules." More nervous gig-gling as she set down the shot of bourbon. "No flirting with cus-tomers."

"Right. Like that's never happened in real life." Lonnie grabbed the second shot and gulped it down even faster than the first. "You're too young for me anyway. Not that I wouldn't mind having a youngster like you for a change."

"Hey, I'll be right back," the blonde bartender said timidly. "Gotta take care of the gal at the end of the bar."

"Story of my life."

Lonnie watched enviously as the cute, young blonde sauntered over to a hot brunette at the end of the bar. Finishing her New-castle, Lonnie continued to glare at the two hotties commiserating about something or other, just out of hearing range. Her blood boiling, her jealousy taking ahold of her, Lonnie waved her arms to try to get the bartender's attention. When she wouldn't respond, Lonnie raised her voice in exasperation.

"Check please, miss. Gotta go. Got people to see."

"Sorry, it's just that I haven't seen her—"

"I don't give a fuck about you two not having seen each other in who the fuck knows how long," Lonnie said, spittle spraying the bar. "What are you, a couple of schoolgirls? Jesus. I was here first, and I need my check. Or do you want me to walk out without pay-ing?" Lonnie breathed heavily, her nostrils flaring.

"No need to be rude," the bartender said, clearly horrified. "I'll get you the check."

Without looking at Lonnie, the bleached-blonde bartender slid the check toward Lonnie, keeping her distance, turning her back on her immediately.

Slapping a twenty-dollar bill on top of the check, Lonnie grabbed her jacket and stared at the hottie's backside.

"You young chicks are all the same," she said, hoping the bartender would turn around. "I could fuck you better than she could. I could fuck you like there's no tomorrow. Sadly, you'll never find out how good it could be."

Chapter 5 Sunday Morning

Tilting back in a recliner, Lisa regarded the young woman sleeping soundly on the double bed in Room 8 at the Super 8 Motel in a working-class suburb of Phoenix. She'd fallen asleep on her stomach, fully clothed, about an hour after Lisa rescued her from an uncertain fate with a john. Relying on her keen instincts dealing in the past with predators and ex-cons, Lisa had flashed a phony badge at him in the dark when she'd approached the two. He then ran off like the coward he was.

Listening now to the girl's steady, shallow breathing, Lisa studied her profile, obscured by a wisp of hair, wondering what her name may be. Did she look like a Diane or a Barbara? Perhaps a Cindy or a Kathleen? More likely, she went by some pseudonym like Blaze, or Velvet or even Montana. *Whatever your name, sweet, lost girl, how did you ever end up turning tricks for a lowlife pimp?*

The young woman inhaled deeply, shifting her head on the pillow, causing the loose strand of hair to flutter as she exhaled. Alerted, Lisa got up and moved closer to her, listening to her breathing, waiting for it to return to normal. Carefully moving the strand away from her face, Lisa immediately noticed the hideous breakout on her chin, immediately realizing the cause. Gently stroking her hair, Lisa started when the girl snorted loudly and turned onto her back.

Opening her eyes, the girl asked softly, "Where am I? Who are you?"

"You're alright, honey," Lisa said soothingly. "He's gone and he's not gonna hurt you anymore."

"Who's gone?" she asked, her eyes filled with terror. "Axel?"

"Is that his name, sweetie? Is that the name of your pimp?"

"Pimp? What the hell are you talkin' about?" The girl pushed herself up to a seated position on the bed, clumsily adjusting the pillows behind her back. "Who the fuck are you? What are you doin' here?"

"My name is Hannah, sweetie," Lisa said, using her pseudonym. "I'm here to help you. Axel is gone. Never gonna be—"

"You are *not* here to help," she said, pointing a shaky finger at Lisa. "I can tell. You're just like the rest of them, always sayin' shit and never deliverin' on it."

Ignoring her outburst, Lisa walked into the bathroom and filled a glass with tap water. When she brought it back into the room, the girl had her head in her hands, whimpering silently.

"Here you go, drink up," Lisa said, handing the glass of water to her. "You need to stay hydrated."

The girl looked up at Lisa, her eyes rimmed in red, her sallow skin appearing even more sickly in the ambient light emitted from the desk lamp.

"I don't need no fuckin' hydration, lady," she said, reluctantly taking the glass of water from Lisa. "I need Axel. What have you done to him?"

Concentrating on the millions of minuscule flecks of dust congregating in a streak of light streaming in through the window above the kitchen sink, Loretta Menifee wondered how long it would take to count them all and if she did, would she do it accurately. Needing to take her mind off a dreaded meeting that would take place in less than an hour with her son's social worker, Loretta forced herself to think of anything obscure and nonthreatening if only to clear her mind of what may happen at the end of that meeting. Charlene Mullins-McMillan, LCSW, had scheduled the last-minute conference with her yesterday because, as she so plainly put it, "It's been months since I checked up on you, Ms. Menifee, and I have time tomorrow morning." What Charlene really meant to say was that her boss was getting heat from the big boss downtown and reports needed to be completed before the end of the year.

Loretta recalled hearing a news report on TV recently about the overall failures of the county's social services division—in particular, child protective services. In some cases, years would go by without proper monitoring of children in the system with more than a few kids dying while in the care of their foster parents. Had someone at CPS gotten a wild hair up his ass, zeroing in on single mothers?

A chill went up Loretta's spine as she looked away from the stream of dust and stared at the dishes piled up in the sink. Better wash them before Ms. Mullins-McMillan shows up, she thought, turning the hot water on and running her cold hands through it. *Would she give me a pass again this time, or delve into things that were none of her business? Would she notice that Kendall had bruises on his arms and assume I'd beaten him?*

CHAPTER 6 SUNDAY MORNING

Forgetting she was sharing her double bed with her new beau, Elizabeth flopped over onto her back and stretched out her right arm, poking DJ in the eye with her index finger. Instantly jarred awake, DJ swatted her hand away, then rubbed his eye with his knuckle.

"You don't need any more shooting lessons, babe," DJ said, continuing to rub his eye. "Your fingers are more dangerous than your loaded guns,"

Elizabeth propped herself up on one elbow and looked sheepishly at DJ. "Oh, honey, I am so sorry, I forgot, uh, you were here, and—"

"I'm crushed," DJ said, feigning displeasure, "in addition to being injured."

"No, that's not what I meant, I, uh, it's just that, I'm not used to—"

"It's okay, really, babe. You don't have to dig yourself into a bigger hole." DJ chuckled and stroked the tip of her nose.

Frowning, Elizabeth crossed her arms defensively, looked down at her lap and sulked.

"What's the matter with you all of a sudden?" DJ rolled over, straddling her, his knees pinning her legs, his hands trying to unclench her arms. "Last night you were only *too* happy to practically rape me, and now—"

Elizabeth snapped her head up and glared at him, her nostrils flaring. "Don't ever say that to me again. *Ever!* You have no idea how, uh, what I've been—"

DJ rolled over onto his back, shaking his head, confused. "Don't say what? Rape? You know I'm only joking; it was just an expression." He shook his head. "Look, I'm sor—"

"*Sorry?* How can you even—" Elizabeth stopped, then took a deep breath, holding it for several seconds. When she blew it out noisily through her mouth, she shook her head and slumped her shoulders. Turning toward DJ, she bit her lower lip, then forced a half-smile.

"I'm sorry, DJ. I, uh...it's just that there are some things in my former life that still affect me. Okay? Things I've obviously never told you—never had a reason to tell you till now. So, please forgive me for my, uh, overreacting."

DJ pulled her close, then said softly, "Nothing to forgive, babe. I get it. I really do."

Timothy Benton stared out of the ceiling-to-floor plate-glass window in his private office of his family's successful business, Ogilvie Wealth Management on Wilshire Boulevard in the heart of Beverly Hills, pondering whether to open a package that had arrived via FedEx this morning. Hardly ever coming into the office on a Sunday, Tim stood in front of the expansive window, knowing it would be prudent to come in, having received a phone call from the building's lead security officer earlier in the day.

"Got a package for you, sir and I went ahead and signed for it," Thomas Davis had said authoritatively. "Do you want me to bring it up to your office or hold onto it till tomorrow morning?"

"Who's it from?" Tim had asked.

"No return address other than a FedEx location in Phoenix."

"Phoenix? I don't do any business with anyone in Arizona."

"What should I do with it, sir?"

"How big is the package?" Tim had tried to conceal his curiosity.

"About the size of a shoebox. Should I take it up—"

"I'll be there in fifteen minutes, Tom. Thanks for the call."

Looking east, regarding the skyscrapers in downtown Los Angeles ringed in afternoon haze, Tim racked his brain to recall anyone he knew who lived in Phoenix. No one came to mind, causing him to become a bit more agitated about the contents of the package on his desk. Never one to simply accept things at face value, always suspicious of unexpected or unsolicited items, Tim turned his attention to the box. Scrutinizing it, he now noticed black markings on the side, as if the sender crossed out a previously used name and address from a prior shipment. Not that something like that should call undue attention, but it was as shoddy as it was unprofessional.

Still, unable to contain his curiosity, Tim scooted over to his desk, sat down in his oversized swivel chair and placed his hands on the box. Caressing it as if he were about to bless it, Tim raised the package and lightly rattled it. Hearing nothing loose inside, sensing it was only dry goods—perhaps paper or notebooks—Tim carefully placed it back on the desk. Reaching for a box cutter in the middle drawer, he poised the knife at one end of the box and was about to insert it when his office phone rang. *What the hell? Who knew I was here other than Tom?*

Having only made an initial cut, he removed the knife and placed it atop the package, staring at the phone. Debating whether to answer it or not, Tim's curiosity once again got the better of him, and he submitted.

"Hello, this is Tim."

Lonnie wasn't sure what she sensed first: a shard of bright light penetrating through the blinds and finding her half-opened eyes or the sharp knife cutting through her brain, slicing it to bits. Did she really have that much to drink last night, or was it the combination of ale and Wild Turkey that contributed to her hangover? Stupid, stupid, she thought, not a wise choice. Then, fully opening her right eye, Lonnie allowed the events at the bar last night to come flooding back to her with clarity.

Fucking cunts, she thought, rolling onto her right side to avoid the sunlight. Just who do they think they are? Prancing around, all cunt-like as if they had not a care in the world. All because they're young and hot. Well, *fuck you cunts!* One day you'll be old and fat like me. Then you'll know what it feels like to be unloved, unwanted and alone.

Not that Lonnie was alone, though she may as well be, considering how her selfish girlfriend, Loretta, was trying to cut her out of her life. *All because she claimed I abused her son, which is a total and complete lie. Kids need to be disciplined and Loretta was doing a shitty job of it. Someone had to instill discipline otherwise the kid would grow up to be spoiled!*

Lonnie pressed the sides of her head to alleviate the agony, but the white-hot pain persisted, forcing her to place a pillow over her head. She had to get up and get over to Loretta's place before...before what? She couldn't think with the unrelenting pain in her head. Before Loretta disappeared with the kid and then she'd really have no one in this world to love her.

Chapter 7 Sunday Afternoon

Lisa never had to answer the young woman's question about Axel, as the half-tablet of Xanax she'd crushed and diluted in her glass of water took effect quicker than she'd thought. Watching her sleeping soundly again, Lisa searched the room for a purse or wallet, anything that might hold her identification. When Lisa had freed her from the deadly clutches of her john—who'd been dragging her through the parking lot by her hair—she'd asked the young woman if she had a room. With much difficulty, and while whimpering, she'd whispered, "Eight."

Helping her into bed, Lisa had made sure she was as comfortable as possible, pulling her hair back into a ponytail, throwing an extra blanket on her and then elevating her knees with a pillow. But the girl had immediately rolled over and fallen asleep on her stomach. If that's what made her happy, so be it.

Finally spotting a backpack tossed in the corner of the room, Lisa opened it, finding a small makeup pouch, a sealed plastic bag with an assortment of prescription pills, a half-drunk bottle of water and at the very bottom, a wallet.

"Chynna Leigh Lindley," Lisa said aloud, scrutinizing the Arizona Driver License. "Date of Birth, June 24, 1998." Making you just 19 years old. "Surprise, Arizona." Wherever that was.

"Well, Miss Chynna Leigh Lindley, what the heck is your story and why the hell are you turning tricks?"

Loretta sat in the cluttered living room of her tiny apartment, her arms snugly wrapped around her 8-year-old son Kendall's upper body as he stood tall and proud, awaiting the arrival of his social worker, Charlene Mullins-McMillan. Wearing a green, long-sleeved pullover and jeans, Kendall understood the gravity of Ms. Mullins-McMillan's visit and promised his mother he'd be on his best behavior. He'd assured his mom he would only answer her questions and not elaborate or offer any other information.

"Are you gonna leave me, mommy," Kendall's eyes filled with tears.

"No, no, sweetheart. I'm not going anywhere," Loretta said, squeezing him tighter.

"Is she gonna take me away from you, mommy?" he asked, eyes widening in fear.

"No, baby, no. She's not gonna take you away from me."

Loretta nuzzled her face in Kendall's neck, squeezing her eyes shut, inhaling his boyish scent, holding that position for several seconds after hearing a hard knock on her front door. Straightening up, grabbing his little hand, Loretta bravely walked with him to the door.

"Good afternoon, Loretta," Charlene said cheerfully. "And hello there Kendall. I almost thought you weren't home. I don't think your doorbell's working. Had to knock."

Instantly feeling defensive, Loretta glared at the social worker, but maintained her civility. "Hello Charlene. Nice to see you." After showing her in, she added quietly, "Yes, the doorbell's been broken forever. I don't remember it actually ever working."

Stopping short of sitting down, Charlene regarded several toys strewn on the sofa before looking at Loretta.

"Oh, sorry, let me clear those away," Loretta said unapologetically. Handing them to Kendall, she said, "Be a sweetie and put these in your room."

Tentatively sitting down, placing her briefcase on the floor, Charlene spoke up when Kendall was out of earshot.

"Does he know why I'm here today?" Charlene said emotionlessly.

"Not really." Loretta chewed on her bottom lip.

"'Not really'? What is that supposed to mean?"

"It means, I, uh, didn't exactly tell him. Why you're here."

Charlene pursed her lips before continuing. "Let me put it another way; does he know there could be a chance he will be placed in foster care?"

"*Shh*, don't say it so loud. He already has his suspicions."

"What are suspicions mommy?" Kendall had slipped noiselessly back into the room. "Are they big spiders?"

"Well, there you are. I've been calling all over town looking for you."

"Jesus Christ, Cyndi, can't a man come into his office on a Sunday without having his wife looking for him 'all over town'?"

Cynthia Arrington-Benton, third wife of venture capitalist Timothy Benton, was 13 years her husband's junior and just as high-maintenance as her predecessors. In reality, she was more high maintenance than Tim's first two wives, but who was measuring? Self-important and impatient, Cyndi demanded Tim's undivided attention, lacking worldly confidence despite the fact she'd had at least a dozen separate plastic surgeries performed on her 29-year-old body.

"Well, your cell phone went right to voicemail and I got concerned. I mean, we are meeting the MacAlisters for cocktails at five-fifteen at the clubhouse and it's already three-thirty and I was just–"

"Cyndi, please. Too much information. How many times do I need to tell you to zip it?" Tim breathed hard into the phone as he stared at the mysterious box. "If you must know, I had to come into the office because Tom called to say I had a package here."

"A package? What kind of package?"

"Jesus, Cyndi. Does it really matter? You know nothing about the nature of my business, yet you are always trying to insert yourself into it."

"I'm just trying to be a good–"

"Look, I'm sorry. I was just about to open it when you called." Tim reached for the box cutter again, pressing the tip into the clear tape on the box. "For some reason, I've let this package upset me no end. I don't know why. It's just not like me."

"Oh, sweetie, it's okay. I bet it's a belated birthday present!"

"Why would you say that? My birthday was six weeks ago." Tim slid the knife along the tape, slicing open the box, careful not to accidentally cut anything inside.

"Well, because, ironically, a package was delivered here at home about an hour ago. So, it can't be a coincidence. Obviously two people remembered to send you a gift for your birthday."

"What? Another package?" Tim pulled crumpled paper out of the box, tossing it on the desk. Inside was a shoebox. "Who's it from?"

"Hold on, let me check," Cyndi said, setting down the phone.

While he waited for his wife to return, Tim pulled out the shoebox and placed it in front of him on the desk. Lifting the top, Tim stared at the contents and recoiled.

"I can't find any name. All I see is the city where it was mailed from."

"Phoenix?"

"How'd you know?"

CHAPTER 8 SUNDAY AFTERNOON

Restless to get back on the road, yet concerned for Chynna's welfare, Lisa glanced at her watch and shook her head. Four-thirty. Bemoaning the amount of time she'd already lost to dealing with a drug-addicted hooker and her violent pimp, Lisa told herself she'd wait till Chynna woke up to reassess her priorities. Who knew if anyone would be looking for the young woman or missing her absence at the dinner table? Likely no one. Still, she was a human being and someone's daughter and–

Chynna moaned, stirring on the bed, so Lisa went to her side and lightly caressed the side of her face. Alarmed, she placed the back of her hand on the girl's forehead. Hot to the touch. Was she sick? What types of drugs had she taken today? Although Lisa had found the baggie of pills, she couldn't be sure which ones she'd ingested, if any. Had that pimp shot her up with drugs, Lisa wondered? How long had she been with him?

Too many questions and she had neither the time nor the interest in finding out that much about her other than caring for a human in crisis. Watching Chynna struggle to open her eyes, Lisa looked at her watch again and grimaced. She really needed to leave soon to keep her schedule and be in LA by morning. Monday morning, when everyone would be arriving at work and grabbing their first cups of coffee.

"You...you're still here?" Chynna stuttered, trying to push herself up on one elbow. "What did you–" But before she could finish, she shut her eyes and fell back down on the bed, grabbing her head.

"Yes, I'm still here, Chynna. I wanted to make sure you're okay before I leave." Lisa smiled weakly at her.

"How—?" Chynna shot straight up in bed but was again forced back down. "How do you know my name?"

"It doesn't matter how I know," Lisa said, scrutinizing Chynna, watching her rub her temples. "The only thing you should be concerned with is getting better and protecting yourself from men that do not have your best interests at heart."

"The hell you're talking about, woman. You don't know me. You know nothing about me. How dare you think you can...help me."

"You're right. I don't know you. I know nothing about you. But believe it or not, I care. Deeply. If you only—"

Three loud knocks outside the motel room shocked both Lisa and Chynna. They both stared at the door, waiting for someone to say something.

"Who the hell's that?" Chynna asked, grabbing a handful of bedding to her chest.

"I was gonna ask you the same thing," Lisa said matter-of-factly.

"I'm scared. I think Axel may have—"

"Axel may have what, Chynna?"

"I, uh, I don't know. He may have sent someone to—"

Without warning, the door to Room 8 flew open, banging hard against the wall, its knob taking out a chunk of drywall. Two ratty-looking, 20-something men carrying semi-automatic pistols burst into the room and headed straight for Chynna, ignoring Lisa as if she weren't there. Incensed, Lisa grabbed ahold of one of them, only to be knocked to the floor with an elbow to her midsection. Trying to catch her breath, Lisa writhed in pain as the two scumbags yanked Chynna out of bed and dragged her screaming from the room.

Rising to her feet, Lisa could do nothing but helplessly watch the young woman being thrown into the back seat of a metallic blue, beat-up Camaro. Squinting at the car, gingerly holding her ribs, Lisa made out the last four digits of the New Mexico license plate.

"Mommy. What are suspicions? Tell me." Kendall asked again, having gotten no response. He was still holding a couple of toys.

Staring blankly at her son, Loretta gripped the loose material on the sides of her pants and held her breath. Stymied, she then looked to Charlene for direction before letting out a gush of air.

"Kendall, sweetie, it's nothing," Loretta finally said, edging closer to her son. "Everything's good. Nothing at all to worry about. No spiders, nothing bad at all."

"But mommy, you scared me. I thought you said—"

"Come over here, Kendall, honey," Charlene interjected, pursing her lips again, deep in thought. "You remember me? I know I haven't been here in a while, but last time we played Minecraft together, remember?"

Kendall stared curiously at the social worker, clearly uncertain of her intentions. Accustomed as he was to following directions from those in authority, he moved cautiously toward Charlene, stopping in front of her.

"Are you still playing Minecraft, Kendall?" Charlene said, gently taking the toys out of his hands and placing them on the sofa. "Or have you found another game you like better?"

Kendall looked up at his mother before turning his attention back to Charlene. "I still play Minecraft," he said tentatively, "but I also like Roblox."

"Roblox! Cool. My grandson loves Roblox." Charlene took his hands in hers and stared at him until he looked straight into her eyes. "I bet you're really good at it, right?"

Still unsure of himself, Kendall looked at his mother, who nodded and smiled weakly. "Yeah. I'm good at it. Really good."

"I knew it! You've got strong hands with good tactile ability. So, it's no wonder."

Turning over Kendall's hands to reveal his wrists, Charlene's eyes widened. "You are one strong little boy, Kendall, but I need for you to relax and allow me to look at your arms."

"Stop it, Ms. Mullins-McMillan, "Loretta said, approaching them, reaching out to grab her son by the wrists. "Can't you see you're hurting him?"

"I'm hardly touching him, Loretta. I only want to check out his arms. Last time, I saw—"

"I know what you said you saw last time, but you were wrong." Loretta pawed at her son's wrists to no avail. "It wasn't what you think it was."

"Then what was it in your expert opinion?" Charlene said, finally able to turn Kendall's hands over.

"It was...he was, uh, injured on the monkey bars at school and his arms got bruised. That's all. Nothing more."

"Then, what do you call these?" Charlene raised Kendall's arms. "How did he get these bruises?"

Lonnie was starting to worry. Loretta was purposely avoiding her; she just knew it. Could feel it in her bones. The bitch hadn't returned any of her calls or texts for going on a week now. *What the hell was going on? The bitch had obviously decided to turn her back on me after all I did for her! Take her and her son as a package deal. Now, who in their right mind would take a kid in that wasn't theirs to begin with? No one.*

To clear her mind and rid herself of the hangover, Lonnie had avoided alcohol all afternoon, thinking that would help. While most of the searing headache had dissipated, she still felt like crap and now concluded she should have just maintained her blood-alcohol level from the get-go. And if she had, she'd be coasting by now. Searching her apartment for a bottle of bourbon she knew she had stashed somewhere, Lonnie started opening all the cabinets in the kitchen, alas, to no avail.

Frustrated, she resigned herself to venturing out to the corner liquor store, a quick five-minute walk. Living a couple of blocks north of Manchester Boulevard in South Los Angeles, she threw on sweats, shoved her mobile phone in her pant pocket and headed out the door, anticipating the instant relief she'd feel in about ten minutes.

Not thirty feet from her building, she heard the distinctive sound of an incoming text. Praying it was from Loretta, she snatched the phone and glanced down to see who sent it. With her heart skipping a beat, she smiled when indeed, it was her sweetheart texting her back. There was a God after all, she thought, opening the message.

Loretta: *You've really fucked me up royally Lonnie. Fuckin social worker is here and she's not letting up about the bruises on Kendall's arms. I can only lie so much before she tricks me into saying something I'll regret. She's on to me. She's gonna take Kendall away from me and put him in foster care. I just know it. I'm desperate. Do you understand me? I'll do anything I have to do not to let her take him.*

Stopping in her tracks, Lonnie held her breath, thinking about her response. *How dare she blame me for Kendall's bruises? If she'd only discipline her own child, I wouldn't have had to do it myself.*

Lonnie: *Babe, I've been calling u for a week and this is all u gotta say to me? C'mon. I miss you like never before. Why u do me like* *this? I love u more than life and I only want us to be together. Is she still there?*

Lonnie hit Send and resumed her walk to the liquor store. It took another two minutes for Loretta to text back, just as she turned the corner on Manchester.

Loretta: *She's still here. I can't breathe. I cannot stay here another minute. When she leaves, I'm gonna take Kendall and get the hell outta here. Maybe we'll go to Vegas. I don't know.*

Lonnie read the text as she pushed the door open to Jimbo's Liquors, elated to have finally heard from her lover, but pissed off by the tone of her messages. *Where the hell would she go? She could barely drive herself to the grocery store, much less across state line. Jesus. What's gotten into her?*

Lonnie texted while paying for her bourbon, Old Fitzgerald, a bargain at fourteen dollars.

Lonnie: *Don't leave till I get there, Do you hear me? I'll drive you anywhere you wanna go. Just wait for me.*

Lonnie waited fifteen minutes for a response that never came. "Fuck you, Letta," she said aloud. "You are a real cunt."

Chapter 9 Sunday Evening

Cyndi sat quietly in the passenger seat of Tim's Porsche Boxter as he drove a half-mile to the clubhouse at their gated community in Brentwood. They were supposed to meet the MacAlisters for cocktails at 5:15—ahead of a 6:30 dinner reservation—and it was precisely 5:18 according to Cyndi's Cartier watch. While she took pride in being on time all the time, much of the time she was fashionably late and got upset only when her husband caused their tardiness. Her current agitation was due to Lucia MacAlister's promise to divulge exactly what she'd bought during a recent sexy lingerie shopping spree. Cyndi had been chomping at the bit with expectation all day.

"We're late, you know," Cyndi spat out indignantly as Tim entered the clubhouse's parking lot. "Lucia is a stickler for time. She's gonna be mad."

"Who cares what Lucia thinks? The last time we got together with them *she* was late. On purpose, I might add. Some kind of a meltdown over her shoes."

"Well, I don't remember, but that's not the point now." Cyndi pouted for effect. "The only reason we're late is your obsession with that package. I mean really. Couldn't you have waited till after dinner to open it?"

"No, I had to open it. Getting two packages at the same time—at home and at the office—on a Sunday I might add, well, it was too much for me to bear. I had to know who it was from."

"And did you figure it out?" Cyndi glanced at her watch again. Five-twenty.

"No, not really," Tim lied, pulling into a spot near the clubhouse's entrance. "I was too rushed to figure it out."

"See?" Cyndi turned and glared at him.

"See what?"

"You could have waited till we got home from dinner before you opened it."

"No, I couldn't have. Anyway, never mind. You wouldn't understand." Tim opened the door and jumped out, smoothing the bottom of his jacket.

"You always say that Tim," Cyndi said, climbing out of the car and walking around to the driver's side. "Like I'm some kind of dummy because I don't have a business degree from a fancy university."

"What? What are you talking about? We're late and I thought—"

"Never mind," she said, linking her arm in his. "I think whatever was in that package put you in a bad mood."

Tim stared inquisitively at Cyndi but said nothing, leading his wife toward the clubhouse in silence.

Proud of having easily made her point, Cyndi smiled inwardly, acknowledging her superior manipulation skills.

"That's okay, Timmy. Everything's gonna be alright," she whispered, squeezing her husband's arm. "And I know just what you need later to lift your spirits."

It took Lisa about ten minutes to regain her composure and search the motel room for any valuables, after which she jumped back into her car and headed west toward Los Angeles. Limited in her ability to either rescue the young hooker or identify the vehicle in which she'd been whisked away, Lisa resolved to do both when she returned to California. The odds of Chynna still being alive at that time were slim, but Lisa felt confident she'd be able to track down the thugs that kidnapped her. There was something ominous going on and it smelled to high heaven of human trafficking.

Still, Lisa thought, easily finding the onramp to westbound Interstate 10, she had more pressing issues to occupy her time, primarily her older brother, Tim. The time was nigh to finally deal with the monster who was the bane of her existence; the reason for her new calling, who was undoubtedly living the life of Riley with his third wife, no less. *A real gad about town, you son of a bitch. Does Cynthia even know what you're all about? Probably not, but even if she does, all your money undoubtedly clouded her better judgment and she married you anyway knowing what an abuser you are.*

Your days are numbered my dear brother, so watch your back. What I wouldn't have given to have been a fly on the wall to see the look on your face when you opened the packages I sent to both your office and home. How long did it take for you to figure out who sent it? Had you cleanly scrubbed all the recollections from your mind's hard drive so that you could live a so-called normal life? Or, has the memory of sexually abusing me for years been at the forefront of your mind, rearing its ugly head every time you fuck your wife? Ha! Another fly-on-the-wall moment I would have loved to see. Well, perhaps soon.

CHAPTER 10 SUNDAY EVENING

Frantic, hyperventilating, Loretta thought she'd pass out at any moment if she didn't find Kendall. *Where had he gone? Why had he run away?* Replaying the scene repeatedly in her head, Loretta determined there was absolutely nothing she could have done to prevent her son from bolting out the front door the minute that crazy bitch social worker mentioned the F word: foster care. *Oh, dear God! Where is my baby? You've never done anything like this before, even during her last visit when she asked to look at your back.*

Charlene Mullins-McMillan—the epitome of self-control—was her usual stoic self, remaining calm throughout Kendall's abrupt disappearance, assuring Loretta that he'd be back in a jiffy, needing time to cool down from all the overt attention. While Loretta screamed and paced the room, Charlene told her to maintain her faith in his safe return; an 8-year-old boy would not purposefully wander too far for too long.

"The hell he won't," Loretta spat out venomously. "I know my son and you just confirmed his worst fear. He is a sensitive boy and was deathly afraid of you taking him away from me."

"I'm sorry you feel that way, Loretta, but he would have found out sooner or later," Charlene said evenly, her expression betraying her real feelings. "It was much better for him to find out sooner than later."

"You could have said it differently, and you know it. You are such a—" but Loretta couldn't finish what she meant to say for fear of making things worse. Instead, she punched the sides of her thighs with closed fists, wanting to punish herself, hoping to bruise her legs in the process.

"Your attitude, Loretta, is what gets you in trouble. Your choices are what puts Kendall in danger." Charlene regarded Loretta curiously as she would an annoying fly buzzing about her head.

"Aren't you going to try to find him?" Loretta said, yanking on her hair. "Why are you just sitting there like an idiot?"

"Like I just said, no eight-year-old boy will purposefully wander too far for too long. He's attached to you, Loretta, and doesn't want to lose you. He's just trying to make a statement.

"He'll be back. Soon."

Bent over at the waist, Loretta stared at Charlene, panting like a feral animal, licking her lips, snorting out a puff of air. "No, he won't. He will not come back as long as you're here."

"Well, that may be true, but he will come back. Eventually." Charlene lifted her briefcase off the floor, rose and headed to the door. Turning to face Loretta, she offered a practiced, insincere half-smile.

"Do let me know when he's back. We've got a lot of paperwork to fill out."

The hell I will, Loretta thought before closing the door on the social worker.

Staring at the clock over the kitchen sink, Loretta squeezed her eyes shut, feeling tears pooling. Fifteen whole minutes was an eternity for Kendall to have a huge lead on her.

Sipping her split of champagne, Cyndi slyly eyed Lucia MacAlister, then winked at her co-conspirator. The two women had been feigning interest in their husbands' conversation about municipal bonds, about which neither had a single clue. Lucia giggled and nearly coughed up her Lemon Drop martini, quickly dabbing her chin with her cocktail napkin. Her husband, Donovan, consumed by his discussion with Tim, carried on, not missing a beat.

"You can buy highly rated ten-year munis that'll yield nearly three percent, and that's more than Treasuries and high-quality corporate bonds," Donovan said before gulping down a shot of 12-year-old single malt whiskey. "That's equivalent to a four-percent taxable yield for people like us in high tax brackets."

Tim nodded in agreement, his mind clearly elsewhere, though he did his best to appear interested in his friend's information. While taking small mouthfuls of scotch, he caught a sideways glimpse of his wife's antics with Lucia. Turning his attention back to Donovan, he noticed his friend had stopped talking.

"Right, Donovan, I couldn't agree with you more," he interjected quickly. "I've always said munis are the way to go in this economy."

"Good, good. Glad you agree. For a minute there, I thought you didn't hear a word I said."

Tim smiled sheepishly, then finished his scotch in one gulp. "No, no. I heard every word you said." Tim stared at his empty glass. "Hey, I'll be right back. Gonna get another." He held up his glass and then walked toward the bar.

"Is Tim alright," Donovan asked Cyndi when her husband was gone.

"Huh? Yeah, he's great. Just fine," Cyndi said, her words betraying her expression. "Why do you ask?"

"Oh, nothing in particular. I just felt like his mind was on something else. Something other than what we were talking about."

Cyndi giggled and winked again at Lucia, as if they were sharing a dark secret. Lucia raised her eyebrows at her husband, indicating she had no idea about anything that had just been said.

"Well, he's had a lot on his mind this week, Donovan, not the least of which was a—" Cyndi stopped and smiled, reconsidering what she was about to divulge.

"Not the least of what, Cyndi? Everything alright at the office? I mean, business-wise?"

As if on cue, Lucia poked Cyndi in the ribs, sloshing her martini on her friend's dress, causing more giggles. Cyndi glared at her.

"Darling, have you had your limit already?" Donovan disdainfully said to his wife. "Do I always need to remind you that you cannot hold your liquor?"

"I'm fine sweetheart," she said, lightly touching his arm. "I just got a case of the giggles." Lucia covered her mouth with her hand and chuckled.

"He got a package today—of all days— and it really set him off," Cyndi said, ignoring her friend and finishing her champagne. "A mysterious package from a mystery person."

"A 'mysterious package'?" Donovan repeated, scrunching his nose and twirling the remains of his whiskey. "Who sent it?"

"Well, that's just it. There was no sender's name on the package or a return address."

"Maybe it's from the Unabomber," Lucia said, laughing hysterically, spilling more of her cocktail.

"Maybe you need to stop drinking," Donovan said, grabbing the glass from his wife's hand. "*Now*."

CHAPTER 11 SUNDAY EVENING

Lisa got as far as Tempe before she had second thoughts about leaving Arizona, so she turned around and headed back to the east Phoenix area. As much as she couldn't wait to mete out justice on her brother, she needed to find out what happened to Chynna; to discover if there was something more sinister going on with her and her former pimp than had met the eye. She even considered slinking back into the cowboy bar, hoping to pick the brains of some local folks, pump them for information on anything and everything. Someone in that bar had to be familiar with the underbelly of society; had to have connections with the creatures of the night. Something menacing was going on in the desert and Lisa intended to find out what it was.

Retracing the route in reverse to the cowboy bar in Gilbert—neatly tucked away in a corner of a strip mall—was not as easy as she thought it would be. Still, she eventually found it in the dark, no thanks to the dim lighting on the streets. Sauntering in through the back door, Lisa blindly walked past several men sitting at the bar, seeking an empty seat at the far end. Sliding onto a stool, she hooked her purse underneath the bar and then flagged down the bartender.

"Gin and tonic, please with three limes," Lisa said, slyly eyeing the others sitting at the bar.

"Top shelf or well?" It was the same female bartender from last night.

"Hendrick's, please," Lisa said distractedly, spying one gentleman sitting on the last barstool.

"Fancy tastes, sister," she remarked, reaching above for a glass. "Last night it was only a Heineken."

Lisa turned around to regard the bartender. "Making my way down the alphabet." Lisa chuckled. "Actually, I had intended to leave town last night. Now, I could be hanging around for a while."

"Hmmm, you '*intended* to leave town,'" the bartender repeated, pouring the premium gin. "What made you change your mind?" She slid a coaster across the bar, then carefully placed the drink on top.

"Oh, nothing in particular." Lisa slowly sipped her cocktail.

"Maybe I should rephrase that. *Who* made you change your mind?" The bartender cocked her head toward the end of the bar.

"Huh?" Lisa followed the barkeep's gaze and saw a man nod while touching the brim of his white cowboy hat. "Oh, no. No way. It wasn't—"

"Are you sure? I think you may be in denial. I mean, you did come back here. You didn't go elsewhere and there are *tons* of bars in the area."

"Look, I know it may seem like that, but I have no interest in him. Honestly." Lisa took a long sip of her drink, then stared straight ahead at the bottles of booze lining three mirrored shelves behind the bartender.

"Suit yourself, sweetie, but you'd be missing out on a rockin' good time."

Lisa smiled and pretended to be intrigued by the variety of liquor in the quaint country-western bar. Then, realizing she was stubbornly shutting off the best networking connection in the establishment, she changed her demeanor and engaged with the bartender.

"You know, you're probably right," Lisa said enthusiastically, draining her drink. "I should really be more open to trying new things; new experiences."

"Great! Glad you're reconsidering."

"Me too." Lisa set her glass down on the bar and extended her hand. "Hi. My name is Hannah," Lisa said, her pseudonym rolling off her tongue with ease. "What's yours?"

"Linda Lou," the bartender responded, her big smile revealing even bigger teeth. "So nice to meet you, Hannah. Want a another?"

"Sure. Why not? I'm pushing my boundaries tonight. Getting out of my comfort zone."

"Nuthin' wrong with that, hon." Linda Lou placed a fresh Hendricks and tonic in front of Lisa. "Cheers!"

"Cheers!" Lisa took a long swig, then shivered. "Wowza! That's one mean drink."

"I like to keep my customers happy and coming back for more."

Lisa smiled and took a deep breath. "Anyone ever kid you about your name?"

"Oh, you mean like the chick in the song?"

"Yeah. Not a very common name."

"Neither is Hannah. Are you parents religious or something?"

Lisa took another gulp before looking Linda Lou in the eye. "No, not at all. My mom was actually a stay-at-home alcoholic and my dad's a workaholic, so I suppose you can say they pretty much pray at the altar of consumerism."

"Oh, well, then maybe I shouldn't have made you such a strong—"

"It's quite alright. I didn't inherit the addiction gene. I think it skipped my generation. Anyway, unlike my mom, I can take it or leave it." Lisa sipped her cocktail before changing the subject. "So, tell me, the guy in the white hat, Jared, right? What's his story?"

"Yes, Jared. Well, he's probably the most eligible bachelor in Gilbert." Linda Lou's eyes twinkled. "A real catch for the right gal."

"Is that right?" Lisa said with forced conviction. "What line of work is he in?"

"He's, um, a headhunter. You know, a recruiter. He sells people for a living."

CHAPTER 12 SUNDAY NIGHT

Loretta refused to let go of Kendall, cradling his head, rocking him in her lap, placing tiny kisses on his forehead. He'd returned home shortly after Charlene left, signaling to Loretta that he'd not ventured far, simply waiting for the social worker to leave their apartment. None of it mattered now. All she cared about was his safe return.

"I'm sorry I scared you, mommy," Kendall said, raising his head. "It's just that I didn't want that lady taking me away from you."

"It's okay, sweetie. I was scared, but I forgive you. All is good now. You're home. Where you belong."

"Is she gonna come back again?" Kendall buried his head in his mother's arms.

"No sweetie. She's not coming back." *Not if I have anything to say about it.*

"But what if she does? How are we gonna keep her out?"

"Don't worry, my sweet. Mommy always has a plan."

Desperate to talk to her lover, Lonnie impulsively called Loretta, but her call went directly to voicemail. *Bitch turned off her phone. You can try to avoid me,* Lonnie thought, instantly inflamed, *but you cannot hide from me forever. I will track you down no matter where you go. I am relentless.*

Then, as quickly as contempt consumed her, she let it subside, turning 180 degrees, sending her lover a brief, emotionless message, steering clear of anything that may push her buttons to freak her out.

Lonnie: *Hey, I know u got a lot on your mind and all, so I won't add no more stress to ur life. I'm actually thinking of taking a few days off. Work said it'd be OK. I'll keep in touch. Stay safe, babe!*

Certain this softer approach would put Loretta at ease, maybe even compel her to let down her guard, Lonnie had to wait only five minutes to get a response.

Loretta:*Hey. Thanks for checking in. I've been a wreck but am determined to save myself and my son from this fucked-up system. We'll be heading out tonight, driving through the desert. Who knows where we'll end up??? I'll text you when we land somewhere.*

Enraged once more, Lonnie stared at her phone and bit her lower lip. *Sure, you will, babe. But I won't have to wait for that, 'cause I will follow your ass wherever you go. Remember: I am relentless.*

"So, what was up with Lucia," Tim said as he and Cyndi drove home from the clubhouse. "She was in rare form tonight."

"A little too much to drink," Cyndi said, staring out the window. "You know she cannot hold her liquor."

"Yep, just like my mom," Tim said. "She always embarrassed my dad in public when she had too much to drink. Which also embarrassed me."

Cyndi turned to glare at him. "No, it's nothing like your mom. For one, Lucia is much, much younger. And two–"

"Of course, it is, darling," Tim interrupted. "My mom drank when she was young. Started younger than Lucia is now. What did you think, she only started drinking when I married you?"

"What? Are you trying to imply that your mom started drinking because of me? That she didn't approve—"

"Oh, will you stop being so goddamned sensitive? That's not what I meant, and you know it."

Cyndi sighed, trying to ignore her husband's callousness.

"Anyway, she was just in a giddy mood. Being silly and the booze heightened her silliness."

"Oh, do tell, darling," Tim said hitting the remote to open their front gate. "What got Lucia so silly?"

"Well, she'd gone down to West Hollywood and bought a few toys on Santa Monica Boulevard." Cyndi smiled.

"Toys? Why on earth would that put her in a silly mood?"

"Because she had to disguise herself before going into the store, for Pete's sake." Cyndi snorted, trying to suppress a laugh.

"'Disguise herself' when buying toys? That's odd, I must say. I mean, who would disguise themself when buying presents for their nieces and nephews?"

"No, darling. She wasn't buying children's toys, for Pete's sake. She bought *sex* toys. For her and Donovan."

CHAPTER 13 SUNDAY NIGHT

"So, Linda Lou tells me your name's Hannah," said Jared, the man in the white cowboy hat, speaking with an indistinctive Southern accent as he slid onto the barstool next to Lisa. Less threatening up close, Jared exuded a small-town naiveté, his big-box clothing covering a soft, plump body that likely hadn't seen a gym since high school. "Nice biblical name for such a mod gal."

"Absolutely," Lisa said, not missing a beat, checking him out with a sideways glance. "My mother came from a long line of bible thumpers."

"My name's Jared," he said, extending a cold, damp hand. "Nice to meet you."

Lisa forced a half-smile as she shook his hand, quickly retracting it when he held on too long. "Yes, Linda Lou mentioned your name to me, too."

"First of all, I owe you an apology, for last night. For calling you a–"

"No apology necessary," Lisa said, interrupting him. "Already forgotten. Let's start fresh."

"Thanks," Jared said, nervously taking a long slug of his beer. "You grow up in the Bible Belt?"

"Just 'cause my mom's family was a bunch of Bible thumpers, doesn't mean *I'm* from the Bible Belt. Nope. I'm a big-city girl."

"Well, I never met another Hannah before, though I've met plenty of Rebeccas and Ruths. And they were all from Oklahoma."

"Where I come from, we have plenty of girls named Hannah, Ruth, Rebecca, and Rachel. We even have a couple of Jezebels, too." Lisa knocked back the last of her second gin and tonic, slamming the glass a little too hard on the bar.

"Now there's a name you'll never hear in Oklahoma. I'd just *love* to meet a Jezebel. Just once in my life! *Please*, Jesus!"

"Really? And, why's that?" Lisa eyed him closely.

"Well, she'd probably be a real good fuck." Jared laughed heartily, staring Lisa in the eye.

"Well, if nothing else, you are an honest man, Jared," Lisa said evenly, feeling the hair on the back of her neck stand on end.

"Oh, I hope I didn't offend you, Miss Hannah. It's just that I believe in speaking my mind. All the time."

"No offense taken, Jared. As I just said, you're an honest man. To a fault." Lisa raised her glass, forgetting it was empty. "Cheers!"

"And you my sweet, need another drink," Jared said enthusiastically. "Linda Lou, another round. On my tab."

"Thank you, Jared, but I think I've had enough."

"Getting coy on me now, my little one?" Jared leaned over and breathed heavily on Lisa's neck. Recoiling, Lisa noticed an unusual tattoo on his right wrist, but the lightning was too dim for her to make it out clearly.

"Don't want to get pulled over by the cops in a strange town now," Lisa said convincingly, smiling at Jared. "Hey, make you a deal. I'll have another, but only after I get a little bite to eat. Deal?"

"Deal."

Loretta got as far as Indio before her car overheated and she was forced to pull off Interstate 10. Tired, hungry and anxious, she glided south on Monroe Street below the speed limit desperately searching for a motel. Biting her lower lip, Loretta scanned both sides of the wide avenue till she saw a broken, flashing neon sign on the opposite side of the street. Quickly puling over to her left, she made a U-turn at the next light and backtracked to the motel.

Two and a half hours prior, she had hastily thrown whatever belongings she could gather within fifteen minutes, tossing it into her dilapidated Chevy Cavalier. She then coaxed Kendall into the vehicle, telling him they were going on a cross-country adventure.

"Are we going to Disneyland, mommy?" Kendall had asked when they'd gotten onto the freeway in Culver City.

"Not this time, sweetheart. Maybe on the way back."

"But I thought you said we weren't coming back to LA." Kendall had appeared dejected.

"You never know, sweetie," Loretta had said convincingly. "We may come back after everything settles down a bit."

"What about Aunt Lonnie?"

"What about her?" Loretta said, stiffening, diverting eye contact from her son. "I thought you said you were happy she and mommy were no longer friends."

"Yeah, I did. I don't want her around anymore. She's not a very nice person."

"I know sweetie." Loretta had started to cry, and rather than having her son see her unhappy, she sniffed back her tears as if she had a runny nose. "She turned out to be a not-so-nice person."

"She was always mean. Even when you thought she was nice. Like in the beginning."

"I am so sorry, baby. You have no idea how sorry I am."

"It's okay, mommy. I forgive you."

It took Loretta several minutes to stop crying, which miraculously occurred when she reached the congested part of the highway requiring unobstructed vision. As she concentrated on the road, she silently prayed to any gods that would listen, allowing her precious little boy to survive that disastrous mistake of a mate in Lonnie.

"What's the matter darling? I thought you'd like a little diversion from the usual, um, missionary position."

Cyndi enthusiastically assumed the dominant role in bed tonight, having donned a lacy, red teddy with a garter belt holding up red lace stockings. The fact she wore no panties was beside the point to her obviously disinterested husband. What seemed to bother him was the oversized plastic phallus she held in her hand and which she poised near his rear end. Squirming away from her, Tim, clad only in a bath towel, slammed his body against the headboard, crossing his legs, fearing being penetrated by a humongous inanimate object.

"What's the matter, you ask? Have you gone mad? That thing looks like a horse's dick. What the hell are you planning to do with it?"

"Oh, c'mon, honey, why are you so skittish?" Cyndi crawled over to Tim, growling like a feral cat. "Why not give it a try?"

"You've really gone off the deep end, Cyndi," Tim said accusingly, moving to the edge of the bed. "You will not insert that thing into any of my bodily cavities."

"What? You mean you actually thought I wanted to use this on you?" Cyndi rolled over onto her back and laughed hysterically.

Tim glared at her, his eyelids fluttering in confusion. "Then why the hell are you holding that thing? Why the hell did you buy it in the first place if not to–"

"Oh my God!" Cyndi screamed, shaking her head. "I thought you'd have figured this out by now."

"Figured what out?"

"Do I have to spell it out for you, darling?"

"Was this Lucia's idea for God's sake? Is this what she's into now? Jesus Christ, Cyndi. This, this *thing* has her fingerprints all over it." Tim slid off the bed and secured the towel around his waist. "It has to be her, that fucking boozer *cunt*. Poor Donovan. Look what he has to put up with!"

Cyndi shot up and glared at her husband. "I cannot even dignify that with a response. How cruel and judgmental you can be."

"It's the truth, Cyndi and you know it. I don't know why you want to emulate her. She's common and crass and a cunt, like I just said."

"I don't want to emulate her. I just want to be free to be myself." Cyndi grabbed the dildo and rolled off the bed. "I wanted *you* to use this thing on *me*. I was just...trying to get you to do something new. That's all."

Tim continued to glare at his wife, clearly lost for words. "You can ask me to do almost anything, Cyndi. Just not that."

Tim shuffled into the bathroom and shut the door.

CHAPTER 14 SUNDAY NIGHT

Lisa sized up the cheeseburger on the plate in front of her and pondered how she'd daintily, and in a ladylike manner, get her mouth around it and not appear to be a ravenous pig. The two gin and tonics had worn off by the time their food arrived at the diner on the opposite side of the strip mall, leaving her famished and cranky. Not really caring what Jared thought of her eating habits and wanting nothing better than to pick it up and devour it like a guy would, Lisa decided at the last moment to cut it into bite-sized pieces.

"You actually eat a burger with a knife and fork?" Jared said, scrutinizing her every more. "Do you also eat chicken like that?"

"Sometimes," Lisa said, chewing her first morsel. "It depends."

"Depends on what, Hannah?" Jared took a huge bite of his cheeseburger, squirting out mustard and ketchup on either side. He then shamelessly wiped his mouth with the back of his hand.

"On how messy it is. Or, who I'm eating with."

"Oh, you don't have to stand on ceremonies with me, Hannah baby," Jared said, chewing with his mouth open. "I'm a laid-back kinda guy. What you see is what you get."

"I definitely see that, Jared. I get the feeling you're a real honest man."

"It's a good thing, right?" More opened-mouth chewing.

"Yes, it is." After taking a few more delicate bites in silence, Lisa demurely looked him in the eye.

"Say, Jared, I have a question for you. Since I'm new in town and really don't know anyone, do you, uh, have any ideas for me, you know, socially speaking? I'm a single gal and would love to get involved with other, like-minded people. You know what I mean?"

Jared's eyes lit up and he stopped chewing mid-bite. "'Like-minded people'?" he repeated, a chunk of ground meat whirling on his tongue.

"Yeah. I'm an active girl and I like to keep busy," Lisa said, studying his fleshy face. "Gotta few more weeks of work in Phoenix and I sure don't want to spend all of my time in an office. I certainly don't want to miss out on any fun parties or anything."

"Funny you should mention parties," Jared said, taking a moment to swallow. "There's a good one on Wednesday. In Tempe, at the Marriott. Always brings in attractive folks."

"You mean I have to wait three days before I have any fun?"

"No, no. Of course not." Jared squirmed, his eyes widening. Then, looking off to his left, he added, "Where's your office? Maybe I can—"

"Why don't you give me your number and I'll call you tomorrow." Lisa winked at him.

"Huh? No nightcap? You promised me you'd let me buy you another drink?"

"You can just pick up this tab and we'll call it a night."

Lisa dabbed her lips, then set her napkin on her plate. Grabbing her purse, she slid out of the booth and extended her hand. "It's been a pleasure, Jared. Thanks for the cheeseburger and the amazing conversation."

"That's it?" Jared poked around in his jacket pocket, producing a bent business card. "Here you go. My cell's at the bottom."

Lisa glanced at the worn card with a handwritten number inscribed below a thick, black mark. "Thanks. I'll call you."

"Where do you work? What do you do?" Jared had another mouthful of cheeseburger churning around in his mouth.

"I'll call you," Lisa said, nonchalantly walking out of the diner.

"C'mon, baby, let's go check into the motel," Loretta said, urging Kendall out of the car. "We'll stay the night and then get back on the road early in the morning. I think we can make it to Arizona with no more problems."

"Arizona? Where's that? I thought we were going to Disneyland."

"No, baby. I told you maybe we'd go to Disneyland on the way back."

"But mom! I wanna go now!" Kendall slumped in the back seat, refusing to budge.

"We will, sweetie, I promise. Just not this week. Okay? Now, c'mon."

Kendall grudgingly followed his mother to the motel's front office, where he found a beefy tabby cat to play with while Loretta checked in. Placing 65 dollars in small bills on the counter, Loretta told the clerk it was all she had. The weathered woman eyeballed the money, then swiftly scooped it up and handed her the key to Room 13.

"Thank you," Loretta said softly, before grabbing Kendall and slipping out of the office. She walked like a woman heading to the gallows, fearing the outcome while needing eternal rest.

When the two had settled into the room, Loretta flopped onto the saggy bed and turned on the TV, perusing the lineup using a remote held together with duct tape. Immediately bored, Kendall decided he needed a soda, so he scrounged his mother's purse for some change. Too tired to complain, Loretta simply asked what he was looking for.

"I wanna get a Coke in the machine outside," he said enthusiastically.

"I don't really want you drinking Coke, sweetie. Too much sugar and caffeine."

"What's caffeine?"

"It'll keep you up all night. Get juice instead."

"I'll get a Dr. Pepper then."

"Same thing. Sugar and caffeine."

"I'll be right back, mom."

"Be careful, sweetie. Keep the door open a bit so you can get back in."

"Okay, mom."

Chapter 15 Sunday Night

Lisa sat in her car for six minutes before Jared emerged from the diner and got into a white pickup truck. From where she sat, it looked like a Ford, one of those oversized vehicles with "dualies" only a guy with a small penis would drive. Waiting for him to pull out of the lot, Lisa scrutinized his Oklahoma license plate and scribbled down the number. Guess he was being honest when he said he was an Oakie, Lisa thought. An open book indeed.

Following at a safe distance behind him, Lisa wended her way through several residential neighborhoods till she noticed him impulsively pull over to the curb in front of an apartment building. Parking two cars behind Jared's, she watched him jump out of his vehicle and hustle to the entrance where he pressed a keypad and waited for the door to buzz, allowing him in. Clearly not his apartment.

Confirming her hunch, Jared emerged within three minutes pushing along a skimpily-clad young woman—possibly a teen—toward his truck. Opening the front passenger door, he unceremoniously shoved her inside, then slammed the door, looking up and down the street before hopping back in and tearing away from the curb.

Lisa followed them on surface streets for what seemed like four or five miles, at which time, Jared erratically turned into the subdivision of a large golf community that encompassed both sides of the street. Thankfully, it wasn't a gated community. Cautiously tailing him, Lisa meandered through the main road for another half-mile till Jared turned left into the driveway of a sprawling, two-story home. With his engine running, Jared waited a few moments for the girl to jump out before he backed out and sped away.

More interested now in the goings-on inside this house, Lisa allowed Jared to get away, knowing she'd easily find him whenever she wanted to. He was an open book, after all. His impulsive and careless actions indicated he may be self-medicating with both booze and drugs. His manic behavior at the bar and later at the diner pointed to an erratic human being needing constant stimulation. Stick with him, she told herself, and discover the ugly underbelly of the Valley of the Sun.

Loretta gave in to her drowsiness and started to nod off, her head bobbing, her chin repeatedly hitting her chest, startling her awake each time. She'd open her eyes for no more than two seconds only to feel them weighted down again, forcing her to close them once more. This happened several times and even the drone of the television couldn't keep her awake. It wasn't till her head slipped off the pillow with her face aiming at the floor that she woke up with a start.

Pushing herself up to a seated position, she assessed the room to make sure everything was in order. She called out for Kendall, but he didn't answer. Concerned, but not yet worried, she slid off the bed and shuffled in a daze to the bathroom. Knocking on the door, she called out his name, but still got no answer. Now a little more awake and a lot more agitated, Loretta burst into the empty bathroom, emitting a squeak as she stared into the darkness.

Turning around, she rushed to the door, which was slightly ajar. *What the hell? Hadn't Kendall returned with his soda?* Pulling it open, she nearly wrenched her shoulder, feeling the pressure of someone on the outside pushing it open. Stumbling back a foot, she strained to right herself before coming face-to-face with the female intruder.

"Just where do you think you're going, Letta?"

Horrified, realizing it was Lonnie, Loretta tried to prevent her from entering, but was overpowered. Try as she might, Loretta soon gave in, allowing her former lover to enter the room. Thrusting Loretta onto the bed, hovering over her, Lonnie's face was within inches of Loretta's, breathing foully on her.

"Where is he?" Lonnie said, pinning both of Loretta's arms to the mattress.

"I-I don't know," Loretta stuttered. "He went out for a soda and hasn't returned."

"You're a lying bitch, Letta," Lonnie said, pressing harder.

"I'm not lying, Lonnie. He's not here."

Lonnie raised her left hand, backslapping the left side of Loretta's cheek, causing Loretta to whimper in pain.

"He's not here, Lonnie, I swear. Despite what you think."

"Once a lying bitch, always been a lying bitch," Lonnie said before striking her hard again, this time with a fist to her jaw.

Sneaking a peek inside the opened door, Kendall, a can of Dr. Pepper in his hand, witnessed his mother being beaten to a pulp by the woman who claimed to not only be his aunt, but to loving him more than life itself.

CHAPTER 16 MONDAY MORNING

"Good morning, Mr. Benton. I placed Saturday's mail on your desk next to the, uh, box. I wasn't sure what you–"

"Thank you, Angie," Tim replied self-consciously, eyeing his secretary suspiciously. "You didn't, um, touch the box, or move it, did you?"

"No, no sir, I didn't. I just wasn't sure if it was something you wanted tossed or saved, so I decided to leave it to your discretion."

"Yes, well, I'll handle it. Nothing for you to be concerned with." Tim rushed past Angie, heading toward his corner office at the end of the hall. Then, reconsidering his abruptness, turned on his heels and hustled back to the reception area.

"Good morning, Angie," he said breathlessly. "Sorry for being rude. It's only seven-fifteen and already things are becoming a cluster–"

"No need to apologize, Mr. Benton, I know how much you have on your mind, especially on Mondays. I'll make sure your coffee is delivered post haste."

"Thanks, dear." Tim forced a painful smile, keeping it plastered on his face as he hurried to his office.

Spying the pile of mail next to the shoebox, Tim glanced at the handwritten letter on top, scrutinizing it up close. No return address. Again. *What the hell is going on? Is someone trying to gaslight me? Make me fear for my life? When have I ever been this paranoid? Never.*

Methodically hanging his suit jacket on the back of his door, he jumped when his landline rang. Rushing to his desk, fumbling with the receiver, Tim brought it up to his ear in time to hear Angie saying something about an emergency call from his mother's housekeeper.

"Yes, yes, Angie, put her through," he said, absentmindedly poking his hand into the shoebox filled with memorabilia.

"Good. You're already in the office," the female voice said. *"I wouldn't expect anything less from a workaholic like you, Timmy."*

"Who is this? My secretary said it was an emergency call from my mother's housekeeper. You don't sound like Margarita."

"Margarita? Is that her latest housekeeper's name? What happened to Adelia? Did she go back to Mexico?"

"How dare you call me at work!" Tim fell back into his oversized swivel chair.

"Calm the fuck down, Timmy. It's not good for your blood pressure. Save your ire for when you'll really need it."

"You, you, you–"

"A stutterer now? I'd have never guessed stuttering–of all things–would end up afflicting the high and mighty Timothy Benton."

"You don't scare me, Lisa. Nor do your childish pranks. Do you even know what I've accomplished in my life? How *powerful* I am?" Tim wiped the sweat off his brow with the back of his hand.

"Your fear or lack thereof doesn't concern me, Timmy, nor do your so-called accomplishments and power. You could be King of LA for all I care, and you'd never impress me. All I want from you is to publicly admit what you did to me all those years ago. Then, when I'm good and ready, I'll go away."

Tim now dabbed at his upper lip, thick with perspiration. Slinking down into his chair, he swiveled it around to face the window. "You will stop this stupid game. *Now.* You will stop sending me shit from yesteryear, or else I'll—"

Lisa forced a laugh before interjecting, "*Or else what? You'll kill me? That's a laugh. You couldn't kill me any worse than you did decades ago. But let me tell you something, Timmy Boy: I wouldn't hesitate to kill you. In a heartbeat! That's what you should be thinking about. You should really fear me killing you!*"

"You're one crazy bitch, you know that? You'll be sorry if you try to intimidate me any further. That, I guarantee." Tim shook as he watched a crow dart through the air. A blue jay appearedout of nowhere, dive-bombing the crow, who flew away in fear. Tim shivered involuntarily.

"*Public apology Timmy, for all your colleagues and ex-wives to hear.*"

"You're crazy. I won't listen to another word."

"*Oh, and let's not forget poor little rich girl, Cynthia. Yeah, she deserves to know what an evil and weak motherfucker you really are.*"

Lisa basked in a few moments of glory, having just given her brother Tim a bit of his own medicine. The pompous pervert had been caught off-guard, unprepared for her attack. *Good. Let him wonder about my next move. Let him feel uneasy, always looking over his shoulder, wondering when and where I'll strike. Let him feel compelled to be more attentive to his wife; for all he knows, she may be the target of one of my attacks, too.*

With no idea of my ultimate intention, he's going to be squirming until I get back to California, no matter when that may be. Daily phone calls—both at home and at the office—should do the trick, as well as a few more packages to remind him of our youth. By the time

I'm ready to inflict my justice, dear brother, you'll be shitting your pants every time the phone rings!

Back to the business at hand, Lisa double checked an address in her GPS, then followed the indicated route for about three miles. Having gathered invaluable information last night after tracking the girl who'd been dropped off by Jared at that private residence, Lisa sensed she was onto something big. Perhaps something huge. Perhaps even human trafficking. Sex slaves involving underage girls.

Returning to the apartment building where Jared had picked up the girl, dressed sleazily in a Che Guevara tank top, ripped jeans and her hair spiked with gobs of gel, Lisa scanned the directory for any names that would pop out at her. Anything unusual sounding or an apartment with several different last names. There were 18 apartments, nine units listed side by side in two columns. Buzzing one with the names–Jenson/Martin/Abdul–Lisa waited for someone to answer, only to be connected to voicemail after seven rings. Disconnecting, scanning the directory again, she saw two more apartments with two names each, and then finally, another with four names listed: Johnson/Petrie/Cisneros/Campbell. Perhaps that's it, she thought, pressing the buzzer with her knuckle.

Waiting for someone to answer, Lisa leaned against the wall and, facing the lobby, watched someone hustling from the elevator toward the glass doors. Hanging up before anyone answered, Lisa caught the door with her toe as the person ran outside, easily slipping into the lobby. She had no idea where to go, but good fortune greeted her when a young woman emerged from the elevator, talking animatedly on her mobile phone.

"Hey, sorry to bother you," Lisa said, tapping the girl's arm, "but I've forgotten what apartment Miss Johnson lives in."

Sliding the phone away from her ear, the young woman gazed annoyedly at Lisa. "You mean Carissa?"

"Yeah, Carissa. I'm friends with her mother and, seeing they don't get along too well, she'd asked me to drop this off." Lisa produced a thick envelope from her purse. "She's worried about her, you know, paying the rent, and, uh, doesn't want her to know who it's from, but—"

"Did you want me to give it to her?" the young woman said, pressing her cell phone against her jacket.

"Could you?" Lisa asked, feigning enthusiasm.

"Well, I'm actually in a rush," she said, looking at her phone. "Actually, I'm late. Why don't you just go up and give it to her yourself. Apartment three-oh-three. I'll call her now and tell her to expect you."

"Thanks. You're a doll!"

Chapter 17 Monday Morning

Kendall boarded the Space Mountain ride at Disneyland, sneaking on the gondola with two other kids and their parents, who didn't seem to mind the intrusion. Marveling at the flashing blue and white lights, he eagerly awaited being tossed into the star-lit, black abyss and feel the G-forces press against his small body. Unafraid of the whip-like acceleration of the rollercoaster, Kendall raised his arms whenever the cart descended, copying his new-found friends, feeling his stomach drop to his feet. He loved every minute of it and couldn't wait to thank his mother for finally taking him to the best Southern California attraction ever!

But when he got off the ride and said goodbye to his new friends, his mother was nowhere to be seen. Panicked, he looked all around, but all he could see was a throng of adults blocking his view. And now, tall people were converging on him, closing in so that in addition to not being able to see, he could barely breathe. He felt as if his throat was closing up so that no air could get into his lungs. He was suffocating!

Struggling to lift his hand to his mouth, he finally succeeded, reaching inside, trying to clear his airway. Then, it hit him: he'd been breathing in pieces of cotton. At least that was what he thought. It was so dark he couldn't be sure. Twirling a piece in his hand, he inspected it up close, but it was still too dark to tell. Escaping the throng, he searched for some light, and finding a sliver coming through an open door, he held the cotton up for inspection. But it wasn't cotton after all. It was just lint floating in the air.

He called out for his mother, but she didn't answer. He called out again and then felt someone nudge his side. Who are you? he thought he said to the woman, but she didn't respond, she just stared at him.

"Who are you?" he asked again, squinting at the dark-haired woman.

"No hablo inglés," she said, which sounded like gibberish to him.

"Where's my mommy?" he asked, ignoring the strange sounding words coming out of her mouth.

"¿Dónde está tu madre? Cómo aquí?" she said empathetically, setting down a large bin of laundry as she walked toward him. "Tu debes haber tenido un mal sueño, cariño." She reached out to him, stroking his hair.

Digging his heals into the makeshift bed atop an industrial dryer, he scooted away from her, wrapping his body in sheets that had been haphazardly strewn about.

"Where's my mommy?" he cried out, tears rolling down his cheeks.

"Bebé, no llores," she said, shaking her head. "Déjame llevarte a la oficina. Allí hablan inglés."

And then, it all came together, his eyes widening in realization, his tears drying up. Tossing the sheets aside, he hopped down from the dryer, dabbed at his eyes and then scrammed out of the laundry room. All he knew was he had to get as far away from the motel as he could.

Tim contemplated calling the police to report Lisa's harassing and threatening phone call, then reconsidered when he thought about possible repercussions. Not only would he need to tell them about the two packages she'd sent–containing photos and trinkets from their youth–but he'd be compelled to explain why she demanded a public apology. He'd be forced to divulge his ugly past—or at least a sanitized version of it—and who knew what that would lead to?

Jesus what a fucking mess she's thrown me into, Tim thought, scrolling his mobile phone's address book. Who could he call to help him out, who could apply some real pressure to that bitch to make her go away and stay away? Stopping at the Ps, Tim pressed his old buddy Jock Preston's number, then pushed back in his chair as he waited for him to pick up.

"Jock, dude, how are you? Long time no talk," Tim said jovially when his friend answered.

"Timmy? Is that you? What the shit's goin' on with you? Where you been all these months?"

"Well, you know how it is with family life, right? The wife's always on my back to go here, go there. I swear that woman can't sit still!" Tim chuckled for effect. "Now, her latest obsession is taking tennis lessons. *Together!*"

"I hear ya dude. Brandi's been on my case to sign up for dance lessons. Salsa dancing for God's sake! I mean, what the shit? Me, salsa dancing? She just doesn't get it that white dudes don't take dance lessons, much less salsa dance lessons." Jock laughed so hard he nearly chocked.

"No kidding?" Tim said, feigning interest, dying to get to the point of his call.

"Would I kid about something like that?" Jock laughed and then cleared his throat.

"No, of course you wouldn't." Tim stopped to redirect the conversation. "Say, not to change the subject, but I need your advice."

"You need my advice? That's a switch. What's up?"

"Well, it's my sister, Lisa. She's surfaced after all these years. After estranging herself from the family many years ago."

"Surfaced? Wow, I almost forgot you had a sister. Jesus. Sorry. Is she okay? I mean, I hadn't heard you mention her in so long, I really—"

"Jock, it's not what you think. She's not—" Tim said, stopping before divulging too much. "She's not up to anything good. Actually, she's trying to make my life miserable. That's why I need your advice."

"Whoa, dude. Heavy. What exactly do you mean by she's trying up to make your life miserable?"

"She thinks I, uh...she wants me to apologize for some *fantastical* things she said I did to her when we were kids."

"Oh, siblings are always doing shit like that. Specially sisters. Can't forgive and forget. They have to dredge up shit from 30 years ago cause their feelings got hurt." Jock snorted.

"It's not that. It's actually more than that. I, uh, was pretty shitty to her when she was young. But now, Lisa just wants to blow it all out of proportion. I don't know, maybe her sex life is fucked up and she blames me, which is ridiculous!"

"Oh, for Christ's sakes! Chicks and their sexual issues. Always blaming someone for their lack of sex drive, lack of orgasms, whatever. I mean I go through this with Brandi all the time. Her wanting me to do all of these—"

"Jock, stop! It's not that."

"Then what is it? Spit it out?"

Tim heard someone enter his office and when he sheepishly turned around to see who it was, he saw his father standing by the door.

"What's this about Lisa?" his father Todd said, his visage solemn.

"Jock, I gotta go. I'll call you back later."

Chapter 18 Monday Morning

A horrific stench on the third floor immediately assaulted Lisa's olfactory senses when she exited the elevator. Covering her nose and mouth with her hand, she inched her way down the hall, noticing the door to Apartment 303 ajar. *Was this the origin of the vile smell permeating the floor? What was going on inside?*

Nudging the door open a bit more with her foot, Lisa rapped lightly on it, peeking inside to see if anyone was there. Neither noticing nor hearing anyone, she slowly removed her hand from her face and was once again pummeled with an atrocious scent. Sneaking inside, she called out Carissa's name, but got no response. Inching deeper into the apartment, Lisa heard low murmuring emanating from one of the bedrooms. Two, perhaps three voices speaking softly and congenially. Standing still, she tried to decipher the conversation, only able to make out a few words and phrases: "*...phony...piece of shit...fuck him...he'll get what's coming to him...*"

Heading toward the bedrooms, she walked past the kitchen, noticing dishes piled up and a basket full of laundry near a closet door. Peering around a support wall, she watched a cockroach scuttle the across the breakfast nook before running through some lines of white powder sprinkled on a shiny object. Spotting another roach scurrying across the sink, Lisa shuddered before hearing a loud crash in one of the rooms followed by an angry male voice.

"*What the fuck, you stupid shithead. Now look what you've done. You owe me big time, bitch!*"

"*It was an accident, Zack. Like I did it on purpose.*"

"You're nothing but a stupid ho, you know that?"

"A ho that brings in more money than you'll ever earn."

"Still a ho, bitch."

"Stop it you two. Seriously, bro. Leave her alone."

"Who's talking to you, fuckhead?"

Sensing imminent volatility, Lisa scooted back to the apartment's front door and pretended she'd just arrived. Banging hard on the door, she called out Carissa's name and this time, she heard a female voice answer from inside the depths of the pad.

"Yeah, who wants to know?"

"Hey, Carissa, it's Hannah Clark," Lisa shouted. "Can I talk to you?"

"I don't know any Hannahs," Carissa yelled back. *"What the hell do you want?"*

"I just wanna talk to you, if I could."

Silence, then bare feet padding on the carpet before a young woman poked her head out of the door, her bloodshot eyes staring down Lisa.

"Whadaya want, Hannah?" Carissa said lethargically, leaning against the door for support.

"I'm actually a friend of Jared's. He said you may have work for me."

Carissa stared at Lisa for a long while, clearly as high as a kite. She wiped her nose with the back of her hand before jerkily straightening up. "Jared never mentioned you. I don't know what you're talking about."

"You know Jared," Lisa said, chortling. "He musta forgot with all that's on his mind."

Sniffing, wrinkling her nose, Carissa coughed loudly before wiping her nose again. "Whatever. I can't keep up with him." She stared at Lisa again, her eyes glazing over.

"Can I come in?" Lisa said tentatively. "Or are you, uh, otherwise, indisposed?"

"'Indisposed'? Like what does that even mean?"

"Is someone else here with you?"

"Yeah, so?"

"I just didn't want to interrupt anything, you know–"

"Who the fuck are you?" A heavy-set male had appeared at the door, throwing his ample weight in front of Carissa, shoving her aside. Naked from the waist up, his belly protruded like a ripe watermelon.

"Oh, hey, what's up?" Lisa said nonchalantly. "I'm Hannah. Jared said I should talk with Carissa about work."

"Work?" Watermelon Man eyed Lisa suspiciously. "What kinda work?"

"Yeah, work. Over at the mansion." Lisa hoped her wild guess and self-assured attitude would give her entrée into their seedy lifestyle.

"Oh, were you the one that couldn't make it last night?" Watermelon Man said, now keenly interested.

"That's me!" Lisa smiled broadly flashing a lot of teeth. "Can I come in?"

"What the hell's going on, Tim?" Todd Benton leaned on his son's desk, glaring down on him.

"What do you mean, dad?" Tim retracted from his father, biting his lips.

"Your sister, Lisa. What the hell's going on with her?"

"I, uh, she's, uh...I don't really know."

"Stop your damn stuttering, son and tell me what you were just talking about!" Todd sprayed Tim's desk with spittle.

Eyes widened in fear, Tim trembled, anxiously thinking what to tell his father. Steadying himself, he swallowed hard and squeezed his eyes shut.

"Lisa is back," he said tentatively, keeping his eyes closed. "Well, not exactly back, but back. She called me. Just a few minutes ago."

"She's back but not back. What the hell's that supposed to mean? She's either back or she's not back. Which one is it?"

"I don't know," Tim said, slowly opening his eyes. "If I had to guess, I'd say she's close by, maybe not in LA but...I don't know. She certainly didn't volunteer that information."

"What did she want? Whatever she said to you obviously upset you."

"She's harassing me."

"About what?"

"The past, dad. The past." Tim shook his head.

"Are you shitting me?" Todd's eyes narrowed.

"No. I'm telling you the truth." Tim took a deep breath before continuing. "She threatened me."

"Threatened? How?"

"She wants a public apology or else."

"Or else what?"

"I don't know. She didn't exactly spell it out."

"Should we be worried, Timothy?"

Unable to look his father in the eye, Tim just nodded, staring at his hands.

Chapter 19 Monday Afternoon

Kendall had made it as far as the convenience store at the end of the block before turning around and heading back to the motel. At least it was warm and safe in there, he thought, and the lady speaking a funny language was probably gone by now, cleaning rooms. Sure enough, when he pushed the laundry room door open, it was empty, except for piles of clean sheets and towels.

Spotting an overhanging shelf with an alcove under it, Kendall edged over to check it out. Perfect size for him to hide in later when he needed to sleep. But, with the sun still out, he knew he had plenty of time before it got dark. In the meantime, he'd look for something to eat. Searching the room, he noticed a small microwave atop a table in the corner and a tiny refrigerator on the floor next to it.

Hungry, weak and disoriented, Kendall opened the fridge, spotting a large container of liquid the color of which he'd never seen before and a plastic bag with several pieces of fruit in it. Moving the container to the side, he noticed a plate wrapped in foil; someone's lunch or dinner. Then, he saw a McDonald's bag. Reaching into the back of the refrigerator to pull it out, he felt someone tap him on the shoulder and then speak to him in a stern voice.

"And just what do you think you're doing little boy?" A woman about his mother's age, dressed in a light blue uniform, wagged a condemning finger at him.

Startled, Kendall fell onto his backside and cowered in the corner. Shielding his head with his arms, he stared at the floor, waiting for her to strike him.

"Where's your mommy? Hasn't she fed you today?" she said with compassion. "What room are you in?"

Keeping his head covered, Kendall refused to talk to the woman, much less look at her.

"Look, sweetheart, I'll be happy to give you the McDonald's bag if you just tell me what room you're in. I promise. And I also promise not to hurt you."

Sitting erect, letting his arms fall to his side, Kendall regarded the woman for a long moment before saying, "Thirteen. I'm in room thirteen."

"Okay, then. See, that wasn't so hard." She reached down and grabbed him by his arm, lifting him up to a standing position. "You're a clever little one, I must say." She snatched the bag out of the refrigerator. "Here you go, though you may want me to nuke it a bit before you eat it."

He gave her a strange look, then shrugged his shoulders. After heating up the hamburger and fries, she handed Kendall the bag and steered him out of the laundry room.

"C'mon, sweetheart. We're going to find your mother. She must be frantically worried about you."

"No, you can't go into that room," Kendall said, stopping in his tracks.

"Why not?" the woman asked, clearly confused.

"Because my mommy's dead. My aunt killed her."

Lisa slid low on the sofa taking a hit off her vaporizer, staring slyly at Carissa. Pretending to keep the smoke in her lungs, she exhaled slowly, her cat eyes slits as she exuded a convincing mellowness. Carissa had been prodding her to partake of their illicit stimulant–crystal meth–that she and Watermelon Man (Zack) and another guy, who called himself Bonzo, were smoking, but to no avail. Cautious and protective while playing her role as "Hannah" exquisitely, Lisa told them she preferred her own drug of choice, which she'd brought along.

"See," she'd said, producing her purple-colored vape pen. "This is what makes Hannah happy. Sativa." She then offered the trio a Cheshire Cat grin as she pretended to slip into a euphoric state.

Indeed, in her line of work, Lisa required the proper tools of the trade, depending on her audience. And because tonight's gallery demanded "Hannah" morph into a sleazy, drugged-out hooker in order to be taken seriously, she had no issue assuming that role. Knowing without doubt this threesome was involved in a least one nefarious venture–prostitution–Lisa came prepared with the faux drug to compliment her fake persona.

"So, what's this Zack was telling me?" Bonzo interjected, passing the pipe to Carissa, eyeing Lisa suspiciously. "You friends with Jared?"

"Yeah, I'm friends with Jared." Lisa took another hit from her vape pen, gazing dreamily at the ultra-thin Bonzo.

"How you know him?"

"Met him through a mutual friend," Lisa answered seamlessly. "She knew I was lookin' for work, so she introduced me to him. Match made in heaven." Lisa licked her lips and rolled onto her side, her .22 concealed-carry pistol cutting into her hip.

"Who's the mutual friend?" Zack said, interrupting, grabbing the pipe from Carissa, who stared mutely at Lisa.

"Linda Lou," Lisa said, sounding bored.

"Linda *who*?" Zack and Bonzo said in unison.

"That's her name. Linda Lou. She's a bartender."

"You dance? Or you just like lay there and look good?" Bonzo chuckled.

"I do whatever the money demands. Know what I mean?"

Zack and Bonzo looked at Carissa, who had somehow snagged the pipe away from Zack and now had it between her lips. Drawing a big hit, she fell back onto a chaise lounge and stared curiously at the ceiling.

"So, when are we gonna go to the, uh, *mansion*?" Lisa asked, one hand grabbing her crotch while the other went to her mouth.

"You mean The Manor? Why you in such a hurry to go over there?" Zack asked, reaching for the pipe Carissa still had in her hand.

"Yeah. Whadaya know about The Manor anyways?" Bonzo added, gazing lustily at Lisa.

"I know I can make a shitload of money there," Lisa said, keenly aware of the skinny guy's intention. "That's what I know. That's all I care about."

"Is that right?" Bonzo scooted closer to Lisa, kneeling near the sofa, his hands now on her thighs. "Then why don't I help you get in the mood, little lady. Little *Hannah*. I'm good like that."

As Bonzo slid his right hand up Lisa's thigh, his mobile phone chimed, startling everyone, especially Carissa, whose eyes widened in fear. Remaining calm, trained to not overreact, Lisa pushed herself into a seated position as an annoyed Bonzo answered his phone.

"Speak of the devil, it's Jared," Bonzo said, nodding at Carissa. "He's on his way over."

CHAPTER 20 MONDAY AFTERNOON

"Yes, Cyndi. I'm busy. I'm at work. When I'm at work, I have lots of things to do, like run the office. But I suppose you wouldn't understand that having never worked a day in your life."

"Wow, dear, is that any way to talk to your wife?"

"I'm...it's just that...I'm sorry, dear. Look, it's been a rough day and it doesn't look like it's gonna get any easier. My dad's—"

"What did you mean by I've never worked a day in my life? I take care of the home and let me tell you, that's a full-time job. And don't forget, when you met me, I was a management trainee at the bank, and if it weren't for me marrying you, I'd still be—"

"Cyndi, please, you're comparing apples and oranges again, and besides, it's not the point." Tim stopped, taking a deep breath before saying something he'd really regret and pay for later tonight. "Look, sorry dear, it's my dad, he's uh...and that damned package, or rather *those* damned packages. All of this has taken its toll on me. I can't seem to cope." Tim sniffed back tears.

"Oh, honey, I had no idea these packages would be so worrisome. What was in them, anyway? Why are they so—"

"And then my dad, man, he's on my case, making it worse. He...he, just doesn't understand me. I don't think he ever will."

"Who sent you those packages, Tim? You never did tell me."

"He's so damned stubborn, you know? He just doesn't–"

"Tim, are you even listening to me?"

"Yes, of course, I am, Cyndi. What?"

"What, you say? Oh, never mind. You just don't seem to feel comfortable telling me about the packages for some reason. About who sent them."

"It's not that."

"Then what is it? You can tell me anything. I can help you."

"I seriously doubt that, but thanks anyway," Tim said, his mind drifting off. "It's something that happened a long time ago, that just doesn't want to go away. I thought it was buried long ago, but it seems to be rearing its ugly head again."

"What's rearing its ugly head?"

"My sister. Lisa."

"You have a sister?"

Naomi Nichols, head of housekeeping at the Motel 8 in Indio, had searched the property high and low for the last two hours for the little man that had led her to Room No. 13 and the awful discovery that lay within–his mother's battered body. Upon opening the door, Naomi had let go of the boy's hand, pushing him aside, inching her way toward the blood-soaked bed. From a safe distance, she tried to make sense of the unrecognizable woman lying half-on and half-off the double bed. Shielding her mouth with her hand, Naomi burned the scene in her memory, then called the police from the phone in the motel's office.

Once the detectives and the crime scene unit showed up, 20 minutes after her call, Naomi had directed them to the room, allowing them the privacy to do their work, which took nearly three hours. Intending to tell them about the boy when they'd completed their work, she purposefully omitted it, knowing things would become even more complicated for everyone involved. She hoped to find the kid hiding in some cubby hole on the premises while praying he'd come back once he realized he was in unfamiliar territory. *Where would he go? He and his mother were not from the area, so running away wouldn't be a wise choice for him.* Still, kids did strange, unexpected things. If she did find him, she'd figure something out, when she could think more clearly.

But the little guy was nowhere to be found and Naomi was beginning to worry. After dark, Indio could be rather seedy. It had neither the upscale resorts and amenities found in desert communities to the west—like Rancho Mirage and Indian Wells—nor the classy people those places attracted. He'd be in danger for sure and wouldn't last one night.

Returning to the laundry room at 4:30—cleared by the sheriff's department to resume business as usual in all of the other rooms except Room No. 13—Naomi loaded a cart-full of sheets, towels and bathroom sundries to begin her last round of the day. Pushing the cart into the breezeway, she heard a scraping sound emanating from within the laundry room. Was it a rat scurrying around or had the little man returned to his favorite hiding place?

Elizabeth had hoped for a session at the new range with DJ this afternoon, but when he'd swung by to pick her up, one thing led to another and before she could resist, she'd allowed him to coerce her into the bedroom, where they finally consummated their relationship. Feeling secure in her feelings for the younger man, confident he wouldn't hurt her physically or emotionally—like her deceased husband, Jim had done till she ended his life several months ago—Liz allowed him to seduce her in the sultry afternoon heat of her apartment on the Westside.

Their bodies sticky with perspiration, Elizabeth and DJ lay flat on the small double bed, their legs intertwined, likely to be stuck together forever.

Chapter 21 Monday Afternoon

Lisa's gut instinct told her to run, ditch the group before Jared dropped by and saw her hanging with the degenerates—two pimps and their prized whore. But the more she thought about it, the more she realized the time already spent with this group would have been all for naught. She sensed she was getting close to discovering something significant, so abandoning the mission now would be ill advised. Stick it out, she told herself. *Make up a juicy story for Jared to swallow and she'd be "In Like Flynn." Literally and figuratively.*

Continuing to play the role of a stoned floozy, Lisa stumbled to her feet and asked where the restroom was. "I gotta piss like a racehorse," she said to Bonzo, winking, knowing the effect she had on the loser pimp.

"Right down the hall on your left," Bonzo said, grabbing her ass as she sauntered past him.

Lisa flashed him an affected smile and then ducked into the bathroom. Making sure the door locked, she quickly looked for an escape route, should she need one. A small window above the toilet might do in a pinch, even though she was on the third floor. Placing a few layers of toilet paper on the seat and, hovering above the toilet, she forced herself to urinate from a standing position, though she really didn't need to go. Best to make use of it while she had the chance.

She washed her hands and splashed her face, then heard voices after she turned off the faucet. Shaking her hands to air-dry them, she tried to catch the gist of the conversation, straining to make sense of what she heard.

"...she's here right now? What the fuck is she doing here?"

"She said you told her about working at The Manor," Zack said. "That there'd be work for her there."

"What? I never talked to her about that. I mean, I just met her the other night. How the hell did she end up here? What the hell's going on?"

"What do you mean? She came to see Carissa about the job." Zack sounded suspicious.

"What job? I never talked to her about a job," Jared said, clearly irritated.

"You sure? Why can't you use her at The Manor?" Bonzo spoke up in defense. "She's fucking hot, Jared. We could make a shitload of money off her."

Lisa zipped up her jeans, leaning against the bathroom door.

"Sure, she's hot, but she's never worked for me before. I have no idea what she's—"

"I knew that bitch was up to no good," Carissa interjected, suddenly lucid. "There's something fishy about her."

Ready to bolt, Lisa eyed the window, noticing it was cracked open a few inches.

"Oh, stop with your whining and jealousy," Bonzo said. "The more the merrier."

"Fuck off, Bonzo. You're not the one goin' out there night after night dancing your ass off for a few measly bucks."

"Complaining now, bitch?" Bonzo's voice rose, echoing off the ceiling. *"We'd be happy to cut off your endless supply of crank if we're such dicks."*

Silence, then Jared's voice again.

"Where the hell is she anyways? We gotta get moving. I have a meeting with Boris in an hour."

"She's taking a leak—"

"I'm right here, Jared," Lisa said, sauntering out the bathroom. "What's up?"

Short of wasting her time cruising the streets of Indio in search of an 8-year-old boy, Lonnie Dautremont opted to proactively check out any gaming lounges in the area. A natural hideout for a boy of any age, especially one hiding from authority. Quickly realizing the word "gaming" would generate results for the numerous Indian casinos in the region, Lonnie still scrolled through all of the hits her phone search brought up till she found one that could be a possibility: Jamie's Game Shack in Bermuda Dunes, roughly three miles west of her location.

Could a child cover that amount of territory on foot? Of course, why not? But would he even know there'd be a gaming lounge close by, much less know how to locate it? Likely not, but it would be worth a shot. The kid was on the run, and she had to get to him sooner than later; before law enforcement or CPS got their grubby hands on him.

Hopping into her car, Lonnie connected with Highway 111, the more direct and logical choice to zigzag toward Bermuda Dunes. It would also afford her a street-level view of the Valley's main drag, which in turn would afford possible people sightings not offered on Interstate 10. When she reached Washington Street, she turned right and checked her phone's GPS for the first driveway after Fred Waring Drive. Jamie's Game Shack would be on the left, tucked away in the northwest corner of a spacious strip mall.

With more time than patience, Lonnie parked in front and then hurried into the establishment, seeking the manager.

"He's not here now, he's at lunch," a tattooed twenty-something with a buzz cut said. She sported a gold nose ring in her left nostril and a badge that read "Sal."

"When's he due back? It's kind of an emergency." Lonnie nervously scanned the dozens of stations occupied by mostly teenage boys.

"Well, I can help you. I'm the assistant manager."

"Sal, is it? Is that short for Salvatore?" Lonnie snickered.

"No. Sally," she said, turning red. "But don't you dare call me that."

"Whatever, Sal. Do I, of all people, look like I'd be judgmental?" Lonnie smirked, looking to her left at a row of Xbox stations.

"So, Sal. I'm trying not to be too worried, or, um, *alarmed*, but my eight-year-old nephew is missing." Lonnie leaned on the counter, inching closer to Sal, pressing her fingers on the glass. "He just wandered away from his mom and me like 10 minutes ago, from the burger joint down the way. We thought maybe he'd moseyed over here, knowing his love of playing Minecraft.

"Have you seen a kid that age in here just now?"

Sal peered at Lonnie inquisitively, then squared her shoulders, addressing her with authority.

"I seen a couple of youngsters come in about an hour ago with their mom, over there," Sal pointed to her left, "but no kids have came in in the last ten minutes."

"Really? Shit. His mom is just sick, but I'm the calm one, you know? He has to be in this strip mall, I mean how far could an eight-year-old go?"

"Where's his mom?"

"Oh, she's off looking in the other direction, in some other stores. We're trying to be efficient, covering a lot of ground."

"You want me to call the police?"

"Uh, no, not yet. Like I said, I'm not worried, yet. I'm sure he's in one of these store fronts. I'm not panicked. He's not the type to just run off."

"But he just did. Aren't you worried someone may have kidnapped him?"

Lonnie's eyes widened before she got a grip on her emotions. "No, absolutely not. We've taught him to punch dudes in the nuts if he ever feels threatened. So, no. He wasn't kidnapped."

"Okay, then," Sal said, peeking beyond Lonnie at a customer who'd just walked in. "Feel free to look around, if you like."

"I will." Lonnie turned to go. "Thank you anyway."

"You sure you don't want me to call the police? There's a sheriff's station around the corner and they can be here in five minutes."

But Lonnie didn't answer, hightailing it out of Jamie's Game Shack before any cops showed up.

Chapter 22 Monday Afternoon

"Yes, Cyndi. I have a sister."

"When were you going to tell me? Or were you just gonna keep it a secret forever?"

"It's not that, I mean, I never meant to keep it a secret," Tim stuttered, desperately trying to find the right words. "It just never came up. It's just that she's been—"

"Never came up. We've known each other for five years and 'it just never came up'?"

"Well, yes. Basically. There was no reason to bring her up."

"What else are you not telling me, Tim? What other secrets are you hiding from me?"

"Nothing, dear. I swear. That's it."

"Sorry, but I don't believe you."

"Please Cyndi. I swear. She's been out of my life...out of my family's life for ten-plus years. She's, uh, *different*. Not like us; you and me. I have no idea what she's been up to. I have no idea why she decided to contact me now—"

"Well, that's just weird, Tim," Cyndi said, agitated. "If one of my siblings cut off ties with my family for whatever reason—and believe me, it would never happen, but as a hypothetical—I can assure you

someone, if not most of my family members would know what that person has been doing and where that person had been living. Weird. Plain and simple."

"Okay. I admit it. My family is weird."

"That's not gonna cut it, Tim. You're not getting out of this one so easily."

"I'm not looking to get out of anything. *Jesus.* Why did you call me in the first place?"

"Honestly, I can't remember. And, considering what you just revealed to me, it certainly doesn't matter."

"Oh, c'mon, Cyndi. I'm sorry. I really am." Tim inhaled sharply. "Look, we had a bad falling out years ago and she was the one to walk out on the family. It was nothing—and I mean absolutely nothing—that we did. It was all her. She's weird. She never fit in...never wanted to fit in with our family. The only girl with three brothers. Even our own mother never got along with her."

Cyndi's ensuing silence caused Tim instant discomfort. He then panicked and overreacted.

"Are you there, Cyndi? Did you hear what I said? It wasn't my fault. It was all on her. She left. End of story."

"No, Tim, darling. It's only the beginning."

Naomi inched slowly toward the supply shelf in the back, near the cubby hole into which the little boy had crept earlier. *Was he back or was it a filthy rodent hiding within?* Pushing aside a pile of towels, hoping a rat wouldn't lunge at her, she was pleased to discover there were no rodents living within. But there was no human hiding there either. Where had the little guy gone?

Perhaps it was time to call the authorities to report the disappearance of the boy. Well, not just his disappearance, but the fact that the deceased had a son with her at the time of her murder. What good could come of her hiding the fact that a child under the age of 10 was missing? Nothing. And, if anything untoward happened to him, she'd be guilt-ridden forever.

Disappointed but still holding out hope, Naomi nonchalantly pushed her fully loaded cart toward Room No. 1, the closest room to the front office. Preoccupied with the events of the day—the most pressing of which was finding the boy—Naomi was also dog-tired from working more than 10 hours straight. All she wanted now was to finish her shift so that she could finally go home and get some rest.

Deep in thought, Naomi at first didn't notice a heavyset woman scurrying from a truck, which had been parked at a haphazard angle near the office. Nor was she aware that the woman was wielding some sort of weapon in her left hand. When Naomi finally realized her life may be in imminent danger, she used the cart as a shield, bracing for an attack.

As the woman rapidly approached, clenching the unidentifiable weapon up high in her hand, Naomi rammed the cart into her, knocking her down, forcing her onto her back. Subduing the woman with the cart, Naomi held firm, pinning the zaftig woman, rendering her immobile.

"Get off me, bitch, or I'll sue your ass!" she said kicking the cart, her arms flailing, the instrument knocked out of her hand.

"Who the hell do you think you are, causing such a ruckus?" Naomi said as she heard sirens in the distance. She then saw flashing red lights appear down the street.

"Let me go. I cannot be arrested," the woman hissed. "They will never take me alive!"

"What the heck are you doing here, Hannah?" Jared said boister-ously, surrounded by his posse. "You are definitely full of surpris-es, young lady."

"Well, yeah, I guess you could say that." Lisa proffered a sheepish grin, lowering her head submissively.

"How did you even know where to find Carissa?" Jared glared at her. "No, no, no. Wait. Wait. How did you even know who Carissa was?"

"Sixth sense, Jared," Lisa answered too quickly, looking Jared in the eye. "You know I'm super intuitive. Good vibes and all that. It's the reason you sought me out in the first place. Remember?"

"Yeah, of course I remember." Jared nodded his head while Bon-zo and Zack turned in unison to face him.

"She's a phony bitch," Carissa spat out venomously, hyper alert and agitated. "I could tell the moment I laid eyes on her. I have a sixth sense about things, and *I'm* super intuitive." Carissa pointed an accusatory finger at Lisa.

"Shut the fuck up, Carissa," Jared said, shoving her aside, causing her to stumble and fall onto the sofa. "Watch yourself. You're a stu-pid, replaceable bitch. And at this moment, Hannah is looking like a good replacement."

Carissa rubbed her scrawny arm while glaring at Jared. She wiped her nose with two fingers, sniffed several times and then stared at the floor.

"Don't listen to her, Hannah. She's a dumb cunt with no common sense. If she weren't so good at sucking cock, I'd have sent her packing a long time ago."

While Zack and Bonzo both laughed, Carissa cowered on the couch. Lisa kept a detached look on her face, fearing she'd betray her real feelings if she replied to Jared. She didn't have to wait long for a cue from the ringleader.

"C'mon, Hannah, let's get goin'. I can't wait to introduce you to Boris and Grigory over at The Manor." Jared gently took hold of Lisa's arm, leading her toward the front door. "They've been begging me for some new blood and looks like I'll be delivering on that promise tonight."

"Sure thing, Jared," Lisa said, ambling out of the apartment before stopping abruptly in the hallway. Facing him, she said, "But, do you mind if I follow you in my car? I have some really important stuff inside and I can't leave it parked on this street. Gotta be able to keep an eye on it."

"Uh, I guess so," Jared began before being nudged in the back by Zack, who was shaking his head. Gripping her arm tighter, Jared jerked her closer so that he was now breathing in her face. "Can I trust you, Hannah? I mean *really* trust you?"

"Of course, you can, Jared. I'm here, aren't I?" Lisa said, her eyes aflame with passion. "I could have bolted earlier if I didn't really want to be here. Right?"

Chapter 23 Monday Evening

Kendall hugged his knees and buried his head in his lap, waiting for the woman to leave the laundry room. She had become annoying, thinking she could boss him around, make him come out and then make him listen to her, just like Aunt Lonnie used to do. *What was wrong with grownups? Why do they always have to force us kids to do things?*

Luckily, he'd been able to expand his hiding space, pushing it farther back and shielding it with more bedding, so that the woman would never be able to find him, much less hear him. And the best part? He'd never run out of bedding or towels. There was a never-ending supply in here! In fact, Kendall had more room inside this hiding spot now than he did before; he even had room to eat the food he'd snagged from the convenience store down the block.

Even though he was crafty enough to find food and drink, had a bed and a bathroom of sorts as well as protection from the elements, he knew he couldn't go on like this forever. He'd need more clothing, a real place to live, fun things to do, and of course, a mommy. *Why did Aunt Lonnie have to kill mommy? I thought she loved her!*

Settling in to eat some of his snacks, Kendall twisted the top off the Sprite bottle just when he heard sirens in the distance. Were the cops coming for him? Would they be more clever than the cleaning woman was and figure out where he's hiding? *Oh, no. I must be really, really quiet and not let them find me.* He then covered himself in a blanket and silently chewed his Fritos.

"Lonnie Dautremont, you are under arrest for the murder of Loretta Menifee," a Riverside County Sheriff's deputy said to Lonnie, still pinned underneath Naomi's housekeeping cart. "You have the right to remain silent and refuse to answer questions. Anything you say may be used against you in a court of law."

"Get off me, you brute! I haven't done anything wrong!" Lonnie shouted, struggling with the much bigger male deputy, unable to squirm out of his grasp. "And learn how to pronounce my name, *asshole*. It's *Dough*-tre-mont, not *Doo*-tre-mont, moron!"

"You have the right to consult an attorney before speaking to the police—"

"Fuck you! I'm gonna sue your ass for false arrest!"

"...and to have an attorney present during questioning now or in the future." The deputy secured the handcuffs on Lonnie's left hand. "If you cannot afford an attorney—"

"Are you listening to a word I said? Ouch! You're fucking hurting me. I haven't done anything."

"...one will be appointed for you before any questioning, if you wish." The deputy now cuffed her right hand. "If you decide to answer questions now without an attorney present, you will still have the right to stop answering at any time until you talk to an attorney."

"I know the fucking Miranda Warning by heart, *dickwad*, so you can shut the fuck up."

"Knowing and understanding your rights as I have explained them to you," he continued, pulling Lonnie up to her feet, "are you willing to answer my questions without an attorney present?"

"Fuck you, pig! I ain't answering *shit*!"

"I'll take that as a no, then. You'll be appointed an attorney once we process you."

It was neither a coincidence nor an accident the sheriff's department knew where to find Lonnie Dautremont, having been tipped off by a young arcade worker named Sal Stanfill, who, suspecting nefarious behavior on the part of a person who'd wandered into the game shack in which she worked, mindfully wrote down the license plate number of the vehicle in which she'd driven off. Recalling certain TV shows about deadly women—that often spoke of the arrogance and carelessness of criminals—Sal pleaded with the deputy to come to the establishment and dust for fingerprints.

"I'll be willing to bet my life that this woman is wanted for some crime or another," she'd told the person on the phone. "She was up to something evil and if I had to guess, or use my sixth sense, I'd say it involved domestic violence."

Sal had explained to the investigator who'd shown up at Jaime's Game Shack that the woman claimed she was looking for her 8-year-old nephew, who'd run off as she and the child's mother were eating at the hamburger joint in the mall.

"Her story sounded fishy from the get-go, and got even more contrived as she went on," Sal had told the investigator. "It really sounded like she was making it up as she went along.

"Then, when I asked why she was so calm, considering a kid was missing, and didn't she think he may be kidnapped, she sloughed it off. Said she taught him to kick men in the nuts if he were ever approached by a stranger. But the coup de grâce was when I volunteered to call the police for her, she adamantly said no, and then just up and left. Like a bat outta hell."

And, in true karmic fashion, a most unlikely heroine would turn out to be the catalyst to break a case that hadn't even begun. Matching fingerprints with the ones taken in Room 13 of the Motel 8 in Indio, the Riverside County Sheriffs easily solved the murder of Loretta Menifee, who sadly, was in the wrong place at the wrong time.

CHAPTER 24 MONDAY EVENING

Cyndi poured herself a glass of Pinot Grigio and sat down at the kitchen table. Grabbing her mobile, she poised her finger atop Lucia McAlister's number, ready to call her best friend, needing advice before Tim came home. She felt like a ball of raw nerves: betrayed, confused and incensed. How could her husband keep such a secret from her? And, if it was so easy for him to hide the fact he had a sister, what else was he hiding from her? At their wedding three years ago, there'd been no mention of a sister not being able to attend, only one of his brothers, Jason—who lived in northern California—who couldn't make it. She'd met his parents and the second oldest brother, James, who ended up being the only Benton who made her feel welcome. His mother, Saundra, the family's unabashed boozer, had kissed her on the lips during the reception and his father, Todd, hugged her mightily, as if he were welcoming a new poker pal into the fold. Yet not one Benton ever brought up a sister.

What had Lisa done to be shunned by this eccentric family? Better yet, what had the family done to poor Lisa to force her to cut ties? Cyndi refused to believe it was all Lisa's fault, as it was always a two-way—

"*Hello?*" Lucia said for the third time.

"What? Who is this?"

"*It's me, Lucia. You called me.*"

"Oh, shit, Lucia. Sorry."

"*What's the matter? You sound spaced out.*"

"I am. Sorry. I'm a mess. No, actually, I am really pissed off now."

"Why? What's going on?"

"I just found out that Tim has a sister. Lisa is her name. How's that for a surprise?" Cyndi sipped her wine. "What a fucked-up family."

"A sister? Really? Where is she? What does she do?"

"Who the fuck knows? All Tim would tell me is that she's been estranged from the family for a decade or more."

"Wow. That's heavy. What made him bring her up? Like out of nowhere?"

"It wasn't out of nowhere. It's more like...she contacted him. Got him all riled up."

"Contacted him? You mean she called him?"

"Uh, no. She sent him a couple of mysterious packages."

"You're talking in circles. I'm confused."

"So am I. I don't know much more than that." Cyndi gulped down half her glass of wine. "Lisa sent him two packages. One here at home and one to his office. Yesterday, Sunday of all days. So fucking weird."

"What were in the packages?"

"That's just it. He won't tell me."

"Oh, my God, girl, you're right. He is most definitely hiding something from you."

"I know. Right? I feel so, so, betrayed. So, empty." Cyndi sighed loudly.

"What can I do to help?" Lucia said, sniffing loudly, preoccupied.

"Wanna come over?" Cyndi whined.

"Uh, give me a couple minutes. I gotta kinda sneak out."

"What do you mean 'sneak out' for God's sake? Just tell Donovan you forgot something over here and you'll be right back."

"It's not that, it's just that I'm not exactly speaking with him at the moment." Lucia sniffed again.

"Too much drama, Lucia. Jesus. If you have to sneak out, then forget it!"

"I'm sorry. He's still sore at me for drinking too much last night."

"So, you're snorting coke instead?"

Lisa wrapped her arms around her body as she stepped into The Manor's cavernous entry hall, the marbled floors, walls and ceiling maintaining a bone-chilling temperature. Looking around, Lisa recorded in her mind every piece of furniture, statue, lamp and wall hanging in case she needed to recall it at a later date. Jared beamed importantly while Zack and Bonzo kept their wary eyes on an angry Carissa.

"Come here, Hannah, you poor thing," Jared said, pulling her by the waist. "You're shivering. You skinny little thing, you. You need to put some more meat on those bones of yours." He laughed heartily, directing her up the spiral staircase. "Next time we go out to eat, I'm ordering you a huge plate of fried chicken and mashed potatoes!"

"I eat plenty, Jared. I just have a high metabolism." Lisa followed his lead, daintily taking one step at a time, mentally recording it all.

"Hey, what's upstairs? Where are you taking me? How come Zack and Bonzo are staying behind?"

"What's with all these questions, baby girl?" Jared smiled lasciviously at Lisa. "You can trust me. I'm not gonna do anything to ya. I trusted you to drive yourself over here, didn't I? So now you gotta return the favor and trust me. Right?

"C'mon. I wanna introduce you to Boris and maybe Grigory, if he's here tonight. They're gonna *love* you!"

"Who's Boris?" Lisa asked dispassionately, now checking out the lavish second floor, which had a loft overlooking the entryway. "Is he your partner in crime?" Lisa giggled demurely.

"You could say that to me, doll, but please don't say that to Boris. He's Russian and may not understand that you're only joking." Jared forced a laugh before continuing down the hall, pulling Lisa along by her hand. "Boris is a genius businessman. From *Voronezh*, if I'm pronouncing it right. I think that's near Moscow, but hell if I know. I'm terrible with world geography."

Lisa felt the hair on the back of her neck stand on end, though she pretended to act like nothing was out of the ordinary.

"Wow, Russian! That's awesome. I've never actually met a real Russian."

"Then you are in for a treat. He loves beautiful women and you, my dear, are an exemplary example of a gorgeous female."

"Is that right?" Lisa forced a smile.

"Sure is. And he treats his women well. Especially the beautiful ones. The ones he calls *suchkas*."

"*Suchkas*? What does that mean?"

"It's an endearing word for beauties in Russian," Jared said, winking.

"Then how does he treat the not-so-beautiful ones?"

"There are none. They're all beautiful. One more beautiful than the next. You'll see."

"Okay then, I can't wait to meet him. I love men with accents."

"And he'll love you, little one."

"*Suchkas.* Then, I'll be his new *suchka.* That's a good thing, right?"

"The best!" Jared winked again.

Lisa looked up and down the hall. "I gotta use the ladies' room. Where's the closest restroom?"

"You sure pee a lot." Jared laughed, shaking his head. "Right over here," he pointed across the hall to a closed door. "Here, allow me."

Jared opened the door, flicking on the light. "Here you go, doll. I'll be waiting right outside for you."

"Thanks, Jared." Lisa quietly closed the door, turning the lock, breathing a sigh of relief. "Fuck," she said under her breath. *What the fuck am I getting myself into?*

While sitting on the toilet, Lisa noticed another door on the opposite side of the bathroom, just beyond the shower stall. What the hell? Could someone be spying on her? Flushing the toilet, she tiptoed to the door and gently turned the handle. Pulling it open, waiting to come face to face with a peeping Tom, she couldn't immediately tell what she was looking at. Then her eyes adjusted, and her stomach nearly dropped to her knees.

Chapter 25 Monday Evening

Leaving Ogilvie Wealth Management after 7:00 p.m., Tim purposefully took a circuitous route home to avoid any possible confrontation with his wife—productive or contentious. Taking a lengthy detour through Bel Air to clear his mind, Tim turned up the music in his car in an

attempt to elicit a joyous vibe. Sadly, no genre of music seemed to work: not hip hop, not techno, not even classical. Frustrated, he settled on a middle-of-the-road light jazz station.

There was no excuse he could think of that would appease Cyndi regarding Lisa, nor would she be ready to forgive him for conveniently excluding the fact he had a sister. What was he supposed to tell her? That Lisa was the one to choose to not have a relationship with him because he'd routinely sexually assaulted her for years while they lived under the same roof? That he'd targeted her for his own selfish and sick sexual gratification, even when he had plenty of girls at school throwing themselves at him? And the worst, most shameful part of the omission—if he'd reveal everything to his wife—would be admitting he had continually attacked his sister knowing full well their own parents knew what he was doing and did nothing to stop it. Oh, yeah, that would make total sense to a prissy society chick like Cyndi!

Oh, God, what am I going to do? How will she ever forgive me for this horrible, horrible mistake I made? And, going forward, will she expect me to make amends to Lisa so that we can all be one big, happy family? Damn, he thought, taking a hairpin turn too wide and having to over-correct his steering, it's all going to shit in a hand basket. *She's going to put two and two together and then realize my sexual inadequacies may be related to incest and not her and she'll for sure want a divorce and I cannot get divorced again no matter what. Dad's not gonna approve of another round of alimony and—*

Tim twitched, jerking the car, nearly hitting the curb with the right front tire when his mobile phone emitted a shrill instrumental of "New York, New York," signifying it was his father calling. Switching to his car's Bluetooth, he answered the call.

"Were your ears burning, dad?"

"What? What are you talking about?"

"I asked you if your ears were burning. I was just thinking about you."

"Is that right? Well, I hope it was all good." Todd Benton cleared his throat and then inhaled loudly through his nose before continuing. *"Listen, I don't have time for chit-chat at the moment, but I wanted to know if you've heard anything else from Lisa."*

"No, nothing else," Tim said, accelerating into a straightaway on Sunset Boulevard. "But now Cyndi is on my case about it."

"What do you mean? You told Cyndi about Lisa? She knows? Everything?" Todd sounded anxious.

"No, no. Cyndi just knows that Lisa exists. That she's my sister. She's peeved about it, too."

"Then why the hell did you tell her?"

"I don't know. It just came out."

"Noting just comes out, son. Why did you tell her?"

"I don't know. I shouldn't have, but she knows how to push my buttons, get me to say things I don't want to."

"Not *good, son, not good at all.*" Todd breathed out heavily into the phone. "*What are you gonna do about it? Do you have a damage control plan?*"

"A 'damage control' plan? Not really. I was hoping you would—"

"*I don't know what to tell you, son. I've got my own problems to deal with, not the least of which is your sister also sent me a memento of sorts.*"

Tim was silent, digesting what his father just said. "A 'memento'?" Tim finally said, his voice cracking. "What'd she send you?"

"*An eight-by-ten photo of her standing over a man lying on the ground, the heel of her booted foot pressing into his gut.*"

"Yeah, and? Is that all she was doing in the photo, just standing over him?" Tim's voice quavered, and he was barely able to steer his car.

"*She was holding a semiautomatic pistol—looked like a SIG forty-five—aimed precisely at the man's head.*"

"That was always her favorite gun." Tim giggled nervously, unable to control himself. "Bitch could shoot that gun better than most men I know."

"*That's not all, Timmy. A pool of blood surrounded the guy's head. The guy was dead. Dead as a doornail. I'd...I'd venture to guess Lisa killed him.*"

"Wow, I'd have never guessed Lisa would turn out to be—" Tim was now completely unhinged, his voice wavering. Easing up on the accelerator, downshifting, his car immediately slowing down, he said, "Why on earth would she send you such a thing?"

"*The man in the photo kind of resembled you. In fact, he really looked a lot like you.*"

"You're shitting me!" Tim had a death grip on the steering wheel, his knuckles turning white. "Why are you telling me this?" Tim let out a feral howl.

"Do you really need me to spell it out for you, son?"

"So, where the fuck is hot *suchka* you bring me?"

Boris Labirov sat in a lavish, red velvet, knock-off French Provincial, high-backed armchair, picking his teeth, looking more like a nouveau riche Russian mafioso stuck in a time warp at Livadia Palace than an authoritarian Soviet politician making peace with Allied Forces. With a plate full of Russian delicacies strategically placed atop a small marble end table—herring, pickles, black bread, *salo* and vodka—Boris chewed with an open mouth, neither offering Jared a bite nor excusing his bad manners for eating in front of him. Par for the course, his bodyguard, the pony tailed Grigory, sat in the corner, his stool tipped precariously, his wary eyes narrowed as he stared at the hick from Oklahoma.

"She's in the bathroom. Had to take a piss; bad, she said." Jared snorted nervously. "I think she wanted to powder her nose before she met you."

"Powder nose? What this means?" Boris glanced sideways at Grigory and snickered.

"It means, boss, that she wanted to look good for you. Wanted to freshen up. Not that she didn't already look good, but—"

"Bring her in. *Now.* I am busy man." Boris tapped his watch with a greasy finger. "No time for bitches who are late."

"Yes, sir. I'll just go see what's keeping her." Jared turned on his heels.

"Go. Bring her in. I have client coming in few minutes." Boris stared at his diamond-encrusted Rolex, then wiped its crystal with his napkin. "Client wants sexy, skinny bitch. New *suchka* he never seen before. Tired of same old, same old, as you say."

"Got it, Boris. I'm all over it." Jared hustled to the door.

"One more thing. Make for sure you get ID from her. Passport. Whatever she have in purse. Last time you forget and I lose good *suchka*. She run away. Free to tell world about me." Boris smiled, satisfied with his polished crystal. "Boris very angry about that. Still."

Jared turned to face his boss, offering him a weak smile. "That won't happen again, sir, ever. I promise you that."

"Better not. I have many other pimps do good job for me, I use them instead. I can find some other *suteenior* like that," Boris snapped his fingers, startling Jared. "Specially black ones, or how you say, *African American*. They real happy work for me. I treat them good, better than own black mens." Boris exhaled noisily and then swabbed a cube of *salo* on a chunk of black bread, biting viciously into it.

"Russian *chernyy khleb* best in world," he said holding the bread aloft. "You Americans have no appreciation for anything black. It's always white bread. Who cares about white bread? Dime a dozen as you say." Boris finished the bread, chewing loudly before swallowing hard. He then washed it down with a long swig of vodka.

"You, Jared, dismissed!" he said, slamming his glass on the table. "Bring her to me now."

Jared quietly slipped out of the room and tiptoed down the hall.

Lisa stared into the darkness of the room adjacent to the bathroom, waiting for her eyes to adapt. Fearless, expecting to come face to face with a peeping Tom, she reached for her pistol, tucked neatly in her bra holster, placing it against her right thigh. While she couldn't immediately tell what she was looking at, she soon realized it was no peeping Tom, nor was it a male at all. There were five tall posts haphazardly bolted to the floor onto which chains had been attached. Quickly assessing the bizarre scene, Lisa saw that only one post was being used; a scantily clad young woman chained to it, incapacitated. Moaning, writhing in pain, the woman, splayed out on the bare floor, was reaching out to Lisa, unintelligibly begging for help.

Lisa felt like she'd stepped into a hallucinogenic film, and at any moment, a kaleidoscope of snakes would slither in rainbow colors toward her, ready to devour her. They'd entwine her and she'd be trapped, not able to escape because they'd be coming from all angles. Shaking off the thought, Lisa, her gun at her side, inched slowly toward the girl, whose post was in the middle of the room.

"Please. Help me," Lisa heard the girl say, barely audible. "Help me."

"I'm here, honey, I'm coming to help." Lisa moved tentatively in the dark, sweeping the room with her eyes as she made her way to the young woman.

"Please...help."

Grasping the chain as she bent down to the girl's level, Lisa immediately noticed a large padlock securing it to the post. "Damn," she said under her breath.

"Over there...on the wall," the girl said faintly. "The key."

Rising, Lisa hurried to the wall by the door to the bathroom. Snatching the ring of keys, Lisa had to try only three keys before one of them worked. Momentarily relieved, Lisa touched the girls' forehead, feeling its heat, her hair matted and wet. "I've got to get you out of here."

"Please. I...I'm...really sick."

"Can you stand up for me?" Lisa asked softly, helping her to her feet. "That's a good girl. Good job."

"They'll...Boris...will see us." The young woman's knees buckled.

"Where is he, do you know?" Her gun now secured in her waistband, Lisa helped the girl stand erect.

"In his...den. Across...the hall. I think."

"Is there another way out?" Lisa scanned the room, noticing a shard of light on the far end.

"Yes, over...there. It...leads to...back stairs—"

"Can you make it?"

The girl looked into Lisa's eyes, and even in the shadowy light, Lisa sensed her deep gratitude.

Chapter 26 Monday Night

Lonnie sat on the hard slab bench in her jail cell in downtown Indio waiting for her court-appointed lawyer to show up. Every joint in her body ached, especially her upper arms and neck from being tossed around by that dickwad cop who arrested her. Why had she been so careless? She'd always been able to cover her tracks well in the past, never leaving a trace of herself behind, much less a clue.

Shifting her weight off her butt, she lay down gingerly, trying in vain to find a comfortable position. Pulling her knees to her chest, she squeezed hard in the hopes of having even temporary relief. Nothing but pain in her right shoulder. *Fuck! When's the lawyer getting here?*

Shooting straight up, stretching her spine, Lonnie tilted her head back and closed her eyes. When she brought her head back down, she opened her eyes to the pleasant visage of a handsome woman dressed in a navy-blue suit and what her mother would to call smart pumps. Next to the woman stood a rotund female corrections officer with short-cropped hair and a butch attitude to match.

"Lonnie Dautremont," the suited woman said without hesitation, "my name is Molly Benedict. I'm from the Riverside County Public Defender's office. They told me you needed a lawyer. Seems you're in a bit of trouble."

Speechless, Lonnie continued to regard the conservatively dressed, forty-something blonde attorney lugging a heavy briefcase. Opening her mouth to speak, Lonnie then shifted her gaze to the guard.

"First of all, I don't *need* a lawyer, I *asked* for one," Lonnie said confidently, still staring at the corrections officer. "Second, why didn't you come and get me when my lawyer showed up? Isn't that the protocol?"

"She's here now, Dautremont, so what's your beef?"

"My beef is that a jail cell is nowhere to have a private conversation with your attorney."

"Lonnie, it's quite alright," Molly interjected evenly. "We'll be meeting in an interview room in just a minute. I asked Ms. Collins to show me your cell. I wanted to see it first-hand. It's all good." Molly smiled sincerely.

Officer Collins unlocked the cell, leading Molly inside. "Careful, Ms. Benedict, the prisoner isn't very–"

"Nice to meet you, Lonnie," Molly said, ignoring the guard, extending her hand.

"Nice to meet you, too," Lonnie replied, shaking her lawyer's hand while glaring at the guard. "I may be in jail, but I'm no criminal, Mizz Collins."

"C'mon. Let's get to know each other."

Lonnie followed Molly out of the cell, with guard Collins shadowing her from behind.

While his mother's killer was plotting her defense with her public defender a mere three miles away, Kendall settled in for the night in the laundry room of the Motel 8, keeping warm by tightly wrapping himself in a combination of bedding–sheets and blankets–just out of the dryer. He had no idea what time it was, though it had been dark for a few hours. It would have been about the same time his mother always started to put him to bed. With nothing else to do and his eyelids heavy, Kendall, lying on his right side, tucked his hands under the pillow and slowly drifted off to sleep.

Tim stealthily slipped into his home via a side entrance—cognizant of not making a sound—stepping inside an eclectic rumpus room filled with all sorts of entertainment paraphernalia. Hustling to his gun safe wedged against the back wall, he rotated the safe's combination lock, ending on the number 36. Listening for a click, he then pulled the handle down and toward him to open the door. Unable to suppress a smile, Tim regarded his arsenal of firearms—long guns and pistols of every caliber imaginable. If he accomplished nothing else in his life, he could rightfully say he did firearms well. Beauties all of them, some were dearer to his heart than others for a variety of reasons, though many served a purpose greater than merely looking good; they were meant for self-protection.

Eyeing the SIG Sauer .380 with custom grips, Tim slid it out of its spot in the case and brought it to a workstation next to the gun case. Regarding it lustfully at every possible angle, Tim thought of the damage it would do to his vindictive sister, should she decide to move forward with her spiteful plan. She may have been a good shot as a teen, but she'd never come close to competing with a real man like him. One who'd been practicing on a regular basis as an adult. *Dad may have appeased your fragile fifteen-year-old ego with plaudits and over-the-top encouragement every time we went to the range, but you've likely had no further firearms engagement since. How dare you even think to threaten me when I've always been the crack shot of the family?*

Returning to the case, Tim retrieved a box of .380 ammo, then filled the pistol's magazine with eight bullets. Pulling back the slide, he made sure one popped into the chamber. Satisfied, he grabbed a gun bag that would fit the SIG, re-locked the safe and shoved the bag into his waistband. Fastening the bottom button of his suit jacket, he turned to leave, intending to sneak into the main part of the house without his wife knowing what he'd done. His plans were thwarted when he saw Cyndi, dressed in a flimsy chenille robe, standing by the door.

"What are you doing, dear?" Cyndi said evenly, her eyes narrowed.

"Nothing, really," Tim said casually. "Just wanted to check if I locked the safe properly the last time."

"The 'last time'? What does that mean?" Cyndi took a few strides inside the rumpus room.

"It means what it means. There's nothing to be read into what I just said."

"Sneaking home late, not coming in through the garage, seems unseemly, wouldn't you say?"

"I don't know what your problem is today, Cyndi, why you're on my case." Tim brushed past her. "I am not 'sneaking' into my own house. Sheesh."

"The hell you aren't." Cyndi grabbed his arm and was immediately spun around when Tim tried to shake her off. "Ow, you're hurting me!"

"Then don't try to stop me from coming into my own home." Tim glared at her, then added, "It's been a long day and I need to relax before I'm attacked verbally by my wife."

Cyndi silently followed him into the hallway that led to the main part of the house, then watched as he started for the kitchen, then abruptly turned and headed upstairs instead. As he moved toward their bedroom, Cyndi hastened her gait and was on his heels in seconds.

"Why won't you talk to me?" she whined, rubbing her sore arm. "Why are you avoiding me?"

"I am not avoiding you, dear," Tim said, entering his walk-in closet. "I'd like to relax before I'm interrogated."

"Oh, for God's sake, Tim! I am not interrogating you." She plopped down on the bed, watching him undress, noticing him take out a satchel from his pants and placing it on a shelf above his head. "Why did you take one of your guns from the safe?"

Unbuttoning his shirt, Tim slowly turned around to face his wife. "If you must know, I've been feeling vulnerable walking in the underground garage at work. I think I should be prudent and prepared if something—"

"Is someone trying to kill you?" Cyndi shot up, her hand covering her mouth. "Oh my God, Tim. Have you called the police?"

"You see darling, this is why I don't tell you certain things," he said, throwing his shirt into the hamper and unzipping his pants. "This is why I'm secretive. I don't want to worry you about every little thing."

"But I do." Cyndi sauntered over to her husband, wrapping her arms around his neck, her robe loosening as she pressed her body against his. "I'm a worry wart, I suppose, but I also don't want to be left out of your life, you know, from important things."

"You're not left out; I can assure you that." Tim held her for a long moment as she nuzzled her face in his neck.

"But you did, darling," Cyndi said, breathing into his neck.

"Is this about Lisa?" Tim pushed away from his wife, removing his trousers as he stared her down.

"Why don't you show me what she sent to you?" Cyndi said, sounding childlike.

"Is that what you want?" Tim arched an eyebrow. "Be careful what you ask for, darling."

Chapter 27 Monday Night, Late

Scurrying quietly down a dimly lit staircase in the rear of The Manor, then finding the back door the girl had alluded to, Lisa helped the frail young woman outside. Now, Lisa had to gain her bearings and locate her car, which she'd parked on the street. Just another minute or two and they'd be on their way–

Hearing three loud successive bangs coming from inside the compound, Lisa grabbed the girl by the waist and instinctively led her around the left of the property, following a flagstone pathway, illuminated by moonlight.

"Are you okay, honey?"

"I'll make it," she said softly, hobbling, trying to keep up with Lisa's long strides. "I'm gonna make it."

"Sorry to push you, but we don't have much time. That sounded like gunfire."

Feeling her hesitate, Lisa urged her along, understanding and empathizing with her fear.

"What's you name sweetie?" Lisa said, spotting a wrought iron gate up ahead.

"Mo-Monique."

"Nice to meet you, Monique. Wish we'd met under different, uh, better circumstances.

"My name is Hannah," Lisa said easily, opting to maintain her fake identity in Arizona. "I am your angel. Sent to rescue you and—"

"My f-friend—"

"What friend?" Lisa hesitated a second.

"Inside. She's inside."

"Was she in the room with you, or in another room in the house?" Lisa jiggled the gate, noticing there was no padlock.

"Other room. I...don't know. Too hard...to remember."

Lisa unhinged the clasp on the gate, opening it, guiding Monique through. "I'm sorry about your friend, but we can't go back in."

Allowing the gate to shut noiselessly, Lisa scanned the area, re-gained her perspective and spotted her car about 50 feet down the street.

"C'mon, sweetie. Let's go. I'll figure out a way to come back and save your friend. We just can't do it now. Trust me on this."

"It's not looking good, Lonnie, not looking good at all," public defender Molly Benedict said matter-of-factly. "Your fingerprints were all over the motel room, same fingerprints the sheriffs found on the counter at Jaime's Game Shack."

"It's a conspiracy, I swear! I did not kill Loretta. I loved her." Lonnie rocked back and forth, shaking her head in disbelief.

"Do you know how many defendants say that to me? Ninety-nine percent of them. They all loved their partners, spouses, lovers. And, in a fit of rage, killed them. It happens. The best we can hope for—"

"I didn't do it," Lonnie said, looking pleadingly at Molly. "You gotta believe me."

"The best we can hope for is temporary insanity. You lost it. It'll be a lesser sentence. We'll plead temporary—"

"What the fuck you sayin'? Are you *nuts*?" Lonnie rose, livid, her eyes bulging. "If anything, it was self-defense. Loretta threatened me and I defended myself!"

The guard hustled over to the table, ready to subdue her prisoner. Molly raised both hands, motioning her to relax, she had it under control.

"Lonnie, please. Sit," Molly said, scooting her chair backwards. "You cannot act aggressively in the interview room, or you'll be removed."

Lonnie begrudgingly sat down, folded her arms over her chest and sulked. She stared at the table, refusing to look at her attorney.

"So, let's try this again, Lonnie," Molly said, shifting in her chair. "You need to trust me on this, otherwise you're going down with a life sentence, there's no doubt in my mind."

"What the hell are you doing, sweetheart?" Saundra Ogilvie Benton asked her husband Todd, who was leaning over the desk in his home office, perusing a strip of negatives, his reading glasses low on his nose.

"Jesus Christ, Saundra. You scared the living shit out of me." Todd straightened slowly, grasping his lower back. Facing his wife, he added, "Why can't you at least announce yourself when you enter a room."

"I'm so sorry, darling, I thought you heard me padding down the hall." Saundra inched closer to her husband, a martini glass unstable in her hand, its colorless liquid sloshing on the carpet. "Are those negatives, dear? Who's in them?"

"Yes, Saundra, they're negatives, like from the Stone Age when people used film in their cameras." Todd continued scrutinizing the strip, wearing protective gloves.

"What are you looking for?" Saundra jerkily lifted the cocktail glass to her lips, gulping down a healthy amount, spilling a bit on her husband's desk. Dabbing the vodka with the sleeve of her robe, she then looked sheepishly at Todd.

"Jesus, Saundra. Must you drink in here? Can't you see this is delicate stuff?" Todd shook his head.

"Who's in the pictures, darling? Is it Timmy?" Saundra licked her lips, preserving every drop of liquor.

"No, it's not Tim, dear. It's not pictures of the boys." Todd ran a gloved finger down the strip, carefully inspecting each frame.

Saundra carelessly set her martini glass on the desk, way too close to the negative strips, and stared at her husband for a long moment. "Don't tell me you're looking for pictures of Lisa. Is that it, Todd? They're pictures of Lisa?"

"Please Sandra, watch where you're putting your drink!" Todd swiped the glass, carefully moving it to the other side of the desk.

"Just tell me, Todd. I have to know," Saundra said, tears pooling in her eyes. "Are you looking for pictures of Lisa?"

"Yes, dammit, if you must know."

"I thought you got rid of them all, years ago." Saundra dabbed at her eyes with shaky fingers.

"Why the hell would I do that? She's my daughter for Christ's sake."

"Because you told me she was dead to you." Saundra squeezed her eyes shut and shook her head. When she opened them, she blinked away residual tears. "I distinctly recall you saying those words, Todd: 'She's dead to me'. I may be a drunk, but I remember everything you've ever said. *Everything!*"

"Jesus, Saundra, I didn't mean it literally." Todd faced his wife, a stern look on his face. "It was the heat of the moment, Saundra. Jesus. After all she put us through back then. I was pissed off, okay? She had no right accusing Tim of all those things." Todd fell back into his chair, his white-gloved hands gingerly holding his head.

"She had every right accusing him because it was all true! And it was my fault for not protecting my child; my darling daughter who was an innocent being till that wretched son of ours got his filthy hands on her!" Saundra breathed heavily, her hand placed on her heaving chest. "I need to lie down. I think I'm going to faint."

Todd shot out of his chair, accustomed to his wife's predilection to both drama and illness. "Are you alright, dear?" he said, edging toward her, placing his hand under her elbow. "Here, let me help you."

Saundra yanked her arm out of her husband's grasp, stumbling backwards, nearly losing her balance, righting herself in time, her robe falling open at the bottom.

"Let go of me, you motherfucker! Your filthy hands are the same as your son's. Acorn doesn't fall too far from the tree!" She grabbed the skirt of her robe, wrapping it around her waif-like body.

"Please Saundra. Let bygones be bygones. It's all over and done with," Todd pleaded, an excruciating look on his face. "Everyone is happy now. Everyone is living a good, successful life, so why dredge up—"

"*Happy*, you say? Except for Lisa and me! God knows I'm not happy and I'm sure my baby girl isn't either." Saundra walked around the desk to retrieve her martini glass. "The unspeakable things Tim did to her, in this very house! Oh, my God—"

"And you think you're completely innocent? Ha! Is that what you're trying to tell me? That it was all my fault for letting him? You are more delusional than ever, dear."

Saundra picked up her glass and glared at her husband. "I'm going to find my baby girl, mark my words. And, when I do, you and your sorry-ass son will regret the days you were born. And that's a promise you can take to the bank."

CHAPTER 28 MONDAY MIDNIGHT

Waiting until Tim passed out on the day bed in his home office, snoring away blissfully for about 20 minutes, Cyndi sneaked into the garage in search of her husband's private effects. Which meant, she was on the hunt for anything she could find concerning his sister, Lisa. Photos, letters, trophies, certificates; anything at all that would help her understand an unknown relative. Indeed, Lisa was a relative of hers by marriage whether her husband liked it or not. And the more she thought about this mysterious sister, the more intrigued she became and the more she wanted to know everything she could about Lisa.

Whimsically choosing a specific cabinet on the eastern wall of the garage, Cyndi, dressed in scruffy sweats, alighted a stepstool and started scanning the upper shelf. Thankful her husband was neat and organized, having labeled all his storage boxes on the sides facing out as well as on the top, she pulled out the boxes, reading each one, before deciding none—with labels such as Tax Returns 2013 and Mortgage Papers 2014—had anything she'd be interested in.

Moving to the next shelf, Cyndi quickly slid out the boxes, reading the following labels: *School Report Cards*, *Marksmanship Certifications*, *School Notebooks* and *School Tapes*. Likely nothing worth sifting through, she told herself. The shelf under that one had more school notebooks and certifications as well as one marked, *Correspondence*. That could mean anything, she thought, sliding it out from behind the one with notebooks in it. The fact it was behind a box and not in front could indicate something or nothing at all. Using a box cutter, she slit open the tape and peered inside. Lots of old, handwritten letters packed neatly into numerous piles, separated by rotting rubber bands. *Wonder why he separated the letters? Were they divided by person or year?*

Placing this box on the floor, Cyndi started removing banded letters, staring at the return addresses, seeing if any one of them caught her fancy. After perusing several piles, she determined they were banded by year, not by senders, meaning she'd have to figure out what year Lisa graduated from high school, then backtrack from there a few years if he'd corresponded with anyone about Lisa.

If Lisa were about 30, then she'd have graduated high school in 2005, give or take a year. On a hunch, Cyndi reached in and pulled out three piles: one each from 2002, 2003 and 2004. A good place to start and if she found nothing, she'd then move on to 2001 and 2005. Arbitrarily choosing a pile postmarked in 2002, she flipped through the letters till one caught her attention. It was addressed to the archdiocese in Los Angeles, written in beautiful script, likely a woman's handwriting. The letter beneath had the return address of the Los Angeles archdiocese, causing Cyndi to wonder which came first, the letter to or the letter from?

Dropping to the floor, removing the first letter, Cyndi felt her mobile phone vibrate against her leg precisely as she read the opening line. Pulling it out of her sweatpants pocket, she stared at the name for much too long before answering it.

"Hello Todd. It's very late," Cyndi whispered. "Why are you calling me at this hour?"

"*Hello Cynthia, dear. It's Saundra, not Todd.*"

"Saundra? Well, this is a surprise."

"*Yes, well, I suppose that would be accurate, dear.*" Saundra coughed three times before
clearing her throat. "*I apologize for being such a goddamned hermit. I haven't exactly been a good mother-in-law, have I? But then who wants a meddling mother-in-law? Certainly not the third wife of my first born.*"

"I'd hardly say you're the meddling type, Saundra. I mean, you're quite the opposite."

"Well, you don't have to be so nice to me, Cynthia. I deserve to be treated like shit if truth be told. I have been such a terrible, terrible mother. I can hardly stand myself any longer." Saundra began to cry.

"Please Saundra, you don't have to do this; you don't have to cry. I have no qualms with you. You've done nothing to me—"

"But by omission, I have. You see, all along you have probably been the only sane Benton in the family, in this world really. I mean it sincerely."

"Saundra, please. Is there something the ma—"

"'The matter'? You mean you don't know? Your hubby hasn't said anything to you?" Saundra laughed hysterically.

"I'm sorry, but I'm not following you."

"Hasn't the fucker mentioned his sister has surfaced? Oh, pardon my French." More laughing.

"Well, actually—"

"See that's what I'm talkin' about, Cynthia, dear child. You do know. And I bet he was coerced into telling you, right? Didn't just come out in normal conversation, right?"

"Actually," Cyndi said, staring at the archdiocese's letter, tears starting to pool in her eyes. "He was coerced. He received a package. Actually, two packages from Lisa."

"So, I hear. So, I hear." Saundra coughed again. *"Oh, you're so sweet and pure, Cynthia. I only hope the bastard hasn't perverted you yet."*

CHAPTER 29 MONDAY MIDNIGHT

Livid, his suspicions confirmed, Jared punched his fist through the wall in the holding room from which one of his recent recruits had escaped. Wincing in agony, he glanced at his hand, watching blood ooze from his knuckles. Now what would he tell Boris? That his latest and greatest *suchka* had not only double-crossed him, but released another one in their keep? From what he remembered, it was Monique that Hannah had taken. The sweet teen he'd met at the rodeo last week, who was in the holding room, waiting to be initiated. Indeed, she was to have been inaugurated by a special Russian who was due to arrive at The Manor tonight.

And, how the hell did this happen? I knew I shouldn't have trusted you, Hannah, or whatever your real name is. Where have you taken Monique? Better not be thinking of calling the police on us. Not a wise decision if you do—"

Hearing Boris yelling his name—pronouncing the J like a Y—Jared cringed and sucked on his knuckles to ease the pain. *Fuck you, Boris, I'll be there when I get there. But first, I have to come up with a believable excuse as to why—*

Blinded by a bank of fluorescent lights coming on, Jared was immediately assaulted by Boris' raspy voice piercing the air. "What the fuck you doing? Where the fuck is *suchka* you brought? Where the fuck is girl from rodeo?"

Trying to regain his composure, Jared had to wait till his eyes adjusted to the onslaught of luminescence before figuring out his boss' location. Slowly turning toward the bathroom door, he glimpsed Boris' large, silhouetted frame filling the small space.

"Nu? Where are *suchkas*?" Boris shouted. "Both of them."

"They're, uh, both freshening up now," Jared said, uttering the first thing that came to mind. "They're in the bathroom down the hall."

"Get them, now," Boris yelled even louder, his opened jacket revealing a holstered Heckler & Koch .45 compact pistol. "You better not be pulling leg."

"I am not pulling your leg, Boris," Jared said, his voice breaking. "I actually saw them scampering down the hall together."

"Scampering? Scam-per-ring? Is this how you talk now, like baby?" With his thumb, Boris flipped the latch on his holster, reaching in and grabbing his pistol. Aiming it at Jared, Boris laughed heartily, clearly enjoying seeing the fear in his underling's face. "I don't believe you for second. Go find the bitches and bring them back to me."

Jared's eyes twitched nervously. "Okay, boss. I'll go find them."

"Better come back with them or else." Boris kissed the barrel of his HK45, then placed it back into the holster. Without saying another word, he turned and slogged back to his opulent den, calling out for Grigory to bring him another bottle of vodka and some more *charnaya ikra*—black caviar.

Lisa drove in silence, watching Monique's head bobbing to the motion of the car, the young woman's will to stay awake surpassed by her desperate need for sleep. Needing to quickly figure out her next move, Lisa instinctively headed to her motor hotel in Tempe, lifting her sleeping waif out of the car, then carrying her to the room. Ever vigilant, always mindful of being followed, Lisa invariably sought a room that could be accessed through a back entrance.

Gently laying the girl down on one of the double beds, Lisa covered her with a blanket, then locked the door with both the chain and deadbolt. Padding over to the dresser, picking up the television's remote, she scanned through the limited stations offered, quickly settling on a local Phoenix station, running an old 60s movie. Not so much interested in the film as she was in it helping to induce sleep, Lisa quickly became comfortable in the armchair in the corner of the room, one eye on her charge and the other on the TV.

Her eyes and head heavy with sleep, Lisa allowed herself the luxury of nodding off when she was startled awake by a change in the program's sound level: the station had suddenly switched to a newscast. Curious, she forced her eyes open, seeing a weather graphic, listening to the broadcast:

"...flash flood warning throughout the Valley this morning and into the afternoon. Move to higher ground if rapidly rising water is seen or heard and do not attempt to cross flowing water..."

Forcing herself up, Lisa went to the window to see if it was raining. Nothing yet, but she thought it would behoove her to leave the area sooner than later and avoid a possible catastrophe. Sitting back down in the cushioned chair, she then noticed the graphic had changed and now an image of a young woman appeared in a box at the lower right-hand corner of the TV screen.

"Friends and family of a Cave Creek teen missing since October are planning to hold a candlelight vigil tomorrow night at the Cave Creek Regional Park at six o'clock," the female anchor said matter-of-factly, staring deadpan into the camera. *"The Arizona Republic reported that the search for Brittany Leigh Brandson, seventeen, continues and that loved ones want to get the word out about her disappearance. Maricopa County Sheriff spokeswoman, Jane Ward said investigators have found no sign of the teen but are continuing to search for clues. Brittany's mother, Sylvia, is heartbroken and—"*

A chill shot up Lisa's spine as she thought of the girl Monique mentioned back at The Manor, wondering if by remote chance this Brittany was the same person. People went missing all the time, and teenage girls often run away from home because parents have rules about boyfriends they don't want to follow. Still, what if Brittany was indeed her friend? Dare she wake her up now to ask?

Regarding a still sleeping Monique, Lisa rose and inched over to the bed, the reporter droning on about the location of the vigil and who to contact to volunteer to search for the teen. Kneeling bedside, Lisa stroked Monique's hair, wondering what evil may have already befallen her. Suddenly Monique jerked, opening her eyes.

Scooting up to a sitting position, pulling the blanket up to her chin, her jaw dropped, staring at the television. Pointing a long finger at the screen, Monique burst into tears, shaking her head, burying her face in the covers.

"What is it, sweetie?" Lisa asked softly. "What's the matter?"

"Brittany," she said through tears. "Brittany."

Chapter 30 Tuesday Morning

Arriving at the office before 7:00 a.m., happy to see his secretary Angie wasn't yet in, Tim quickly slung his jacket on the back of his chair, then retrieved his gun bag containing the SIG Sauer .380 from his briefcase. He lay it carefully on his desk, then glanced at his watch: it was still way too early to make the phone calls. Wary of Angie overhearing his conversations, Tim would now have to deal with her in the office when the time came to make those calls. Whatever, he thought. *Pick your battles; there are too many other pressing issues to concern yourself with.*

Sliding the SIG out of the bag, grasping it in his hand, he admired the custom grips, loving the way the gun fit so well in his hand. Smiling to himself, he flinched when his office phone rang. Placing the pistol on his desk, he absentmindedly lifted the receiver.

"Timothy Benton."

"*Good, you're in,*" Todd Benton said breathlessly. "*I need to talk with you. Got any lunch plans?*"

"I do now, apparently. What's up, dad? You sound out of breath."

"*It's your mom, Tim. She's gone off the deep end. I mean, it's really bad this time.*"

"'Off the deep end'? She's been off the deep end for as long as I can remember." Tim nabbed the SIG, admiring it, delighting in it. "Why is this time any different than any other time?"

"*It just is. I can't go into it now. Meet me at The Blvd Lounge at eleven forty-five.*"

"You're not coming in first?" Tim brought the gun up to his nose, inhaling the pleasurable fusion of gunpowder and oil.

"No, *I have an appointment before lunch.*" Todd said dismissively. "*I'll see you at the Lounge. Be on time.*"

"Yes, sir," Tim said after hanging up. Shaking his head, he tried half-heartedly to imagine what his alcoholic mother did this time to piss off his dad. Walk into his man cave? Trip on the carpet and spill her martini all over his white couch?

Hearing Angie enter the outer office, Tim hastily shoved the SIG back into the zippered gun bag, sliding it in the bottom drawer of his desk. Grabbing a sheaf of paper out of the same drawer, he nonchalantly strode to the copier and shoved the paper into the tray. On cue, Angie stuck her head in his office and offered him her best feature, a glowing smile.

"Good morning, Mr. Benton. Happy Tuesday!"

"Good morning, Angie. Happy Tuesday indeed." Tim hustled back to his desk, sat down and added cheerily, "I'm meeting my dad for lunch at the Beverly Wilshire. He won't be in this morning, so hold all of his calls."

"Yes, I know. Mr. Benton Senior already called to tell me that."

"He did? Oh, well, then why didn't you say something?" Tim stared at her, annoyed. "What else did he tell you already?"

"Uh, that I need to prepare the conference room for a meeting at two-thirty. Order some individual mineral waters—you know, the pricey Italian kind—and some Earl Gray tea."

"Who's coming in at two-thirty?" Tim eyed her suspiciously.

"Mr. Weinstein and his partner Mr. Mizrahi. Plus, both their paralegals."

Tim glared at Angie. "What the hell for?"

"Well, since they're his trust and probate attorneys, I'd venture to guess it has something to do with his trust."

Son of a bitch! "Oh, I see. Well, then, I guess you have your work cut out for you today." Tim laughed nervously. "I hear those two can be demanding."

"Yes, they can be, but they are thorough, otherwise your dad wouldn't pay them all that money." Angie turned to leave, then stopped when she reached the door. "Ever wonder why all the attorneys in Beverly Hills are Jewish?"

"It's not just Beverly Hills, Angie. It's all over." Tim anxiously shuffled a stack of files on his desk. "They certainly have that profession locked up."

"My mom says it's a cultural thing with them, you know, going into law. What do you think?"

"What?" Tim looked up at her, preoccupied. "Oh, I suppose she's right. They have high expectations. And they love money."

"Mr. Benton, that sounds kind of, uh, racist."

"What? Whatever; you know what I mean. Us *goys* also love money, so we're even."

"Well, I better get back to work."

When Angie finally closed the door behind her, Tim sat back, fuming, unable to concentrate. *What the fuck is dad going to discuss with his trust attorneys?* Tim thought, opening a drawer and pulling out the package that Lisa had sent him. Staring at its contents, he felt a shiver run up his spine, forcing him to put his jacket back on.

Jared had been out for hours, cruising up and down the boulevards infamous for hookers plying their trade, even checking out a few hotel lobbies, hoping to find Hannah and Monique who'd escaped from The Manor. Knowing in the pit of his stomach he'd sooner find a needle in a haystack, Jared made the tough choice of stopping his search after just three hours before heading back to face Boris.

Ascending the stairs to the second floor of The Manor, ambling down the hall to Boris's den of iniquity at a snail's pace, Jared began formulating a couple of plausible reasons for Hannah and Monique running away. One, Monique had suffered a miscarriage and Hannah, being a typical caregiving woman, took it upon herself to get her to a hospital. Or, two, Hannah forgot something in her car, and she needed an accomplice to help her get it out...*Oh, God help me. What the hell am I thinking?*

The only real answer to his dilemma would be to come clean with Boris and beg forgiveness, promising replacements—double the replacements—so that he'd have an even bigger supply of *suchkas*. Yes, that was the answer, he thought, rapping lightly on the outer door to his lair. Patience, clarity, courage, he mumbled to himself, waiting for Boris' gruff voice to emanate from the depths of his den. Sweat oozed from his brow and trickled down his cheeks as he awaited a response. He knocked again, three times in rapid succession, then called out Boris' name: still no answer. Beads of perspiration seeped from the back of his head, pooled at his neck, and then started to trickle down his back.

"Boris, I've got some good news for you," Jared said, his voice quavering. "May I come in?"

Without warning, the door opened, and Jared came face-to-face with the ape-like Grigory, his presence ominous, the Russian's head twice the size of any man Jared had ever seen, his hands easily able to crush another man's skull with little effort. Standing at least 6 foot 8, the Neanderthal gazed down menacingly at Jared.

"What the fuck you want?" Grigory spat out, his breath smelling of garlic and fish. "Boris sleeping."

"I, uh...Boris was expecting me back," Jared said, self-consciously shrinking in fear. "He was very eager to hear–"

"Boris sleeping. You not hear me right?" Gregory picked his teeth with a long pinky nail.

"Yes, I heard you," Jared said, feeling a layer of perspiration encase his body. "It's just that–"

"Go home," Grigory commanded, shoving Jared with one of his beast-like hands. "I tell Boris you want to see him. He call you later. Understand?"

"Yes, yes, Grigory," Jared said, stumbling backwards. "I understand."

Turning to leave, Jared breathed a sigh of relief, knowing he had a few more hours to concoct a viable plan. Boris' hangovers were legendary, taking upwards of five hours to sleep off.

CHAPTER 31 TUESDAY MORNING

Aware of the imminent danger in returning to The Manor to rescue Brittany, Lisa administered a sedative to the girl's loyal friend, Monique, one that would allow the frail and distraught woman to sleep undisturbed during the risky abduction. While filthy scum such as Boris may intimidate the likes of Jared—who aspire to attain similar lows—they certainly never scared Lisa, who'd seen it all during her law enforcement career. The Borises of the world may have oversized egos and disproportionate opinions of themselves, surrounded by bodyguards with automatic weapons, but Lisa had a few things they'd never possess: patience, perseverance and a sixth sense to sniff them out.

Arriving back at The Manor just before 11:00 a.m., Lisa parked down the street, keeping an eye out for Jared. Retracing her footsteps, she retrieved her pistol from her bra holster, then stealthily walked the perimeter of the property till she found the back door she and Monique had used as an exit. Astonishingly, it was unlocked, so she slipped in easily and quietly climbed the back staircase, wary of any opened doors along the corridor leading to Boris' den. Dodging an introduction to him earlier, she didn't know what he looked like, and he wouldn't be able to recognize her, either. Still, she knew exactly where he'd be and felt confident she'd recognize him the moment she saw him.

Spotting the bathroom door as well the entrance to Boris' den directly across from it, Lisa slowed her gait as she tiptoed closer. Controlling her breathing, releasing the safety on her SIG, Lisa reached for the door handle to Boris' den and slowly turned it clockwise. Pushing it open, she was instantly assaulted by an amalgam of stale cigarette smoke and fish. Fanning away the stench, she crept quietly into the dimly lit, elaborate room decorated with ornate European furnishings, including animal skin rugs under tables and in front of sofas and chairs. Looking right then left, not seeing anyone inside, she innately navigated the room, heading diagonally toward the far corner where she noticed the outline of another door.

With her SIG Sauer .45 at the ready, she glided toward the corner of the room, passing a large coffee table filled with half-eaten crepes and caviar as well as a square mirror with faint white markings. A near empty vodka bottle lay atop the table, three empty glasses nearby while a champagne bottle lay tipped over on one of the rugs, a dark discoloration underneath it. Hearing the faint sound of music, Lisa quickened her pace, following her instincts, heading straight for the door. Scanning the room behind her, satisfied no one was there, she grabbed the door handle and turned it.

Carefully pushing the door open, she stepped into what appeared to be a supply room, with metal shelves lining the walls and an old wooden desk in the center. Loud, foreign pop music blared from a radio on the desk, on which a disheveled, ponytailed giant of a man lay on his side, snoring blissfully. Something about him told her this was not Boris, this humongous blob of a man who exuded all the qualities of a bodyguard.

Lisa inched closer to the man, strategically standing at an angle behind him, hiding from view, placing the barrel of her .45 on his right temple.

"Hey, fuckhead, wake up!" Lisa yelled, watching the behemoth's chest expand and contract, still snoring away, unaware he had a visitor.

"I said, wake up fuckhead! I don't have all day."

At that, Grigory snorted, opened his eyes and tried in vain to sit upright. Realizing he had a gun to his head, he lay back down and snorted, seemingly trying to clear his airways.

"Who the fuck are you, bitch?" he said, coughing.

"None of your fucking business," Lisa seethed, jamming the gun hard against his temple. "I don't answer your questions."

"*Suchka* think she tough like man," Grigory chortled, trying to take a peek at her.

Lisa kept a steady pressure on his head. "Where is Boris?" she yelled into his ear. "Is he here?"

Grigory forcefully laughed so hard, he started coughing again, nearly choking. Bringing his hand up to his mouth, he spit green phlegm into it, then wiped it off on his pants.

"Where's Boris? I don't have time to listen to your bullshit, so give it up. *Now!*"

Breathing raggedly, sounding asthmatic, Grigory couldn't stop coughing and it seemed to Lisa he may keel over and die at any moment. When he finally caught his breath, he said, "Boris sleeping. Other room."

"Get up dickwad and take me to him." Lisa moved the gun's barrel to the center of his back, urging him to get up.

With great effort, Grigory hopped off the desk, stood on wobbly feet, and, instead of backtracking through Boris' den, ambled to a corner of the supply room.

"Where the hell you taking me?" Lisa asked warily. "You better be taking me directly to him, otherwise I have no problem putting a bullet into your head right now. Watch your step. I have killed for lesser offenses. I am dead serious."

Lisa felt Grigory stiffen at the word "killed," so he knew she meant business. After exiting the supply room and meandering through another back hallway, Grigory stood in front of a door, knocking three times.

"Борис, вставай! Тут одна сука хочет тебя видеть. Я понял, что это срочно. Не пытайся умничать. у неё есть пушка! поторопись! она угрожает пристрелить меня, если я не подчинюсь!"

"Boris, vstavay! Tut odna suka khochet tebya videt'. Ya ponyal, chto eto srochno. Ne pytaysya umnichat! U neyo yest pushka! Po-toropis! Ona ugrozhayet pristrelit menya, yesli ya ne podchinyus!"

"I didn't understand a word of what you said, but you'd better not have tried to pull anything funny with me," Lisa said breathing into his massive back. "I'd just as soon kill you anyway. You are meaningless to me."

"I told him to get up, someone here to see him. I swear," Grigory said with difficulty, omitting he'd called her a bitch. "I told him is urgent and not to try anything stupid. He come now. You can hear for yourself."

"What else did you say?" Lisa seethed. "A whole lot more shit came out of your mouth than what you just said."

"I say you have gun to my ribs, and to hurry because you no play around; you kill me if I don't...uh...I, uh, don't know word in English."

Lisa then heard heavy footsteps from behind the door, increasing in sound as the person got nearer to the door. "Act cool or you're toast," Lisa commanded when she heard the door handle turn. "And I'm not talking about bread."

Peering around Grigory's gargantuan body, Lisa's jaw dropped when she saw who answered the door.

CHAPTER 32 TUESDAY MORNING, LATE

With no recourse but to wait for her public defender, Molly Benedict, to contact her on Friday, Lonnie Dautremont resigned herself to her immediate fate: sitting in a jail cell, biding her time alone. Having no interest in speaking with any of the other inmates awaiting trials of their own, Lonnie avoided the other women, preferring to sulk in private. Barring a miracle or an escape, she would be going away for a long time, so what was the point in making friends with anyone?

Still, there had to be a way out, she thought, racking her brain to come up with an idea. She was too clever not to create an escape plan. She had to think of something as the possibility of spending the rest of her life in prison was not an option. So, with time to spare after breakfast, she opted to utilize one privilege: making a phone call. Dialing the number of a childhood friend with whom she hadn't spoken in a long while, Lonnie thought fondly about Darlene Sampson and their relationship back in high school. Darlene was the type of gal who would give anyone the shirt off her back if they needed it, with no questions asked and no expectations of reciprocation.

After listening to the recording indicating the call was coming from a penal institution, Lonnie was ecstatic upon hearing the voice of her longtime friend.

"What the fuck, girl, you in the pokey?" Darlene said with a throaty laugh. *"What the fuck you do this time?"*

"Dar, it's so good to hear your voice," Lonnie said, her own voice cracking with emotion. "I, uh, it's not good. Not good at all. The cops say I killed someone. Murder. I, uh—"

"What the hell you talkin' about, girl? Murder?"

"Yeah, it's not...it wasn't...*murder*...I loved her. It was an accident. I didn't mean for it to happen."

"Lon, you gotta watch what you say on the phone, you know? They're tapped. There's people listening in to our conversations."

"Yeah, well, let them!" Lonnie shouted, startling two other women in line waiting to use the phones. "I'm not sayin' nothing that ain't the truth, ya know?"

"Look, I hear ya, but you know what they say: Anything you say can and will be used against you in a court of law."

"You seem to know that line by heart." Lonnie laughed humorlessly.

"Stop it. Everyone knows it." Darlene breathed out loudly. *"Look, ya know I love ya, but since I'm payin' for this call, get to the point. Please?"*

"Will you come visit me? Please? Pretty please? I know you don't got a felony or an arrest warrant out for ya, right?"

"No, I don't." Darlene chuckled.

"So, then come. No reason they cannot let you in to see me."

"Sure thing, Lon."

"I know it's a long drive, but I'll make it worth your while. Promise!"

"You will?" Darlene laughed freely, then added, *"Can't wait to find out what my reward will be."*

"Tomorrow morning? Please? You could even stay overnight at a cheap motel. Just down the street. That way you can see me two days in a row. Whatcha say, hon?"

Lonnie felt as if her feet weren't touching the ground on the way back to her cell.

The Blvd Lounge inside the Beverly Wilshire Hotel would have been an extraordinary treat for the average person living in LA, but Timothy and Todd Benton were anything but average. For them, the restaurant was a regular lunch destination for men of their social and economic stature. Sauntering into the hotel's lobby at precisely eleven forty-one, for fear of being late and angering his father, Tim spotted the elder Benton leaning against a pilar, deep in conversation with a young gentleman sharply dressed in a three-piece, pinstripe suit.

"Hey dad, what's up?" Tim said breathlessly, approaching the two men, having rushed into the hotel after dropping his car off at the valet.

"Timothy, please say hello to Branson Wilmington. He's one of the junior partners at Weinstein Mizrahi. Just ran into him in the lobby. What a coincidence, right son?"

"Sure is, dad." Tim shook the younger man's hand, carefully checking out the attorney's attire. "Nice to meet you, Branson. Will you be joining us for lunch?"

"Oh, no, no. I'm waiting for a client, myself." Branson smiled congenially at the younger Benton, then turned his attention back to Todd. "Great seeing you, Todd, and good luck this afternoon.

"Pleasure to meet you, Timothy." Branson smiled again.

"Please, call me Tim."

"Tim." Branson turned, then, spotting his client coming into the lobby, hustled to greet him.

"I thought Jews only hired other Jews,' Tim said sarcastically, nodding in the attorney's direction.

"Keep your voice down, Tim," Todd seethed through clenched teeth. "What's the matter with you?"

"Oh, stop it dad, he can't hear me." Tim chuckled while continuing to regard Branson Wilmington from a distance, a smile forming on his face. "He's just not what I would expect a Jewish law firm to hire, especially a firm like Weinstein Mizrahi."

"Lower you voice, Timothy," Todd whispered, as the two scurried into the restaurant. "You can't talk like this in Beverly Hills, where a majority of folks are of that faith." Todd shook his head. "And what the hell is a 'Jewish law firm' supposed to mean anyway? Jesus, son. This is twenty-seventeen for God's sake, not nineteen fifty-five."

"Never mind, dad. It's not important. I'll try to refrain from sounding like an anti-Semite. For now." Tim followed his father as a hostess seated them at a table in the middle of the room. After a busboy set down two glasses of ice water, he turned to face his dad. "So, what's going on with mom? Why invite me out for lunch to talk about her?" Tim sipped his water.

"I invited you to lunch because, one, I didn't want to talk about this in the office and, two, I need to look you in the eyes when I tell you what's going on. Why you mother's scaring me so much. It's...it's...just *awful!*"

Tim reached for one of the rolls that had just been delivered by the same busboy, slathering a generous amount of butter on top. "Okay, shoot, dad. I've also got a heavy workload today, so I'd appreciate you getting to the point." Tim bit into the roll and chewed three times before adding, "Quickly."

Todd glared at his son. "I'm buying and I'm your father, so show some respect. I'll take as long as I see fit."

Tim stopped chewing as he regarded his dad. "Okay, sorry."

"Anyway, your mother is really losing it. I think the booze has finally done her in." Todd sipped his water slowly before continuing. "She's threatening me—actually both of us—with what you did to Lisa all those years ago."

Tim swallowed the last of the roll. "What do you mean 'threatening' you? Like, what the hell is she gonna do about it now?"

"She intends to find Lisa, and I guess, apologize to her and beg her forgiveness."

"So, why should you or I be worried?" Tim reached for another roll and a pat of butter. "Who cares? Let the two reconnect. No skin off my back."

"Are you dense or what?" Todd bit into a roll, chewing as he glared at his son. "She threatened *us*, said we'd regret the day we were born."

"It's just the booze talking, dad. Like she has any real power to do us harm?" Tim chortled, chewing the remaining piece of roll.

"Good afternoon gentlemen," the waiter said, appearing with a notepad and pencil. "Anything to drink?"

"A Maker's Mark for me, straight up, please," Tim said forthrightly before his father could swallow the last bit of his roll.

"Iced tea for me, please," Todd said, looking sideways at his son. "With two slices of lemon."

"Must you indulge in alcohol this early?" Todd shook his head. "We've got both Weinstein and Mizrahi at two-thirty. I need you clear-headed."

"Got to take the edge off when I meet with the two *Heebs*."

"When did you become such an anti-Semite? I never raised my kids in this manner. Rather disgusting, actually."

"You never did, but mom's side of the family is, how shall I put it—"

"Speaking of your mother, I need you to talk some sense into her before she does something."

"Actually, Cyndi and I were planning to take her out to dinner one night this week."

"Is that so? Then make it tomorrow. Or even better, how about tonight?"

Tim watched the waiter gently set his bourbon down on a monogrammed paper napkin bearing the initials of the restaurant, TBL. Sipping his drink, feeling the wondrous effects of the alcohol on his central nervous system, his eyes caught two men being ushered to the table to their left; one of them, the dashing Branson Wilmington. Gazing at him too long, Tim blushed when Branson looked his way and smiled. Tim then self-consciously gulped down the rest of his bourbon, arming himself with a false sense of bravado he'd need later that afternoon.

Chapter 33 Tuesday Afternoon

"Cynthia, dear, how are you?" Saundra said, sounding empathetic and sober on the phone. "I apologize profusely for my weepy call last night. Sorry dear; I doubt I was making much sense. It's just that, I was in a *mood*. Do you forgive me?"

Taken aback, flustered and confused, Cyndi was unable to get her brain in gear to find the right words with which to address her mother-in-law. Breathing deeply, she centered her body and mind, then opened her mouth, praying for the best.

"Saundra, it's quite alright. We all have such moments. Really," Cyndi said cheerfully. *"It was nice to hear from you yesterday. You can always feel free to call me even if you're in a 'mood'. Funny, actually I was just thinking about you."*

"Really? What made you think about me of all people? Don't get me wrong, I'm grateful to have my beautiful daughter-in-law think about me, it's just—" Saundra's voice trailed off.

"Oh, it's all good, sweetheart," Cyndi chuckled heartily. *"I had a serious conversation with Tim and one thing led to another and your name came up and I said I—actually we—hadn't seen you in such a long time and it would be wonderful to have lunch, you know, or dinner, you and me, to catch up on things. Girl things."*

"What a sweet suggestion, dear. I would definitely love to meet you for dinner. In fact, I'd love to take my beautiful daughter-in-law out to the country club; show you off. Give all those old geezers heart attacks." Saundra snorted loudly, then laughed frenziedly.

"Oh, Saundra, you are too much. You are a riot! Tim's gonna love hearing we're going to dinner."

"I do hope that spoiled brat first-born of mine is treating you right, because if he's not, he'll have to answer to me," Saundra said, coughing. "As you well know, I am a hard-nosed, tough WASP-of-a-bitch no one wants to mess with!"

"Saundra, you are certainly full of surprises," Cyndi said calmly, betraying her feelings. *"I, uh, could definitely learn a lot from you. Definitely."*

"You have no idea, dear. I am a wealth of vital information."

Lisa's jaw dropped when she came face-to-face with Jared, not Boris, who she'd assumed was in this private room in the back of a maze of hallways in the rear of The Manor. Keeping her wits about her, not betraying her serious demeanor, she gripped Grigory by the arm, twisting it just so to make him shriek in pain. Lest he think she was becoming weak, Lisa jabbed her .45 deeper into his midsection and pushed his large frame through the door, startling Jared.

"What the fuck? What are you—" Jared stuttered, stumbling backwards.

"Where's Boris?" Lisa shouted authoritatively, using Grigory as a shield, pushing herself and the hulk into the candlelit room. "What have you done with him?"

"He's not here." Jared watched in disbelief as the woman he knew as Hannah manhandled Boris' bodyguard. Then, turning his attention to Grigory, he said, "What are you...why are you letting her push you around like this?"

"Shut the fuck up, Jared," Lisa said, gripping Grigory's arm even tighter. "I don't answer your questions."

Lisa scanned the room, a veritable mess, similar to Boris' den with tipped alcohol bottles everywhere and drug paraphernalia strewth about the floor. Colossal candles, strategically placed around the room for ambiance, adorned shelves with other objects of various art. Even an antique wooden hutch with a marble work area, at the far wall, had several lit candles on it, reflecting eerily in its mirrored back. Shuddering, Lisa thrust Grigory onto a filthy, sex-toy strewn couch, training her pistol on him, but keeping an eye on Jared.

"Since you insist on playing games with me, I'll give you one more chance before I mete out the punishment I had in mind for Boris on his blubbery bodyguard." Lisa glared at Jared, her gun now poised on Grigory's head.

"Hannah, what the fuck? What are you talking about?" Jared said, visibly shaking. "I thought we'd become fast friends. Was that all a lie back at Carissa's apartment?"

"Did you hear a word I said?" Impatient and tired, Lisa shot a round into the ceiling, blasting a light fixture to pieces, causing chunks of drywall and glass to rain down on Grigory's head. Both men cowered, covering their heads from the debris.

"Do I have your attention now?" Lisa yanked on Grigory's ponytail, training her gun once more on his head.

"Crazy bitch," Grigory shrieked, shaking his head. "Just answer her question, moron."

"Fucking Christ, man," Jared yelled, dusting off flecks of drywall from his sleeves. "What the fuck is wrong with you?"

"I already told you I don't answer your questions, dickhead," Lisa said, pulling on Grigory's ponytail, causing his head to tilt back. "Now, I'm really losing my patience, so you have exactly three seconds to tell me where Boris is if you want to live another day."

"Do what she say, man," Grigory cried out, holding the sides of his head. "She mean business. She kill us both!"

Jared cringed, then looked away, scanning the room. Redirecting his attention back to Lisa, he looked pleading at her. "He's really not here. I swear. He's, uh, no longer with us. I, uh—"

"What the fuck, man?" Grigory craned his neck to try to look at Jared. "Where is Boris? I kill you!"

Ignoring Grigory's remarks, still yanking his hair and pressing her gun against his head, Lisa glared at Jared.

"What the fuck does that mean, 'he's no longer with us'?" Lisa spat out venomously, hearing low-pitched moaning coming from somewhere in the room. "What the hell was that sound?" She searched the room for movement.

"N-nothing, I don't hear nothing." Jared backpedaled toward the antique hutch, reaching behind him with his hands, blindly feeling his way.

"*That*, dickhead," Lisa said, nodding toward the hutch. "Sounds like a female crying."

A foot away from bumping into the hutch, Jared shook his head wildly as he inched backwards. Livid, Grigory continued to wail about Boris' whereabouts. Ever alert, sensing something amiss, Lisa let go of Grigory's hair.

"Stay put," she warned the bodyguard, walking around the couch, her gun still pointed at him. "Or else."

Gliding sideways across the room, keenly attentive to Jared's movements toward the hutch, her gun trained on Grigory's head, Lisa heard the moaning increase with intensity, most certainly emanating from inside the antique bureau. His body now flush with the hutch, Jared reached behind him, attempting to open one of its three doors, his hand desperately trying to grab the handle. Inches from an unarmed Jared, Lisa closed in on him, trapping him, more interested in who was inside the hutch than in Grigory running out of the room or coming after her.

"Move away from the hutch, Jared," Lisa said, discerning the moaning was indeed coming from inside. "Do you doubt I'll use my gun again? Are you really that stupid?"

Still trying to open the hutch's door, Jared's hands fumbled wildly with the handle as he now looked past Lisa, something catching his attention, his eyes widening with consternation. Finding the handle, pushing it down, Jared wrenched the door open, stepping aside, causing Lisa to look within and momentarily forget about her captive. Hearing heavy footsteps behind her, she alertly swung her torso around just as the giant bore down on her. Releasing two rounds into the behemoth—who fell backwards with a resounding thud—she then immediately trained her weapon on Jared, who was attempting to crawl inside of the hutch.

"Stop, hands up, Jared, or I'm going to shoot you," Lisa shouted, her .45 strategically aimed at his head.

Ignoring her commands, Jared clawed at the opened door, trying with all of his might to get inside the hutch, but his frenetic actions prevented him from getting any traction. Kicking him in his ribs, sending him reeling off-balance in the other direction, Lisa watched in horror as Jared knocked over several candles in his attempt to regain his bearings. Fearful the candles may start a fire, Lisa, still cognizant of the moaning woman inside the bureau, scooted inside, shocked to realize it was another trap door leading to another room. *What the hell?*

CHAPTER 34 TUESDAY AFTERNOON

Flustered, distracted and curiously aroused, Tim rushed back to his office after his peculiar lunch with his father. Assuring his dad Cyndi would take Saundra out to dinner tonight, Tim rose to leave precisely at the moment the waiter brought the outrageously expensive check. The whole family was slowly losing a grip on reality, and he wanted no part of their insane devolvement into the abyss. Having enough problems of his own, Tim needed a new diversion, and he knew exactly what that would be. Meeting the handsome Branson Wilmington today at the restaurant was more than a serendipitous occurrence: it was outright destiny.

Perusing Ogilvie's database of business contacts, Tim easily found Branson's direct phone number and before he would lose his courage, he found his fingers punching in the lawyer's number on his cell phone. His heart beating wildly, his thoughts racing, Tim momentarily lost his voice when he heard a female say, "Mr. Wilmington's office, Maura speaking."

"Uh, oh, yes. Mr. Wilmington, please. Timothy Benton calling from Ogilvie Wealth Management."

"Of course, Mr. Benton. Please hold."

Four full seconds seemed more like four minutes as Tim waited to hear that velvety voice of the Gentile, junior partner of the Jewish law firm, Weinstein Mizrahi.

"Tim, what a coincidence, I was just about to dial your office," Branson said enthusiastically. *"How was lunch?"*

"Wow, really? Ha, indeed. A real coincidence." Tim chuckled nervously, feeling butterflies in his stomach. "Lunch was fine, you know, kinda quick as your partners will be here in about an hour.

"Have you changed your mind about accompanying them this afternoon?"

"Oh, it's not a matter of changing my mind, Tim, I actually wasn't included in today's meeting. Just the two managing partners today."

"Well, a shame, really, as I was hoping to show you around our office." Tim cringed the moment those words left his mouth, thinking he sounded too sterile and corporate.

"Another time, I suppose, but I'd rather get together with you under more casual circumstances, you know?"

What the hell did he just say? Get together? With me? "Uh, yes, well, sure, why not. Do you golf?"

"I'm a tennis guy myself, switched about three years ago. Tennis is more dynamic for someone with a sedentary job, you know what I mean?"

"Sure do and I'd love to get back on the courts myself." Tim looked up when his secretary appeared at his door. "Hey, gotta let you go, but this is my cell. Give me a call later this week, okay?"

"You got it, Timothy. Enjoy the rest of your day."

"Tim. Please call me Tim."

"It's okay, Brittany, you can come out now; I'm here to help you. I won't hurt you."

Lisa discovered the missing teen and friend of Monique stashed away in a hidden room accessed through the antique bureau. She appeared to be lucid and visibly uninjured, though Lisa had no doubt she'd been mentally abused—and likely routinely raped—by Boris and his gang of pimp thugs.

Brittany stared wide-eyed at Lisa for a several seconds, hesitating, clearly uncertain if she could trust this unknown woman. Then, realizing this could be her one and only chance of escaping from captivity, she crawled like a scared animal on her hands and knees, sniffling, still moaning softly till she reached Lisa's open arms. Embracing the frightened teen—dressed only in a torn, nylon dress with mismatched socks—Lisa felt her shaking uncontrollably. Lisa
held her longer than necessary to assure her sincerity.

"My name is Hannah Clark," Lisa said, again using her pseudonym. "Your friend Monique told me you were held captive here, too. I rescued her last night. She's doing alright and eager to see you." Returning her SIG to her shoulder holster, Lisa helped Brittany straighten up. "Are you able to walk with me through the mazes in this house to my car outside?"

"I, uh, think so," Brittany said breathlessly.

"Are you in any physical pain?"

"My, ba-back hurts. A lot." Brittany placed a trembling hand on her lower back.

"Okay, sweetie, I'll help you out of here. Just follow me."

Placing her left arm around Brittany's waist, Lisa took her right hand in hers and then assisted her in stepping over a still sprawled-out Jared. Unconcerned with him waking up till they were well on their way to the hotel, Lisa suddenly smelled something burning, a mixture of paper and synthetics. Looking beyond Jared and the hutch, she saw smoke rising from a smoldering heap of fabric that had been tossed next to the hutch. Carefully avoiding the fabric, pulling Brittany away from it, she flinched when the heap instantly ignited, flames reaching up about three feet and now spreading horizontally.

"Oh, my God," Lisa said, pulling Brittany to their right to avoid the flames. "We've got to hustle out of here before this place is torched."

Skirting around the various objects strewn on the floor, the duo leapt over the gargantuan Grigory, splayed out in front of the couch. Scampering toward the door, Lisa guided Brittany through the labyrinth of hallways and rooms within the house until they found the main staircase. Clearly finding her second wind, Brittany kept up with Lisa as they burst out of the residence through the front door.

Standing on the sidewalk for a few moments, Lisa watched as the flames found their way to the windows on the second floor. Grabbing her phone, Lisa punched in 911 and reported the fire.

CHAPTER 35 TUESDAY AFTERNOON

Venturing out from his hiding place just once since he'd hunkered down yesterday, Kendall was craving some fried chicken, so after the woman had made her cleaning rounds in the morning and sat down to eat lunch outside, he sneaked out and wandered down the street to a Kentucky Fried Chicken. Using street smarts he learned from his mother, he stopped a nice-looking young woman about to enter the eatery and asked her to buy him a couple of pieces for him.

"My mommy's in the laundromat over there," Kendall said, teary-eyed, pointing across the street, "and now she doesn't have any extra money to buy me lunch. Will you please get some for me?"

"You poor thing," the woman said, patting his head. "Of course, I'll buy you some chicken."

Quietly thanking her, snatching the small bag out of her hand when she exited the establishment, he then turned on his heels and scooted down the sidewalk, disappearing into a throng of pedestrians. Content for the moment, Kendall wended his way back to the motel where he sneaked back into the laundry room when the woman was busy speaking in another language to one of her coworkers.

Snagging a cold can of Coke that had been left unattended atop a cabinet, Kendall crawled back into his hiding place and raven-ously ate his fried chicken with gusto, hidden under the covers. Smacking his lips in delight, he never heard the woman re-enter the room, and was horrified when she pulled back the covers and stared at him disgustedly. With a chicken leg still hanging out of his mouth, Kendall sprang from his makeshift bed, only to be subdued by a short, dark man wearing blue trousers and a white shirt with a name inscribed above his breast pocket.

"Get off me," Kendall cried, kicking the man, chewing the chicken he'd just bitten off. Fighting with all his might while gripping the chicken leg that still had more meat on it, Kendall wriggled this way and that, all for naught as he was no match for the fully grown adult male.

Dragging the child kicking and screaming to a van parked in front of the laundry room, the man tossed him into the back bed, then quickly shut the door, locking it with the remote in his hand. Trapped inside, Kendall banged on the metallic sides, unable to see a thing outside. Hearing the man and woman speaking in that same strange language, he could not see them gesticulating wildly with their hands, pointing in different directions. After what seemed to Kendall like several minutes, the duo got into the van: the man behind the wheel with the woman sitting shotgun. Kendall—separated by a locked inside door—peered at them through a small glass window, pleading with them to let him out.

Turning to regard the child, the woman immediately looked away when her eyes met Kendall's, clearly guilt-ridden for what she and her cohort had done. The man and woman continued to speak fast and furious about where they would go and what they would do with the homeless child. And it wasn't long after getting onto Interstate 10 that they exited at Jackson Street, pulling into the first available gas station.

Laying low, biding his time inside the van while the man went inside the service station, Kendall crawled to the back and pushed on the inside door handle. Amazingly, it unlocked the latch, allowing him to kick it open. Bursting out of the van to freedom, Kendall ran as fast as he could, the sun blinding him as he escaped into the desert.

At precisely 2:22 p.m., Marcus Weinstein, his partner Benjamin Mizrahi and two female paralegals entered the lobby of the Ogilvie Wealth Management building on Wilshire Boulevard, taking the elevator up to the seventh floor where Tim's and Todd's offices were located. When the probate attorneys and their entourage stepped out of the elevator, eager-beaver Angie Lockhart, secretary to both father and son Benton, cheerfully greeted the foursome, ushering them immediately into the conference room where bland refreshments awaited them.

"Todd and Tim will be in momentarily," Angie said to the senior attorney, Marcus Weinstein, flashing her perfect white teeth. "Please, help yourselves to the beverage of your choice."

"Tim will be joining us today?" Marcus asked, straightening his jacket lapels, glancing sideways at his partner. "I thought it was just going to be Todd."

"Oh, well," Angie said, a puff of air uncontrollably escaping her mouth, "that's what I was told." Nervous, she absentmindedly rearranged the bottles of Italian mineral water on the shiny, gold Chinese trays, thinking of what to say next. Then, serendipitously catching the eye of Ben Mizrahi, she blinked several times before adding, "Well, maybe that's what I assumed. Maybe I thought I heard Mr. Benton senior say it. Excuse me."

Blushing, Angie quickly exited the conference room and hustled to Todd's office, running right into Tim as she rounded a blind corner.

"Jesus, Tim, sorry!" she shrieked, bouncing off her younger boss. "I was just—"

"Just coming to get me?" Tim said, beating her to the punch.

"Uh, no, not really, I was—" Angie looked off in the distance, self-consciously patting down her hair. "Were you supposed to be at this—"

"I'm not late, am I?" Tim asked, glancing at his watch. "Is that what you were going to say? Because according to my Rolex, which is never wrong, it's exactly two twenty-nine."

"No, you're not late, it's not that. You're not supposed to—"

"Angie, what the hell's gotten into you today? Are you feeling alright?"

Looking up at Tim with narrowed eyes, Angie's attention was diverted when she caught sight of the elder Benton hastening down the hall.

"Yes, I'm fine Tim," she said. "Nothing a little shot of espresso can't fix." Turning to head back toward her office, Angie added, "I'll be right back."

"Where're you going, Angie?" Todd asked, approaching the two. "Will you please take Tim into the conference room and introduce him to Mr. Weinstein and Mr. Mizrahi? I need to make one quick phone call and I'll be right in. Please apologize for me."

Angie looked quizzically at the elder Benton, then shrugged her shoulders. "Certainly, Mr. Benton. My espresso can wait."

Angie and Tim walked in silence to the conference room, where they found the legal foursome sipping their beverages: Marcus Weinstein drinking Earl Gray tea and the other three drinking mineral water. All four looked up when Angie and Tim entered.

After introducing everyone and letting them know the senior Benton would be along in a few minutes, Angie excused herself, slipping out to the lobby to get her afternoon espresso.

"So, Tim, I hear you met one of our junior partners today at The Blvd Lounge," Marcus Weinstein said forthrightly. "He had only nice things to say about you."

Caught completely off guard, Tim eyed the distinguished lawyer, unable to suppress a smile. "He did? Well, I, I was impressed with him as well. Bright young man, indeed."

"He mentioned the two of you may be getting together for some tennis at the club." Marcus slyly eyed his partner, who was draining his mineral water bottle.

"Uh, well, I hope I can live up to his standards," Tim said sheepishly. "I haven't actually played tennis in a very long time."

"I'm sure you'll be just fine." Marcus winked involuntarily.

"So, what did I miss?" Todd said, rushing into the conference room.

"Nothing much," Ben Mizrahi responded. "We hear your son will be playing tennis with our junior partner, Branson Wilmington."

"He what?" Todd looked confused. "We ran into him at lunch, but, I didn't realize—"

Embarrassed, Tim quickly changed the topic. "Dad, we're not paying these gentlemen to critique my tennis game, but rather offer their expertise on what they do best: probate and trusts."

"Exactly right, son. Probate and trusts." Todd glanced at Marcus, then quickly turned to face Tim. "Speaking of which, I'm glad you're able to sit in on our meeting. In this way, it's going to be a lot easier to—"

"A lot easier to what? Why am I getting the feeling there's a punchline coming and that I'm the butt of it?"

Todd flashed his son a look that said more than he could ever utter with words: *Don't be so goddamned sensitive, Timothy. Not everything is about you. Time to grow up and smell the coffee.*

When he was certain Tim got his message loud and clear, he turned his attention to the law team and officially began the meeting. Sitting close to their clients, the two lawyers silently motioned to their paralegals to begin taking notes. Reaching into his brief-case, Ben Mizrahi brought forth a thick folder labeled "Ogilvie Wealth Management" and laid it on the table. He then immediately reached back in and retrieved another, smaller folder labeled "Benton Family Trust."

Tim immediately scrutinized the second folder, his brow fur-rowing in curiosity. About to ask a question, Tim was interrupted by his father.

"I know Tim still has a few client appointments this afternoon, so for his benefit, and the sake of brevity, why don't we get down to the real reason I arranged this meeting today," Todd said, his gaze on his attorneys. "Marcus, will you please concisely verbalize the gist of my amendments?"

"Amendments?" Tim exclaimed, shooting up in his seat, glaring first at Marcus, and then at his dad. "Amendments to what exact-ly?"

"Tim, please let Mr. Weinstein explain, and then after he's fin-ished, you may ask any and all questions you have."

Annoyed and agitated, Tim slipped back down into his chair and folded his arms across his chest. Todd smiled at his lawyer, nod-ding for him to begin.

Marcus cleared his throat, sipped a bit of tea, then commenced.

"Todd has made some significant changes to the family trust and since Timothy," Marcus stopped to acknowledge the younger Ben-ton with a nod, "is the executor of the trust, it is incumbent upon me to inform him of those changes."

Once again, Tim shot up, keenly aware that something crucial was about to be revealed. Unfolding his own arms, he gripped the sides of the chair, his knuckles turning white.

"So, in accordance with my client's wishes, I have added the name of a fifth sibling to the trust, that of Lisa Margarethe Benton. Although she'd been omitted from the first draft of the trust, I have now–"

"What the damn fuck are you doing dad?" Tim shouted, now standing, hovering over the conference table, glowering at his father. "What the fuck is going on here?"

Chapter 36 Tuesday Evening

"Thank you for meeting me for dinner on such short notice, Saundra. I really appreciate it."

Cyndi daintily sipped her white wine as she regarded her mother-in-law painstakingly nurse a vodka gimlet in a martini glass. At her husband's suggestion, Cyndi booked a last-minute dinner reservation at the Wilshire Country Club. Offering his regrets for not being able to join the women, Tim complained of a splitting headache, brought on by a longer-than-usual meeting in the late afternoon. Sitting across the table from Saundra, Cyndi sensed acute melancholy in the older woman, even as she seemed to relish every drop of her cocktail.

"You are welcome, dear daughter. It is such a pleasure to be in the company of a young, vibrant and beautiful woman."

Cyndi bristled at being called "daughter," assuming her mother-in-law purposefully left off the "in-law" designation to inspire trust as well as induce her to drop her guard. Taking another mouthful of wine, she carefully placed the glass down on the table and took a deep breath.

"Thank you, Saundra." Cyndi waited for Saundra to down the last of her gimlet before continuing. "You know, I wanted to ask you something, if I may. About Lisa."

Saundra stiffened as she carelessly placed her martini glass next to her dinner plate, unaware she'd missed the table's flat surface by half an inch, causing it to tip over. Ever alert, Cyndi caught it before it keeled over and broke.

"Oh, pardon me, dear, I, uh, was distracted for a moment...so sorry," Saundra said, reddening, touching the sides of her hair. "Now, of course you can ask me anything you want. What is it you wanted to know about Lisa?"

"Well, it's just that seemingly out of nowhere, Lisa's name has come up this week, and not just once or twice," Cyndi said, twirling the stem of her wine glass, "but several times. Before yesterday afternoon, I didn't even know he *had* a sister. That you had a daughter. So, you can understand, from my point of view, it's really confusing."

Saundra warily regarded Cyndi, pursing her lips, clearly thinking of the right words to say. Then, spotting the waiter out of the corner of her eye, she waved her arm in the air, trying to catch his attention.

"Another vodka gimlet, please," Saundra shamelessly shouted across the room.

Cyndi's eyes widened as the waiter approached their table. "Yes, Mrs. Benton? May I bring you another drink?"

"Yes, you may young man. Another vodka gim— No, I've changed my mind. Make it a vodka martini. Belvedere, straight up. Three olives."

"Absolutely, ma'am."

Saundra squeezed her eyes shut, then reopened them, reflexively grabbing her empty cocktail glass. Shaking her head, she pulled her hand back, smiling at Cyndi.

"Through no fault of her own, my darling little girl, Lisa, became estranged from the family many years ago. You see," Saundra stopped to dab her eyes with her napkin, "she was...she *thought* she was doing the right thing to distance herself from me and her father. From the whole family. Because of what happened. What Tim did to her."

"What Tim did to her? What does that mean? You're scaring me." Cyndi stared blankly at Saundra.

"I'm sorry, dear, I didn't mean to scare you," Saundra said, nervously twisting her forefingers together. "It's just that...it's about time I came clean and admitted *my* fault in this...*all* of this."

"Here you go, Mrs. Benton," the waiter said, appearing out of nowhere. "Belvedere martini, straight up. Enjoy."

"Thank you," she said, forcing a smile. "We'll be ready to order in about ten minutes."

Saundra paused, gulping down half of her cocktail, waiting for the waiter to retreat out of hearing range. Sliding one of the olives into her mouth, she allowed a smile to creep across her face. "Look, it's no secret, I like my liquor and sometimes I get, oh, how shall I put this?" She paused to chew the olive before adding, "I get complacent—Yes. I think that's an accurate word. Complacent and single-minded in caring only about keeping my body filled with enough vodka to dull the pain. *All* the pain. The pain of my failure as a mother.

"Am I rambling? I guess I'm not doing a very good job of explaining myself." Saundra's eyes glazed over as she took another swig of her martini. She then popped the remaining two olives into her mouth.

"I, uh, wouldn't say...no, you're not rambling, Saundra. But this is all a shock to me. Like I said, I only found out about Lisa yesterday, after being married to Tim for three whole years! After being a part of this family for even longer than that. I'm just not understanding the dynamics of the Benton family, I guess." Cyndi finished her wine, then desperately searched for the waiter.

Saundra chuckled, turning the stem of her glass, staring at the base, mesmerized by the candlelight's reflection in its cut facets. "'The dynamics of the Benton family'. Is that what you'd like to know?" Saundra looked up, staring at her daughter-in-law. Downing the remaining liquor, she breathed out noisily through her mouth. "Well, is it?"

"Another glass of Pinot Grigio, miss?" the waiter asked softly.

"Yes, please." Cyndi answered, staring straight ahead.

"And another Belvedere martini for me, son." Saundra interjected straight away, the right side of her mouth turning up creepily as she ogled the young man. "Oh, for God's sake, don't look at me that way. I'm not driving. My beautiful daughter-in-law is." Saundra winked at the waiter, who quickly disappeared.

"Saundra, look—"

"No, Cynthia, dear, let me finish. I need to. It'll be *cathartic*." She inhaled deeply through her nose, then exhaled through her mouth. "My son, Timothy, your loving husband, is, for all intents and purposes, a very damaged person. So, when I tell you this, it's...please take it with a grain of salt. Alright?" Saundra eyed Cyndi.

Cyndi nodded, anxious to hear the punch line. Looking into Saundra's eyes, she saw that the older woman was crying. "Look, you don't have to," Cyndi said, gently touching Saundra's hand. "Not now, anyway."

"Oh, yes I do. It's about time. I allowed it to happen because I was so wrapped up in what the Monsignor did to him. Years earlier."

"I'm really not following you now."

"The *Monsignor*, baby. He raped by boy. For years." Saundra allowed her words to permeate the air. When she was satisfied its effect had lingered long enough, she added, "Then my boy did the same to Lisa. He raped his own sister, for Christ's sake."

CHAPTER 37 TUESDAY EVENING

While his wife was being schooled by his own mother about his secret childhood past, Tim was on his own mission of discovery: why his father decided to include Lisa as a beneficiary of the estate. Why, he wondered, after all these years of estrangement, had his otherwise intelligent and commonsensical father opted to bring his daughter back into the fold?

Livid, obsessed, unable to concentrate on anything other than the fact his sister would be getting proceeds from a company she never worked at, Tim headed to the garage in search of anything he could arm himself with to show his father why he was making a terrible and tragic mistake. With an attitude that needed adjusting and a focus that craved clarity, Tim foolishly poured himself a generous double-shot of Wild Turkey from his private stash, hidden in a cabinet on the eastern wall of the garage.

At first, he merely sipped the bourbon, kicking back in an old, wooden rocking chair, admiring his carefully organized shelves. Then, something caught his attention; something was out of order. A box was not precisely lined up on the top shelf. Had someone been in here snooping through my private files, he wondered? Did his father have the nerve to do so, or was it his intrusive wife, who got a wild hair up her ass after forcing him to reveal he had a sister?

Reaching for the box, he pulled it down, setting it on the floor. Someone indeed had been snooping in here, he thought, gulping down half the bourbon. Feeling his face flush, Tim sat on the ground and rifled through the files inside the box, intent on discovering just what had been seen and read.

Jared remained motionless on the wet soil, long after several bodies were pulled out of The Mansion and the fire trucks left. Having crawled away from the fracas and hiding behind the bushes that bordered The Mansion, Jared was able to elude first responders from noticing him. Staring in disbelief at the devastation, he tried to recall the events that transpired before the mysterious, fast-spreading fire started. Hannah had appeared, holding a gun on Grigory, of all preposterous things! How had she–? Then, feeling something jam him in the temple, and passing out. *Then what?*

He'd awakened to the smell of burning flesh–Grigory's flesh–and smoldering fabric. What the fuck? Then, desperately crawling on his belly through the labyrinth of hallways and rooms in the house of carnal pleasure Boris had built, barely ahead of the spreading flames till he finally reached the main staircase that led downstairs and to safety. How he made it out alive by the skin of his teeth was nothing short of a miracle. *Now what?*

Without a clue as to where he would go and what he would do next, Jared tried to regroup mentally and physically. Other than his lungs burning, he had no obvious injuries, and was easily able to get to his feet. Tapping his pant pockets, he breathed a sigh of relief as he felt his keys and wallet. And then it all came together: *Hannah. She was the instigator, the one to break into The Manor in search of that wimpy girl, Brittany. Where had those two gone? Where was that con artist Hannah–or whatever her real name was–staying?*

With now two teenage female victims in her care, Lisa realized she had bitten off more than she could chew. Without a doubt in her mind, she had an obligation to save the two girls once she knew about their precarious situations. Still, her focus was to eliminate the predators who enslaved them; kill the sadists who fulfilled their sick dreams by sexually abusing them.

While she was certainly elated she'd shot and killed that goliath piece of human excrement bodyguard to Russian pimp Boris, the big boss himself was nowhere to be found. His whereabouts was of more concern to her at the moment than almost anything. Jared, on the other hand, was of no consequence, as he most likely perished in the fire she'd seen engulfing the large structure when she escaped with Brittany.

Having watched the two friends reunite earlier in the day, hanging on to each other for dear life, crying into each other's necks, Lisa's short-lived contentment only increased her longtime craving. As happy as she was to have saved these two innocent girls from enslavement, she hungered to return to her own, familiar backyard, where she could pursue her missions without distractions and diversions, no matter how noble they seemed.

Now quietly perusing the Internet while the teens slept soundly, Lisa started when she heard a scratching sound outside the motel room door. Sitting erect, listening for further sounds, she placed her laptop on the edge of the bed and retrieved her gun from her purse in the top dresser drawer. Pulling the slide back on her .45, checking for a round in the chamber, Lisa inched noiselessly to the door and waited. Hearing the sound again, she carefully peered through the curtains to see whether a human or animal was making the noise. With all that had occurred in the last few days, she wouldn't be surprised if one of those scrawny pimps was coming around to hassle her. Or do worse.

Steadying her nerves, her heart beating wildly, Lisa checked through a tiny slit in the curtains but saw no one there. Holding her breath, sliding the chain off its track at the top of the door, she quietly unlocked the deadbolt and swiftly opened the door. Letting out a huge sigh, dropping her gun to her side, she started laughing uncontrollably when she spotted a cute opossum scurrying away toward the motel's office.

Chapter 38 Wednesday Morning

Darlene Sampson, longtime pal of Lonnie Dautremont, coasted into the Coachella Valley at 6:45 a.m., arriving at the Indio jail by 7:11. Eager to see her friend to find out the circumstances of her arrest—not to mention to hear about the surprise Lonnie had in mind for her—Darlene was whisked to a bank of telephones within 10 minutes of substantiating her credentials with the corrections officer at the reception desk.

Giddy with anticipation, Darlene sat on the edge of a hard, blue, plastic chair behind a glass wall, looking to her left, waiting for Lonnie to emerge. When Lonnie finally rounded the corner, she looked nothing like Darlene remembered: heavier, grayer, waddling toward the glassed-in area with a frown on her face. Darlene instinctively rose to greet her, expectantly placing a hand on the grimy glass.

Trying to crack a smile, Lonnie gingerly sat down on an equally uncomfortable plastic chair and stared at her friend on the freedom side of the glass for a long moment before picking up the phone. When she finally placed the phone to her ear, she started crying.

"Thank you, Dar," she said, sniffing back tears. "I didn't know who else to call. You're a good egg. A real genuine human being."

"Oh, Lon, of course I'd come. Of course, I'd be here for you," Darlene said, her forehead creased with empathy. "You're one of my dearest—"

"Look, I know it's been a while, and I wouldn't blame you one bit if you have stored-up resentment for me."

"Nothing could be further from the truth, Lon. C'mon. You're in jail, for Christ's sake. Of course, I'd come and offer whatever support I could."

Lonnie offered Darlene a half-smile, dabbing at her eyes with her fingertips. Sneaking a peek at a guard walking behind her, Lonnie quickly averted her eyes when she was silently prompted by the CO to turn back around.

"Hey, how long did it take you to drive in?" Lonnie asked seamlessly, as if nothing was amiss, and they were two friends shooting the breeze in a bar. "Hope there wasn't too much traffic."

"Nah, not long at all, Lon. I made it in great time." Darlene forced a smile of her own, feeling the conversation had suddenly become stilted. "I even had plenty of time to check into the motel down the street, like you suggested. Motel Eight."

"Wow, cool. You really did make it in good time." Lonnie got quiet for a moment, biting down hard on her bottom lip, trying to stifle more tears. But it was too late: she'd begun crying in earnest. "Hey...sorry," she squeaked, unable to clearly enunciate her words. "I just...don't know...how I can thank you."

Darlene pressed her hand on the glass and Lonnie copied her on her side.

"Hey, did you happen to see any kids running around the motel?" Lonnie asked, looking around self-consciously, cracking her neck from side to side.

"No, why would you ask something like that?" Darlene let her hand slip off the glass.

"It's just, uh, oh, nothing. I was just hoping you'll be comfortable there with no rambunctious kids running around, bothering you. That's all." Lonnie looked away.

"You know me, I can sleep through an earthquake." Darlene waited for Lonnie to face her again before continuing. "Hey, Lon, you got a good lawyer? She's gonna get you off, right?"

"How'd ya know it was a woman?"

"Just knew. Is she good?"

"She's a public defender. Seems to know her stuff."

"But Lon, it's murder one."

"But, Dar, it was an accident."

Lounging at home with a cup of coffee, glancing at the headlines in the paper, avoiding the office for as long as he could, Tim unfolded a piece of paper and stared at the writing inside: Branson Wilmington's cell phone number. Self-conscious, he looked behind him, praying Cyndi was still sleeping. She'd come home late last night after having dinner with his mother, and Tim had been fast asleep when she'd finally come to bed. He'd assumed the two women had enjoyed themselves beyond anyone's imagination, including imbibing in multiple cocktails, thus Cyndi's tardiness this morning. *Good for them. The last person I want to confront this morning would be my wife, terrible as it sounds. She can give me all the details of dinner with mom later today, if at all.*

Staring at the piece of paper, Tim wondered if it would be appropriate to call Branson this early. *Of course, the junior partner would be awake by now, and likely already in the office. What am I thinking? Why am I acting like a giddy schoolboy? Would it be presumptuous of me to expect him to take my call now? I'm not even a friend of his and he may think—*

Ignoring logic, listening to his heart instead, Tim punched in Branson's number and counted the rings till he answered. Four.

"Good morning, Branson, Tim Benton here. Hope I'm not calling too early." Nervous staccato laugh.

"Good morning, Tim. Nice to hear from you," Branson said breathlessly. *"Just getting into the office now. Taking the stairs. What's up?"*

"I checked my calendar and I have some free time this afternoon to hit some balls. You free at all today?"

"What time were you thinking? I have clients coming in at two for an hour, but I will have to check what I have afterwards."

"I am wide open, buddy. Decided to take it easy today after a shitstorm went down yesterday."

"Oh, wow. Sorry to hear that. Nothing to do with our firm, I hope?"

Tim was silent for a moment, wisely choosing his words. "No, of course not. Your partners are awesome." Tim involuntarily chuckled. "No. Something that happened right afterwards. It'll all blow over. Eventually."

"Let me call you back after I check my schedule," Branson said, a door squeaking in the background. *"If not tennis today, maybe we can meet up anyway, at the clubhouse instead. For a drink."*

"Honestly, dude, that sounds a lot better." Tim let out a sigh of relief. "I could sure go for a nice, cold one later."

"Terrific, then. I'll get a hold of you right after lunch, cool?"

"What sounds a lot better, Tim?" his wife said, sneaking up behind him.

"Cyndi!" Tim exclaimed, his finger shaking as he tapped his phone to end the call. "How long have you been standing there?"

"Long enough." Cyndi regarded her husband suspiciously. "What the hell's going on with you, anyway?"

Chapter 39 Wednesday Morning

Lisa woke up with a neck ache, having fallen asleep crumpled on the motel room's floor, her SIG Sauer in her hand. Stretching, rotating her head one way and then the other, she heard something pop, and felt immediate relief. Looking at the two teens still sleeping, Lisa smiled, recalling the opossum last night, who was scratching outside their motel door. Although it was just a hungry marsupial, next time it could be one of those ruthless pimps. Best thing she could do for everyone involved would be to drop off both girls at the nearest police station as soon as they woke up.

There was nothing to be gained by appointing herself their guardian; the girls would now be in good hands. They'd give law enforcement the details of their abductions and subsequent imprisonments, and then get much needed psychological therapy to move on to have productive lives. Lisa had more pressing issues to deal with like finding Boris and of course, making it back to California to confront her brother, Tim.

Having penned a quick and concise letter to the police right before she fell asleep, Lisa felt it was a perfect explanation for why two teenagers—one who'd been reported missing since October—were being delivered anonymously to law enforcement. Rereading it, Lisa decided to make one correction: deleting the mention of her staying in a motel.

To whom it may concern,

I am a good Samaritan, who wants to remain anonymous, that happened to be driving in an upscale neighborhood last night when I saw two young women running down the street half naked. I stopped and picked them up, took them home with me overnight so they could get some rest, then acted upon my civil responsibility, turning them over to the police. One of the girls, I believe, is Brittany Leigh Brandson, who was reported missing in October. The other girl is Monique, and I never found out her last name.

From what I can gather, they were abducted for the purpose of prostitution and kept captive in a mansion in an upscale neighborhood. From what little information I could piece together, they had two main pimps: a Russian named Boris and his colleague in crime, Jared. The reason they were able to escape was due to a fire that likely killed several people, including Jared. But I wasn't able to confirm any of it.

Please be gentle on them; they are hurting and quite damaged for their young ages.

Sincerely,
Concerned Citizen

Arriving unannounced at Ogilvie Wealth Management at 9:20, Saundra confidently sauntered past the main reception counter and continued down the hall to the left to Angie Lockhart's desk, standing silently until Todd's secretary finished a phone call. Smiling at the younger woman when she finally looked up, Saundra opened her mouth to speak, but the professional secretary beat her to the punch.

"Good morning Mrs. Benton," Angie said cordially. "How lovely to see you on this fine day."

"Good morning, Angie dear. I would normally agree with your assessment of things, however this particular day is neither fine nor am I feeling lovely."

"Oh, Mrs. Benton, I am so sorry to hear—"

"Plus, I am in no mood for chit-chat. Please buzz my husband that I am on my way to his office. Now." Saundra offered the woman an ersatz smile before adding, "Do you know where the name Ogilvie came from?"

"Uh, not really—" Angie's face flushed, and she immediately cast her eyes to her desk.

"Well, I figured Todd's omission was intentional. Why would he give credit to my father when he wants everyone to believe he founded this firm?"

Angie stared wide-eyed at Saundra, unable to respond.

"I'm sorry, dear," Saundra said sincerely. "I really didn't mean to make you feel badly. Or stupid. It's not your fault you never thought to ask about the Ogilvies."

Smiling once again at her husband's employee, Saundra turned and shuffled down the hall, humming softly to herself.

Fumbling with her phone, Angie immediately dialed her boss' extension, breathing shallowly, perspiration breaking out on her brow.

"Mr. B, your wife is on her way to your office. There was nothing I could do to stop her. Please don't be mad."

But it was too late, as Saundra, even in her advanced years and with the chronic effects of alcoholism, was too clever and slick. She arrived at her husband's desk as he was hanging up the phone.

"Saundra, what—"

"Am I doing here? Is that what you were going to say?" Saundra effortlessly slipped into one of the luxurious armchairs facing her husband's desk.

"No, dear, I was about to say, what a nice surprise to see you." Todd nervously shuffled a pile of papers on his desk.

"Cut the bullshit, Todd. You're a terrible liar. You're just as shocked as Angie was." Saundra opened her purse and fished out an electronic cigarette.

Todd curiously regarded his wife. "It's not bullshit, darling. Any day my wife surprises me with a visit is a good day."

Saundra took a hit from her e-cigarette, blowing out a plume of vanilla-scented vapor. Ignoring her husband's comment, she smiled warmly at him.

"I had a wonderful dinner last night with Cynthia, you know, our beautiful daughter-in-law. She is such a sweet and genuine woman." Saundra eyed Todd as she took another toke. Blowing it out, she added, "I'm so mad at myself for not doing it sooner. And more often. Sometimes I am blinded by what's directly in front of me."

"How long have you been smoking, Saundra?" Todd stacked the pile of papers on its end, smoothing out the edges. "It's not exactly something I'd associate—"

"Did you hear a *fucking* thing I just said?" Saundra glared at him.

"Yes, dear. I heard every word you just said. Cyndi is such a sweet and genuine—"

"You're fucking useless. You know that?" Saundra tucked her e-cigarette in her jacket pocket and squared herself in the armchair. "Funny story. I was curious if your staff knew the origination of this firm, so I asked Angie if she knew where the name Ogilvie came from."

"What's your point, Saundra?" Todd absentmindedly placed the stack of papers on his desk.

"She didn't know, of course, and it seems you've forgotten, as well. If it weren't for my father's hard work in building this firm, where would you be today?" Saundra glared at her husband. "Just curious, dear."

"Have you been drinking, darling?" Todd asked, cocking his head to one side.

"I'm as sober as a judge, Todd, and my mind is as sharp as a tack."

"Was there a point in you coming in this morning? I was sincerely trying to be loving and kind, but once again, you've made that impossible."

"Of course, there was a reason, dear. You didn't think I came in here for my health, did you?"

Saundra rose and ambled over to her husband's desk, standing right next to him. Leaning in close to his left ear, she whispered mockingly, "I came in here to tell you that I told Cyndi everything."

Todd flinched, then rolled his chair away from her. Searching her face, his jaw moving from side to side several times, he finally said, "What do you mean you told her 'everything'?"

"Just what I said. 'I told Cyndi everything.'"

"Everything." Todd nodded involuntarily, as if he were counting off the sins one by one.

"Yes, dear," Saundra said unflinchingly, walking to the armchair to retrieve her purse. "She now knows what kind of a psycho pervert she's been married to.

"It was about time."

CHAPTER 40 WEDNESDAY MORNING

"Cyndi, you're overreacting to some imaginary thing you *think* you heard."

"Don't insult me, Tim. I know what I heard." Cyndi's chest heaved as she tried to catch her breath. "'I could sure go for a nice cold one later'. What the hell's that supposed to mean?"

"Oh, for Pete's sake, Cyndi. I was talking to one of our firm's lawyers." Tim shook his head. "Prior to you sneaking up on me, I was telling him I needed a reprieve from the shitstorm that happened yesterday."

"'Shitstorm'?" Cyndi's eyes widened. "What the hell are you talking about?"

"Well, I was going to get around to telling you, eventually, but since you bring it up now, I suppose now's as good a time as any."

"Tell me what?"

Keenly aware he was now in control, Tim purposely slowed down the conversation, waiting for his wife's undivided attention. After a long moment he continued.

"My father, in his infinite wisdom, has decided to rewrite his trust."

"Okay, so, why is that so bad? I mean, you're his first-born son and right-hand man in the business, so–"

"Let me finish, Cyndi. It's bad alright." Tim circled the kitchen, letting his words sink in. "Outrageous, even, because he has decided to include my sister in it. Lisa is now getting her share of the Benton Family Trust, which includes, of course, Ogilvie Wealth Management's millions."

"You mean she wasn't included before, from the beginning?"

"No, she wasn't, Cyndi. As I mentioned to you the other day, she's been estranged from the family for years."

"I know, but still. I thought, as a sibling–"

"Don't think so much, dear. Thinking can be a dangerous proposition."

Cyndi stared at her husband, appearing to forget what she was about to say. Then, regaining her train of thought said, "Why would this upset you? I mean, she is your flesh and blood, your sister, even if–"

Stopping abruptly, her hand clasping her mouth, Cyndi looked like she would be sick. Running out of the kitchen, she left without saying another word. Tim, at first, thought she saw the error of her ways, till he put two and two together and went chasing after her. Finding her leaning over the sink in the downstairs bathroom, Tim went to her side, tentatively placing his hand on her waist.

"Get your hands off me," Cyndi barked, flinching. "Don't touch me!"

"Cyndi? What he heck's wrong? What's gotten into you?"

Cyndi slowly turned around to face her husband. "Are you kidding me? Do I need to spell it out for you?"

Looking deep into her eyes, Tim instinctively knew that she knew. Everything.

"What did my mother tell you? What did that crazy bitch tell you?"

On her way out of Ogilvie Wealth Management, Saundra slipped unnoticed into a vacant office near the reception area. Sliding behind the unused desk—which offered an inoperable computer and functional telephone—Saundra picked up the phone's receiver and punched in a number she'd copied down from the Internet earlier. With gloved hands, she lifted the receiver to her ear and counted two and a half rings till someone answered.

"Pat Healy, please," she said when the attendant answered.

"Who shall I say is calling?"

"Saundra Ogilvie."

"One moment, Mrs. Ogilvie."

"Saundra, dear. What a pleasant surprise," Pat Healy said enthusiastically. *"How's the family?"*

"Hanging in, at times by the skin of our teeth, Pat." Saundra exhaled audibly. "Seriously, would I be calling you if everything was good?"

"Saundra, I'm hurt. I thought we were friends, going way, way back to junior high school."

"You honestly remember those days, Pat?" Saundra chuckled.

"Now, you're really driving a knife through my broken heart. You had to know how big a crush I had on you back then."

"You did? I honestly can't even remember." Saundra giggled nervously. "I cannot even remember what I had for dinner last night. Oh, wait, I do. I went out with my gorgeous daughter-in-law to the country club. What a looker she is. Tim doesn't deserve her, the son-of-a-bitch."

"You were a looker back then, too, Saundra. And you knew it. I think you even taunted me with your looks. Subconsciously, I'm sure." Pat snorted, laughing. *"Why did you have to go and marry Todd Benton? What did he have that I didn't have?"*

"A penis, Pat."

"And, that penis got you pregnant. All the more reason you should have been with me instead."

"You always were the class clown, Pat. Still a funny gal after all these years."

"So, what can I do for you? You just said you wouldn't be calling you if everything was good."

Saundra suddenly couldn't speak. Her throat tightened and her eyes welled up with tears. "I need for you to find my daughter, Lisa. Please, Pat. I'm desperate."

CHAPTER 41 WEDNESDAY AFTERNOON

Lisa returned to the motel after dropping off the teens at the police station, packing up what little she had and throwing it haphazardly into her car. Quickly assessing the room to make sure she didn't forget anything, Lisa left the key on the dresser, then backed out of the room. Feeling something hard and metallic against her lower back, she froze, waiting for someone to say something.

"I knew if I bided my time, I'd catch up with you eventually, *Hannah*," Jared said, exhaling hot, alcohol-laced breaths on Lisa's neck. "And looky here? I've done just that."

"What do you want from me, Jared?" Lisa said calmly, betraying her surprise that he was alive and well.

"First, I wanna know who the fuck you really are, *Hannah*. I don't think for one second that's your real name," Jared said, pushing her inside the motel room. "Then, I wanna know why you targeted me. And, I don't have all day to wait for an answer, so let's get cracking."

Lisa allowed Jared to push her back into the room, where he shoved her onto the bed, then kicked the door closed. Falling face-first, she twisted herself around at the last moment, landing on her back. Rocking back all the way, she brought her knees to her chin, and using her momentum, rolled to a sitting position, forcing her feet into Jared's midsection. The impact forced his gun to fly out of his hand and twirl in the air before landing against the wall behind him. Comprehending a second too late what had happened, Jared pawed the air in a vain attempt at retrieving his gun.

With Jared distracted, Lisa got to her feet and landed a punch to his gut. Bending over in pain, Jared now received a karate-chop to his neck, compelling to him to double over in agony. Scooting to the wall, grabbing Jared's Glock 9mm, Lisa adroitly jabbed it into his neck, forcing him up to a standing position, twisting his right arm behind his back.

"What the fuck is wrong with you?" Jared shrieked in pain. "What do you want from me?"

"Shut up, Jared," Lisa said, reaching behind her back for the handcuffs hooked on her belt loops, slapping them first on his right wrist, then on his left. "I don't answer your questions. You answer mine."

Lisa shoved him onto the bed, where he landed uncomfortably on his left side. Looking as if he were trying to right himself, Lisa kicked him hard, forcing him to remain in that awkward position.

"Stay right there, Jared and listen up." She came around to the side of the bed so that he could see her. Standing over him, holding the 9mm above his head, she said, "You're just a piece-of-shit cog in the wheel, I suspect. Someone I couldn't care less about. What I really want is your boss."

"My *boss*?" Jared said, struggling to talk.

"Yes. Boris. Where is he?"

"I...uh, I have no idea."

Lisa pistol-whipped him upside his head, forcing him to involuntarily shriek. "You're lying, dickwad. Where is he?"

"I swear, I don't know." Jared winced in pain.

"Try again, asshole. Think hard. I'm willing to spare your life if you tell me where he is. otherwise, I have no compunction to kill you both. No skin off my back."

Jared was quiet, clearly mulling over his fate. Tilting his head up to Lisa, sneaking a peek at her through his disheveled hair, he breathed out raggedly, gasping for air.

"I'm, uh, not too sure, but I think I may know where he may be hiding."

"Hiding? Where?"

"In Surprise. North of here. Near Sun City."

"Get in the car. We're going for a ride."

Unable to concentrate at work, worried about both his wife's and mother's new attitudes, Tim kept checking his cell phone to see if he missed a call from Branson Wilmington. If anyone would be able to distract him from the current shitty situation with his family, it was the junior, *goyishe* partner of the Jew Law Firm. What luck to have been at the right place at the right time yesterday to have met the man of his dreams! He was a godsend; an angel sent from above to divert his attention away from all the clusterfucks that had befallen him this week.

Tim buzzed Angie and told her to hold all of his calls till further notice; to take messages for him and to tell his clients he'd call them back in the morning. If it were a true emergency, he told her to put them through to his dad.

"Your dad? Are you sure that's okay?" Angie asked in an unusually whiny, accusatory voice.

"Angie, don't question my decisions, alright? You work for me; I don't work for you."

It was a good thing Tim couldn't see Angie roll her eyes and shake her head, otherwise he may have been inclined to fire her on the spot. Responding with a terse, "*Yes, Tim,*" Angie simply hung up the phone and resumed filing away client folders. Satisfied, Tim swiped his mobile phone off his desk and punched in Branson's cell number.

Staring at his wristwatch, counting the rings, Tim thought it was the perfect time to follow up with the attorney; it was neither too early nor too late. Three fifty-five.

"This is Branson," the velvety-voiced hunk said after five rings.

"And this is Tim," he responded, wondering if Branson knew who was calling or if the lawyer always answered his phone by identifying himself by his first name only. "How's it going?"

"Tim! How are ya?" Branson said, chuckling. *"Wow, good timing. I just got out of a meeting I thought would never end."*

"Yeah, I know what that's like. I've been avoiding meetings all day today," Tim said, laughing nervously. "After what happened yesterday, well, I'm all *meeting'd* out."

"Yeah, and I've got a slight headache now, but nothing that a nice cold one can't cure."

"Where did you want to meet?"

"How about Clancy's on Olympic. A bit off the beaten track but with plenty of parking in the back."

"Clancy's. Wow. Haven't been there in ages." More nervous laughter. "Sounds good. What time?"

"How about four forty-five? Does that work for you?"

"Perfect, Branson. See ya then."

On his way out of the office, Tim thought he passed Angie's desk without her seeing him, but she'd turned at the last moment and caught him sneaking out the door.

"Tim, I put through a couple of your clients to your dad, like you said to do, and he wasn't too thrilled about it," Angie said with forced conviction. "You said it would be—"

"Just do your job Angie and stop analyzing things. We have analysts here who get paid a lot of money to analyze."

Tim flashed her an ersatz smile and skipped out of the office.

CHAPTER 42 WEDNESDAY AFTERNOON, LATE

Undeterred in his decision to include his only daughter in the family trust, feeling absolved of any previous guilt, Todd continued to obsess about what Saundra taunted him with when she'd left the office earlier that morning. *Did she mean to imply she'd spilled her guts to Cyndi, told her all their dirtiest family secrets? Jesus, Saundra; what were you thinking, woman? More important, what did Cyndi now think about the Benton family?*

Damage control, Todd thought as he dialed his daughter-in-law's number from his cell phone, was now a top priority, trumping even the trust's final draft. He had to be meticulous in his articulation to Cyndi so that she would understand first what happened to Tim all those years ago, and second, why he did what he did to Lisa afterwards. It was quite complex, he'd tell her, actions that cannot be simply explained in a sentence or two. The poor boy, through no negligence by his parents, fell victim to the Monsignor, then to the Archbishop, who–

"Cyndi, dear, it's Todd. I hope I've reached you at a good time," Todd said smoothly, surprised his daughter-in-law answered the phone. "Is this a good time?"

"*As good as any, Todd,*" Cyndi said evenly. "*I do have an appointment in twenty minutes, so I have to leave in about ten.*"

"Okay, great. I won't keep you long, dear. It's been a long time since–"

"*What's on your mind, Todd?*"

"Look, I won't waste your time or mine with ancillary chit-chat, alright? I'll get right to the point." Todd inhaled sharply before continuing. "Saundra mentioned to me that you two had a lovely dinner last night. Which, by the way, warms my heart immensely. She also said that she divulged some things to you, some very personal things pertaining to Tim. Things that undoubtedly shocked and likely repulsed you.

"The reason for my call is to ease your mind about not only what she said but *how* she said it."

"So, *are you the good cop to Saundra's bad cop? Or is it the other way around? Hard to tell which side of the plate any Benton is batting from these days.*"

"Cyndi, I don't blame you at all for being angry and hurt. You must feel blindsided, for God's sake. To find out your own husband was sexually abused by the very clergy who were supposed to protect him. Who were held in high esteem as protectors of children."

"*Are you fucking kidding me? Is that all you got, Todd? Where were you and Saundra when this was happening to Tim? Huh, where?*" Cyndi breathed loudly into the mouthpiece. "*Even worse, and more sickening, where were you and Saundra when Tim was raping his own sister, Lisa?*"

"It's not what you think, Cyndi," Todd said pathetically. "It wasn't like that."

"*No, I'm sure it wasn't. I'll bet it was far worse. No wonder Lisa estranged herself from the family. I'm surprised she actually never brought charges against Tim. I know I would have if that had been me and my own flesh and blood was raping me. What a piece of—*"

"And that's exactly why I am rectifying things with Lisa. Right now, as a matter of fact."

"*A little late, don't you think?*" Cyndi said disgustedly. "*How have you and Saundra lived with yourselves all these years?*"

"Look, dear, I am not trying to convince you of anything. I am only trying to tell you that people make mistakes, and then people have to rectify their mistakes. We are only human, after all. I am so sorry—"

"Stop it Todd, you're actually making it worse, you know? I'd have more respect if you'd just admit you were wrong and—"

"That's what I am doing, Cyndi. I was...we were wrong. Terribly wrong. Have you never made a mistake in your life, dear?"

"Stop calling me 'dear'. It's irritating." Cyndi exhaled noisily into the phone. *"Of course, I've made mistakes. But what Tim did was not a mistake; it was a pure evil deed. And what you and Saundra did by not speaking up, by not protecting their one and only daughter, well, that's almost more evil. Completely unforgivable."*

"Please tell me you don't really believe that Cyndi. Please tell me you're a bigger person who has forgiveness in her heart."

"I'm sorry, Todd. I can say nothing of the sort." Cyndi waited a long moment before continuing. *"I've gotta go, Todd. I'm happy for Lisa. I have a feeling she may actually be the only sane one in the Benton family."*

"How far is it to Surprise?" Lisa asked as she drove northwest on Highway 60, Jared securely cuffed in the back of her 4Runner, low on the floor.

"I don't know, about twenty, twenty-five minutes." Jared mumbled, unable to see where they were.

"What the hell's Boris doing all the way out here anyway?" Lisa asked, scanning the highway for cops. "You'd better not be taking me on a wild-goose chase."

"Why would I do that?" Jared moaned uncomfortably. "I'd only be shooting myself in the foot, for lack of a better expression."

"You still haven't answered my question. What's a Russian lowlife pimp doing in a place that sounds like a retirement community where the most exciting activity at night is bingo?"

"You'd have to ask him that. I have no clue."

"Well, he's not here so I'm asking you, Jared. You're one of his field service experts, who scouts the sidewalks of the inner city for ripe, new meat. Seems the only *suchkas* he'd find in Surprise would be old enough to be his grandmother."

"Maybe his babushka lives there. Who the fuck knows?"

"'Babushka'?"

"Yeah, his grandmother. I thought for sure you'd know that word. Thought you were this worldly chick who spoke a few languages." Jared tried to chuckle, but it came out more like a hacking cough.

"Did he actually tell you he has contacts in Surprise?" Lisa asked, ignoring his attempt to demean her. "Or are you just guessing for the sake of stalling?"

"All I know is he let it slip one day he had to drive up to Surprise for business, he said, and he put me in charge."

"Head pimp for the day? You lucky dog." Lisa chortled.

"I paid my dues. I command respect from the girls and their handlers."

"'Handlers'? I'll bet you do," Lisa sniggered, noticing a black and white in her peripheral vision. "*Fuck*, a cop," she seethed. "Get down and throw that blanket over yourself. Don't say a fucking word. You hear me?"

Jared mumbled incoherently as the cruiser slowed and slid behind Lisa's 4Runner. Within seconds, flashing red lights swirled and Lisa saw in her rearview mirror the cop pointing for her to pull over to the shoulder of the highway. "Fuck," she said again, sliding Jared's gun under her seat.

"License and registration, miss," the no-nonsense policeman said when he'd approached her car, his eyes obscured by reflective shades.

Lisa calmly reached over to her purse on the passenger seat and retrieved her driver's license from her wallet, then took the registration out of the glove compartment. "Here you go, officer," she said, handing them to him.

"Do you know why I stopped you, Miss Benton?" he asked, gazing at both documents.

"I honestly have no idea." Lisa searched the policeman's face while he stared at her driver's license. "I was driving the speed limit, for sure, so, I'm not really–"

"You were weaving in and out of lanes, Miss Benton."

"Oh, sorry," Lisa giggled nervously. "I was looking for a piece of paper on the passenger seat, that I had written directions on."

"You were driving like you were impaired. Have you been drinking?"

"Absolutely not! In fact, I don't touch the stuff. Not good for training."

"'Training'?' he asked, peering over his glasses at her, a smile forming on his lips. "What kind of training?"

"Marathon training. That's why I'm in Arizona. Training in the dry heat."

"Is that right? I ran the LA Marathon this year. Nearly didn't make it. They changed the route and it's a little longer. Threw me off a bit." The officer removed his sunglasses.

"LA's still on my list. Maybe next year." Lisa smiled sincerely, cocking her head to one side.

"Awesome. You really should." He placed her license over her registration and held them in the air for a moment. "You still living at the same address on Shadow Lane in Fallbrook, California Miss Benton?"

"Yes, I am, officer," Lisa said, swallowing hard.

"Here you go," he said handing her documents back. "Be careful. You should really use a GPS, you know."

"You're right officer." Lisa's smile never waned.

Lisa waited for the cop to return to his cruiser before starting up her engine and slowly pulling back onto the highway. Breathing a sigh of relief, feeling her heart pounding in her ears, she also watched Jared in the rearview mirror pulling the blanket off of him.

"Miss Benton?" he asked sarcastically. "I knew you were nothing but a lying bitch pretending to be someone else."

"My identity is none of your fucking business, Jared," Lisa said, realizing she'd now have to eliminate the idiot after all. Once he took her to Boris.

"I shoulda told that cop who you were pretending to be. *Hannah Clark*. He'd have dragged your ass to jail." Jared laughed heartily.

"Is that so? And where would that have left you, moron?"

Jared was silent, unable to respond.

"If I were you, I'd be really careful about what you say from here on out."

CHAPTER 43 WEDNESDAY EVENING

Tim arrived early at Clancy's, grabbing a pint of Guinness at the bar, then slipping into the one open booth at the far end of the pub. Sweating, nervous, he kept his sunglasses on as he awaited Branson's arrival, subconsciously hiding his shame from total strangers who had no clue about his illicit rendezvous. Four thirty-three, Tim noted on his phone, twelve more minutes till he walks through the door. *Shit! Why am I so fucking nervous?*

Gulping a large draught of the stout, Tim scanned the room, filling up quickly with the after-work crowd. More of a local hangout than a posh Westside watering hole, Clancy's drew in a diverse crowd, from young urban professionals to blue-collar workers to secretaries needing reprieves from their overbearing bosses. It clearly offered a laid-back ambiance that put everyone at ease. So, why did he feel so uptight?

Tim took another big gulp, then wiped his upper lip with the back of his hand. Setting his glass down in front of him, he tapped his phone to check the time—4:43—exactly ten minutes since he'd last checked. Why was he acting like a goddamned high school kid, anxiously waiting for his date? Looking up, gazing in the direction of the front door, Tim was startled when Branson appeared at his side, having come around the back of the pub.

"Penny for your thoughts, Timothy?" he said in a low voice, sliding into the booth, opposite Tim.

"Hey, sorry. I didn't even see you come in." Tim felt his face flush.

"And you started without me." Branson chuckled, nodding his head. "Reminds me of a scene in that old Woody Allen movie, Zelig, where he believes he's a doctor who, among other things, teaches a masturbation class. During a session with his shrink, Mia Farrow, he tells her that he needs to get going because if he's not there on time, 'they start without me.'"

Stunned, Tim self-consciously pushed his sunglasses higher up on the bridge of his nose, staring straight ahead, unable to speak.

"Did you ever see it? It was really one of the funniest scenes in one of his funniest movies. Ever." Branson chuckled again.

"Wow, funny shit indeed," Tim said, slowly removing his shades, placing them in his shirt pocket. "Guess I'll have to watch it one of these days."

"What can I get for you?" A waitress had appeared at their table, tossing down two cocktail napkins, causing Tim to blush even more, fearing she overheard their conversation.

"I'll have the same as my friend here," Branson said without hesitation, pointing to Tim's draught. "And two shots of Jameson." Branson winked surreptitiously at Tim.

"I'll have another stout as well," Tim said anxiously. "Thanks."

"Be right back, boys."

Branson raised his eyebrows at Tim, who reciprocated by shrugging his shoulders. Laughing, they repeated in unison, "Boys?"

"Hey, you know it's actually kind of nice to hear that after having to be so fucking *on* all day long," Tim said, finishing his Guinness in one gulp. "You know, having to be 'the boss' all fucking day, exuding a phony persona to all the employees lest they walk all over you. Am I right?"

"Yeah, you are. Though I'm a bit luckier. I don't have nearly as many employees or reports as you have. But I get it.

"That's why I was so happy when you called, wanting to get together, to let loose, just be one of the guys."

Tim searched Branson's eyes, which were sparkling and full of joy. "You seem to be a truly uncomplicated, happy person. Me, on the other hand—"

"Here you go, boys. Two Guinness and two shots of Jameson. One or both of you are true-blue Irishmen."

Tim and Branson both smiled congenially, then eagerly lifted their shot glasses to make a toast.

"To a new friendship, Tim. To new adventures. To us! Cheers!"

"Cheers," Tim said timidly before downing the whiskey, overwhelmed by Branson's zeal.

Branson slapped his shot glass on the table and immediately grabbed his pint of Guinness. After taking a long draught, he set it down and looked seriously at Tim.

"To respond to your assessment of me, yes. I am genuinely uncomplicated and happy. Why not? Life's too damn short to not go for the gusto."

"You're right, you know. It's just that I get so, so sick and tired of—"

"When I was thirteen," Branson said somberly, interrupting Tim, "my older brother and younger sister and I were riding in the back of our parents' station wagon when a kid who'd just gotten his driver's license broadsided our car at forty-five miles an hour. My sister died from internal injuries; pronounced dead at the scene. One minute she was there, the next gone; like that." Branson snapped his fingers.

"Oh, wow. I'm so sorry. I didn't mean to sound—" Tim hung his head in shame.

"It's okay. I wasn't trying to make you feel guilty. All I'm trying to say is cherish every moment. Love your family. Love your friends."

"I, uh, really do try," Tim said, guzzling his stout for a full three seconds. "But it's not always possible." Feeling lightheaded when he put the glass down in front of him, he looked Branson in the eye and asked him unabashedly, "Why did you recount that specific scene in a Woody Allen movie, the one about masturbation?"

"Oh, I don't know, trying to be funny, I guess. Break the ice. Probably because you started drinking without me." Branson took a long swig of Guinness before adding, "Did that offend you in any way? Did I offend you? Because I thought for sure—"

"No, Branson, you did not offend me. Not at all. In fact," Tim said, polishing off his second Guinness, "it turned me on."

Locked in her tiny, private office off the kitchen's oversized pantry, lounging on a red velvet daybed, Saundra filled her tumbler again with Grey Goose as she stared at the phone, willing it to ring. Certain her childhood friend, Patricia Healy, would come through for her in her hour of desperation, Saundra silently prayed while she drank herself into a stupor. Her last hope in locating her daughter, Pat was not only a longtime friend, but the founder of one of the most successful private detective agencies in Los Angeles: Healy and Associates.

Having utilized Pat's services to locate the priest who abused Tim, Saundra had been astounded by the speed with which Pat achieved results. Undoubtedly helped by the fact her parents personally knew the Monsignor from their local diocese, Pat exposed a total of three LA-based priests who'd sexually abused 23 boys and 11 girls—all of whom were stealthily and shamelessly "relocated" to other dioceses on the East Coast.

A tenacious detective who allowed nothing to stand in her way, Pat vowed to find Lisa no matter how long it took. Believing her friend's promise, Saundra forced herself to remain positive, even as she felt herself drifting off to sleep. Staring at the near empty bottle of vodka, seeing double, she couldn't recall if it had been unopened when she started drinking earlier. If she had drunk that much liquor in one sitting, it was a wonder her liver still functioned. Losing her coordination, Saundra attempted to take a long swig, but instead, jammed the plastic tumbler too hard into her mouth, forcing the expensive French vodka to spill out of both sides of her mouth.

"Goddamned shit," she said aloud, wiping her mouth with her sleeve. Reaching for a flimsy napkin on the coffee table, she dabbed the spilt liquor on her robe to no avail. "Goddamned shit fuck," she said as she tossed the napkin in the air.

Setting the tumbler on the coffee table in front of her, Saundra leaned back on her daybed and started to cry. Her life was shit starting with her egomaniacal and unstable husband to her evil first-born son, Tim. The only family member she could now trust—Cynthia—was not even blood, for God's sake, but family, nonetheless. When did everything go to hell in a hand basket? she wondered, dabbing her eyes with her fingertips. *When the hell did all of my children decide I was no longer worthy of respect, no longer a valuable member of the Benton clan?*

Oh, well, fuck the Bentons. Low-life, nouveau riche, elitist turds. They can't hold a candle to the Ogilvies anyway. Oh, what the—

Loud ringing in the distance startled her. *Is that my phone or am I hallucinating?* The ringing continued unabated until Saundra rolled off the daybed and onto the floor, where she noticed her landline tucked underneath the bed. Reaching for it, she breathlessly answered it on the fifth ring.

"Hello, this is Saundra."

"*Hi doll, it's Pat. Hope I didn't wake you.*"

"Patricia! Oh, my goodness, no! I am so happy you called." Saundra got to her knees, then pushed herself onto the daybed, rolling back, all the while balancing the phone in her hands. "In fact, dear, I have never been happier to receive a phone call in my life."

"Thanks, sweetie. Kind of you to say that. I just hope—"

"No, it's not me being kind. It's the truth. So, what have you got for me? Good news about my daughter?"

"Well, yes, sort of. And I wanted to call you immediately."

"What?" Saundra asked spiritedly. "What did you find out?"

"Well, I discovered an address under the name of Benton in Fall-brook—that's in San Diego County—and a vehicle registration as well. But both are under—"

"Oh my God! Really?" Saundra said, before becoming quiet for a long moment as she digested what Pat just revealed. "So close, yet so far away."

"Yes, but interestingly, both the house and the vehicle are under Jason Benton's name. Not Lisa's."

"Jason's? Wow. Interesting indeed. So, what does this all mean?"

"Well, I'm not sure, yet. Remind me again who Jason is, Saundra."

"My son. The one closest in age to Lisa. He lives up north. Also abandoned the family because of the whole Tim scandal."

"Right. Anyway, Jason and James Benton are on the home's title, so it's possible two of your sons may know where Lisa has been living."

"Why do say 'may'?" Saundra said anxiously. "Aren't you sure?"

"Well, I found out that Lisa Benton was a parole officer for several years, until about May or June of this year, reporting to a field office in Oceanside, near Camp Pendleton. Fallbrook to Oceanside is about twenty miles. So, it could be very possible that she had been living in the house in Fallbrook, owned jointly by Jason and James."

"I'm speechless."

"Are you in contact with James? Where does he live?"

"Yes, from time to time. I mean more than with Jason. He lives in Orange County. Rancho Santa Margarita."

"Right, so it would then make perfect sense to me that Lisa had indeed been residing at the Fallbrook home while she was working in Oceanside."

"'While she was working'? What do you mean, she's no longer living there?" Saundra swallowed a huge gulp of vodka from her tumbler.

"Well, I don't know if she is or not. Sometime during the summer, she fell off the radar completely. I can't find anything on her since this summer."

"So, this is really not good news at all, right Pat?" Saundra shouted angrily. "You're really no closer to finding my baby than you were this morning."

CHAPTER 44 WEDNESDAY EVENING

Lisa pulled off Highway 60 at West Bell Road and headed west, hoping Jared was giving her the correct directions as she had no flipping idea in the world where she was. Still moaning in pain, Jared told her to look out for a change in the street name, to West Sun Valley Parkway after crossing over Highway 303. Lisa mumbled cursorily and drove steadily, watching for the bisecting highway. Lots of rock lawns and golf courses, Lisa noted as she drove, anticipating her meeting with the human trafficking ringleader.

"Did you cross three-o-three yet?" Jared asked from the back, disturbing Lisa's silent assessment of the area.

"Coming up on it now."

"Okay, then look for the third street, I think, which should be Happy Trails. Take a right on that street. It'll take you into a golf community."

"Is there any type of community here other than golf?" Lisa asked facetiously.

Lisa watched for the sign to Happy Trails, turning right as she was instructed, onto what looked like an entrance into a gated community. Just as she was about to ask Jared what to say at the guard shack, he spoke up.

"Pull over and un-cuff me," he said matter-of-factly. "They'll never let you in if you're not already pre-approved or on a list from one of the residents."

"Bullshit, Jared. I'm doing nothing of the sort."

"If they see me, they'll just wave us in," Jared said pleadingly. "You won't get in on your own. Guaranteed."

"Watch me, asshole." Lisa drove straight ahead toward the guard shack.

"You're a real cunt, you know?" Jared said indignantly. "Get ready to turn around. See if I care."

"Your opinion of me is insignificant, but in this case, I'll take the 'C' word as a compliment."
Lisa accelerated a few feet, then slowed to a stop. Turning around to look at Jared, she said, "Say a word and you're as good as dead. Understood? Lay down low, dickwad."

Lisa moved forward toward the gate, slowing again as another car was waiting to be allowed in. A guest, she noted, as the guard placed a placard in the lower left corner of the driver's windshield. Quickly pulling her V-neck top down to reveal what little cleavage she had, Lisa pushed her boobs together to make them appear larger than they were. Satisfied, she inched up slowly to the guard, rolling her window down, licking her lips.

"Good evening, sir," Lisa said in a sultry voice. "How are you tonight?"

"Excellent ma'am," the guard said, approaching the driver side of her car. "And a pleasant evening to you as well. Who are you here to see?"

"Boris, of course," Lisa said, slyly checking the guard's name plate. "I'm a bit early, Randall, but he's most definitely expecting me."

"Certainly, ma'am. What is your name?" Randall grabbed a clipboard with a long list of names on it.

"Carissa."

"Last name, Miss Carissa?" Randall scanned the list.

"No last name. Just Carissa. I'm just a girl with one name." Lisa smiled seductively, then giggled. "Do you want me to help you find my name?" Lisa unbuckled her seatbelt and pretended to get out of her vehicle.

"Oh, no need for that, Miss Carissa. I'm sure you're on the list. Just having a hard time finding it now."

"Here, let me help," Lisa said, pushing her upper body out of the window, her breasts at the perfect angle for the guard to see. Running her right hand down the length of her neck and onto her chest, Lisa let it rest on her left breast as she feigned looking for her name on the list. "Wow, so many names tonight and I can't for the life of me find little old me." More giggling before letting her eyes find Randall's.

When he looked up, he was staring at Lisa/Carissa, now leisurely twirling a hank of hair on one finger. "Can't seem to find your name, Miss Carissa. How do you spell it?"

"'C' as in cat, 'A' as in apple, 'R' as in real," Lisa said, touching her left breast again. "'I' as in imagination–"

The phone inside the shack rang, compelling Randall to jog back inside. With no time to lose, Lisa waved at him as he spoke on the phone, and when she got his attention, winked animatedly. Confused, clearly unable to multitask, Randall hit a button on his desk, and the heavy wrought-iron gate swung open. Lisa waved goodbye as she drove inside the development.

"What's the address, motherfucker." Lisa demanded of Jared, pulling up her top to its original shape. "I don't have all night."

Rattled awake after being slammed into the opposite side of the truck, Kendall pushed himself off the padding and felt grateful for having chosen this vehicle over others that may not have

been as safe. After escaping the couple in the van by busting out the back, Kendall walked for miles until he found a truck stop near a freeway offramp. Cruising unnoticed among the semis, whose drivers were either snoozing in their cabs or eating inside the convenience store, he chose a smaller truck parked away from the others because the hatch was ajar and easy to push open. Neither concerned with the direction the truck was headed nor with what the driver was delivering, Kendall just wanted to get as far away from the place where his mother was killed and hopefully find a new mom.

Unfamiliar with the contents inside the truck, unable to see much because of the darkness, Kendall had scootched along the left side and found a heap of soft packing materials on which to lie. Sinking comfortably into the stack, he had fallen asleep before the driver had returned. Though he'd awakened slightly with the revving of the engine, he'd easily fallen right back to sleep.

He had no idea how long he'd been sleeping when he was startled awake by the driver slowing down unexpectedly, causing him to go flying in the opposite direction. Now crawling back to the stack of packing materials, Kendall sunk back down, covering himself, trying to go back to sleep. With no light seeping into the truck, he assumed correctly that it was still nighttime; still time to sleep.

As he was lulled back to sleep, Kendall prayed for a new mother, one that would never be taken away from him; one that would finally take him to Disneyland.

CHAPTER 45 WEDNESDAY EVENING

Tim rolled over onto his stomach and felt the warmth of the winter's sun on his back. Turing his head to his left, he let the sun penetrate his face, feeling utterly and apologetically self-indulgent. How long had it been since he allowed himself the luxury of doing something so sybaritic, so taboo? How long had it been since he purposely ignored stacks of paperwork on his desk during a weekday in favor of doing absolutely nothing? He could neither remember nor care, though it was likely way back when he was first married to that society girl his parents fixed him up with who had small tits, a flat ass and thought sucking dick would send her straight to hell. He'd somehow talked her into going to a swingers' party in the Valley. Yeah, that was the last time he did something so reckless without regard to the consequences.

Aware now of a slight breeze on his bare skin, he smiled and inhaled deeply, luxuriating in the sensation, not wanting it to end, not wanting to go back to work and face reality. Had he really gone on vacation to Jamaica mid-week, finally succumbing to the temptation of a nude resort? And where was Cyndi? He hadn't seen her for a few hours. Had she found some studly black man with a gigantic cock to send her to heaven forever?

Who gives a shit? he thought, turning his head to his right so that the other side of his face could absorb the warmth. And so, what if she did? It would relieve him of his husbandly duties, something he'd been sorely lacking these past few months. Or was it years? *Who knew? So long as she leaves me alone, she can go after every black cock on the island for all I care.*

Soft, firm hands now caressed his butt, causing him to get hard and moan in pleasure.

"Who is it?" he asked quietly, keeping his eyes shut, enjoying the massage. No one answered, and instead, the hands came around his sides, slipping underneath, grabbing his manhood. Shrieking in ecstasy, Tim raised his butt to allow the person more room to stroke him. Whoever this was, they were expertly handling him, lightly scratching his balls with their fingernails, sending him over the edge.

Unable to control himself, wanting to prolong the pleasure, Tim pushed off the lounge chair and turned over onto his back. Keeping his eyes shut, he reached out to grab ahold of this person, but could not touch them, even though he sensed their presence hovering over him. Frustrated, he tried to force his eyes open, to finally see who it was, but his eyes felt like they'd been glued shut. Screaming in an amalgam of pleasure and pain, he finally willed his eyes open, but the onslaught of light blinded him to everything around him.

"What the fuck?" he said, pushing himself up to a sitting position. Slowly, his eyes began to adjust, and he was able to make out the shape of a man straddling him. "Who the fuck—"

"Tim, it's okay, you were having a wild dream. It's me. Everything's good."

Staring in disbelief at the naked man sitting astride him, Tim opened his mouth to scream, but nothing came forth. Squeezing his eyes shut, he exhaled noisily and shook his head.

"What the...did we? Am I...what did—"

Branson smiled crookedly at Tim, grabbing his hands, lacing his fingers together with Tim's.

"Don't you remember anything, Tim?" Branson said, nuzzling his face into Tim's neck.

Tim flinched, shaking his head, trying in vain to move away from Branson. "N..no. Remember what?"

Branson leaned back, sitting atop Tim's thighs. "Wow, you really don't remember."

"Remember what? What the hell happened?" Tim's asked, horrified.

"Relax, dude. It's all good."

"It's not all good if I cannot recall a thing."

Jabbing her .45 into Jared's ribs, Lisa forcefully pushed him up the serpentine pathway of the sprawling home, hyper-alert, ever vigilant. Interestingly, Boris' pad at the Sunrise Grand Villa Estates, was situated just a few short streets off the development's main street, Happy Trails. One would have thought the pimp extraordinaire would have wanted as much seclusion as possible, but there was obviously no accounting for the reckless actions of a criminal.

Secure in the knowledge her rowdy, hustling prisoner wouldn't be able to defend himself, Lisa had warned Jared about not alerting his Russian partner in crime beforehand. Surprise was key in nabbing the leader of a sex trafficking ring and Lisa would not leave Arizona without first eliminating him.

"Just remember to act normal, dickhead, and make him believe you're alone," Lisa said through clenched teeth, gipping his arm, unlocking the cuffs on his hands. "Got it?"

"I got it, bitch," Jared said, rubbing his sore wrists, avoiding eye contact.

"Look at me when you talk to me, Jared, so I know you mean what you say."

Jared lifted his head, smirking. "There! Is that better? Jesus, man. You're too much. Give me a fucking–"

"Shut the fuck up and just go up to the door and knock," Lisa said, thrusting her gun into his gut. "And don't do anything stupid or you're a dead man."

Jared glared at her one last time before turning and limping the last few feet up the path. Ringing the doorbell, he glanced behind him, but Lisa had already disappeared behind a hedge. Waiting impatiently for someone to answer the door, Jared bounced from one leg to the other, looking up at the moths buzzing around the light fixture. When someone finally answered, Jared was nervously wringing his hands, trying to calm his nerves.

"Crystal, is that really you?" Jared asked a skinny, catatonic blonde with stringy hair who'd appeared to be stoned out of her mind. "Are you okay?"

"What the fuck are you doing here?" the blonde said, absentmindedly twirling her hair.

"I need to see Boris, Crystal," he said, glancing beyond her emaciated body. "Can I come in?"

"Boris said not to allow you in." She stared past him at nothing in particular.

"What do you mean? I need to see him."

"Sorry, Charlie. No can do."

"Get out of my way, you stupid, useless slut," Jared shouted, shoving her to the side, causing her to topple over with a thud.

Lisa shot out of the bushes, her prized .45 at the ready as she rushed past the startled blonde, still splayed out on the floor. Unbelievably, Jared had easily disappeared inside the house, despite being exhausted and injured. Unable to stop Lisa, the blonde simply whimpered, throwing her hands up in the air in defeat. Pulsating sounds emanated from another room, while disco lights painted the far walls red, white and pink. Not knowing which way to go, Lisa used her instincts and followed the music, running down a long hallway till she saw a flash of white come out of a room, then quickly disappear again.

"Shit," Lisa muttered under her breath. *Was that Jared?* Continuing on, following the hallway till the end, Lisa arrived at a T, with closed doors on either side. Difficult to determine from which room the music emanated, Lisa naturally chose the left, turning the handle easily, and pushing it open. A ragtag group of degenerates filled the large room, many gyrating to the techno music, others taking bong hits, while still others simulated sex on the floor. The depravity was enough to sicken anyone with a moral compass.

No one seemed to take notice of Lisa—even with her gun drawn—as each was wrapped up in his or her own pleasure-seeking activity. Checking out people as she meandered through the crowd, she spotted a tight group of people huddled at the far wall. Curious, she pushed her way through, slipping between several folks before emerging in the center of the circle where a throne-like chair stood. At first, she didn't know what she was observing, having approached the chair from behind. Inching her way clockwise, she now saw two scantily clad girls kneeling in front of the chair, where a swarthy, naked, sweaty man in his 40s sat. With his eyes closed, the man undulated his hairy body to the music while the two girls offered him oral and tactile pleasure.

Could that be Boris? Was this the piece of shit Russian who kidnapped runaway girls with endless promises just to enslave and abuse them to enrich himself? Watching the girls go down on him simultaneously was more than Lisa could stomach, and she knew she had better use the small window of opportunity afforded her to off him before someone noticed her. With the group riveted to the disgusting show, she sneaked behind the throne and placed her .45 to his right temple.

Leaning in close to him, she asked, "Boris? Are you Boris Labirov?"

Stiffening, opening his eyes, the hirsute one instinctively brushed the two girls aside. Not understanding what had just happened, not knowing who was behind the chair taunting him, he attempted to turn around, but was stopped by Lisa, who jammed the gun harder into his temple.

"Don't move or I'll shoot," she said, loud enough this time for everyone to hear, forcing the crowd to back away and begin to disperse. While the two girls who'd been servicing him simply stood in place, too stunned to react, twenty or so people who'd made up the circle shouted incoherently and started running out of the room, shielding themselves for imminent gunfire.

"Who the hell are you?" Boris said, covering his genitals with both hands. "Let me see you."

Guessing no one in the room would be armed, Lisa boldly came around to face Boris, all the
while poising her gun at his head. "Here I am motherfucker. I am you're worst nightmare."

"The fuck you say," Boris laughed, shaking his head, pointing at her .45. "A pipsqueak *suchka* with oversize gun bigger than her pussy. That is funny. Real funny."

Without hesitation, Lisa fired a round into the floor, an inch from his foot. Nearly everyone in the room scattered, heading for the door screaming, a human funnel coursing through a 3-foot-wide opening. Beads of sweat sprouted on Boris' brow and chest as he froze in place.

"Next outburst from you and I'll make sure not to miss," Lisa said, looking him in the eye. "Now shut the fuck up and only answer yes or no. Understand cocksucker?"

Nodding his head affirmatively, Boris stared dumbfoundedly at Lisa. Shifting his weight on his throne, he crossed his legs in an obvious attempt to hide his genitalia, then leaned on his elbow, propping up his chin on his hand. By now, the two girls had slipped out of the room with the rest of the crowd, leaving Lisa and Boris alone in the room. While the techno music droned on, louder now than it had been with a room full of people, Lisa inched closer to the man she thought she'd never find, much less capture. Up close, stripped of his clothing, dignity and power, he looked like any other predatory creep she'd ever seen: overweight, sweaty, smelly and crude. The only difference with Boris was his Russian accent.

"Just answer yes or no. Are you Boris Labirov?"

Boris glared at Lisa before answering. "How you know my name?"

Lisa aimed her pistol at his foot, and before she pulled the trigger, Boris shouted, "Yes! I am Boris Labirov."

Raising her gun again to his head, Lisa continued. "Have you been trafficking young girls for sex?"

Once again Boris glared at his captor, hesitating to answer her question.

"Have you been trafficking young girls for sex?" Lisa repeated, louder this time, shouting over the music. "Do you not understand the question? Is there a language barrier?"

Embarrassed, enraged, Boris' face reddened and sweat broke out across his upper lip. He opened his mouth, but only something inaudible came out. Impatient, Lisa aimed her SIG Sauer at his left foot and pulled the trigger, the blast shattering his foot, the sound ear-splitting over the blaring music. Screaming in pain, Boris grabbed his foot and started shouting at Lisa in Russian.

"Is there a language barrier now, Mr. Labirov? Or am I making myself perfectly clear?"

Rolling onto the ground, grasping his bleeding foot, Boris moaned while Lisa stood over him, waiting for him to respond.

"Say it, Boris, or the next bullet goes through the other foot. Have you been trafficking young girls for sex?"

"Fuck you, bitch," Boris howled, writhing in pain. "I don't need to tell you anything."

"Okay, then have it your way." Lisa moved closer to Boris, standing over him, the gun aimed at the top of his head. "I'll just assume the answer to my question is 'yes' since you're having such an adverse reaction to me. I actually couldn't care less what you think of me, and you calling me names is of no significance. The only other question I have is what role—"

"Fuck you *suchka!*" Boris said, rolling on the floor, never aware of another person entering the room.

"How does Jared—"

"You're in over your head, Miss Benton," Jared said, walking toward them, a gun pointed at Lisa. "You've just involved yourself with something beyond your pay grade, *well* beyond your understanding. You shoulda left well enough alone. Thought you could play with the big boys and now—"

Lisa ignored Jared's aggressive posturing and intentionally walked toward him, her .45 aimed at his core. He appeared more haggard than when he'd escaped her watch at the front door, likely from having just ingested some drugs.

"Stop right there, Hannah," Jared said, shakily pointing his gun at Lisa's chest. "Another move and you're dead."

"Fuck you, Jared," Lisa said authoritatively, inching closer to him. "*You're* in way over your head."

"Fuck me?" Jared's hand shook uncontrollably.

"Yeah, that's right. Fuck you," she said releasing a slug into his right thigh, hoping she hit his femoral artery. "I'm your worst nightmare, the bitch you never wanted to encounter because I'm a way better shot than you."

Watching him fall onto his right side, she stood over him, menacingly waving her SIG Sauer over his head. "By the way, my name is Lisa Benton and I'm the singular purveyor of cosmic justice. Just thought you should know before I blow your brains out."

After emptying two slugs into Jared's head, she returned to a squirming Boris and did the same to him. She then nonchalantly exited the home without encountering anyone else, promptly calling 911.

"Two dead bodies at Sunrise Grand Villa Estates off Happy Trails," Lisa said unemotionally to dispatch when she got back into her vehicle, using a burner phone for such occasions. "Both involved in sex trafficking. You're welcome. You may want to check on the degenerates hiding inside who were attending a party of some sort when the shooting began."

CHAPTER 46 WEDNESDAY NIGHT

"Tim, I've been calling you for hours. Where the hell are you?"

Cyndi hung up the phone, having left Tim five messages, unable to reach her husband for the past five-plus hours. Not usually prone to panic when Tim didn't come home when he said he would, Cyndi was now assuming the worst. Something definitely was not right tonight. She felt it in the pit of her stomach.

Was he having an affair? she wondered, knowing that was un-likely, as he hardly ever commented on other women, much less glanced twice at a hot female when they were out in public. Was he having a late meeting at the office? Again, not likely as he would've told her so. Was he having a showdown with his dad over the newly revised trust that included Lisa? Now that was definitely a possibility.

Or perhaps he was having an in-person encounter with Lisa, af-ter all these years, having somehow located her. That had to be it. Nothing else would come close to explaining his absolute absence for more than five hours. Grabbing the phone again, Cyndi pressed redial just as she heard Tim coming through the back door. Ending the call before it rang, she rushed through the kitchen to cut him off at the pass, hating herself for being so obsessive.

"Where have you been? I've been calling you for hours."

"Can I come in, please, before you start interrogating me?" Tim brushed past Cyndi on his way to the kitchen.

"'Interrogating'? I'm not the one who's been incommunicado for five-plus hours."

"It's been a rough day, okay? I can't expect you to understand." Tim opened the liquor cabinet and grabbed the bottle of Bushmills. He then poured two fingers into a glass and downed in immediately.

"You haven't expected much from me lately, so why would you now? Oh, don't bother answering that. It was a rhetorical question."

Tim poured himself another double shot of whiskey, sat down on a stool and faced his wife. Lifting his drink, inaudibly toasting her, he then gulped it down before slamming the glass down on the counter.

"I'm sorry," he said, looking Cyndi in the eyes. "I fucked up. I should have called you. I should have had my phone on. I was in a meeting till late with a client, then, he wanted to get a bite and then one thing led to another–"

"You are a terrible liar, you know that? And, worse? You insult my intelligence. But of course, you've never given me credit for having *any* intellect, since I never graduated from college."

"Will you please stop putting yourself down? I never said anything of the sort–"

"Don't you dare change the subject. I couldn't care less right now what you think of my IQ."

Cyndi, who'd been standing by the alcove to the pantry, approached Tim and stood menacingly at an angle to him. "The topic of conversation is you being out for hours without even a peep as to where you were."

"I just told you where I was and the fact you don't believe me is your problem."

"Wow, you're unbelievable." Cyndi glared at her husband, shaking her head. "You know what I think you've been up to?"

Tim blanched, his eyes betraying his thoughts. "Please do tell, Cyndi. Can't wait to hear your brilliant deduction."

"I think you've found Lisa and confronted her, threatened her with...what, I don't know. But you've found her at long last."

Tim chortled, nearly coughing. "You really do have a wild imagination; I'll give you that much." Tim shook his head while continuing to chuckle. "Found Lisa. If only that were true."

Counting nine rings, Pat Healy was about to disconnect the call when she heard a click on the line and a faint voice answer *"Hello."*

"Saundra, is that you?"

"Who's this?"

"It's Pat, dear. Pat Healy. Are you alright? I hope I didn't wake you up."

"Patricia, darling. No. I mean, yes, but it's alright. I was just dozing a bit. You can call me anytime."

"I'm sorry. But thank you. I thought maybe you were peeved at me for not having anything concrete on Lisa, for it seeming to be a dead end, for it seeming as if–"

"No, no, Patricia. No darling. You are doing all you can, I know it. And, soon enough, you're going to call me with some good news. I just know it."

"Saundra, I've not let up since our last conversation. I've been on the phone for hours in my determination to find Lisa, and I actually do have something concrete. Absolutely."

Saundra fell silent for a long moment, then said, *"Concrete? What is it, dear?"*

"Earlier this evening, Lisa was stopped on an Arizona Highway Patrol Trooper. She was driving—"

"Arizona? What the hell? Is that where she's living, in the desert?"

"Well, that's not entirely clear, but if I had to guess, I'd say no. She's not living there."

"How can you be so sure?"

"Because she confirmed her address in California to the trooper, after she'd given her driver's license to him. She lives in Fallbrook, dear. The same address as the house owned by Jason and James."

"But she's in Arizona right now, correct? How do we know when she'll be back in California?"

"We'll wait for her to return. I have one of my guys already on his way to San Diego County."

CHAPTER 47 THURSDAY MORNING

Sensing the truck slowing down, Kendall opened his eyes and moved the packing materials away from his face, immediately noticing light seeping through the back door. Morning, he thought, just as the truck's driver turned right and hit a pothole, sending him sliding sideways and onto a pile of boxes. Hungry, anxious to get out, Kendall felt happy when the driver pulled to a stop, engaging his air brakes and opening his door.

Silent stillness and heat instantly permeated his space, causing him to feel disoriented and lightheaded. Everything started closing in on him and he felt he had to get out of the truck, or he'd suffocate. Crawling over the boxes, he lunged for the hatch, pulling it with all his might to the right, flipping it over in seconds, disengaging the lock. Breathing hard, anticipating freedom, Kendall slid his fingers under the door and pulled up as hard as he could. Gliding it open barely a foot, the door stuck on its rails, but it was enough height for Kendall to squeeze his small body through.

Tumbling out, landing on the asphalt of a huge parking lot, he stood, then spun around, breathing in the fresh morning desert air, tinged with the distinctive scent of chamise shrubs. Trucks were parked all around, lined up in diagonal lanes for as far as the eye could see. And at the far end of the lot, a one-story building displayed a familiar logo at the top. Food, he thought, the scent of coffee and fried offerings wafting by him as he headed in that direction.

Slipping inside behind a rotund man whose ill-fitting t-shirt couldn't cover the lower half of his ample belly, Kendall headed straight for the packaged sweet rolls near the candy, helping himself to two packs of cinnamon buns. On his way over to the cashier, he snagged a chocolate milk from the refrigerated section and then snatched a bag of Taki's Zombies from a display rack. Without adult supervision directing him to the cashier, and with seven customers waiting in line to pay, auspiciously shielding the youngster from management's eyes, Kendall slipped outside unnoticed, disappearing into the maze of trucks.

Propping himself up against the huge tires of a semi, Kendall gleefully washed down two sweet rolls with the chocolate milk. He then tore open the bag of Taki's and munched on a few of the super spicy chips before realizing he needed something else to drink. Leaving behind an unopened package of sweet rolls and the Taki's, he jogged back into the convenience store in search of a cold beverage. Searching rows of sodas and sports drinks, he settled on a chartreuse-colored beverage with a wide-mouth opening on the top shelf. Unable to reach it, he asked a tall man standing next to him to get it for him.

"Thanks," he said softly, avoiding eye contact with the man, grabbing it quickly from his grasp.

"Hey kid, where's your mom?" the man asked as Kendall zigzagged through the store. "Hey kid! You need to pay for it."

But Kendall had already slipped out of the store between two customers who were entering, once again avoiding payment. Opening the bottle on the run, his mouth parched, he took a large gulp of the electrolyte-laden sports drink as he meandered back to the semi, happy to find his food was still there, undisturbed.

If Saundra thought she'd scooped her husband in finding out where their long-lost daughter was living, she would soon be dismayed to learn she'd been outwitted by a much craftier and determined competitor. Todd had hired his own private detective firm to locate Lisa, just a couple of days before his wife had called her childhood friend, Pat. Neither had bothered to tell the other for fear of being berated or belittled, though both had their own self-ish reasons for finding their beloved daughter.

Learning that Lisa had indeed been spending a few weeks in Arizona, Todd had also been privy to the fact she'd been living in a home in Fallbrook owned jointly by two of his sons, Jason, a CPA and James, a personal injury attorney. Interestingly, James—with whom he had a decent relationship—never bothered to mention this to him, though perhaps it was Jason—with whom he had little contact—who'd actually rented the property to his sister unbeknownst to James. Whatever. The details didn't matter to him. All he cared about was finding his daughter so that he could give her the good news about her inheritance.

What Todd did find curious was his PI's discovery that Lisa had disappeared from Fallbrook for about three months during the summer, neither residing nor working in northern San Diego County at that time. It was as if she'd fallen off the face of the earth only to reappear for a couple of weeks in October before disappearing again and then turning up in the Phoenix area a month later. Her mysterious comings and goings were odd, he'd thought, but there must be some solid reasons behind her recent wanderlust. Perhaps she'd taken a vacation this summer and met a potential mate who lived in Phoenix, which would explain both absences easily. Hopefully, she'd found love and followed this fellow to his hometown, where she met his family, and they all got along, and Lisa and her beau were going to live happily ever after. Hopefully, when he finally located her and was able to communicate with her, she'd tell him she was the happiest girl in the world because she was about to get married!

And what timing it would all be. Another wedding in the family. Saundra would be thrilled.

Saundra. Fuck. She was definitely not herself lately; absolutely up to something, likely involving Cyndi, luring her into her web by divulging family secrets. What was she thinking telling Cyndi things she needn't ever know? All the ugly things about Tim—the abuse by the priests and his abuse of Lisa. And the fact he actually had a sister! Jesus. What a disaster. And now, Cyndi likely wants nothing to do with me!

Regardless, Todd maintained his positive perspective, praying his daughter indeed had a good life after separating herself from the family and that her life was about to become even better! She was going to be married!

Lisa had enough gas to drive about 33 miles before she needed to refuel. She hated the long stretch between Phoenix and the Coachella Valley, straight, flat for the most part and nothing but cactus and sand. Boring as shit and colorless, limiting depth perception and alertness. According to the signs, the next closest service station would be in Tonopah, Arizona, a dusty town of 2,000 situated along Interstate 10 with the requisite Main Street and store front buildings dating back 80 years.

Taking a left as she exited the freeway, Lisa ducked under the freeway overpass heading toward a service station farther away from the highway, just as a precaution. You never know, she thought, cutting the engine, who would be looking for me. Sliding her credit card into the slot on the pump, she then selected the gas and inserted the handle into her tank. Locking her doors with the remote, she hopped inside the convenience store to use the restroom, hoping to avoid stopping again until she was well into her home state.

By the time she got back to her car, there were a few people milling around the pumps in her row, pointing this way and that, animatedly talking to each other, though making no sense. Annoyed, but not interested in finding out what got them all in a tizzy, Lisa snatched the receipt from the pump and slid back inside her vehicle. Caught up in something dramatic, several people continued to mill about, impeding her ability to leave the station, forcing her to aggressively inch forward and virtually push them out of her way with her car.

"What the hell's the matter with people?" Lisa said aloud, shaking her head, as if anyone
could hear her and offer her an answer.

Happy to have at last gotten back on Interstate 10, she easily forgot about the crazy people back at the station as she merged into traffic, heading straight for the fast lane. Not half a minute later, she heard movement in the back of her car, like a small animal scurrying for food, scratching the floor for something to eat. Carefully turning around to see what it was, Lisa saw a heap of navy-blue squirming, something alive trying unsuccessfully to hide from view. Swerving wildly to get to the right shoulder of the freeway, Lisa abruptly stopped her vehicle, threw the transmission into park, unlatched her seatbelt, and turned to face the intruder.

"Who the heck are you and what the heck are you doing in my car?"

Sneaking out of the house before Cyndi got up and started interrogating him again about last night, Tim drove to his parent's home a few miles away in Bel Air, letting himself in with the spare key he'd had for years. His professed reason—should his dad or mom be awake—was to confront Todd about his decision to include Lisa in the trust, begging him to reconsider before all hell broke loose. But his actual goal—should his dad or mom not be at home—was to snag one of his long guns, either the Remington .308 or the Mossberg .30-06 Patriot. Either one of those beauties would be appropriate for what he had in mind. *You did this to yourself dad; you gave me no other choice.*

Walking through the back door leading to the kitchen pantry, he keenly listened for any sounds in the house. Inching into the kitchen, looking for any signs of activity, he smelled neither
coffee brewing nor bread in the toaster. Assuming his dad had already gone to the office and his mother was sleeping off a bender, he turned around and headed toward his mother's tiny office. But a phone ringing in her office forced him to stop in his tracks. Sensing only his pulse beating in his head, he then heard his mother's sleepy voice answer the phone.

"Hello?"

Silence as Saundra listened to the caller.

"Good morning, Pat. No, it's alright, I was just waking up." Saundra yawned before adding, "So, I'll assume you're calling me this early because you have some wonderful news for me, right?"

Continued silence as his mother listened to "Pat" allowed Tim to creep closer to her office.

"Oh, I see—"

Tim now stood at his mother's opened office door, flush with the wall, listening intently to a one-sided conversation.

"So, she's really on her way back to California. I never thought—"

Tim craned his neck, peering into the small room, seeing his mother twisted uncomfortably on her day bed, her back to him, her nightgown askew, her hair a mess. She was now running her fingers through her hair, trying to primp herself as if Pat could see what a wreck she truly was.

"You are, Pat. You are the best. I don't know how I'll be able to pay—I mean *repay*—you for all you've done. For finding my baby. My Lisa. You're a miracle worker."

What the fuck? Mother is engaging someone to find Lisa. What is going on? Is she doing this unilaterally, or is dad in on it? Jesus Christ. This family has truly gone off the deep end.

Backing away from the door, Tim quietly scurried through the kitchen and into Todd's study, where his dad kept his gun safe. Praying that his father never changed the combination lock, Tim tried the numbers he'd memorized as a teen, easily unlocking his father's treasure trove of firearms. He immediately spotted both the Remington and the Mossberg, grabbing both, just for good measure. He then closed the safe and wiped his prints off the lock and door with the bottom of his t-shirt.

Nimbly slipping out of the house, Tim carefully placed the rifles in the trunk of his car and then drove back home, confident his attitude had been properly adjusted; ready, willing and able to take on anyone, especially his wife.

What the hell? Cyndi thought, seeing Tim place two rifles into the trunk of his car, which had been parked in the circular driveway of his parents' home in Bel Air. Cyndi had arrived moments earlier, invited for breakfast by Saundra, and having decided to park on the street in case Todd was still home, was walking onto the property when she noticed her husband. Shocked to see Tim at this hour at his parents' house and not on his way to work, Cyndi hid behind a hedge along the sidewalk until he drove away. Certain he didn't notice her, Cyndi hustled to the back door, as she'd been instructed by her mother-in-law.

"Good morning, gorgeous," Saundra said, a wide smile on her face, a tumbler of liquor in her right hand. "Perfect timing. Come in, dear."

"Good morning, Saundra," Cyndi said, stepping into the pantry. "Thank you for inviting me. Lovely to be here."

"Coffee'll be ready in a couple of minutes, dear. Not to fret." Saundra held up her glass of vodka. "I'm just getting primed for my first cup of java."

"Saundra, you never have to apologize to me for having a cocktail first thing in the morning. I find nothing wrong with it. In fact, I'd do the same if I were in your shoes."

"That's what I love about you, dear. Your fearless honesty. Your forthrightness. The world needs more people like you in it.

"C'mon in the kitchen. Have a cup of coffee. I would normally apologize for not being dressed appropriately, for wearing bedroom attire when I invited you over, but I've been on the phone this morning and didn't have much time to prep. I do hope you can forgive me.

"And I have some *wonderful* news for you."

"Nothing to apologize for, Saundra. It's your home and you can do as you please." Cyndi followed Saundra into the kitchen, sitting on a tan, high-backed leather stool edging a granite bar encircling the sink. Smiling in anticipation of hearing good news, she watched the older woman deftly cut a piece of crumb cake from a fresh coffee ring and place it on a floral-patterned bone China plate.

"Cream and sugar?" Saundra asked, opening a carton of half and half. "Or do you like it black?"

"Black, please."

"I was going to be a smart ass, but since you married my son, there was no point in saying it." Saundra poured the coffee into a matching cup and then handed it to Cyndi. "You know, I used to fantasize about what it would be like to sleep with a black man, and I regret the time I actually had the chance and chickened out.

Cyndi chuckled and took a sip of her coffee. "Why'd you chicken out?"

"Well, for one it was Tim's friend from school and two—"

"You needed more than one reason *not* to do it?" Cyndi nearly spit out her coffee.

"Dear, if you would have seen him, believe me, you would have also needed more than one reason. This young man was an Adonis. Chiseled, gorgeous, but I digress."

"You're too much, Saundra. I wish my mother was as open and hip as you are, though I'm not sure I'd approve of—"

"Darling, he was a minor at the time, that was my number two reason," Saundra said, taking a swig of her drink. "I may be a loathsome, functioning drunk, but I am not a pedophile. Plus, I was just trying to be funny."

Saundra came around to sit on a matching leather stool next to Cyndi, placing her cocktail on the granite bar. "Time to get serious. You know, I happen to be the luckiest woman in the world right now. And I'm shaking like a leaf." Saundra held out her hands.

"What's going on? I'm confused?" Cyndi's brow furrowed.

"Soon—really soon—I'm going to see my Lisa." Saundra stared wide-eyed at Cyndi, her head now also shaking.

"Wow, Saundra, that is fantastic! What, uh…how did all this happen?"

"Well, I hired an old friend of mine, who just happens to be the best private eye in the Southland. She found her."

"Really? Where?" Cyndi took a bite of the coffee crumb cake.

"She's been living in northern San Diego County, in Fallbrook, for a number of years, but my friend actually found her in Arizona."

"Arizona?" Cyndi asked, chewing daintily.

"Yes, it's, well…she was obviously visiting someone out there, but she's on her way back. Now. This morning, in fact."

"*Fantastic!*" Cyndi smiled warmly at her mother-in-law before adding, "Mind if I join you in a little cocktail to celebrate?"

"Mind? Darling, I thought you'd never ask."

CHAPTER 48 THURSDAY MORNING

Darlene Sampson sat patiently on a hard wooden bench lining the east wall of the reception area at the Indio jail, waiting for Lonnie Dautremont to be roused from her cell and escorted to the prisoners' side of the visitation room. Refreshed and raring to go, Darlene had slept amazingly well at the motel Lonnie suggested, never once waking up during the night for any reason. Hoping to be called soon, she enviously observed several women march toward the visitors' room, a veritable cross section of society from white to black to Hispanic. Some of the women looked like men while others looked too good to be real women.

At last, Darlene's name was called by a burly sheriff's deputy whose gender was indeed questionable. He could have actually been a man or just as easily been a woman identifying as a man. When Darlene got closer, she determined the deputy to be just a plain old butch dyke. Excited to see Lonnie again for the second time in as many days, Darlene slid onto the wobbly wooden seat at cubicle 13, immediately taking out a cloth and a small bottle of rubbing alcohol, cleaning the phone's handset thoroughly. By the time she finished, Lonnie had arrived looking even more haggard than she did yesterday.

"Hey, girl, you don't look too good," Darlene said empathetically. "What's up?"

"Can't sleep in this shithole. That's what's up." Lonnie squeezed her eyes and shook her head. "Jesus fucking Christ. The noise in this place will make anyone go insane."

"Sorry, hon. Wish you weren't in here. Wish I could—"

"Hey," Lonnie interrupted, rubbing her eyes, quickly changing the subject, "did you happen to see any kids at the motel?"

"Kids? Uh, no. No kids. In fact, I slept like a baby last night. Thanks for recommending the place."

Lonnie glared vindictively at her friend. "Do you even have an iota of sympathy for me? How can you bring up the fact of how great you slept last night while I was stuck in this hell hole? Shit. Be real."

Darlene took a deep breath and changed the subject. "Did you speak with your attorney yesterday after I left?"

"No, I did not speak with Molly. Guess she's got more important clients to represent."

"I'm sure she'll be here today," Darlene said, trying to sound cheerful. "I just have a good feeling about it."

"You're sure a giddy little bitch today. What'd you drink this morning?" Lonnie shook her head again.

"Just a couple of cups of coffee. That's all."

Lonnie licked her lips, then stared inquisitively at Darlene. "As you can see, I'm not in a very spunky mood today. In fact, I'm in a downright fucked-up mood. Probably best for you to go home now. Thanks for driving out all this way. Maybe we can talk another time when I'm in a better mood."

"That's it? That's all you got?" Darlene shook her head in disbelief. "Okay, I get it. I'd be pretty pissed off if the situation was reversed."

Darlene hung up the phone and stood, watching her friend slowly collapse onto the table, still clutching the phone. She felt badly for Lonnie—who was now crying, her body heaving on the table—but she also knew beyond a shadow of a doubt that she did this to herself. There was no one else to blame for her downfall. There was only so much she could do for a friend whose every intention and action caused her life to spiral deeper into the abyss.

Lisa reached behind her seat and yanked on the navy-blue fabric covering a small human being hiding on the floor of the back seat, revealing his frightened face. Yelping in fear, the little person cowered, shielding his face with his arms, shaking uncontrollably.

"Who the heck are you and what the heck are you doing in my car?"

Not speaking, the boy continued to shake, lowering his eyes, pulling away from the woman who was now his captor.

"What's your name?" Lisa asked, lowering her voice, and tempering her mood to engender compliance. "Where are your parents?"

Strong and determined, the boy used all of his might to try to get away from Lisa, kicking the seat back, clawing at her, but quickly gave up as he was no match for her. Sulking, the boy rigidly folded his arms across his chest and pouted.

"Okay, then, if you won't talk to me and tell me who you are and where your parents are," Lisa said, staring sternly at the youngster, "I will be forced to take you to a police station and let them sort it all out."

Hearing the threat, the boy stiffened, straightening up, looking pleadingly into Lisa's eyes. Slowly, he pushed himself up onto the seat until he was sitting erect.

"Please, no, don't take me to the police," he said, shaking his head. "*Please.*"

"Give me one good reason why I shouldn't? You sneaked into my vehicle, and you're obviously not old enough to be on your own."

"You just can't," the boy said defiantly, crossing his arms again.

"Yes, I can, and I will." Lisa turned around and started to buckle her seatbelt.

"No, you can't take me to the police."

"One last time, kid: where's your mother? Tell me or we're headed straight to the police."

"I don't have a mother anymore. She's gone."

"What do you mean she's gone?" Lisa turned around to face him.

"Gone. Dead."

"Dead? Then, where's your dad?"

"I don't have one. Never did."

"So, who takes care of you? Your grandmother? An aunt?"

"Well, my Aunt Lonnie kinda used to but she's gone, too."

"Is she dead, too? I'm getting confused."

"No, I don't think she's dead."

"You don't think so? So, you don't really know, right?"

The boy was quiet for a long moment, trying to formulate his thoughts. Finally, he said forthrightly, "All I know is that she killed my mommy."

"Who killed your mommy, kid? Aunt Lonnie?" Lisa felt the hair on the back of her neck stand on end.

"Yes, Aunt Lonnie killed my mommy. At the motel. In Indio."

Chapter 49 Thursday Mid-Morning

With the two long guns wrapped in blankets snugly tucked under his arm, Tim rushed into his home, praying he would not run into Cyndi and her inquisitive mind. He especially didn't want her to confront him after her tirade last night when he got home late.

Relieved he caught a break, Tim jumped into the shower, tarrying longer than usual, then leisurely dressed, and grabbed a bagel before jumping back into his car and heading to the office. Amazingly, things were falling nicely into place, and by the time he'd finally come face to face with Lisa, after all these years, he'd be ready to take her on. He'd be the better prepared sibling to engage in the final chapter, the last hoorah. And, whatever she thought would happen, she'd be on the receiving end of his wrath.

Skipping into the Ogilvie Wealth Management building, idly whistling a nondescript tune, Tim nodded blindly as he passed his father's office only to be tracked down by Angie before he reached his own office door.

"Tim, um, excuse me," Angie said, tapping him on the shoulder. "Your dad wants to see you. Stat."

Tim turned around and glared at his secretary. "'Stat'? What are we now, working in a hospital?"

"*Now*, Tim." Angie nervously blew a puff of air out the side of her mouth, causing her bangs to flutter on one side. "He's waiting for you in his office."

"Jeez, Angie, okay. Let me just check my voice messages and I'll be right in."

"Now, Tim. *Now*. No time for that." Angie flushed a deep shade of crimson, then turned on her heels and hustled back to reception.

Setting his wallet, keys and cell phone on his desk, Tim noticed a stack of mail piled in the middle of his desk. Curious, he flipped through it, and nothing caught his attention until he saw a thick, odd-shaped, yellow envelope with no return address. *Fuck you, Lisa. Bring it on.*

Shaking his head, ambling down the hall to his father's office, Tim saw a flash of Branson's naked body streak across his path, compelling him to swipe at the phantom image he knew was only in his mind. But the imaginary likeness of his new friend wouldn't disappear, and instead, reversed directions, crossing his path again, and then again, finally evaporating when Tim seemed to walk through it. Shaken, Tim dug his fingernails into his palms and squeezed his eyes shut to rid himself of that intoxicating image.

"Timothy, where have you been? I've been waiting for you for hours."

"Good morning, Dad. Jesus. You sound just like my wife." Tim walked past Todd, taking a seat facing his enormous desk.

"Well, if Cyndi's reaction is the same as mine, I'd say it's definitely something you're doing or not doing that's got us upset."

"Whatever Dad. I'm well past the age of consent, so if you or my wife have a problem with me spending a little quality time by myself, then it's time to get over it."

Todd glared at his son while absentmindedly shuffling a stack of folders in front of him. Pressing the stack with both hands, he offered Tim a half-smile. "Good news and bad news, Timothy. What do you want—"

"Just give me the bad news first," Tim interjected impatiently. "I'd rather save the good stuff for last."

"Okay, son. You got it. Lisa won't be back in California till later tonight."

"That's the bad news?" Tim regarded his dad incredulously. "Fuck! What's the good news?"

"I found Lisa. I found out where she lives. Right under our noses, for crying out loud. All this time."

"What do you mean 'under our noses'?"

With the boy sitting shotgun, Lisa sped west on Interstate 10 toward Indio, her brain working overtime on determining what to do with the kid who just told her his mother was killed by a woman he calls Aunt Lonnie. With no father in the picture and no other relatives he knew of, the kid was now basically an orphan, and would, without a doubt, become a ward of the state. His lot would be cast into the foster care system, from which any number of misfits and morons could become his temporary guardians. What a future! What an awful fate awaits this innocent youngster.

Glancing his way for a fleeting moment, Lisa noticed him nodding off, succumbing to the warmth of the sun and the motion of the car. Good, she thought, sleep my darling boy, you need your rest. *You certainly didn't deserve any of this.* Not the single mother who may have had a hard time caring for you or for a relative whose selfish actions robbed you of your only parent. *What the hell was wrong with people? Jesus! One more injustice in this world!*

How was she going to handle this once she got to Indio? Take him to the local police or Highway Patrol station, drop him off hoping he'd have a great life from here on out? *Shit!* Lisa shook her head, trying to think of a solution. Maybe she should keep driving to LA, then take him to a child protective services office there.

That would make more sense, rather than stopping off in the place where his mother was murdered.

Unconsciously, Lisa had slowly taken her foot off the accelerator while placing a death grip on the steering wheel. Wait just a freaking minute, she told herself, releasing her hold. *If his mother was murdered in the motel in Indio, how long ago did it happened? Did it happen in the room, outside or in a car? Did the aunt hunt them down having dinner somewhere, bringing them back to the motel to murder the mother? Did the kid witness the murder? Did they all live nearby, or were they visiting the Coachella Valley? Fuck! Too many possibilities and nothing was coming together.*

Impulsively pulling off the freeway when she saw a McDonald's up ahead, Lisa eased into a parking spot in front and cut her engine. It took a minute for the boy to realize they'd stopped. Opening his eyes, he smiled at Lisa when he saw where they were.

"Hey, kid. My name's Lisa. What's your name?" Lisa asked, smiling back at him.

"Kendall. And I'm eight years old."

"Are you hungry, Kendall?"

"Very hungry."

"I bet you can't even remember the last time you ate."

The boy shook his head as the smile dissipated.

"C'mon. Let's get something to eat," Lisa said, sliding out of the car. "I'm famished, too."

While they ate Big Macs and fries, Lisa gently coaxed him into revealing personal information, like his mother's name—Loretta—where he and his mother lived—Los Angeles—where Aunt Lonnie lived—sometimes with them, but most of the time somewhere else—why they were in Indio—vacation—and the name of the motel in Indio where Aunt Lonnie killed his mother.

"Do you remember the name of the motel?" Lisa asked gently, strategizing a plan of action.

"Yes, Motel Eight. We were in Room Thirteen."

"Was Aunt Lonnie with you the whole time, or did she come later than you and your mommy?"

"She came later. I never saw her until—" Kendall squeezed his eyes shut as tears started to flow.

"Oh, Kendall, I am so sorry," Lisa said, reaching out and touching his hand. "I didn't mean to make you cry. I'm just trying to figure out—"

"She told me she loved mommy," Kendall said, crying hard now. "She told me she loved me, too. She said we were going to be a family. I believed her."

Lisa's compassionate stare did not betray her inner thoughts. She got it. Loud and clear. A lover's quarrel, a jealous rage that turned deadly. She now knew she had to stop in Indio to not only search for clues but to mete out justice.

CHAPTER 50 THURSDAY AFTERNOON

Lonnie sensed her public defender, Molly Benedict, was ignoring her in favor of other, sexier cases to come across her desk; ones that would bring her fame and praise from her boss, no doubt. Why focus on a plain, old self-defense murder case when you had notorious gangbangers with facial tattoos to defend? Having called Molly three times in two days, Lonnie was convinced she'd only hear back from her attorney once the hearing was set.

Lying on her bed, her cellmate relaxing above her reading a magazine, Lonnie chewed on her nonexistent fingernails till she bit too hard and two of them bled. Jumping up, lunging toward the sink, she washed her hands till the bleeding subsided, then fell back onto her bunk, bored and anxious. If she didn't get out of jail soon, she'd go crazy for sure. In fact, she was already going insane with no one to talk to much less commiserate with. Her cellie seemed to be a fucking deaf-mute. *Of all fucking people to be paired up with, why did I get her?*

Hearing a whooshing sound coming from down the hall—as if two nylon bags were brushing against each other—Lonnie sat up, placed her feet on the ground, and waited for the guard to come by. Wondering if today would be her lucky day—*"Your lawyer has arrived and has requested a meeting, Dautremont"*—she instantly became hopeful, changing her attitude as if her life depended on it. And it did.

Nearly losing hope after several minutes went by without hearing or seeing the guard, she was about to lie back down on her bed when she heard the whooshing sound resume. In seconds, a rotund corrections officer approached her cell with an envelope in her hand.

"Dautremont, a letter for you," the CO said, sliding the envelope through the bars, waiting for Lonnie to come get it.

"Who's it from?" Lonnie asked enthusiastically, grabbing it from the CO.

"Your lawyer."

"What's it say?" Lonnie reached inside the envelope and pulled out a letter.

"Hell, if I know," the rotund one said irritably as she continued on her route. "Read if for yourself."

Glancing at the short letter, Lonnie allowed a smile to appear on her heretofore sour face.

"Hey, Mute. Listen to this," Lonnie said aloud. "My attorney's coming to see me today."

"Lisa's been living in Southern California all this time," Todd said, sitting behind his huge desk, smiling widely at his son. "In Fallbrook, a small town in northern San Diego County."

"I know where Fallbrook is, dad. So, what's your point? Why's that good news? She was the one who estranged herself from us, from her family. We were always—"

"Well, I think she had good reason to do so. And now that I've had time to really think about it, I can't say I blame her."

"Really? So, who do you blame, huh? Me? Mom?" Tim shifted uneasily in his chair.

"If anyone, I blame myself. For a lot of things. I was—and still am—the man of the house. I should have done a lot of things differently." Todd reshuffled the stack of folders, staring at them as if they held all of life's answers. "I am to blame for not addressing her issues at the time they happened, for allowing it to go for so long, for not doing anything about your mother's drinking—"

"Mom would have been a drunk no matter what you did or didn't do. Jesus. And Lisa," Tim shook his head, "she had a wild imagination. Lots of what she *thinks* happened to her never happened. I am *not* a monster."

"Look, as much as I'd like to, we can't put the genie back in the bottle. What was done is done. It's all water under the bridge, and that's why I have to make it right by her. To rectify all of my mistakes."

"Well, you're got a helluva way of doin' that, dad. Whatever." Tim pushed off the chair, then immediately sat back down when he saw his mother and wife enter the office. They both looked haggard and worn, like they'd wiled away the last few hours with non-stop drinking.

"Saundra, Cynthia." Todd looked up, shocked. "What the heck are you two doing here?"

"Is that any way to greet your wife and your daughter-in-law?" Saundra sauntered into the office holding Cyndi's hand, as if she were a small child. "Show some goddamned respect, would you?"

Saundra led Cyndi to a plush chair on the other side of her son, giving the younger woman a slight nudge, then walked to her husband's desk and sat on the edge.

"No point in keeping it a secret anymore," she said, slurring her words, glaring down at him, "so I'll come right out and say it. Lisa's coming home tonight."

Todd looked quizzically at his wife, then gazed at Tim, who was eyeballing Cyndi. "Yes, I know, darling. I was just telling Tim the good news."

"The what—? How, uh, did you know?" Saundra stared at Todd incredulously.

"I've had a private investigator looking for her." Todd beamed proudly.

"The fuck you say?" Saundra glanced sideways at Cyndi, then turned to glare at her husband. "*I've* had a private investigator looking for her. We couldn't have been looking for her at the same—"

"Great minds think alike," Cyndi said, giggling, sneaking a peek at her husband.

"Public intoxication for a female is quite unappealing, Cyndi," Tim said, seething. "Especially for someone of your upbringing,"

"Oh, Tim, you are such a party pooper." Cyndi waved her hand at him and giggled uncontrollably.

"Ignore him, dear, he's just jealous," Saundra said, then without missing a beat, turned her attention back to her husband. "Todd, what's this about you hiring a private investigator?"

"I sure hope my mother isn't influencing you to become an alcoholic like her." Tim glared at his wife, shaking his head.

"I hired the best PI money can buy, Saundra. You remember Guy Simonsson?"

"You really believe someone can *turn* you into an alcoholic?" Cyndi said too loudly. "That's the dumbest thing I ever heard."

"Who? I don't remember any Guy person. I just can't believe we both hired someone at the same time to find Lisa. What a waste of time and effort and money, we could have joined forces and—"

"You're all ridiculous and incoherent," Tim said, frustrated, rising, heading for the door. "I'm *outta* here. You're all *nuts*. Fucked-up! You all deserve each other!"

Tim stormed out of the office before anyone could stop him, much less understand why he was so upset. Todd, Saundra and Cyndi were thrilled that Lisa was found, no matter who initiated the search for her, yet Tim deemed her imminent arrival as a disaster in the making.

"Was it something I said?" Cyndi asked, giggling, clearly inebriated. "Now, he's never gonna come home."

"What are you talking about, dear?"

"He didn't...last night, he came home...really late and—"

Todd's cell phone rang, startling all three of them. Nabbing it off his desk, he glanced quickly at the Caller ID and then immediately connected the call.

"Yes, Guy, we were just talking about you," Todd said, listening intently for a long moment before smiling and nodding. "Wonderful. Wonderful. Thanks very much."

"What?" Saundra asked, scooting off the desk, standing in front of her husband.

"She's back in California. Just passed through the agricultural inspection checkpoint about thirty minutes ago. Won't be long now."

CHAPTER 51 THURSDAY AFTERNOON

"Dautremont, time to get your shit together, your presence is needed elsewhere." The same rotund corrections officer who'd brought her Molly's letter, was now shouting from three cells away.

"My presence?" Lonnie's eyes lit up when the CO appeared in front of her. "Is my lawyer here?"

"How the fuck should I know?" the CO said mockingly, unlocking the cell door. "All's they tell me is to get you to reception."

"What else could it mean?" Lonnie said, giggling. Staring at the CO cuff her hands, Lonnie
studied her plump face then added, "Aren't you even a little bit happy for me? Admit it, you are." Lonnie winked at her, as they headed toward reception.

"To be perfectly honest, Dautremont, I couldn't give a rat's ass about you. You're just another criminal in jail waiting to be tried and convicted." The CO yanked on Lonnie's wrists, urging her along.

"That's a helluva thing to say to me when you don't even know me." Lonnie glared at the woman. "I'm innocent, you know. I didn't do anything illegal."

"Yeah, right. You and everyone else in this joint is innocent."

"I don't know about everyone else, but I know I am. You'll see. Just wait. I'm gonna beat this shit. And I'll come back to prove you wrong."

"I ain't waiting for nothing, Dautremont" the CO said, stopping at the reception counter. "Checking in Lonnie Dautremont," she said to the female guard inside the office. "She's all yours."

"What's going on, where's my lawyer?" Lonnie watched the heavyset CO waddle off without saying another word. "Where's Molly? She was supposed to be meeting me here today."

"Who?" the guard asked, looking down, jotting notes into a ledger.

"Molly Benedict. My attorney. She said she was going to meet me here today. She wrote me a letter earlier."

"Letter?" The guard finally looked up, regarding Lonnie disinterestedly.

"Yes, it's in my cell. Can I go back and get it to show you?"

"No, there's no need for that."

"Why the hell not? What's going on?" Lonnie looked pleadingly at the guard. "Where am I going?"

"Calm down, Dautremont. You're going to court for your hearing. You should be happy. I'm sure your attorney will be there. Nothing to get all worked up about."

"Hearing? Wow. No one told me shit." Lonnie craned her neck to see what the guard was writing.

"We tell you as you need to know. Not before."

"You people like keeping us in the dark like mushrooms."

"Here you go, Dautremont," the guard said, handing her a legal-size paper. Take this and walk straight ahead. The van is waiting for you right outside the double doors."

Thankful to be out of Arizona relatively unscathed, yet eager to get back to business, Lisa forced herself to drive the speed limit after crossing into California, wanting to avoid any attention from the California Highway Patrol. She was on a new mission now, thanks to a chance encounter with a runaway kid whose mother had just been murdered. To think she'd be meting out justice, once again, on her way to her *coup de grâce* in Los Angeles made her smile.

"So, tell me again, Kendall, so I understand correctly. Your mother, Loretta and your Aunt Lonnie, were sometimes living together? Is that right?"

"Yes, sometimes she lived with us and other times, like after they had a fight, Aunt Lonnie wouldn't be around for a few days. Then she'd show up and act like everything was alright. Like nothing ever happened."

"Is that right?" Lisa said gently, not wanting to spook the child or get him to clam up. "When Aunt Lonnie came back, after a fight, did she bring anything with her? You know, to make your mom feel better?"

"You mean like flowers?"

"Yeah, like flowers."

"Yeah. Flowers. And also wine. She liked to drink wine."

"Who, Aunt Lonnie?"

"No, my mom. She never really bought it herself. She said it cost too much to buy the good stuff."

"Oh, I see. She's right about that!"

"She did buy cheap wine, but then she would tell me it gave her a headache."

"Right again. Your mom was a smart woman. Say," Lisa said, changing the subject, "what is Aunt Lonnie's last name?"

"Dough-tre-mont." Kendall pronounced it phonetically. "I don't know how to spell it, if that's what you're going to ask."

"Oh, no, that's okay. Dough-tre-mont. Sounds French."

"She's not French. She's American, like you and me."

"You're funny, Kendall, you know that?"

CHAPTER 52 THURSDAY AFTERNOON

His anger boiling, his head on the verge of exploding, Tim opted to cool his heels by calling his new friend, Branson to find out if he'd meet him for a tête-à-tête later at Clancy's. Not that he wanted to drown his sorrows in alcohol, and then be tempted again to engage in taboo sex. He desperately wanted someone to talk to; someone who would listen to him and validate his frustrations and not make him feel like they were all a figment of his imagination.

As he drove home to change his clothes, he scrolled through the recent calls on his phone, tapping Branson's number, waiting for that silky voice to answer, "Hello." But when the call went straight to voicemail, Tim's heart sunk, and he almost disconnected the call before leaving a message. Disappointed, he allowed two seconds to lapse before uttering a word.

"Oh, hi Branson. It's me, Tim. Bummer I missed you. I was hoping you'd be free later to meet me at Chancy's. Another brutal day at the office. Will fill you in later. Anyway, let me know. Either way, I'll be heading over there about four forty-five. Uh, catch up later, man. Bye."

Ending the call, Tim felt foolish, thinking he rushed his message. It was way too assuming. What if Branson had plans? It wasn't as if they were an item and Branson was breathlessly waiting for him to call, at the ready, at his beck and call. Nonsense! What was wrong with him, he thought, shaking his head, taking a hairpin turn on Sunset. He'd only just met him this week and then—though he had no memory of it—jumped into the sack with the hot attorney and junior partner of his father's trust lawyers. Jesus! What had gotten into him? Was he finally succumbing to his true sexual identity–being gay–or was this a crazy diversion to get away from his annoying wife? Was it simply a matter of the right place, time and person? He'd had sex only with women all of his life–except for the fucked-up priests who molested him–and now Branson enters stage left and easily seduces him, making him totally question his evolving sexual identity! *Oh God, what am I going to do–*

Taking another tight turn on Sunset, Tim heard a distinctive ding, signifying a text coming in. Grabbing his phone, tapping the Message icon, he saw it was from Branson, and though he couldn't read the whole thing, saw it was only two lines. Grateful to have to stop at the light up ahead, Tim looked down at the message, feeling his chest tighten.

Got your VM. Sorry, dude, got plans tonight.
Maybe tomorrow? Enjoy, Branson.

What the fuck? Plans? With whom? Why is everyone dissing me?

Cyndi had a pounding headache as she drove Saundra home following their strange meeting at Ogilvie Wealth Management. Attributing most of the pain to the morning cocktails she'd shared with her mother-in-law, she also knew a good part of her stress arose from trying to deal with the peculiar goings-on of Tim. He was up to something untoward, she was certain, though she couldn't put her finger on it. Biting her lower lip, she held her breath, then blurted it out.

"Saundra, I've been meaning to ask you something. Something difficult for me to–"

"Ask away sweetheart. Ask me anything. I am an open book." Saundra tipped her head back, leaning against the headrest.

Cyndi breathed out a draft of air, then tightly gripped the steering wheel. "Okay, it's just that I don't want to sound like a whiny, wimpy bitch with no self-esteem."

"Please darling. You're none of the above."

"Okay. I caught Tim sneaking into the house this morning carrying a couple of rifles. And last night, he came home late. *Really* late."

"So, you think he's a hitman? Is that it?" Saundra chuckled, straightening her head, turning to regard her daughter-in-law. "Sweetheart, Tim has his faults—and there are many—but moonlighting as a killer is not one of them."

"Saundra, this is a serious matter. Please. Of course, he's not a hitman, but last night he came home really late and smelled of booze and—"

"Booze and what, dear?"

"Booze and sex. *Sex*, Saundra. He had sex with someone else."

"'Someone else'? You mean he had sex with another woman?"

"No, not really, Saundra."

"What the hell are you inferring, then?" Saundra turned ice cold.

"I think you know, unless you want me to spell it out."

"So, he's a homosexual? Is that it?"

"I-I don't think...I don't know. I thought he loved me."

"Then, why the rifles? What does him having sex with a man have to do with guns?"

"I have no earthly idea. I was hoping you could tell me."

Chapter 53 Thursday Afternoon, Late

"There's the motel we stayed at," said Kendall, pointing to his left, across the street. "We were in room number thirteen. It was in the back."

Lisa quickly sized up the Motel 8 as she passed it on her left, a median with low-lying plants running the length of the street impeding a turn into the property. Able to make a U-turn a block past the motel, Lisa then glided into the motel's lot, parking near the motel's office.

"Wait here, Kendall. I'll only be a minute."

"Okay. What are you gonna do?"

"Just ask the manager a few questions. Please stay in the car. I won't be long, I promise."

Alert and ready for action, adrenaline coursing through her body, Lisa boldly entered the office, hearing a bell ding above her. Spotting a door behind the counter slightly ajar, Lisa looked inside just as a woman dressed in a generic work uniform emerged.

"Hello, checking in?" said the woman, rubbing her hands on the sides of her black slacks.

"Uh, no. I just have a question for the manager. Is he or she in?"

"She's not here right now. She had an outside appointment. She'll probably be back in an hour or so."

"Oh, darn. I can't wait that long. Have to get back to LA."

"Can I help you with something? My name is Naomi Nichols and I'm her assistant manager. Been here since she came aboard, like fifteen years ago."

"Well then, maybe you can." Lisa regarded the middle-aged woman with lovely brown eyes and high cheekbones. "I was hoping to get any information you have on a woman who stayed here this past week with her young son, who was brutally—"

The woman's eyes instantly filled with tears as she bit down hard on her lips, trying to stop herself from crying. Squeezing her eyes shut, she shook her head as tears rolled down her cheeks.

"The poor woman," she finally said, sniffing back tears. "I was the one who found her. It was just awful. I was also there when the cops showed up."

"I know, honey, I'm so sorry you were the one to find her." Lisa reached out across the counter, lightly touching her arm.

Blinking away the remaining tears, the woman grasped Lisa's hand and then looked her in the eye. "Are you related to her? Is that why you're here?"

"I am actually godmother to Kendall, her son," said Lisa, the lie easily rolling off her tongue.

The woman squeezed Lisa's hand, shaking her head. "The poor kid. I think he witnessed the whole thing. And now he's gone. Poof! disappeared into thin air after sleeping in the laundry room for two nights. I just hope he's okay...God only knows."

"Sleeping in the laundry room? Oh, no...my poor godson." Lisa offered the woman a forlorn look.

"Did you just drive out here from LA?"

"No, actually I was returning from Arizona. I heard about it on the news."

"Then you must hurry and get over to the police station, right down the street," she said, letting go of Lisa's hand and pointing to her right. "Tell them about your godson missing and find out what's going on with that woman who killed his mother in cold blood."

"Did they arrest someone already?"

"Oh, yes; the same day. Ironically, I was the one to find her, too, snooping in the motel afterwards. Held her down till the cops arrived a few minutes later."

"Wow. That's some story. What jail is she in?"

"There's only one jail in Indio. Adjacent to the police station, down the street."

Tim strolled into Clancy's as if he didn't have a care in the world. He summoned up his courage and strode cockily to the same booth he and Branson occupied last night, sliding in all the way to the wall. Resting his right leg at an angle on the bench, spreading out his right arm on the back of the seat, he perused the clientele, once again a mix of professional types and blue-collar guys just getting off work. There has to be one person here this evening I could get to know, he thought, willing to talk to me, listen to me and agree I've been dealt some very bad cards for a very long time.

Watching a threesome of suit-clad men enter and take their seats at the bar, Tim quickly scrutinized each one, determining in seconds any one of them would be a waste of his time. Stuck-up dicks, he reasoned, incapable of telling the truth, each one of them trying to outdo the other with embellished stories of questionable conquests of women they seduced recently. God how boring, he thought as a duo of jeans-clad men with work boots entered the watering hole, laughing loudly, sliding into a booth next to him. Good looking guys, but not hot like Branson. Next?

"Hey, how are you?" The waitress who'd served him and Branson last night had appeared at his table, tossing down two cocktail napkins.

"Oh, hey, good. How are you?" Tim stared at the second napkin.

"Good. Your friend joining you tonight?"

"Nah, he's got other plans. It's just me."

"Cool. Same as last night?"

"Uh, yeah. Why not?"

"Be right back."

Tim's neck tightened, forcing him to rotate his head clockwise, then counterclockwise. Swiveling his head to his left then to his right, he caught a glimpse of another professionally dressed threesome striding into the establishment, this one composed of two females and a male. Assuming they all worked together, Tim watched as the hostess led them to the booth just beyond him, closest to the rear of the bar. Engaged in a conversation, the threesome looked his way before slipping into the booth, with the man politely nodding at him.

Impressed, Tim nodded back and then proceeded to evaluate the attractive man. Tim thought the man fell short of being classically handsome, but he sensed a unique quality that made him irresistible. He looked to be in his mid-30s, though Tim was admittedly terrible in determining people's ages. He'd been known to be off by as many as 10 years, so this dude could be anywhere from 30 to 40. Sporting a thick shock of black hair, shapely eyebrows over dark eyes, and matching dimples in each cheek, the hottie had a cocky playfulness about him, akin to...*Branson!*

Oh, for fuck's sake! Stop it! I cannot get the prick out of my mind. Lowering his leg, pivoting his body, Tim now faced the other booth and was in a direct line of the hottie's vision. *Oh, my God, he's staring right at me!* Feeling his face flush, Tim was grateful when the waitress appeared with his pint of Guinness and a shot of Jameson.

"Thanks, hon," said Tim absentmindedly, quickly offering her a half-smile before turning his attention back to the man in the booth. But now, the hunk was fully engaged in conversation with his work peeps, the two chicks. *What the hell were they talking about and why did they all look so joyous and carefree? Why can't I be that easygoing and happy?*

Tossing the shot of whiskey back then chugging his stout, Tim attempted to be nonchalant, wanting to exude an I-don't-give-a-shit attitude for the guy to see, just in case the guy thought he was desperate for attention. Time to play hard to get, for once in my life. Sneaking a peek, Tim was disappointed again when the dude kept on talking to the women without even looking his way. *Was it all a figment of my imagination that he even noticed me at all?* Now, with the same waitress at their table taking their orders, the guy was completely out of Tim's line of vision. *Damn! What fucked-up luck.*

Downing half his pint in three huge gulps, Tim flagged down the waitress the moment she finished taking their order. Ambling over with a big smile on her face, she bent at the waist, sliding her palm across the table, stopping at Tim's left hand.

Winking at him, offering him a full view of her ample cleavage, she then lifted her hand to reveal a small, folded piece of paper.

"Looks like you've got a new fan club, honey," she said in a low voice, nodding her head toward the other booth.

Swiping the note off the table, glancing at it quickly before refolding it and stuffing it in his front pant pocket, Tim's mouth quivered with excitement. Then, calming a bit, he allowed a wide smile to appear on his face.

"Looks like you've just earned yourself a new name."

"What's that, hon?" she said straightening.

"Lady Luck!"

CHAPTER 54 THURSDAY AFTERNOON, LATE

Drawing from her years of experience in law enforcement, Lisa confidently strode into the reception area at the Indio jail, knowing exactly what she needed to do to get access to one of their prisoners. Donning a professional suit and carrying a brief-case—both of which she fortunately had among her belongings in her car—she headed toward the female desk sergeant, looking like any other attorney visiting her client.

"Co-counsel for Lonnie Dautremont," said Lisa authoritatively, expecting to be ushered to a side entrance for attorneys.

"She's still in court," the desk sergeant said glancing at a manifest and then at her watch. "Should be back in about forty-five minutes. At about five."

"Oh, darn. I came as fast as I could, but I had to meet with a bail bondsman about another case." Lisa offered her a crooked smile. "Seems I need to clone myself to keep up with all these criminals these days."

"No argument from me about that. Do you want to wait, or do you have someplace else you have to be?"

"Well, actually, I could sure use a cup of coffee. Any good coffee houses around here, and please don't suggest Starbuck's."

"Yes, right down the street, half a block down, Callahan's Coffee. They've got some tasty deserts, too, and the best ice cream in town," she said, pointing to her left. "Unless you want to brave a cup of our delicious brew."

"Thanks, I'll take your suggestion and try Callahan's. See you in forty-five minutes."

Lisa could barely feel her feet touching the floor as she turned on her heels to leave the station. Forty-five minutes was more than enough time to prepare for taking down the scum who murdered the single mother of the little boy waiting patiently in her vehicle for justice.

"Hey, Kendall, I want to get you a nice treat," said Lisa, hopping back into the car. "How about an ice cream?"

"Really? Yeah! I want two scoops of chocolate in a waffle cone."

"You got it little buddy. And I know just where to get that for you." Lisa started her vehicle and headed down the block.

"Wow. You're in a really good mood all of a sudden."

"Indeed I am. It's a special day today. For you and for me. For many reasons. One day you'll understand."

"Did you find out where Aunt Lonnie is?" asked Kendall, as Lisa hung a U-turn in the middle of the street.

"As a matter of fact, I did." Lisa looked over at him and smiled.

"Well, where is she?"

"She's exactly where a murderer needs to be."

"In jail?"

"Yes, sweetheart, in jail."

"Forever?"

"Let me put it this way: she will never be able to hurt you or anyone ever again."

"You promise?"

"More than promise, my love. I guarantee it."

Lonnie Dautremont sat shackled in the third row of a 12-passenger van that this evening held only three inmates. Looking out the window, she stared covetously at the goings-on outside on the street. Pressing her cheek against the cool, dirty glass, she pursed her lips as she lamented her lost opportunities. Opportunities that should have been hers only three short days ago. *Why had everything gone to shit so quickly? Why had Loretta betrayed me after all I did for her?*

Unable to come up with any logical answer, Lonnie instead mindlessly stared at traffic, projecting her thoughts on the near future and how she intended to beat the charges filed against her. Soon enough, she thought, watching the endless stream of cars coming toward her, she'd be acquitted of all charges, released from jail and back on her feet. Her life would be restored, and she'd find love again. Someone even better than Loretta!

Loretta certainly didn't deserve me, after all. I gave her my all and what did she ever offer me in return? Nothing but the baggage that comes from having to support a little shit like—

Lonnie leaned forward in her seat as far as she could move, watching a mother and her young son walking on the sidewalk, laughing, eating ice cream cones. Uppity bitch, Lonnie thought, dressed in her fancy business suit, taking your kid for a treat to appease him for always leaving him at after-school care because you have to work. *Fuck you and your ilk, bitch. You're all the same. Think you're better than the rest of us. Just wait till I get out of here and put all you bitches in your place.*

Getting a closer look at the mother and son as the van got into the left-hand turning lane to enter the jail's lot, Lonnie scrutinized the boy and was stunned at how much he looked just like Kendall. Of course, it wasn't him; it couldn't possibly be him, because this kid was with his mother, not Loretta. "Loretta," she said aloud, staring at the woman walking with her son, hating her even though she didn't know her from Adam.

When the van turned into the lot, Lonnie lost sight of the woman and her kid, which was just as well, as her ire was about to send her over the edge and want to strangle someone; anyone. Forcing herself to calm down, breathing steadily and evenly, Lonnie eased back in the seat just as the van approached the guard shack. Purposefully ignoring the corrections officer who stuck his head into the vehicle for a visual head count, she shut her eyes, trying to visualize lying on a beach in Hawaii, a Mai Tai in her hand. Soon, soon, she told herself.

But when she sensed the driver had parked the van in the underground garage, cutting the engine, she leaned forward and rested her head on the back of the seat in front of her, not wanting to budge. Dreading to hear the driver's loud voice telling them to ready themselves to be released from their shackles before exiting the van, Lonnie was instead greeted with utter silence. Sitting up, opening her eyes, she saw an empty van. No driver and no inmates. *What the hell? Where had everyone gone?*

Even stranger, she now heard the distinctive clicking of high heels on cement, echoing off the low-ceilinged garage, rhythmically hustling closer to the van. She wasn't sure if she heard the clicking stop before she saw the woman enter the passenger side of the van, or after the woman had entered, pointing a huge pistol at her head. And then it all came together as it registered in her brain. It wasn't just any woman, but the very same woman who'd been eating the ice cream cone with her son on the sidewalk.

"Who the fuck are you?" Lonnie asked, more confused than afraid.

"Your worst nightmare."

CHAPTER 55 THURSDAY EVENING

Tim unfolded the note and re-read it for the third time. A crooked smile formed on his face as he glanced at the guy sitting in the next booth with the two women. Oddly, the guy wasn't looking at him, but was instead laughing with the two chicks. Was he getting shy, playing coy and hard to get? Or were the three of them plotting their next moves, which included seducing Tim into a threesome, or a foursome? God, no, Tim thought, cringing. *Please don't let that be the case.*

Looking down at his hands, folding the note and slipping it back in his pocket, Tim jerked his head up just as the guy turned to look his way. Paralyzed by the man's allure, Tim offered him a weak smile, which he seemed to accept by allowing his beautiful brown eyes to shine. Then, as quickly as he engaged with Tim, the man abruptly looked away, seeking comfort and confirmation from his coworkers. Neither able to comprehend the dude's behavior nor properly assess his intentions, Tim opted to ignore him and finish his stout. If he were really that immature, then Tim wanted nothing to do with him. A little coquettish playfulness was one thing, but downright mixed messages was confusing and mean. Let things play themselves out—

"Hi there, I was wondering—" the hot dude had suddenly appeared at his table, standing off-kilter, one hip jutting out seductively, his hand strategically placed on his waist.

Catching his breath, feeling his face flush, Tim's eyes widened in delight. "Wondering what?" asked Tim, his words coming out in hot puffs of air.

"Um, my friends were wondering if you'd like to join us," he said, visibly uncomfortable, switching his hitch to the other hip. "I mean, you're all alone and—"

"You noticed?" Tim chuckled as he admired the younger man. "So, your friends want me to join you guys at your table? What about you? Do you want me to join you and your friends?"

"Yeah, well, me too," he said, ignoring the perspiration forming on his brow. "What do you say?"

"I'd be inclined to say, 'why not'?"

"Great," he said, noticeably relieved. "Linda and Maureen are going to be thrilled, especially Linda."

"Why's that?" Tim glared at the man, confused.

"Because she thinks you're hot."

"Linda thinks I'm hot?" Tim's right eyebrow arched.

"Yeah, that's why she wrote you that note. The one the waitress passed to you." Perspiration now instantly sprouted on the young man's upper lip.

Embarrassed, but grateful he hadn't yet made a complete fool of himself, Tim said a little too quickly, "Of course, man, and I'm flattered. Really."

Sliding out of the booth, he stood up, towering over the hot dude. "Excuse me for a moment. I'll be right back."

"Okay. We'll be waiting for you." The guy offered a weak smile as Linda and Maureen turned to watch Tim sauntering toward the restrooms. Sitting down, the guy swiped a napkin off the table and dabbed his brow.

"Well, is he coming back?" Linda asked, breathing heavily.

"I guess."

"You guess?"

"Next time, do your own dirty work, Linda. It's just weird for a guy to approach another guy and practically beg for him to—"

"You did good. I'll buy you another drink."

Unsettled after her awkward conversation with Saundra about Tim on the drive home earlier, Cyndi called her mother-in-law, seeking resolution.

"I got to thinking after I got home about something that should have been fairly obvious to everyone involved," Cyndi began, hoping to express herself properly and empathetically. "What if—and I mean hypothetically, of course—Tim really was—is—gay because of the molestations by those priests all those years ago. Haven't you or Todd ever thought of that possibility?"

"*Well, of course we thought about that, dear,*" said Saundra, slurring her words. "*It was the first thing we thought could happen to him, but then of course, he started to, uh, molest Lisa, so we pushed that theory aside. For a while.*"

"What do you mean for a while?"

"*Well, when Tim went away to college, and, thankfully, left Lisa alone, he didn't really have a girlfriend for the longest time, you know, so Todd and I often wondered if, you know, he ever would find one and get married. We were concerned—*"

"Concerned he'd turn out to be gay, but not concerned that he'd fucked-up your daughter?" Cyndi shocked herself by what she just said but couldn't stop herself from asking. "Sorry to be so blunt, Saundra, but it has to be said if you ever want to come to terms with it."

"No, *don't apologize, dear. It does have to be said; I'll be the first to admit it.*" Saundra sniffled a few times before continuing. "*I deserve to be berated, accused, slammed, whatever you want to call it. As his mother, it was up to me to do something about it, and I didn't.*"

"What about your husband? What was Todd doing during those years?"

"*Working, making money and schmoozing with clients. Sexual abuse was not something we wanted to talk about, much less to confront. Still, it was up to me, as his mother—*" Saundra noisily slurped her drink.

"Anyway, it's not my intention to beat a dead horse, but I thought you'd want to know that Tim is not home and has not called, so I have no other choice than to think he's got some action on the side. I think he's finally come to terms with his sexuality and come out of the closet."

"*You're his wife, so I'd be inclined to believe your instincts, dear.*"

"Yeah, well." Cyndi took a deep breath. "There's something else I wanted to mention. About the rifles."

"*Rifles?*" Saundra said, accentuating the two syllables. "*Oh, yes. Rifles that he'd sneaked into the house earlier. I recall you mentioning this. What of them?*"

"Call me paranoid, but I think he's preparing himself for a showdown. This weekend."

"*Showdown?*"

"Yes, with his sister."

Chapter 56 Thursday Evening

"Who the fuck are you?"

"I already told you; I'm your worst nightmare." Lisa grabbed ahold of Lonnie's waist shackles, pulling her out of the van. "Let's get moving. I'm not here to answer your questions."

"You can't do this to me," Lonnie said, resisting Lisa's extraordinary strength. "You're not with the jail. Look at how you're dressed. Where's everyone else?"

"You're a little dense and stubborn, I see. Pay attention." Lisa yanked her hard, causing her to stumble, leading her toward her 4Runner parked on the other side of the lot.

"Where are you taking me?" Lonnie's voice now quavered with fear.

"I just told you I don't answer your questions."

"Where's that kid you were with? What have you done with him? Is he your son?"

Lisa ignored Lonnie's continuous questions, tugging her diagonally through the lot. When they approached her car, Lisa hit the remote, a chirping sound echoing loudly throughout the covered garage.

Leading her captive to the front passenger door, Lisa pulled it open with her free hand, revealing Kendall sitting inside. The youngster flinched as he regarded Lonnie, scooting away from her.

Lisa then prodded her captive to look at Kendall for a long moment before saying anything.

"Who is this person, Kendall?" Lisa urged him gently, smiling at the child. "It's okay to tell me. She's not going to hurt you; I promise you that."

"It's Aunt Lonnie," said Kendall tentatively.

"Very good, sweetheart. And what did she do to your mommy the other day?"

Kendall hesitated, then said forthrightly, "She killed my mommy."

"What the fuck you saying, Kendall? I loved your mommy."

"Watch your language, the kid's been traumatized enough by you."

"He doesn't know what he's talking about. He's a kid, for God's sake."

"I saw you kill my mommy," Kendall said, louder this time, pointing a shaky finger at her. "You did it."

"Well, there you have it, Miss Dautremont, guilty as charged. No need for a drawn-out trial and eventual conviction only to have the taxpayers of California fund your room and board in state prison for the rest of your pathetic life."

Lisa yanked her away from the child, leading her to the back of her SUV.

"Get in," Lisa commander her, opening the back hatch. When Lonnie resisted, Lisa shoved her inside.

"What are you going to do to me?" Lonnie demanded as Lisa secured her to a metal bar with a set of hand cuffs. "You're never going to get away with this, bitch!"

"I've gotten away with much worse, Miss Dautremont. You have no idea." Lisa reached into a duffle bag, retrieving two bandanas, promptly inserting one into Lonnie's mouth, tying the other around her head to secure the gag in place. "I could kill you right here and now, or you can comply and go with us for a little drive. Pick your poison."

Lonnie Dautremont fell silent as Lisa exited the police station's parking lot and headed toward the westbound onramp to Interstate 10.

Tim startled his wife when he walked into the kitchen, finding her on the phone. Stunned, Cyndi mumbled incoherently into the mouthpiece, then placed the handset carefully back onto the base. Sheepishly regarding her husband, she quickly assumed an indignant pose.

"So, you decided to come home, I see," said Cyndi, glaring at him for a few seconds before adding, "Where have you been? Oh, never mind, I'd prefer not to know."

"'Prefer not to know'? What the hell does that mean, anyway?"

Cyndi shook her head, looking down at the floor.

"You think I'm like every other guy out there, sneaking around, going to a strip club or something?" Tim's chest heaved with every breath he took.

Whipping her head around to stare at her husband, Cyndi said evenly, "No actually, I don't."

"You don't? Then why did you say you prefer not to know where I was? And why are you looking at me like that?"

Cyndi shook her head. "I guess I meant to say, I'd prefer not knowing what I *think* you've been doing. If that makes any sense."

"Sense? It makes no sense at all. Speak English. Please."

Cyndi slid onto one of the barstools, folding her arms defensively across her chest. "I've been wondering about your...I've been having a hard time reconciling your–"

"There you go again, not making any sense whatsoever."

"Sorry, it's just–"

"Just spit it out, for Christ's sake!

Unfolding her arms, Cyndi spread her hands out on the counter, staring at her perfectly manicured red nails. Rapidly blinking her eyes, she bit her lips before opening her mouth. "Are you having an affair?"

"What? Is that what you've been thinking?"

"As a matter of fact, yes. I have."

"Now you've really gone off the deep end," Tim said, pacing the floor. "Last night you accused me of confronting Lisa–with what, I still don't know–and tonight, you've decided I'm having an affair.

"What's it gonna be tomorrow? Accusing me of burying bodies in the back yard?" Tim snorted contemptuously.

Cyndi watched her husband pace in front of her. "That's a very strange confession to make."

"Who's confessing? I didn't confess to anything." Tim stopped in front of her. "I'm just trying to point out how ridiculous your accusations are. So ridiculous that you might as well *accuse* me of killing people and burying their bodies in our backyard."

"Well, I'd not be too far off if I did. I saw you sneaking two rifles into the house this morning. What was that all about?"

"About?" Tim echoed, turning red, unconsciously backpedaling into the wall behind him.

Then, as if saved by the bell, his cellphone emitted a shrill sound. Fishing the phone out of his pocket, he stared at the caller ID, freezing, alternating his stare between his phone and his wife.

"Aren't you going to answer your phone? Or are you just going to let it ring?"

Tim swallowed hard, allowing three more rings, then swiped the face of his phone, all the while gazing at Cyndi.

"This is Tim," he squeaked, looking off in the distance. "Oh, hello Branson," he said calmly, keeping his eyes fixed on an invisible mark on the far wall. "Yes, I'm fine, and you? It's a little late, but I understand the gravity of the situation...Oh, no, not at all...Yes, I can...In the lobby...Of course...I'll see you there shortly."

"Branson?" Cyndi said venomously. "Who the hell is he?"

CHAPTER 57 THURSDAY NIGHT

Wanting to avoid any mishaps in unfamiliar territory in the dark, Lisa considered driving directly to Los Angeles rather than taking a diversionary route in order to dispose of the trash that was putrefying her vehicle. The irony that one of her two passengers—in need of immediate redemption—was being exposed to the toxicity of the other—in need of swift retribution—was not lost on her. So, she opted to complete her mission in the Coachella Valley; to mete out justice in the same place the vile creature committed her despicable crime.

With the horizontal orange glow rapidly fading over Interstate 10, Lisa chose an arbitrary exit between Rancho Mirage and Palm Springs, which would afford her privacy to perform her clandestine act. Recalling a frontage road called Varner—running the length of the freeway till it reached the town of Desert Hot Springs—Lisa drove for several miles, turning north on an unlit side street. Using her high-beams, she navigated through an area with deeply-tracked, low-lying hills on both sides—created by off-road motorbikes and quads. Soon, she arrived at a spot in unincorporated Riverside County on the outskirts of Desert Hot Springs.

Parking off the road on a slight grade, her SUV's rear tilting down, Lisa turned off the engine and regarded Kendall, half-asleep in the passenger seat. She smoothed the hair away from his angelic face, then caressed it, whispering for him to wait in the car for her, she'd be right back. Adroitly slipping out of her business attire and donning sweats and sneakers, she watched Kendall's eyelids flutter, assuring her he would stay put. Only then did Lisa slide out of her vehicle and open the back hatch.

"Out, Dautremont," Lisa said, shining a flashlight in Lonnie's eyes, unlocking the handcuffs she'd previously attached to the metal bar. Yanking on her waist restraints Lisa added, "Time to go for a little walk."

Securely gagged, Lonnie simply groaned in protest, unable to verbalize her feelings, clearly fearful of what awaited her. Unable to avoid her inevitable fate, Lonnie trudged along a dirt path lit only by the single beam of Lisa's mag light, wriggling and moaning to no avail.

"Stop your whimpering, Dautremont. It's not going to sway me one iota to have mercy on your soul," Lisa said, jamming her trusty .45 SIG Sauer into her captive's back. "By the way, did you show any mercy at all to your lover Loretta when you were using her as your own human punching bag? It's how I imagine you murdered her, with your bare hands, right?"

Lonnie merely groaned, shaking her head vehemently.

"Tell me, did you restrain yourself even a little bit, thinking how much you loved her with each blow to her head?"

Trudging up a hill, shining her light on the carved-out tracks created by years of off-road vehicles, Lisa arrived at a location remote enough in which to exact her justice. Untying the bandana, Lisa removed the gag, allowing Lonnie to speak any last words in her own defense.

"Fuck you, bitch!" Lonnie spat out, breathing heavily. "Who do you think you are to snatch me away from jail and bring me up to this godforsaken place under cover of darkness?"

"I already told you I don't answer your questions, Dautremont." Lisa said, moving in closer to Lonnie. "But since I'm feeling rather joyous tonight, I'll break from tradition and tell you this, so you'll have something to think about as you take your last breath: I was put on this earth to avenge the abuse and deaths of voiceless victims, who did nothing to deserve their fates, many of them murdered at the hands of people who professed to love them."

"What the fuck? Who died and made you queen of revenge?"

"So, how did you do it? With your bare hands?" Lisa repeated her question, ignoring Lonnie's comment. "Or did you shoot Loretta in the heart that you broke? Huh, which one was it?"

"For the last time, I didn't murder Loretta. I loved her. It wasn't like that. It was self-defense."

"'Self-defense'?" Lisa snickered, removing another set of hand-cuffs from her belt loop, snapping one end onto Lonnie's right wrist, the other onto a tree branch. "Well, the good news is you won't need self-defense out here, only self-preservation. Let's see how long you last out here in the wild, where no one'll hear you crying for help."

"No! What the hell are you doing to me?"

"I'm actually showing you a lot more compassion than you ever showed Loretta. Hey, don't be afraid; chances are someone may actually find you out here. I mean, it's not like you're in the middle of nowhere."

"Fuck you, you fucking bitch!" Lonnie screamed, jerking her tethered hand. "You're not going to get away with this. Just you wait and see."

"What are you going to do, report me to the police?" Lisa turned and started walking back to her vehicle, leaving Lonnie in the dark.

"Yes, I will, as a matter of fact, when they find me here like this," she said trying to raise her hand. "They'll be coming after you."

Lisa turned back around to face Lonnie, shining a beam of light on her. "And just who will you tell them did this to you, the boogeyman?"

"Branson? He's one of our trust attorneys. Why are you so upset and, uh, suspicious?"

"Upset? You need to ask?" Cyndi fumed, shaking her head. "I mean, I don't know any other woman who would just sit back and watch, uh...no, *allow*, her husband to just come and go as he pleases."

"'Allow' her husband? Have you completely gone bonkers?" Tim shook his head. "You're really something else, you know?"

"Lucia would never tolerate that from Donovan, but she wouldn't have to because he'd never do that to her. He respects her too much."

"Donovan? Ha! You don't know him as well as you think you do. He's a pla–"

"You're sick."

"As much as you think I'd like to stay here and play this he-said-she-said game of yours, I really have to get a move on." Tim turned on his heels and headed out of the kitchen.

"Oh, yeah, you're meeting 'Branson' in the lobby," Cyndi shouted indignantly as her husband walked away from her. "I know what you're up to, Tim and it's disgusting!"

Chapter 58 Friday Morning, Early

Lisa coasted into the Los Angeles basin in the wee hours of the morning, her passenger buckled up in the back of the 4Runner, sleeping snugly. At the moment, she had no idea what to do about Kendall, whether to call Child Protective Services, or take him to a police or fire station. Whichever tack she chose, she acknowledged, the kid would end up in foster care, no picnic under the best of circumstances. What a damn shame, she thought, navigating through an interchange maze of three freeways just south of downtown Los Angeles—one going west, one northwest and the other heading due north. What would become of this sweet boy?

With no immediate plans for him, she knew without doubt she'd make the right decision when the time came. Even though she'd been annoyed at first when the kid had stowed away in her vehicle, she'd come to like him, shocking herself in the process. Most kids Kendall's age were annoying little buggers that got under both your feet and your skin. But Kendall had such a sweet and caring disposition, with a calming effect on her. In more ways than one, she was going to miss the little guy when the time came to turn him over to the authorities.

Her vision immediately assaulted by the hideous graffiti covering freeway overpasses and barrier walls welcoming her to the City of Angels, Lisa concomitantly felt a definite shift in her attitude. She had to refocus quickly if she were to successfully perform her ultimate mission: dealing with her brother Tim. Which meant she'd have to get Kendall settled in somewhere
very soon.

Continuing on Interstate 10 through South LA, Lafayette Park and Cheviot Hills, she heard Kendall stirring in the back just as she reached for her mobile phone to make a call. Tossing the phone back into her purse, Lisa opted to take the next exit, Washington Boulevard, and attend to her young passenger's needs. She pulled over but keep the engine running.

"Hey buddy, what's up?" said Lisa, turning around to face him.

"Hey Lisa," said Kendall, sitting upright, rubbing his eyes. "I'm hungry. What time is it?"

"Oh, it's about three o'clock in the morning. A little early for breakfast, but I bet we can find a McDonald's somewhere that's open twenty-four hours."

"'Twenty-four hours?" Kendall echoed Lisa's words, shaking his head. "That's a really long time."

"Yes, it is, but it's a good amount of time for people like us that want to eat at a really odd time."

"What does 'odd time' mean?" Kendall looked out the window, staring up and down the dark street.

"It just means it's a different time from normal. That's all."

"Hey, I know a place we can eat that's open twenty-four hours."

"You do?" Lisa smiled.

"Yeah. *Ships*. It's on this street, I think. Or on another one close by."

Lisa narrowed her eyes, pursing her lips. "Really? *Ships*?"

"Yeah. My mommy and I used to go there when she wanted to splurge."

"Did you live around here?" Lisa asked, intrigued.

"Yeah. A few streets down there," he said, pointing straight ahead.

"Near *Ships*?"

"Yeah. I wanna get a big cheeseburger and fries there."

"Then, let's get moving, kiddo!"

Unable to sleep, her husband still out at the ungodly hour of three a.m. with the mysterious Branson, Cyndi sneaked into her husband's closet in search of the long guns he'd brought into their home. She'd start there, she told herself, then work her way down to the garage if she couldn't find them in the house. The most logical place for him to stash them would be his gun case, but Cyndi had a hunch they'd be in a place more readily accessible. His actions of the last few days indicated he'd become desperate, compelling him to use more reckless measures.

Ferreting in his overly organized closet, Cyndi found no guns, only clothing and shoes, so she went downstairs to the rumpus room, where Tim kept his gun safe and where he stored miscellaneous entertainment paraphernalia like his old turntable and record albums. Ambling to the gun safe, Cyndi placed her hand on the combination lock, shutting her eyes, trying to recall the sequence of numbers. Gently turning the dial, clockwise once, stopping at 13, counterclockwise, stopping at 31, then clockwise again, ending on the number 36, Cyndi pulled the handle and smiled. Not because she was happy, but rather because she remembered a simple combination of numbers Tim never thought to change, which were also easy to remember.

Cyndi shook her head at the assortment of guns before her, every caliber that he'd collected over the years, most of which remained in the safe for...what? Posterity? That was a laugh. There would be no children to pass anything down to, much less firearms. Why the hell did he need all of these, for crying out loud? It had to be a simple obsession, like women who collected shoes, even after running out of shelves on which to store them! Not seeing the new rifles, Cyndi shut the door, spun the lock, and crouched on her haunches. Damn, she thought, rolling over, propping her back against the wall. *Where did he put them?*

After treating Kendall to a cheeseburger and fries at *Ships*, Lisa compulsively attended to two of three important tasks: one that would determine whether she would return to the desert to complete unfinished business, and the other that would afford her the time necessary to accomplish that task. First, she accessed the state's database seeking information on Lonnie Dautremont. Stunned at what she discovered, she next called her protégé, Elizabeth Canton, to watch Kendall for a day or so while she finalized her *coup de grâce*. If there was anyone in the world she could trust to not ask questions, it was Elizabeth, whom she'd chosen and groomed to be her successor. Prefacing her request with minimal information as to how Kendall came into her life, Lisa explained she would eventually deliver him to social services for the professionals to sort out.

"Kendall, sweetie, say hello to my good friend, Elizabeth," Lisa told the youngster when they arrived on Elizabeth's doorstep. "She's like a sister to me and a very cool person, with lots of toys for you to play with, right Liz?" Lisa winked at her friend, who got the hint.

"Hi there Kendall, so nice to meet you!" Elizabeth patted his shoulder, leading him inside her apartment. "We're gonna have a splendid time together. I've got lots of toys, and what I don't have, we can go out and get."

"Do you have Xbox One Minecraft?"

Elizabeth shot Lisa a look, then smiled at the youngster. "How 'bout we go to the Microsoft store in the mall and play it over there?"

"Cool. Thanks!"

"Thanks Lizzy, and have fun, Kendall." Lisa bent down and gave him a quick hug. "I promise to be back soon. Just gotta get some work done before the day's over."

"Okay, Lisa. Don't hurry back. I think me and Lizzy are gonna be plenty busy today, right Lizzy?"

When Lisa was back in her 4Runner, she opened the Maps App on her phone and searched for her brother's address.

Chapter 59 Friday Morning

A jagged, horizontal shard of sunlight, outlining the sawtooth mountain range to the east, landed perfectly across Lonnie's face, forcing her awake with a start. Shielding her eyes with one hand, she painstakingly pushed herself up with the other, only to discover she was restrained. Handcuffed to a tree branch.

"*Fuck!*" she screamed, hoping someone would hear her. "Fucking bitch, you'll pay for this. If it takes me a lifetime. You'll pay for this!"

Yanking hard on her restrained hand, the metal cuff cut into her skin, leaving a red welt. How difficult would it be to wear down the tree branch and break free? she wondered. A couple of hours? Rising slowly, she was at least able to slide the cuff up the branch, allowing her to stand fully upright.

Unstable, trying to gain her bearings, Lonnie brushed sand off her right side and looked all around: not a sign of humanity or anything that resembled a building. To the west, a low-lying hill obscured anything that could be beyond—if indeed there was something on the other side other than more hills, sand and dust. To the east—although blinded by the sun—rolling sand dunes as far as the eye could see. *Jesus. Where did she drop me off? Will anyone ever find me? Fuck this all to hell! I'd gladly return to jail if this is to be my fate.*

"Someone, anyone. Can you hear me?" she yelled at the top of her lungs; her throat now raw. "*Fuck! Fuck! Fuck!*" she said, slumping down to her knees.

Tears rolled down her cheeks as complete terror set in. This was no dream; it was a real-life nightmare. No one was going to find her and there was no way on earth to get the handcuff off. She dabbed at her eyes with her fingertips thinking, *God must really hate me to allow this to happen.* Propping her back on the tree's trunk, facing west, she stared straight ahead, racking her brain for a solution. Her stomach growled loudly right before she heard a car's engine in the distance. Unable to decipher from which direction the vehicle was coming, she stood, prepared to flag down the driver. Quickly forgetting her despair, she became freakishly giddy with hope.

Weary from a lack of sleep and wary of his wife catching him once again sneaking into the house, Tim parked in the driveway and sat in his car for a few minutes contemplating a viable explanation for being gone all night. Of course, Cyndi wouldn't believe anything he proffered at this point, short of him being taken hostage by ransom-seeking aliens.

Paralyzed with apprehension, biting his knuckle, Tim silently berated himself for his propensity to crumble like a cookie after returning home from another clandestine rendezvous. He had the guts to pursue the taboo deeds, yet he was unable to stand up to his wife afterwards. Thinking long and hard about it, he realized he'd routinely picked a fight with Cyndi right before storming out of the house, making it easier to leave. Returning to the homestead following the illicit activities dredged up shame and guilt, and no matter how hard he tried to justify his actions, shame and guilt—without fail—reared their ugly heads.

Okay, just go in there and act like the head of the household that you are and ignore any comments from her, he told himself, sliding out of his car, quietly closing the door. *Act like the boss, for crying out loud. Don't allow her to push your buttons or scold you like a child.*

Still, his stomach flipped, and his heart pounded wildly as he walked through the back door, holding his breath, waiting for Cyndi's high-pitched voice to come screeching from the kitchen. But it never came; the house was silent; his ears aware only of his pulse throbbing in his head. *What the fuck? Where is Cyndi?*

"Cyndi, are you home?" Tim called out, ascending the stairs, un-buttoning his shirt, then peeling it off. Not waiting for an answer, he looked left to right at the top of the landing, half-expecting his wife to surprise him from behind. Shrugging his shoulders, balling up the shirt, he ambled into the bedroom and threw it into the hamper in the master bathroom. Ripping his trousers off, he kicked them sideways toward the closet's ceiling-to-floor mir-rored doors, intending to pick them up after his shower. Passing his wife's section of the enormous bathroom to the left, he ca-sually sauntered by without peeking inside. He then strode into his custom-built shower and its eight pulsating jets of water, four each on opposing sides.

Whistling as he lingered luxuriously amidst the multiple streams of water, Tim wanted to stay in that zone forever, but knew he'd better get into the office sooner than later before his father over-reacted and called his cell phone. Drying off, he glanced at the dig-ital clock on the vanity and breathed a sigh of relief when he read 7:13. With everything he'd experienced in the past six hours, he'd completely lost track of time. No need to rush now, he thought, toweling off the last few drops of water from his back as he walked past Cyndi's bathroom.

Intent on dressing quickly and then stopping at Starbuck's on the way to the office, Tim halted when he caught sight of his wife's white terrycloth robe on the floor surrounded by streaks of red on the white tile. Swiveling awkwardly to his right, Tim now noticed it was more than mere streaks, but a veritable rivulet of crimson liquid flowing from the direction of his wife's side of the bathroom. *What the hell?* Feeling nauseous, he wrapped the towel around his lower body, creeping slowly into the depths of her chamber, following the red viscous flow to its source: Cyndi's shower. Through the shower door's beveled glass, Tim saw three distinct colors—beige, red and black—covering the basin. Fearful of opening the door to see what lay inside, he tried to get a clear im-age through one of the singular vertical panes of glass.

Whether it was the terror he felt in the pit of his stomach or his eyesight playing tricks on him, Tim could focus only on the black object, which looked like a rifle. Feeling lightheaded, ready to pass out, he leaned against the glass door trying to regain his composure. But his heart continued to race at an outrageous speed and his breath caught in his throat. *Where the fuck is my mobile? I need to call the police. There is no way I can open this door and remain sane.*

But the weight of his body pushed the shower door open and before he could react, he found himself lying atop the lifeless body of his wife. Screaming, writhing in the slippery, gooey mess, he could get no traction and was forced to remain on top of Cyndi's bloodied, naked corpse. Finally, he gripped the door's metal edge, yanking himself out, leaving behind his blood-soaked towel.

Wobbly, unable to find his feet or take his eyes off his once beautiful wife, now a mangled mess with a few bullet holes in her torso, Tim ran to the sink and vomited what little he had in his stomach. Returning to the shower, he now saw that his first assessment about the black object had been correct: it was indeed a rifle. In fact, it was the vintage bolt-action Remington he'd just nabbed from his parent's home. *What the damn fuck?*

Inching closer, holding his hand over his mouth, he saw a most unusual thing: Cyndi, curled up on her left side with the rifle wedged between her legs. And, as if that prop wasn't enough out of character for his wife, her right hand tightly gripped the barrel, strategically aimed under her chin. *What the fuck? Did she kill herself with my rifle?* Not likely, he thought, counting three bullet entries on her torso. *Did she have more bullet holes on the left side of her body? How many times was she shot? Did the killer pose her like this to send a message? What message? Who'd want to kill Cyndi of all people? Wait...Did the killer mistake her for me, his actual target? Am I responsible for my wife's death?* Tim slunk down to his knees shaking uncontrollably, turning his gaze away from his wife.

Still, as shocked as he was, not a single tear flowed from his eyes. Instead, a nagging question lingered in his mind: "What was she doing with the rifle in the first place?

CHAPTER 60 FRIDAY MORNING

Anticipation getting the best of her, Lonnie nervously hopped from one foot to the other, awaiting the imminent arrival of the vehicle she'd heard in the distance. Her arms tired from holding them up for what seemed like forever, she kept them raised, one arm noticeably lower than the other.

"C'mon, already," Lonnie said aloud, shielding her eyes with her right hand as she bounced excitedly. "I'm here, waiting to be rescued."

Noticing a plume of dust rise in the distance, Lonnie instinctively stretched her right arm again in preparation for flagging down the driver of the car. In her stressed, hyper-attentive state, she couldn't identify the size of the vehicle from its sound, nor did she care; any size would do. And if they were at full capacity, she'd lay across everyone in the back or gladly jump into the trunk, just to be saved. Just to be saved.

But when the car finally came into view, about a quarter of a mile to the south, Lonnie stood, stunned, thinking she was seeing a mirage. *What the fuck? Is that what I think it is? Or is my mind completely fucking with me?* Another 100 feet closer, her hallucination dissolved into reality when she recognized the vehicle. "No, no, no, no, no," she said over and over again. "No, you cannot do this to me and get away with it."

As the car got closer, it maintained its speed, never slowing, moving steadily on the gravel road, straight ahead, straight toward Lonnie. *She's aiming for me, the bitch. She's aiming straight for me. Oh, sweet Jesus! She's going to run me over and kill me with her car.*

Trusting Elizabeth wouldn't mind watching Kendall for as long as necessary, Lisa listened to her intuition to head back to the Coachella Valley. She decided soon after having an early-morning burger with Kendall at *Ships* that she had unfinished business with Lonnie the murderess. Mulling over the type of punishment she'd exact upon her, Lisa realized it was completely inappropriate to leave the lowlife out in the wild to die. The psychopathic killer needed to be terrorized some more before her ultimate *Come-to-Jesus* moment in the desert.

Yet, before she returned to that remote location near Desert Hot Springs, Lisa wanted to make a dry run to her brother's home in Brentwood, a dress rehearsal of sorts before opening night tomorrow. Everything had to fall perfectly into place without a hitch. She'd been running through a few possible scenarios in her mind, and actually being in his home first—to see the layout and escape routes—would make all the difference.

Assuming the coast would be clear, betting he'd already be at work by the time she arrived, Lisa discounted any possibility that his wife would be home. *Certainly, everyone worked outside the home these days, and if she didn't, for some reason, she'd most likely be at a spin class, or at hot yoga at a new-age studio by the beach. That's what gold-digging trophy wives did before meeting their girlfriends for lunch on Melrose Avenue, right?*

When she'd first glimpsed Tim's gated mansion, she'd been revulsed by the ostentatiousness: excessive fountains shooting water at least twenty feet into the air and an immense circular driveway leading up to three tall, marble, Roman columns on either side of the front door. It looked like a bad B-movie set. *What the hell was he thinking, anyway?*

Parking about a couple of hundred feet up the street, then hustling back to her brother's property, Lisa easily scaled the gate and was on the property within seconds. Reaching under her left armpit, she touched her leather holster in which her prized .45-caliber SIG Sauer rested. Hoping she wouldn't have to use it—other than to defend herself—she nonetheless never left home without it, just in case. Noticing no cars in the driveway or any movement around the home, Lisa presumed her initial hypothesis to be correct: *Tim was at work and his trophy wife at yoga. Perfect. No one to interfere with her surveillance.*

Quickly sizing up the perimeter of the mansion in both directions, Lisa noticed a side entrance, likely leading into the maid's quarters or the laundry room. But when she grasped the handle,
it wouldn't budge. Always prepared for this type of situation, she inserted a pick and a tension wrench into the lock, precisely manipulating the pick to feel for the pins inside. With an expert tactile touch, Lisa depressed all five pins in twenty seconds, turning the handle with ease. *No alarm. Good for me; bad for the Bentons.* Slipping into her brother's home, she quietly shut the door behind her and scanned the layout.

Just as she thought, a laundry room to the right and a maid's quarters a few feet beyond. To her left, a hallway leading to the kitchen. Padding through the enormous kitchen and formal dining room, she spotted a spiral staircase to her left, leading up to a wide-open second floor. Alert to any movement or sound in case anyone was home, Lisa sprinted noiselessly up the stairs, looking behind her every step of the way. Unsure which way to turn at the top of the stairs, she followed a lovely lavender scent, to her left again. Trophy wife must have just taken a shower before working up a sweat at the yoga studio, she thought. *Must have a honey on the side.*

Passing the master bedroom, Lisa peeked inside, regarding a mahogany canopy bed with white gauzy-like drapes swathed across. Gauche, Lisa thought, continuing toward the source of the lavender scent. Now entering the opulent his-and-her bathroom, she chose the clearly feminine side to the left, exuding the pungent French herb. A sunken tub under a picture window revealing lush vegetation in the garden was to the right and opposite that, the white, tiled walk-in entrance to the shower area.

Something metallic fell on the tile inside the shower, startling Lisa, causing her to reach for her pistol. Her senses heightened, she proceeded guardedly, listening for any other sounds. *Did something dislodge itself in the shower, having been placed precariously on a shelf a little while ago by the lady of the house? Or was Tim's wife actually home, dressing and getting ready to take on her day? Fuck, have I miscalculated?*

Then, a flash of white to her left and another loud noise, this time sounding like a large metallic object hitting the tile, then bouncing up only to hit the tile two more times before settling in place. Someone had to be in the house, Lisa thought, raising her .45, sweeping it from side to side, ready to take on anyone, even her brother's wife. Inching inside the depths of the cavernous shower area, Lisa waited for someone to show his or her face, demanding to know who she was and what she was doing in their home. Cognizant that even her own brother would not recognize her— she'd altered her appearance tremendously since her near fatal accident the previous year—she would undoubtedly be considered by either one of them an unwelcome intruder and open game.

Silence for a long while until she heard the distinctive sound of a bolt-action rifle and the hair on the back of her neck stood on end. Placing her back to the wall, she counted to three and then shuffled deeper into the room. Hearing the swooshing sound of a glass door opening then closing—probably the shower door—Lisa followed her instincts as well as the lavender scent, arriving at the enclosed shower with its lavish beveled glass door. Uncertain where the person went, Lisa instinctively turned to her right just as a lovely blonde woman in a thick terrycloth robe lifted a vintage rifle and aimed it at her.

"Show me your hands," said the woman in a quavering, meek voice. "Do it now!"

An errant round from the rifle must have been inadvertently discharged by the blonde, ricocheting off the opposite wall, startling Lisa. Looking down the barrel of the World War II-era rifle, Lisa's self-preservation mode overwhelmed her. But before she fired two successive rounds into Tim's wife's torso, she locked eyes with her, sensing the woman knew exactly who she was. Astonishingly, the robed woman didn't seem to be affected by the power of the .45-caliber slugs, though she stumbled toward the enclosed shower, as if she wanted to hide inside, losing her robe in the process. Still gripping the rifle, the woman struggled to pull open the heavy glass door and instead, accidentally pushed it open with her weight, falling inside.

Recognizing the untenable situation, the now naked woman struggled to sit upright, aiming the long gun again at Lisa. With much effort, she pulled the bolt back, emptying the used shell casing, then chambered another round, apparently ready to fire again. Never one to wait and see what would transpire when someone was aiming a gun at her, Lisa released three more slugs into the woman, this time snuffing the life out of her.

CHAPTER 61 FRIDAY MORNING

Mortified by Cyndi's murder, mystified by the fact she was clutching the family vintage, bolt-action Remington rifle in her death pose, Tim turned her body over onto the other side, hearing a clink. Ignoring the source of the sound, he immediately saw the origin of her blood loss: a perfect cluster of three bullet holes on the left side of her upper body. *Jesus fucking Christ! Did a sniper shoot her? What the damn fuck?*

And then he noticed the spent .223 shell casing on the tiled floor, covered in blood. *Cyndi fired a round at her attacker. Was he injured? Where the hell did he go? Oh, my God! I've got to call 911. Immediately. But I've touched the body; I've moved it. They're gonna know I touched her—*

Tim looked down at his hands, a bloody mess, then regarded his towel, smeared with blood as well. *Dear God. I have to shower again and clean myself up. Calling the police will just have to wait.* Throwing the towel into the laundry hamper on his way to the shower, he thought better of it and pulled it out. After cleaning himself up and dressing, he placed the bloodied towel in a heavy-duty plastic bag and hustled downstairs. Dialing 911 as he tossed the bag into the trunk of his car, he waited a full minute for dispatch to answer.

"My wife...my wife...she's been murdered," Tim stuttered through feigned tears.

"Where is your wife, sir?"

"In the shower. Dead."

"*How was she murdered?*"

"Shot. She was shot. Several times with a large-caliber gun."

"*Large-caliber gun? How do you know, sir?*"

"I can see the bullet holes, for God's sake. Anyone can see them."

"*Okay, sir. Detectives are on their way. Don't touch anything. Stay away from the body. Homicide detectives should be there momentarily.*"

What the fuck? Is that what I think it is? Lonnie thought, seeing a red vehicle coming straight at her at a high rate of speed on the gravel road. *Am I hallucinating? Could my mind completely be fucking with me?* Then, recognizing the vehicle, her fear was confirmed: it was the same bitch that snagged her from the jail and brought her up here to die.

"No, no, no, no, no. You cannot do this to me, bitch! You cannot get away with it."

The car maintained its speed as it neared Lonnie, never slowing, moving steadily, straight toward her. *She's aiming for me, the bitch,* Lonnie thought, trying in vain to get out of the way. *She's aiming straight for me. Oh, sweet Jesus! She's going to run me over and kill me with her car.*

Then, as quickly as the vehicle was heading toward her, it slowed to a snail's pace, coming to a complete stop within inches of Lonnie's restrained body. Panting, wiping the sweat from her face, Lonnie wailed savagely as Lisa emerged from her car, holding her prized pistol against her leg.

"Why don't you just kill me, for God's sake and put me out of my misery," Lonnie begged, falling to her knees. "Why are you doing this to me?"

"You did this to yourself, Lonnie, or should I call you Leona, or Letitia, or how about Lola. Yeah, I think Lola was your best pseudonym, wouldn't you agree?"

Stunned, a different kind of fear overtook Lonnie. She sat up straight and glared at her captor.

"What the hell would you know, *Miss White Privilege* who never had to fight for everything she ever had, ever got. You're so out of touch with the rest of us ninety-nine percent–"

"I know a lot more about you than I did a few hours ago," said Lisa confidently. "In fact, I know that you have a rap sheet as long as that tree branch you're attached to, in more states than just California."

"You don't know what you're talking about. I never used any name other than–"

"Lola Demetrius, six months served for breaking and entering in Arizona," Lisa recalled from memory. "Letitia Dominguez, extradited to Florida from California to serve thirteen months in the Dade County Jail for battery on a domestic partner, whom I'm sure you loved. Then we have my favorite, three months served for false imprisonment of another domestic partner, in Modesto, while using the fake name of Leona Price. Well, maybe that's your real name but I digress.

"In all, you've served minimal sentences for violent offenses because of technicalities. Overcrowding. Good attorneys. Whatever. Doesn't matter to me why."

"You really don't know what you're talking about," Lonnie said, looking away. "I was wrongly accused and convicted. That's why I served, as you say, 'minimal sentences.'"

"Deceiving your victims with false identities is truly despicable but not as despicable as being the co-conspirator in killing the child of one of your lovers, while using the pseudonym, Lucretia

Borgia. I mean I really have to hand it to you on that one. I didn't think you were that clever."

"I didn't kill anyone," Lonnie protested. "I've never killed anyone. Why won't you believe me?"

"Nothing's as contemptible as murdering a child, and your lover's child at that." Lisa spat out. "And to not even be charged! Then, letting your lover take the fall. Outrageous!

"Well, let's just say I came back to make sure that justice is finally served."

Lonnie cowered, eyeing Lisa fearfully. "What the fuck does that mean? What the hell are you gonna to do to me?"

"Guess you're not familiar with cosmic justice," Lisa said emotionlessly, lifting her SIG Sauer, aiming it at Lonnie's head. "Let me be the one to introduce you to it."

CHAPTER 62 FRIDAY MID-MORNING

Tim easily summoned a convincing distressed look as he greeted two no-nonsense, suit-clad detectives at his front door. Opening the electronic gate ahead of time, so they wouldn't have to wait at the gate like idiots, Tim allowed the duo to park on his circular driveway.

"Mr. Benton, I'm Detective Heatherly and this is Detective Jorgensen," the beefier and older of the two said with a deep voice. "Very sorry for your loss. May we come in?"

"Hello, detectives, of course," Tim said, his voice quavering. Stepping aside, he allowed the duo inside. "She's, uh, upstairs. In the shower."

"The forensics team should be here in a few minutes. Okay to leave the door unlocked?"

"Yeah, sure thing." Tim regarded Heatherly for a long moment before unlocking the door.

In unison, both men removed thin notebooks from their back pant pockets and fat pens from inside their jackets. In single file, the detectives ascended the staircase following Tim to Cyndi's bathroom. Stopping at the first pool of blood about 20 feet from the entrance to the bathroom, Detective Heatherly arched an eyebrow, seemingly noticing an anomaly.

"Hey, Phil, can you snap a picture of this, right here," he said, pointing to the thickened puddle.

"Sure thing, Stan," Detective Jorgensen said, pulling out his mobile phone.

"What's going on, detectives? Why are you—"

"Nothing to worry about, Mr. Benton," Heatherly said, hustling to catch up to Tim. "The forensics team should be here any minute now."

"Okay," Tim said, maintaining an anxious look. "Right this way, gentlemen. Follow me."

"Please, Mr. Benton. You're going to have to wait outside of the crime scene area. We can't have you contaminating it."

"But I've already been inside. I mean, I found her. I probably contaminated the scene already." Tim shook his head.

"You didn't touch the body, did you?" Jorgensen asked contemptuously.

"Well, I, uh...well, yeah. I did. I mean, I had to see if she was really—"

Jorgensen glanced at his partner, rolling his eyes. "Mr. Benton, it'll be best if you go back downstairs, alright? Listen for the forensics team and then send them up here, will you?"

"Uh, okay. I can do that. But I just wanted to let you know—" Tim stopped when his cell phone rang, emitting a shrill pop music tune. Looking down at the caller ID, he couldn't suppress a smile when he recognized the number. "I gotta take this call. I'll wait downstairs. I promise."

Gliding down the stairs, Tim put the phone to his ear when he was halfway to the first floor, speaking softly.

"Hello!" he said ardently. "I've been thinking about you all morning, since, uh...but haven't had a chance yet to—"

"*What the heck, dude? Haven't 'had a chance yet' to call me? What am I—*"

"Uh, look, something's happened," said Tim breathlessly, sauntering into the kitchen. "Something awful, man. The police are here."

"*What? Your wife confronted you again, looking for a fight? Trying to get you to admit your sins?*"

"Branson, uh, if only it was just that silly and stupid. But you see...it's not. Something awful has happened to her. Just awful." Tim's voice trailed off as he took a deep breath.

"*What's happened? Tell me?*"

"She uh...she's, uh...gone. Dead. She was shot, several times. I, I...don't know what...how...I just found her, when I got back home, after—"

"*What? What the hell are you talking about? Cyndi's dead? That's...impossible. I can't believe it. Who would—*"

"I have no idea. None at all. I mean—"

"*What's going on? You're acting like it's...I don't know. Your wife was just murdered for Pete's sake! And you're not even upset in the least. I can't believe it. What's the deal?*"

"What's the deal, you ask? *Deal?* What the fuck's that supposed to mean? My wife's dead, and I'm not upset enough for you? 'Not even upset in the least'?" Tim breathed heavily as he paced the kitchen floor, shaking his head.

"*Something's really not right with you, ya know?*" Branson said dismissively. "*I, I've gotta go, Timothy. I'm really sorry about Cyndi; really, I am. I'll call you later.*"

The drive back to Los Angeles on Interstate 10 was a blur of muted colors on either side of the freeway with intermittent splashes of brightly colored billboards advertising fast food. Hyper-focused on the tasks at hand, Lisa stared straight ahead, though her body felt tremendous pressure, as if she were in a deep underwater tunnel crossing between land masses. Then, seemingly in no time at all, she was approaching the Los Angeles County line, grime and graffiti covering freeway overpasses and underpasses.

What a clusterfuck, she thought, carefully maneuvering her 4Runner to the far-left interchange in order to remain on I-10. Lisa felt disgusted for having to eliminate Tim's wife, but she'd had no other choice; it was self-defense. Having been in the wrong place at the wrong time, his wife had become the unfortunate victim of collateral damage, even as the actual target remained alive and well. It had to be the conundrum of the day, maybe even the year, she thought, passing through South Los Angeles. Having never met the woman, Lisa had no opinion of her whatsoever, imagining the poor thing had been yet another victim of her brother's guile and chicanery. She had likely been a very nice person, with very good intentions, who'd gotten caught up in the Bentons' web of greed.

Just put it out of your mind, Lisa told herself, approaching Crenshaw Boulevard. *It was you or her and it had to be her. Self-defense at its most basic.* But she wouldn't have had to defend herself if she hadn't been the one to break into her brother's house in the first place.

"*Shit!*" she said aloud, pounding the steering wheel with both palms. Killing an innocent person had not been on her agenda, ever. *How will I ever forgive myself for such an awful act?* If there was ever a time to seek divine guidance, it would be now, she said to herself, seeing the offramp for Robertson Boulevard up ahead.

And, then the answer came to her, quickly and easily: Kendall. That's it! He had to have been put in her life for a real purpose and now she realized what purpose: atonement for all of her sins. She was going to receive redemption through Kendall. She'd now focus all of her energy on seeing to it that the little boy with no mother found his way to a new life. She'd make sure he got a new family. He deserved it after all he'd been through. Who else but a youngster with a big heart who embodied everything she was not: pure innocence. She'd tell him the good news the minute she walked into Elizabeth's house. She'd make the arrangements as soon as possible, calling CPS, creating a viable story for the social workers. They'd commend her for turning him in, after which he'd be just days from getting his forever family. Then, she'd be on her way to finally completing her grand plan.

But as she neared Elizabeth's place, her glee diminished as her mind circled back to Tim and the real possibility—if not, probability—that he'd be questioned about his wife's death. After all, who's typically the first person law enforcement looks at when a spouse is murdered? She had to get to him before that happened. What could be worse than the police interfering with her *coup de grâce*?

Chapter 63 Friday Afternoon

"Has anyone heard from Tim today?" said Todd to no one in particular as he walked past Angie's desk.

"No, Mr. Benton. I haven't heard from him or seen him. At all. Today." Angie's eyes widened as she watched her boss hang a U-turn and head back toward her desk.

"You mean he hasn't called in?" Todd's worried intonation contrasted wildly with the curious look on his face.

"No, sorry, Mr. Benton, he has not. Do you want me to call him?"

"Well, yes. Of course." Todd glared at his secretary. "You should have done that already. I'm actually surprised that you haven't."

"Right away, sir." Angie said, looking down, snatching the receiver and pressing a pre-set button on the phone's base. "I'm sure there's a good reason for him—"

"There better be a *really* good reason."

"Voicemail, Mr. Benton," Angie said, looking sheepishly at her boss. "Went straight to voicemail."

"Then, leave a message, Angie. And call him back in ten."

"Yes, sir. Of course, sir."

"I need him here by two. Meeting again with the estate attorneys. He knows about it, of course. Just remind him. Nicely, but firmly."

Angie spoke softly into the mouthpiece, leaving a cryptic message for Tim to get his butt into the office ASAP.

"Thanks, Angie. Buzz me in ten after you've tried calling him again."

The moment Todd Benton disappeared, Angie was startled when her mobile phone vibrated on her desk. Staring down at it, she shook her head when she recognized the number.

"Where the hell are you?" Angie breathed heavily into the mouthpiece.

"I'm, uh, I'm on my way."

"What's wrong? You sound weird."

"It's, uh, it's Cyndi. She's uh—"

"What's wrong with Cyndi? You're scaring me, Tim."

"I'm so sorry, Angie. She's, uh, gone."

"Gone? Where's she gone to?"

"She's, uh, dead."

"*Dead?* She's dead? Oh my God, Tim. What are you saying?"

"I'll be right there. I'm parking now."

Lisa stealthily followed Tim from his home in Brentwood, ostensibly to his office on Wilshire Boulevard, having perfectly timed her appearance at his home just ten minutes prior to him leaving. Changing her plans to return to Elizabeth's to pick up Kendall, she'd instead reversed her direction, heading to her brother's mansion. And as if by divine intervention, when she'd turned onto his street, she'd noticed a police cruiser speeding away from his home followed closely by a large, unmarked, black sedan. Police work must be done for now, she'd thought, slowing down. They probably cut him loose, telling him he was free to go about his business.

Bingo! There he was turning out of his driveway, heading in the same direction as were the cops, clearly in a hurry. This may be her one-in-a-million chance to track him unimpeded till he eventually stopped at a public place where she could freely stalk him and finally, exact retribution. Nonchalantly hanging a U-turn, Lisa maintained a close distance behind Tim, driving east on Wilshire till he, predictably, pulled into the parking structure of his building. Intent on not losing him in the immense, multi-level structure, Lisa yanked a ticket from the machine at the visitor's entrance, then furtively followed him, watching him pull into his reserved spot, right by the elevators.

Parking in one of the guest spots on the other side, Lisa cut her engine and decided to not go up to Ogilvie Wealth Management but to wait for Tim to return, assuming he'd not be too long. He had to undoubtedly be rattled—perhaps even distraught—from having just discovered his wife dead of gunshot wounds, in his own home! He had to be shaken up, no matter what kind of relationship the two of them had. He was probably just going in to talk to daddy, to try to figure out what he should do now that trophy wife was gone. Would Todd and Saundra be overcome with grief? Or would they be relieved that gold-digging wife number three was finally out of their lives?

Stop it, Lisa told herself, shaking her head. You're being heartless and cruel. *It wasn't even an hour ago that I was seeking redemption for having to kill the very woman I'm now dissing. It wasn't her fault she was in the wrong place at my right time, but there you have it. Sometimes collateral damage is justified. Sometimes killing innocent people...How many times have I used my gun today without reloading? Fuck. Am I getting careless?*

Retrieving her SIG Sauer from her shoulder holster, she quickly released the magazine, counting three remaining bullets. *Shit. I could have been caught utterly unprepared if I had to use it right now.* Recalling she had an extra box of ammo in her glove compartment, Lisa pulled out seven .45 slugs and loaded them into the magazine. She then filled another magazine, just in case, returning both the pistol and the extra magazine to her holster.

Shit! What's taking Tim so long? Lisa glanced at her watch, noting thirteen minutes had passed since she'd parked. *Fuck. Where is he? He may have decided to stay for a while, after all. Maybe he's being interrogated by dad. Maybe mom showed up, too, and they're having a family pow-wow. Jesus, man. I don't have all day to fuck around and wait. Gotta get back to Kendall and sort all of that out.*

Impulsively, Lisa jumped out of her 4Runner, clicked the alarm on and jogged to the elevator. Watching the digital floor indicator above the door illuminate 4, she waited patiently for it to descend to P1. When the doors opened, she quickly scanned the faces of the three people exiting, determining none of them was her brother. Recalling from prior research that Ogilvie occupied all of the seventh floor, she punched 7, leaned against the cool interior, closing her eyes as the elevator whizzed up seven levels in three seconds. The ding compelled her to open her eyes and the first thing she saw was a tall man in a yellow shirt standing to the side waiting for her to get out.

Locking eyes with him, Lisa felt her voice catch in her throat, so she merely shook her head, silently indicating she was not getting out.

"Going down?" he asked, visibly annoyed.

"Yeah," she finally said, recognizing her brother.

CHAPTER 64 FRIDAY AFTERNOON

"Here we are, Kendall. Five-seven-three South Bingham," Elizabeth said matter-of-factly, eyeing her passenger as they cruised by his former apartment. "Are you sure this is the right place?"

"Of course, I'm sure, Miss Elizabeth. I lived here for a few years with my mom."

"Just wanted to make sure." Elizabeth patted his head and smiled. "So do you still want to go in?"

"Yeah, but how are we gonna do that?" Kendall looked dejectedly at Elizabeth. "We don't have a key."

"No key?"

Kendall shook his head.

"No key, no problem, kiddo." Elizabeth pulled to the curb, parked and smiled again at Kendall. "Your Aunt Elizabeth knows just what to do."

"Are you gonna break in?" Kendall's eyes widened.

"Break in? Oh, no, sweetie," she said, laughing. "Aunt Elizabeth never breaks into any home. She doesn't have to. She's cleverer than that."

Kendall stared at her for a long moment before asking, "What do you mean?"

"C'mon. You'll see."

Letting Kendall lead the way, Elizabeth followed her charge to Apartment 3 on the ground floor, scanning her surroundings, making sure no undesirables were hanging around. This neighborhood could be dangerous as it was on the fringes where Crips and Bloods were known to clash.

Elizabeth jiggled the handle to Apartment 3, but it wouldn't open. Telling Kendall she was a magician, she slyly slid a pick and tension wrench into the handle's simple lock, maneuvered the pick, feeling around for the pins. With adept ease, Elizabeth depressed all the pins in seconds and the two were inside the apartment in less than half a minute.

Coughing, covering her mouth with her hand, Elizabeth grimaced as stuffy, rancid odors escaped the apartment. "So, what did you want to get?" said Elizabeth, regarding the toy-littered sofa in the small living room.

"Some clothes and some toys. In my bedroom."

"Cool. Go grab them. I'll look for some bags in the kitchen to put them in."

"Okay, Auntie Liz."

A putrid stench emanating from the kitchen forced Elizabeth to hold her breath while scrounging for plastic bags. Glancing in the sink, she saw the source: food-encrusted plates and bowls sitting in the basin, mold already growing on some. Haphazardly opening drawers, she spotted a few clean garbage bags before being driven from the kitchen and back to the living room.

"Got everything?" she shouted to Kendall.

"I think so. Here." He handed her a pile of clothing, and a Nerf gun while hanging onto a boogie board.

"Planning to surf?" Elizabeth snickered.

"My Aunt Lonnie gave it to me. I never used it. I thought–"

"Sure, kiddo. Of course," Elizabeth said somberly. "I'll even take you to the beach. Later today."

"Really? Cool!"

"Of course. I always say what I mean and mean what I say." Elizabeth shoved the clothing and Nerf gun into one of the bags, allowing Kendall to carry his boogie board. "C'mon, let's get out of here. There's a beautiful day at the beach waiting for us."

Skipping out of the apartment, using his boogie board as a shield, Kendall stopped in his tracks when he ran into a silhouetted woman entering the building. Observing Kendall's impasse, Elizabeth slowly walked toward the two, unable to make out any facial features of the person impeding Kendall's movement.

"Everything okay, sweetie?" Elizabeth called out, approaching the woman, who had just grabbed Kendall by the wrist. "Hey, what are you doing? Get your hands off of him!" Dropping the bag, she rushed to Kendall's side.

"Excuse me, but who are you? Where are you going with Kendall?" the woman asked angrily.

"Who the hell are you is a more appropriate question," Elizabeth said, reaching for Kendall's other hand, now able to get a better look at the zaftig woman.

"I'm his social worker, Charlene Mullins-McMillan," she said authoritatively. "And Kendall has been missing since last Sunday. Actually, both he and his mother have been missing. They missed an appointment with me earlier this week."

"Don't know anything about any missed appointments, Charlene, but his mother gave me permission to take him to the beach."

"You still haven't answered my question. Who are you?"

"A friend. Crystal. Now please let go of him and let us be on our way."

"I'll do nothing of the sort. Where's his mother, Loretta? She wouldn't allow—"

"Go ask her yourself." Elizabeth pointed down the hall.

"I will, but you're both coming with me to sort this out first." Charlene gripped Kendall's arm even tighter, causing the youngster to whine in pain.

Elizabeth eyed the plastic bag filled with Kendall's clothing in the middle of the hall, deciding it would be best to leave it there and hightail it out of the building. "Look, Charlene, give the kid a break. He's got his heart set on boogie-boarding at Venice, and I promised him."

"Once Loretta gives me the okay, you're both free to go on your way." Charlene started to pull Kendall toward his apartment.

With no choice but to show this stubborn woman who was in charge, Elizabeth withdrew her 9mm pistol, which had been holstered on her right ankle, and jammed it into Charlene's ribs.

"We're actually free to go now, Charlene," Elizabeth said, freeing Kendall from her grasp. "Don't make me use this on you."

"What the hell? You're one crazy bitch!"

"I've been called worse, believe me. Now just stay right there, till we're out of sight. Then go check up on Loretta."

Elizabeth led a shaking Kendall out into the sunlight and to the safety of her car.

Riding the elevator down to the parking garage with Tim standing at an angle behind her, Lisa stared straight ahead, rigid, aware of her brother nervously tapping his foot. Her senses heightened, wanting desperately to nab her gun, turn around and shoot him in the face, Lisa tampered her desire by fantasizing about slowly torturing him for hours in the privacy of her home before placing a bullet between his eyes.

Shutting her eyes, biting her lips, trying to remain still, she excruciatingly concentrated on each breath she took till she heard the doors open. But when she reopened her eyes, she noticed Tim had disappeared into thin air! Looking around, she heard screeching tires and smelled rubber before spotting him backing his car out of his reserved spot. Fearing she wouldn't catch up to him in time, she sprinted to her 4Runner, got in and tore out of the garage, conveniently slipping out behind a sports car without paying before the arm came down on her vehicle.

Concentrating intently on keeping up with her brother, Lisa forced herself to quash her emotions and just breathe. While she could normally maintain a steely calmness when tracking predators, she felt differently today with Tim because he was her brother, the one who relentlessly raped her as a child while her parents did nothing. *Okay, just stop it, woman! You're tougher than this. You're a rock star when it comes to focusing on the task at hand.*

Where the fuck is he going? she thought, heading east on Wilshire, staying close in thick traffic. *He lives in the opposite direction, so he's obviously got another destination in mind.* Following him at a safe distance, she had to slip into a right-hand turning lane at the last moment at Robertson Boulevard. *He's venturing south of Beverly Hills, out of his comfort zone. What the hell?*

Patiently driving for another two miles, Lisa nearly missed him getting into the left-hand turning lane at a side street she'd never heard of. Gliding through a yellow light so as not to lose track of Tim, Lisa immediately turned right into a parking lot behind a restaurant. Or maybe it was a bar. She hadn't noticed the marquee while waiting to turn.

What the hell was this place giving away? she wondered, finding one of the last parking spots in the lot. Checking her visage in the rearview mirror before exiting her car, Lisa patted her hair before smoothing her jacket, pulling it taut around her midsection, making sure her holster didn't make a dent. Tarrying just a few steps behind her brother, Lisa sauntered into the establishment through the back door.

Adjusting her eyes to the ambient light inside, she now realized she was indeed in a bar. A
neighborhood dive bar catering to drunks and clandestine tryst seekers.

"Welcome to Clancy's. How many, miss?" the hostess asked, rushing to greet her.

CHAPTER 65 FRIDAY AFTERNOON

"This cannot be happening, Todd. Tell me this is a dream and I'm going to wake up at any moment. Please, I'm begging you."

"It's not a goddamned dream, Saundra, it's real and it's happening. In the pit of my stomach, I knew something like this was bound to happen."

Having taken a cab to the Ogilvie building the moment Todd called her with the tragic news, Saundra now sat in a plush armchair in her husband's office, chewing on the tip of a plastic cigarette holder, trying in vain to calm her nerves. Shifting her weight, moving the cigarette holder to the other side of her mouth, Saundra glared at Todd.

"What the hell's that supposed to mean?" Saundra withdrew a pack of cigarettes from her purse, plucked one out with shaky fingers, then clumsily slid it into the holder. Reaching back into her purse, she withdrew a gold lighter, poising it under the elongated cigarette.

"You're not thinking of lighting that in here, are you? For Christ's sakes, Saundra. You can't smoke in here."

Saundra scowled at her husband sitting across from her. "Well, of course I'm thinking of lighting it, for Christ's sake. Didja think I just went through the trouble of putting it in the cigarette holder for my health? Criminy!"

Todd loudly sucked in air, looking down at the work piled on his desk, mindlessly shuffling a few stacks of paper. "Okay, dear; you win," he said looking her in the eye. "This is not the time for a fight, God knows. We are all on the same team. We need to put our heads together and figure out a plan from here on out."

"But you didn't answer my question, darling," said Saundra, flicking her gold lighter, sucking hard on the cigarette holder, releasing a large plume of smoke.

"What question?" Todd waved away the smoke, annoyed.

"What did you mean when you said, 'In the pit of my stomach, I knew something like this was bound to happen.'"

"It means exactly as it sounds, dear. There was no hidden meaning. I had a bad feeling things for Tim were not going to end well. And it seems my hunch was right all along."

"So, it's all about Tim. Again. Jesus Christ."

"No, Saundra. It's not all about Tim. It's about him *fucking* up. One too many times, and now the chickens have come home to roost."

"Poor, poor Cyndi. No one seems to care the poor girl is dead. *Murdered!*" Saundra took another drag off her elongated cigarette. "Murdered! My God. This isn't so much about him as it is about his wife being murdered, for God's sake!"

"Of course, I care. You care, too. We call care about what happened."

"Cut the bullshit Todd. You didn't give two shits about her. Never did. Called her a gold digger from the get-go.

"Am I right?"

Todd remained quiet for a long while, watching his wife smoke her cigarette, acting and looking like some floozy straight out of a Prohibition Era speakeasy.

"That's unfair and you know it, Saundra," Todd spat out. "God knows I liked her. She was my daughter-in-law. I, uh, you could say I loved her as a *daughter*."

Saundra snorted loudly, turning to face her husband. "I need a drink, dear. Where are you hiding the booze?"

"It's, uh, it's somewhere," Todd said disgustedly, gripping the edge of his desk. "Must you—"

"What's going on in here?" Angie had burst into her boss's office, waving her hand in front of her face. "I smelled smoke, and I uh—"

"How astute of you, dear," Saundra said, holding her cigarette high in the air. "Yes, I am the one smoking. No need to look any further."

"But, Mrs. Benton, you cannot—"

"Cannot what, dear? Smoke? Is that what you were going to say?"

"It's against the law, actually, Mrs. B and we could get—"

"So was murdering my daughter-in-law this morning, but I don't see anyone doing anything about that *real* crime. And honestly, murder is much worse than smoking a goddamned cigarette, wouldn't you agree?"

Angie turned pale, embarrassed, bracing herself against the wall. "I know, Mrs. B. It's just awful news. Tim called me, just a little while ago to tell me. After I was trying to reach him, that is, for Mr. B. He called me back. Anyway, I, uh, I cannot believe it." Angie bit her lips as she continued to use the wall for support.

"Tim was just here to give us the terrible news," said Saundra, shaking her head. "Such a tragedy. Nothing but tragedy for the Benton clan."

"Saundra, please," Todd interjected. "Let me handle this, for God's sake."

"The only thing you're supposed to be handling is fixing me a drink," said Saundra, visibly shaking. "Now, please, dear; if I don't have my fix in two minutes you will have to contend with me going through major withdrawals. And, let me tell you it won't be a pretty sight."

Angie stood in place, against the wall, wringing her hands while Todd glowered at his wife. He then pushed his chair away from his desk, rose, and padded over to an ornate cabinet to his right. Unlocking one of the glassed doors, he removed a bottle of domestic vodka from the top shelf that was a little more than half-full. Nabbing a glass from another shelf, he set them down hard on a side table, causing both women to flinch.

"All I have is Smirnoff, dear, and I know how much of a vodka snob you are. Hope it'll—"

"Oh, will you stop it, Todd? I am only that way in public. When it's vital I *proffer* the right image. The proper Ogilvie image."

Clearly thinking she had to react kindly to the older woman, Angie scooted over to Saundra, bent over, and wrapped her arms around her. "Oh, I am so sorry, Mrs. B," she whispered into her ear, holding her tightly.

Todd regarded the two women as he filled the glass with vodka. "Here's to you maintaining your superior Ogilvie image, darling," he said, handing it to his wife. "Even in the face of catastrophe."

Angie stepped back, self-consciously wrapping her arms around herself. Saundra smiled weakly at the young woman, then grimaced at her husband before snatching the glass from him. "Thank God my medicine has finally arrived," Saundra said, gulping down half the glass. "For a minute I was convinced I would convulse right here in this office."

"Can I do anything for you, Mrs. B?" Angie wobbled nervously on her feet.

"Thanks, dear, but everything's being taken care of, right darling?" Saundra downed the rest of her drink, holding up the empty glass in her left hand for her husband to retrieve, the elongated cigarette in her other hand. "Haven't the police already been there, and hasn't the coroner taken the body away?"

Todd snatched the glass, giving his wife a sideways glare before heading to the hutch. "That's right, Angie, everything's under control. But thanks very much for offering to help. We'll keep you posted on things."

"Oh, okay, thanks." Angie wrung her hands before adding, "I'm so sorry for your loss. I'll just go now. I've got a load of work piled up on my desk." Backpedaling out of the office, she cut away clumsily when she reached the door.

"What a disaster she is, Todd," Saundra said casually, taking the refilled glass of vodka from her husband. "Christ, I thought she had more balls than that."

Todd sat down again, opened his laptop, peeked at his Outlook calendar, then slapped his forehead. "Shit! Lisa is due back this afternoon. Have you heard from your private eye?"

When no answer was forthcoming from Saundra, Todd peered around his computer to see her slumped over the side of the armchair, the empty glass dangling from her one hand, the lit cigarette suspended from the other.

CHAPTER 66 FRIDAY AFTERNOON

"How many, miss?" the hostess repeated, louder this time.

"Oh, just me for now," Lisa said, scanning the room for her brother. "I'll just sit at the bar till my girlfriend shows up."

"Absolutely, miss. Lots of room at the bar."

Sliding onto a barstool, Lisa turned around, her alert eyes catching a man wearing a yellow shirt sitting in a booth near the back of the establishment. Tim. *Who would wear a yellow shirt, for crying out loud? He is truly an egotistical fuck to wear such an eye-catching color when he would be better served wearing something muted to blend into the crowd.*

"What can I get for you?" the male bartender asked, startling her, placing down a white napkin with the bar's name in fancy green script printed on it.

"Oh, uh, I'll have a gin and tonic," Lisa replied absentmindedly, gin being the first spirit that came to mind.

"Well or top shelf?"

"Do you have Leopold's?"

"Sure do, miss."

"Awesome. Wait. Scratch the tonic. Make me a gin martini. Straight up. With three olives. I feel like livin' it up this afternoon."

"I like your style, sweetie," the bartender said, winking at her.

Lisa smiled at the young man, who was undoubtedly gay, checking out his backside in his tight jeans when he turned around. What a damn shame and a waste, she thought before resuming her vigil on Tim in the back of the establishment.

With his back to her so she couldn't see his face, Tim was now ordering from the waitress, using hand gestures to describe something or someone, perhaps. Scribbling down his order, she then walked over to another table, and Tim immediately took out his cell phone, punching in a number. Looking off in the distance, he then quickly placed the mobile back down on the table, never speaking to anyone.

"Here ya go, sweetie," the cute bartender said, placing her cocktail on the napkin. "Looks so yummy. Enjoy!"

"Thanks. It does."

Lisa took a quick sip, enjoying the immediate effects of the juniper-laced spirit, all the while keeping an eye on Tim. Once again, he picked up his mobile phone and punched in a number, possibly calling the same person back. Hounding would be more precise. How on earth a person can casually sit in a bar a few hours after finding his wife murdered and nonchalantly order a drink without a care in the world was beyond her comprehension. You are the worst of the worst, she thought gulping down her drink, coughing from the rush of alcohol.

This time, however, Tim connected with someone as he animatedly spoke using his right hand for emphasis. Even as the waitress delivered his pint of beer, he continued to talk on the phone, ignoring her. When he finally ended the call, he wiped his forehead with a napkin, then picked up his pint and guzzled down a quarter of it.

Something's really got him upset, Lisa thought, carefully sipping her martini. *And it's clearly not his wife's murder. He's gotta have someone on the side, and that's who he just called to join him for drinks.* Piece of shit, she thought, slamming her fist on the bar, shaking her head. Startled, the gay bartender turned to stare at her, and she sheepishly grinned at him, shrugging her shoulders. *Someone's bound to show up any time now. Why else would he have taken a booth for four?*

"How's the drink, love?" asked the hot bartender, forcing her to turn around to face him.

"Lovely, hon." Lisa daintily took a sip. "Thanks."

"Let me know when you're ready for another."

"Sure thing," she said, turning back in Tim's direction to see a man approaching her brother's table.

What the hell? Who else can jack up my plans today? Observing the man hovering over Tim, Lisa was stunned when she saw him wagging a finger at him, admonishing him for something he said or did. *Who is this person? Why is he berating Tim?* Now the man had his hands defiantly placed on his waist, one hip jutted out for emphasis. Desperate, Tim spoke to the man, using his hands animatedly. Then without warning, Tim reached out and grabbed the man by the waistband of his pants. Shaking his head, the man tried to pull away when Tim suddenly grasped him tightly by his hips. Tim's arms shook in despair, trying to get his message across to this person, who seemed anxious to get away.

Unable to make sense of this unfolding scene, Lisa gulped down the rest of her cocktail just as the waitress appeared and told the two men something, likely warning them about their inappropriate behavior. Setting down her martini glass behind her, Lisa got a good look at the man as he stormed out of the establishment, locking eyes with him. Instantly understanding the depth of their relationship, Lisa now knew how she'd ensnare her prey. Thank God for the hot bartender standing behind her.

"Hey sweetie," Lisa said, eyeing the study gay man. "What would it take for you to do me a favor?"

"Depends what it is." The bartender's eyes lit up.

"It involves that cute guy sitting over there, in the yellow shirt, in the corner booth by himself."

"Okay, yeah, he's kinda cute," the bartender said, craning his neck.

"'Kinda'?"

"You gotta know I see *tens* all day long, sweetie."

"Of course, you do. So, without getting a closeup look, what do you rate him?"

"Hmmm, I guess an eight?"

"Is that a question?"

"Huh? No, no. It was, uh, a statement. An eight. Yeah, a definite eight."

"Awesome, dude."

Always concerned about his wife's dignity, especially during a blackout, Todd stubbed out her cigarette, and placed her drink on his desk. He then straightened Saundra's upper body, knelt next to her, heaved her over his shoulder and placed her on the sofa against the wall. He then threw a blanket over her and listened to her breathe shallowly for a few minutes. His momentary sadness was interrupted when Angie barged in, this time with a look of confusion on her face.

"Mr. Benton, sorry to bother you again," she said breathlessly, "but the police are here. Looking for Tim."

"Police? What the hell for?" Todd moved away from Saundra, who continued to sleep soundly.

"I, uh, I don't know. They didn't say. All they said was they wanted to speak with Tim. What should I tell them?"

"I, I don't know right now. Stall them for a minute. Think of something."

"Okay. But should I say you'll come out to speak with them or what?" Angie threw out her hands in exasperation.

"Use your head, Angie, dear. You're the first line of defense for a reason. You'll think of something."

"Yes, sir, Mr. B. I'll think of something." Angie turned on her heals and walked out of the office.

Jesus, Todd thought when he was alone, except for Saundra now snoring away blissfully. *The fucking chickens have come home to roost.*

CHAPTER 67 FRIDAY AFTERNOON

The hot bartender, who Lisa found out was called Hank by his peeps, but who would have been more aptly named Hunk, slithered out from behind the bar and sauntered over to the booth where Tim sat. Looking glum and despondent, Tim immediately looked up when the young hottie placed another pint in front of him.

"I, uh, didn't order this," said Tim, staring at the handsome guy. "You must have the wrong table."

"Oh, no I don't. I actually have the right table." Hank smiled seductively at Tim.

"But I didn't order it."

"It's on the house, man. Cheers. Cheer up!"

"Okay, if you insist. Cheers!" Tim pushed his empty glass toward the bartender, lifted the fresh, full one and swigged the ale, all the while ogling him. "Thanks, man."

"My pleasure," said Hank, discreetly sliding a folded piece of paper toward Tim. "Y'all come back now."

Tim's mouth fell open watching the guy sexily strut away and it wasn't till Hank was back at the bar that Tim noticed the note he'd left. Unfolding it, he read: "*I think you're hot. Text me later for a hookup.* (619) 555-3388. *Hank.*" Stunned, Tim looked around self-consciously, as if anyone inside the establishment could know he'd been slipped a note, much less know what was written on it. He then quickly refolded it, shoving it in his front pant pocket.

Swilling down more stout, Tim glanced back at the bar, locking eyes with a woman who sat there, daintily sipping a martini. *What a shame she has to sit at the bar waiting for Mr. Right to walk in while I get the cream of the crop to proposition me. Hank. Wow. Life is just not fair!*

When Tim finished his beer, he walked past the bar on his way out, deliberately nodding at the bartender, offering him a half-smile. Hank nodded back and winked as he dried a martini glass with a towel. While his head swirled with all sorts of wild sexual thoughts, he noticed that
martini woman had already left. Musta gotten lucky herself, he thought, exiting into the bright sunlight.

Waiting in the parking lot for Tim to leave, Lisa followed him once again as he backtracked across town, likely to his Brentwood home to freshen up before his big date with Hot Hank. *Wow. I'd have never in a million years guessed that the deviant who relentlessly molested me for years, would turn out to be gay. When did all this start? And then why the three marriages? To cover up his true identity? Did his being an altar boy have anything to do with his adult sexual preferences?*

Lisa started when she heard her mobile chime with an incoming text before remembering it was her number that Tim had, not Hank's. *The fucker's so transparently horny and despicably uncaring about his murdered wife he can't even wait to get home before texting the guy. Won't you be shocked when you discover who's behind your impending hookup!*

Taking a curve on Wilshire Boulevard as it edged the Los Angeles Country Club, Lisa heard another text chime and shook her head at the hopeless impatience of her brother, who had no clue who was at the receiving end of his messages. Estimating Tim's drive home was less than ten minutes, she quashed her enthusiasm, opting to check her text messages when she was parked on his street. Let him wait, she thought vindictively. *I'll respond when I'm good and ready.*

Approaching Tim's neighborhood, Lisa slowed to a crawl, wanting to avoid causing him any suspicions of someone tailing him. She was so close now—closer than she'd ever been—to accomplishing her goal, she could practically taste it. She would not let anything interfere with it now. Seeing Tim drive into his compound up ahead, she pulled over, parking a good sixty feet from his property. She'd answer his texts while waiting for him to change.

But when she glanced at her phone, she saw that the two texts were from two different senders, causing her to pause. The first one was indeed from Tim—*Heading home to change. Text U in a few*—while the other was from a number with a 602 area code—*if ur still willing to help, im willing to listen.* It was signed simply "CC." *What the hell? Who the heck is CC?*

Intrigued, but with a more pressing issue at a hand, Lisa quickly texted back CC: *who is this?*
then replied to Tim: *cant wait, big guy. see ya soon! :)*

Feeling both nauseated and exhilarated, she sat patiently in her vehicle, waiting for him to respond back that he was ready to rock and roll. Then it hit her: where would she suggest they meet? Think, she told herself, launching Safari on her phone. *Where, oh where to meet?*
Someplace very public to make him feel comfortable on a first "date," or a cozy, private bar where no one would hear their conversation? A gay bar on Santa Monica or a hotel lobby on Wilshire? For God's sake, woman! What difference does—

The incoming text chime startled her, forcing her to look down.

it's carissa...combs...remember me?

Fuck! What the hell? Of all people to contact me now, the hooker connected to Jared.

Carissa: *bonzo and zack have taken me hostage. they think I had something to do with jareds death.*

Lisa: *What do you want me to do? I'm back in California.*

Carissa: *they're threatening me...*

Tim: *I'm ready big guy. Where are we meeting?*

Quick, think of a gay bar on Santa Monica–

Her phone chimed before she could finish her thought

Tim: *Do U know where the blvd lounge is? Wanna meet in the lobby at 4:30?*

Quickly typing in The Blvd Lounge into Safari, Lisa learned it was inside the Beverly Wilshire Hotel. *Who'd have known that little nugget, other than the pretentious Bentons who likely dine there on a regular basis.*

Lisa: *Yeah, sure. See U there.*

Tim: *Awesome. I'm on my way.*

Carissa: *u still there?*

Lisa: *Have an urgent matter to deal with for the next couple of hours. Can you hang in there? I promise to get back to U.*

Carissa: *hope I'm still alive.*

Feeling badly for Carissa's supposed hostage situation, Lisa had to put the young prostitute out of her mind till later. Besides, she reasoned, how'd she get my number? Carissa could be setting a trap for her, at the bequest of Bonzo and Zack. *Best to stay out of that mess.* Dealing with Tim was her priority now. Once she captured Tim, she needed this operation to go smoothly, avoiding any possible snags. Still, just in case of emergency, she scribbled a generic note that included her name and contact information on it

Like clockwork, Tim jammed out of his driveway ninety seconds later, laying rubber as he whipped his car around the curve, like a teenager rushing to get away from his parents. Hanging a U-turn, Lisa followed him, staying close without being obvious, having lots of experience doing this last summer when she'd track and then follow parolees released from prison. Imagining for a minute Tim was a newly released ex-convict, she felt the same adrenaline rush shoot through her body, affording her a welcome "high."

No sooner did she feel the butterflies in her stomach from the rush than she saw an unmarked police cruiser in her rearview mirror. *Fucking A! How did I miss that?* she wondered, berating herself for her carelessness. *The cops must be here to either arrest him or bring him into the station for questioning.* Homicide detectives are so transparent, she thought: their bland, unmarked vehicles look like they come straight off the fleet lot. *Still, I didn't notice them at Tim's place till they were directly behind me!*

Continuing to follow Tim as he made a right on Barrington, then a left on Wilshire, Lisa also watched the unmarked, dark sedan in her rearview, wondering if they knew she was following Tim as well. *Jesus. What a cluster fuck this could turn out to be.* Once on Wilshire, Tim sped east toward the hotel, making every green light, clearly obsessed with meeting the bartender. Pulling into valet, Tim jumped out, said something to the attendant and rushed inside. Lisa did the same, turning around as she entered the hotel's lobby just in time to see the cops in the unmarked car pull up to the curb, and in the process, inconsiderately block patrons from easily accessing the entrance.

Hustling along to get to Tim before the cops did, Lisa hightailed it for The Blvd Lounge, to the right of the lobby, ducking inside before the cops noticed either one of them. Searching for her brother among the early Happy Hour arrivals, she quickly spotted him at the end of the L-shaped bar in the front of the restaurant. Overwhelmed with emotion, Lisa told herself to slow down, forcing herself to concentrate on each breath as she approached her brother. Unsure how'd she feel when she finally looked him in the eye up close after all these years, she sensed a strange mix of relief and dread.

Noiselessly gliding up to Tim, Lisa saw he was texting frantically, completely unaware of her presence. Hovering over him, motionless, she watched him hit "send" and within two seconds, her own mobile chimed.

Turning around, startled and confused, Tim looked his sister in the eye and said, "What the hell?"

"Get up and follow me. *Now.*"

"Who the fuck are you?" Tim glared annoyingly at her, unaware of her intentions.

"For the moment, your savior."

"Savior?" Tim scoffed. "Not hardly. I'm actually waiting for someone, and you're actually in the way." He waved her off importantly with his left hand.

"Get up, asshole and follow me," Lisa commanded him, sticking the barrel of her .45 into his ribs. "Unless you prefer to be arrested by the cops that have been following you and will be walking in here any minute."

"The hell you're talking about?" Tim glowered at her.

Lisa pointed beyond the restaurant's alcove opening leading to the hotel lobby, where two suited men stood, looking around, seemingly lost.

"Pick your poison, brother. Me or the cops."

CHAPTER 68 FRIDAY AFTERNOON

When the two homicide detectives entered the Beverly Wilshire Hotel, they stopped in their tracks as they assessed which way to go. Looking left toward reception, then right toward The Blvd Lounge, each cop then took off in opposite directions before catching themselves, with the beefier detective walking over to his partner at the reception desk, where they conferred.

"Why would he go check into a hotel?" the heavier of the two, Detective Stan Heatherly asked his partner.

"Why the hell not?" Phil Jorgensen said, shrugging his shoulders. "He's probably freaked out by sleeping in his own house, much worse, his own bed, after knocking off his wife."

"So, you think he skipped into the restaurant to have a bite to eat while he considers his next move?"

"Sure. If he's the cold-blooded killer I believe he is, he's more concerned with feeding his starving self, and having a cocktail or two than getting a good night's sleep."

"You're the lead, so let's go with your hunch."

"It's not a hunch, Stan, it's my gut feeling."

"Okay, then, let's go with your 'gut feeling'. We're wasting precious time parsing words."

Heading toward The Blvd Lounge, Heatherly and Jorgensen looked out the glassed doors as they passed the entrance. At that precise moment, they observed a man and woman get into Tim's Porsche.

"What the fuck?" Heatherly said to his partner, pointing to his right. "He's escaping. With a woman!"

"Fucking shit," Jorgensen said, rushing to the door. "He's a sly motherfucker, that's for sure. Hooking up with a chick just hours after he killed his wife."

"Piece of shit. I swear, I'll never understand human behavior as long as I live."

Grasping Tim by his upper arm, her gun firmly jabbed into his right side, Lisa directed her brother through the restaurant, meandering into the kitchen without so much as a question from staff as to what they were doing there. Sneaking out the back door, she pushed him around the building, toward the front of the hotel, hopeful the cops were still inside The Blvd Lounge asking the wait staff if they'd seen him.

"You can't just order me around," Tim said, resisting her, yet trying to avoid undue attention to himself. "I'm supposed to meet someone now, you know, and when he doesn't see me in the restaurant, he's gonna get suspicious."

"Calm down, no one's gonna miss you." Lisa stopped abruptly, breathing heavily as she studied the hotel's entrance, weighing her options and the possibility that the cops may see them if they come around to the front.

"The hell he won't. I was just texting him when you approached me."

"That person doesn't exist, big brother. I'm in control now."

"What the hell are you talking about?" Tim glared at her.

"There is no 'he', only me." Lisa said, pushing him along.

Lisa inched further along toward the entrance, now steering her captor alongside the cops' vacant unmarked black Crown Victoria. Slyly dropping the note she'd written earlier onto the driver's seat, she then urged Tim toward the parking attendant.

"You're one crazy bitch. Speak English to me."

"You ought to listen better."

"What do you mean 'he' doesn't exist? I met him myself. He's as real as you and me."

"Well, you're half right. I'll give you that."

"Say what?"

"Remember when you sent your last text at the bar, and you heard my phone chime? Jesus. Do I need to spell it out for you?"

Tim abruptly stopped, eyeing Lisa suspiciously. Ignoring him, Lisa spied the entrance as she pushed her brother along nearing the valet post. "We're going for a little ride, you and me."

"Ride? Who the fuck are you anyway? You can't just order me around without any rhyme or reason–"

"Does this forty-five jammed into your waist suggest there is no 'rhyme or reason', brother?"

"Stop calling me brother, will you? What kind of a crazed weirdo are you?

"Stop asking so many questions," Lisa said, approaching the valet. "You'll find out soon enough. Patience, my brother. Now just be calm and hand the guy your ticket. I'm certain you have a *fin* for a tip, right?"

"You're certifiably insane. You will never get away with whatever you think you're doing to me."

"Shut the fuck up and don't make any sneaky moves to get away, or you're a dead man right here and now, get it?"

Tim tried to wriggle away from Lisa, forcing her to jam the pistol deeper into his side.

"I need to hear you say, 'yes', you get it. You won't make any sudden moves to get away."

"Yes, I get it, Jesus!" Tim said, seething.

"Good, now give the nice young man your ticket and a five. Smile, too."

Tim complied as he got behind the wheel of his Porsche, with Lisa jumping in shotgun. When they were both buckled in, she faced him at an angle, poising the SIG Sauer at his ribs.

"So far so good, Timmy," she said icily. "Now be a good son and call dad. Tell him we're on our way."

CHAPTER 69 FRIDAY AFTERNOON, LATE

Stan Heatherly clumsily followed his more agile partner, Phil Jorgensen out the door of the Beverly Wilshire Hotel. Nearly knocking over two elderly, high-heeled women dressed to the nines, Heatherly jumped into the passenger seat while Jorgensen slid behind the wheel. After starting the Crown Vic's engine and pulling away from the curb with a squeal, Jorgensen nervously drove toward the lot's main exit, edging over to the left-hand turning lane.

"Where ya headed? Back to the Benton's palace?" Heatherly asked, looking down at his partner's lap.

"Yeah, isn't that what we just agreed on?" Jorgensen stared at the red light.

"Yeah, but why the heck do ya think he went back home, knowing we're looking for him?"

"He had a chick with him. Reason enough."

"Oh, so he's gonna bang this chick in the same house he just killed his wife? Doesn't compute."

"Why not? The guy's obviously deranged enough to off his wife, so why not get some ass at the one place he feels most comfortable: his own home."

"Nah, I'm not buying it. I think we ought to—" Heatherly looked down at his partner's lap again.

"Why ya keep looking at my crotch?" Jorgensen stared at his partner.

"It's, uh…oh Jesus. I'm not looking at your crotch. I think you're sitting on something. A piece of paper. I don't know if it was there earlier or fell outta your pocket. I saw it right before you sat down."

"How come you didn't say anything before?" Jorgensen creased his forehead as he leaned to his left, pulling out the note from under his butt.

"Here," he said, handing it to Heatherly. "See what it is."

Stan Heatherly slipped on his reading glasses and scanned the handwritten note. Pursing his lips, he stared at his partner and said, "Get over to the right. We're going back to Ogilvie Wealth Management."

"What the hell?" Jorgensen said, looking in his rearview mirror. With no one behind him, he backed up and maneuvered the Crown Vic into the right-hand turning lane. Amazingly, the light was still red, but he could now turn onto Wilshire Boulevard.

"What the hell makes you think he's there?" Jorgensen asked as he zipped through traffic. "Who was that note from?"

"Someone named Hannah Clark who claims she has our perp and will hold him for us till we get to Ogilvie."

"What the hell? Who the hell is Hannah Clark, and more important, what connection does she have to the Bentons, specifically Tim?"

"We're about to find out."

"Where the hell am I, darling, and why the hell did you let me sleep so long?"

Saundra shot up with a start, blinked several times before swinging her legs to the floor. Sitting upright on the sofa against the far wall in her husband's office, she looked questioningly at Todd, who was intensely reading a report on his desk.

"Darling, why'd you let me sleep so long?" she repeated, louder this time.

Todd looked away from his report, staring at the far wall. "You were so tired, dear, and looked so comfortable, sleeping like a baby, I just had to let you snooze for as long as you needed."

"There you go again, lying like a son-of-a-bitch." Saundra yawned loudly, then wrapped the blanket around her shoulders. "Why is it suddenly so hard for you to say I was passed out drunk, and you let me sleep it off?" She chuckled and shook her head.

"Does it really make a difference if I'm brutally honest? What's the difference really, dear? I let you sleep, or I let you sleep it off. Let's not parse words. We have bigger fish to fry, lest you forget."

"Don't be so touchy, darling. It was only an observation, not a judgment. Anyway," she suddenly stopped, looking around for something, and not seeing it, seemed to lose her train of thought. "Anyway, it's not like I'm—"

"Are you looking for your cigarette holder, dear?"

"Actually, I am. Do you know where it is?"

"Right here, dear," Todd said, pointing to a decorative bowl on his desk.

"Oh, thanks, darling. I must have—"

"Mr. B., sorry to interrupt again, but I just got a frantic call from Tim," Angie said, wringing her hands and wobbling on her feet. "He basically said he's coming into the office. Now."

"Oh, how nice of him to come back after leaving so abruptly before," Saundra interjected, smiling at the younger woman. "Like a bat out of hell, actually."

"He said he was bringing someone with him."

"Who dear?" Saundra asked, suddenly perky and wide awake.

"All he said was that it was a woman."

"Be a good son?" Tim repeated, staring straight ahead, gripping the steering wheel, driving toward his office. "Just who the fuck are you?"

"With all of your smarts, you shoulda figured that out by now, big brother," Lisa said, raising the gun to his right temple, brushing the tip of the barrel lightly against his skin, tracing an imaginary line down to his neck.

"Fuck me!" he spat out, swallowing hard, visibly shaking.

"Indeed, brother. Fuck you, figuratively speaking of course, unless you're up to the literal version with my favorite firearm."

Tim stared straight ahead, blinking rapidly, biting his lips. With her free hand, Lisa punched a saved number on her cell phone and handed it to her brother.

"Here, talk to dad. Tell him we're on our way."

"How the fuck am I supposed to do that with you pointing a gun at me?"

"Take the fucking phone and talk."

Tim put the phone up to his left ear and when the line connected, it was Angie's voice he heard.

"Angie, it's me, Tim. Is dad still there?"

"He's on a conference call and asked not to be disturbed. I can get a message to him."

"Yeah. Please tell dad I am on my way to the office now and to wait for me. I'll be there in a few minutes."

"Okay, I'll let him know. What's this about?"

"I can't go into it now, but it's very important. And tell him I'm not coming alone. I'm, uh, bringing a woman with me."

"You got it."

Tim disconnected the call and handed it back to Lisa. "You're one sick bitch, you know that?" Tim sneaked a sideways peek at his sister, studying her visage, clearly not recognizing the woman sitting next to him.

"Speaking of sick—or should I say *dick*—what's up with you batting for the other team?" Lisa interjected vindictively. "All that incessant raping of me back in the day turn you off to women for good?"

Tim turned away from her, now clearly connecting the dots. He stared straight ahead, tightly squeezing his eyes shut for a few seconds. When he opened them, he realized he was drifting into the lane to his right, forcing him to steer the car hard to the left. "I don't know what you're talking about," said Tim, defensively. "You haven't seen me in however many years, and you have the nerve to attack me with such a statement? Jesus. You're even sicker than I thought."

"What's wrong with being gay? Are you telling me you're a closeted gay who's also homophobic? Wow. Just wow."

"Shut up and leave me alone," he said, breathing heavily. "Just cause you've taking me hostage—which is illegal, by the way—doesn't mean I have to talk to you."

"So sensitive. So defensive. What happened to the high and mighty Timothy Benton of yesteryear?" Lisa chuckled to herself.

Shaking his head, seemingly accepting his fate, he said, "I knew you'd come after me one day. Just didn't think you had it in you to do it like this."

"Like what? With a gun? Think you're the only Benton who's a crack shot?"

"'Crack shot'? That'd be pathetic if it weren't outright funny." Tim let out a forced laugh, his voice breaking. "So that's what you pride yourself in these days? What a joke you are."

Lisa raised the gun again to his temple, pressing it hard against his head, causing Tim to flinch and move away from her. "Do you really want to test my shooting skills right now?"

Tim continued to drive east on Wilshire, slowly taking a right turn on a side street before the Ogilvie building, his hands shaking, sweat visible on his brow. As he started to duck into the building's garage, he felt the pistol press harder against his temple, and Lisa's hot breath on his neck.

"Park on the street, right there," she said, nodding with her head.

"My car's not safe parked on the street. Someone may—"

"Just do it." Lisa waited for him to cut the engine before lowering her gun. Tim allowed his hands to fall to his lap, where they shook uncontrollably. Regarding him contemptuously, Lisa added, "So, how does it feel, big brother?"

"How does what feel?" Tim said in a cracked voice, staring straight ahead.

"Fear? Pure, unadulterated fear?

Tim glanced at her, then immediately looked away, staring down at his hands.

"It's okay, you don't have to answer me just yet. I have a strong feeling lots of confessions will be forthcoming when we get upstairs."

Chapter 70 Friday Afternoon, Late

"Who do you think Tim's bringing with him, darling?"

"I have no earthly idea, Saundra, but I'll tell you something: it smells to high heaven. I don't have a very good feeling about this at all."

"Oh, for Christ's sake, darling. Why are you always so full of gloom and doom? So pessimistic," Saundra said, superficially searching the room with her eyes. "Hey, where's my cigarette holder?"

"I am not pessimistic. I am a realist. There's a big difference."

"Whatever. Where'd you put my cigarette holder?"

"It's over here, dear. The realist in me snagged it away from you earlier before you burned down the building." Todd snatched it out of the decorative bowl on his desk and walked it over to his wife. "Here you go, dear. If you must smoke, please stay awake long enough to smoke the whole damn cigarette."

"I promise I will, darling." Saundra fished a pack of cigarettes out of her purse, inserted one into the holder, then ceremoniously lit it with her gold lighter. "So, do you want to know my guess?"

"Your guess for what?" Todd sat down behind his desk.

"My guess for who Timmy's bringing with him."

"Oh, yes. Who, dear?" Todd leaned back in his chair, staring at the ceiling.

"His attorney. A female attorney. I'll just bet he has a female attorney."

"You really think he has an attorney already? What on earth for?"

"Are you serious, Todd? You can bet your bottom dollar he's gonna need one." Saundra dramatically sucked on her slender cigarette holder, blowing the smoke toward the ceiling. "What did you think the police were doing here a few hours ago? They were looking for him to bring him into the station for questioning."

"That's outrageous! To even think he had anything to do with killing his own wife. Preposterous."

"Guess we've just reversed roles now with me being the realist about what's gonna happen to our first born. You know as well as I do the first person the police ever question is the spouse." Saundra puffed some more then stared off into space. "I'm confused, darling. You just told me not two minutes ago that you didn't have 'a very good feeling about this at all'. Why the sudden change?"

"I meant, dear, that I didn't have a good feeling about who our son might be bringing with him, that's all. And also, what he might do because of the situation he finds himself in." Todd shook his head, grimacing. "The probability that the cops think he murdered his wife is what's outrageous to me. I'll never in a million years think he's capable of murder."

"And that's why I know in my gut he got a female attorney. You'll see, darling. A female attorney to dazzle both the detectives and the prosecutor." Saundra smiled devilishly.

"*Prosecutor*? Jesus, Saundra. Aren't you getting a little ahead of yourself?"

"Not at all. I'm being a realist." Saundra smirked before taking a long drag on her cigarette.

"Okay, dear. You've made your point about being a realist. Enough."

"I'll refrain from saying I told you so when he walks in with his female attorney."

Todd opened his mouth to respond, then quickly closed it, shaking his head again and rolling his eyes. He then rose and walked over to a cabinet near where his wife was sitting on the sofa. With his back to the door, Todd didn't see or hear Tim and Lisa enter. The siblings stopped and stood quietly just inside the office.

"See, I was right, darling," Saundra said importantly. "Timmy got himself a female lawyer."

Tim and Lisa rode up silently in the elevator, her SIG Sauer .45-caliber pistol rammed into her brother's ribs. When they reached the 7th floor, Lisa nudged him out, following him to Ogilvie Wealth Management's reception desk and the startled face of Angie Lockhart. The odds Angie suspected Tim was being coerced from behind by this unidentified woman was even money, as Angie was simply relieved to see him.

"Hello Angie, we'll just go straight through to see my dad," Tim said emotionlessly. "No need to let him know."

"Okay, Tim." Angie looked questioningly at Lisa, who simply nodded when she passed her.

As they proceeded down the hallway, Lisa held a tight grip on his right arm while pressing the gun into his side. "No sudden moves or outbursts when we get inside dad's office or you're dead meat," she said jamming the barrel deep within his flesh. "Don't even think for one minute I'm joking. I have no qualms about doing it. None. I've been fantasizing about it for years."

"Then just kill me now," Tim seethed. "Do it and let's get it over with. My life is shit now anyway. I don't care anymore."

"You think I'm gonna let you off that easily? After all you did to me? You're dreaming, pal. You need to suffer before you're extinguished."

"You're insane. You'll never get away with it. The cops will come after you. *You're* dead meat."

"The cops will come, but not for me, big brother."

Tim thrust his shoulder forward in defiance, trying to pull away from Lisa, compelling her to yank even harder on his arm and press the gun deeper into his flesh. "You really shouldn't test me like the moron you seem to be. You are clearly clueless about the damage I can do."

"I already told you I don't care anymore. It's over. For me *and* for you."

"Where's dad's office? We seem to be walking forever."

"Right here. The next door on the left."

"It better be, otherwise—"

"Why are you doing this? I just don't understand. After all these years, you get some wild hair up your ass and have to, what, punish me?" Tim was shaking again.

"Open the door, walk in casually, as if it's the most natural thing in the world," Lisa said, lightly shoving him.

Turning around to give her a dirty look, he forthrightly gasped the handle of his father's office door and pushed it open.

Entering quietly, Tim and Lisa stopped just inside the room, letting the door automatically shut behind them. Saundra, not hearing them but aware of something amiss, turned to see her son, flanked by a woman, standing by the door. Locking eyes with the woman, Saundra smiled and said, "See, I was right, darling. Timmy got himself a female lawyer."

Hearing his son's endearing moniker, Todd jerked around to see who was there.

"She's not my lawyer, mother, she's actually–"

"Tim, who is this person? What the hell's going on?" Todd asked, perplexed.

"Timmy's right, Saundra," Lisa quickly interjected. "I'm not his lawyer and I'm certainly not advocating for him in any way. I'm just along for the ride, to make sure justice is served."

Saundra sat upright, striking a pose with her elongated cigarette, eyes ablaze as she stared at the mysterious woman. "What the hell are you talking about and how the hell do you now my name?"

"Tim, who is this?" Todd interjected. "Who have you involved in our personal affairs?"

"And why is she holding a gun to your ribs?" Saundra started to rise, but fell back onto the sofa, hitting her head on the wall. "Something's not right in the state of Denmark."

Chapter 71 Friday Afternoon, Late

Detective Phil Jorgensen pulled into the underground garage of Ogilvie's building, slipping into an open spot by the elevator. Stan Heatherly, hoping to get a head start on reaching the lift, released his seatbelt before his partner cut the engine. Riding up in silence, the two locked eyes halfway through as if telepathically transmitting information to one another that had previously been left unsaid.

"What are the odds this Hannah Clark person is the one we saw him leaving the hotel with?" Heatherly asked, stepping out of the elevator first.

"Pretty good, I'd say," Jorgensen said, catching up to his partner. "Still, what is her connection to him? Is there something deeper here, like a connection to the Bentons in general?"

"What I'm thinking—and I really think this could be viable—is she could very well be the jilted lover, who was promised a life with Tim after he offed his wife. Maybe he's been pussyfooting around the issue, and she's had enough of his lies."

"Wow, man. You either really have a wild imagination or you've been watching too many TV reenactment shows."

"Neither. It's called having a nose for detective work. You'll develop it, too, hopefully, with a few more years under your belt."

Jorgensen politely nodded to his senior partner and walked up to the reception counter at Ogilvie.

"You're back," Angie said nervously, biting her lips, recognizing the two detectives.

"Yes, we are, Miss Lockhart," Jorgensen said, reading the gold name plate resting in front of her on the counter. "We'd like to speak with Timothy Benton, please."

"Uh, oh," Angie stuttered, clearly flummoxed. "What's this about?"

"We'd like to speak with Timothy Benton," Jorgensen repeated. "Will you please get him for us?"

"Tim?" Angie swallowed hard.

"Yes, please get him for us."

"Let me see if he's here," she said, shuffling sideways, her eyes firmly planted on Jorgensen's face.

"Great. We'll wait right here."

Heatherly watched the receptionist flutter away like a hummingbird, her tiny, invisible wings propelling her down the hall. When she was out of sight, he took a seat against the wall and near a coffee table with an array of business magazines. Jorgensen paced the open space, contemplating the situation.

"She's buying time, dont'cha think Stan?" Jorgensen said, abruptly stopping in front of his partner. "I mean she's obviously hiding something, if not outright covering for Tim."

"Probably. But I can't blame her. The Bentons must have her on a short leash and she's scared to death to contradict anything they do or say."

"Yeah, but don't folks know things always come back full circle? It's not like you can hide anything forever."

"Oh, cut her some slack before you jump to any conclusions," Heatherly said, leafing through a magazine. "Boss man probably tells her to screen all his calls; check in with him first before letting anyone know he's in his office."

"Whatever. At this point I couldn't care less. We've wasted enough time already today." Jorgensen resumed his pacing, then stopped once again in front of Heatherly. "If she's not back in ten seconds, we're going in to find him."

Heatherly slapped the magazine down on the table. "What if she comes back and tells us he's not here. Then what?"

"You're the one who chose to believe the note from this Hannah person. Not me. I wanted to go back to his home. Where I still think he is."

"Give her another minute. Then we'll–"

Angie reappeared without so much as making a sound, looking like she'd just seen a ghost.

"Where's Mr. Benton?" Jorgensen asked, his eyes narrowed, his brow furrowed.

"Well, he's not, um, exactly–" Angie flushed, shaking her head.

"Not exactly what?" Jorgensen approached her aggressively, backing away grudgingly when Heatherly stood and reached for his arm.

Angie cowered in fear, lowering her head. "I was told to ask you to please wait three minutes before going in to get him."

"Three minutes? What the hell for?" Jorgensen spat out, inching closer to Angie. "So, he can have enough time to escape? Not on my watch." Jorgensen started for the hallway, but his partner grabbed him by the sleeve.

"What's going on in there, Miss Angie?" Heatherly asked gently, playing the good cop.

"He's, um, he's with his parents right now. It's all good, gentlemen," Angie said, her voice shaky. "Tim's not going anywhere. I promise."

When the detectives had arrived, Angie noiselessly slipped away from the reception desk, flitting down the hall like Tinkerbell, her feet barely touching the floor. When she arrived at her boss's office, she lightly rapped on the door before unceremoniously entering. What she witnessed unfolding inside was not at all what she'd expected. The blonde woman tightly held Tim by his arm while jabbing something metallic into his waist as her boss and his wife stared in disbelief.

"Oh, I'm sorry," she said, when the foursome turned to face her. "I didn't realize you were—"

"What's she doing in here again?" Saundra said, pointing an accusatory finger at Angie while glancing at Todd. "This is a private matter, and absolutely none of your business."

"Well, Mrs. B, I'm terribly sorry but there are two LAPD *homicide* detectives wanting to see Tim," Angie said, rocking sideways on her pumps. "They're waiting in reception for him. They won't leave till they speak with him."

"Tell them to get the hell out, or I'll call in my debts to the LAPD and they'll come here to yank them out themselves."

"I don't think you understand, Mrs. B. They're not leaving. They're really serious."

"Angie, tell them to please hold on a moment longer. We're just about done here," Lisa calmly interjected, smiling cordially at the secretary, then glancing down at her watch. "Tell the two gentlemen Tim's all theirs. In exactly three minutes."

Angie stood motionless, like a deer in the headlights, staring at the strange woman for a long moment before turning on her heels and shuffling out of the office. Unable to move, the gun pressing against his side, Tim stiffened, sending a pleading look to his father.

"Are you gonna let her do this to me, dad? After all we've been through?"

"You still haven't answered our question: who the hell are you and why are you doing this?" Todd glared at Lisa, clearly not recognizing her.

"Let's all calm down now and not waste precious time," Lisa said, staring at her parents, carefully taking in their visages. "As you just heard me tell Angie, I am turning Tim over to the police in exactly three minutes, minus fifteen seconds."

"Oh, for Christ's sake, girl, why on earth are you picking on our son? What has he ever done to you?"

"Saundra, please, you heard the woman. Let her speak and—"

"'Picking' on your son, you ask?" Lisa breathed out heavily, her nostrils flaring. "That's a very interesting comment. I'll let it pass for now, since time's running out."

Saundra pushed herself up, balancing her frail body by lightly touching the sofa's arm. "Who are you, goddammit, I demand to know right now!"

"I am a blast from the past who knows a thing or two about cosmic justice. One could even say I conceived the term—cosmic justice—having exacted it on others these past few months. Unconditionally, by the way, with no quid pro quo in the process.

"But now, you see, it's my turn. My turn for justice. Redemption. I've been waiting a long time for it. Far too long, in fact." Lisa adjusted her grip on Tim's arm, keeping her gun steady on his waist.

"What the hell are you talking about? Speak English, girl," Saundra yelled, waving a pale, thin arm in the air, wobbly on her feet.

"Justice is the answer. With contrition, of course," Lisa added, ignoring her mother's outburst. "You may think simply making amends may absolve you of your sins—what you allowed to happen all those years ago—but asking for atonement just wouldn't be enough for the gravity of the sins you committed. All of you committed."

"What the hell's wrong with you?" Saundra shouted, pushing herself away from the sofa. "Are you having some kind of a spiritual awakening right here in our office? Are you going to start speaking in tongues?"

"Tongues? No, I'm making a clear statement of fact. You have all sinned. Now you owe me. By the way, your time's almost up."

"Who are you and what do you want? Money?" Saundra inched closer to Lisa. "Because if it's money, then we'll gladly pay. Just leave us the hell alone."

"Money?" Lisa snorted disdainfully, removing the gun from Tim's side and pointing it directly at Saundra, who was now within a few feet of her. "It's always about the money, hasn't it? And about appearances; perception. The Bentons and the Ogilvies; all they care about is appearances, not substance. What others *perceived* went on behind closed doors. What others thought about our little nuclear family. Kids so well behaved. A husband so *very* successful! Everyone always dressed to the nines. Always appearing to be a perfect part of the community, when in reality everything was going to shit in a hand basket. Perception is reality, right, mother?"

Saundra spun her head around to catch Todd's gaze, but her husband wasn't looking her way, instead, he was studying the features of the heretofore strange woman in his office. Whirling back to face Lisa, Saundra opened her mouth, but it took several seconds for her brain to click into gear.

"Who the hell are you? Why did you call me 'mother'?"

Chapter 72 Friday Afternoon, Late

Frozen in place, Lisa stared down her mother, gun still pointed at her, perspiration forming on her upper lip. Lowering the pistol, she turned it on her brother, jabbing it once again into his ribs, feeling him flinch, hearing him moan softly. Readjusting her grip on his arm, she felt its dampness, fully sensing his fear of the unknown.

"Why did you call her 'mother'?" Todd blurted out, staring at Lisa, moving sideways toward a ceiling-to-floor cabinet.

Lisa blinked as she came out of her reverie, cleared her throat and looked directly at her father.

"Well, if you can't figure that out by now, then I can't possibly help you."

"Oh, for crying out loud, dad, don't you recognize your own daughter?"

"What the hell are you talking about, my 'own daughter'?"

Saundra inched closer to Lisa, first scrutinizing the gun, then her face. "The hell you say, son! This person is not my daughter. No daughter of mine would be jamming a gun into her own brother's ribs!"

"Even after all these years, you're still in denial," Lisa said, shaking her head. "What's astounding to me—what you don't even understand, mother—is I could have, and probably should have, killed your son-of-a-bitch son earlier this afternoon and you'd never have known I did it. His life is meaningless to me, because of his unrepentant actions. And because of your unrepentant behavior. All you and dad ever did was cover up for him, enable him to get away with the things he did to me—"

"Unrepentant? Denial? Wha...Who are you, really?" Saundra stopped inches from her daughter's face, still holding onto her cigarette. "You certainly don't look like Lisa. And my Lisa wouldn't talk like this or act like this. Lord in heaven. If it is really you, then we must have really fucked up for you to want to kill your own brother."

Todd remained quiet, continuing to move closer to the cabinet, keeping a close eye on Lisa.

"Time's just about up," Lisa said, carefully watching her dad's movements. "I have other people waiting on me, who need me, who appreciate who I am and what I do for them."

"I can't believe you're Lisa," Saundra said, for the first time calling her by her name, "the daughter I raised and who was located by my friend Pat, and who I was eagerly awaiting to see after all these years. In fact, I refuse to believe you're the Lisa I raised.

"You're a monster! You're inhuman, disgusting, vile, criminal. It's you who should be arrested by the cops, not my Timmy."

"Two detectives will be entering this office at any moment to arrest your darling son, Timothy, for the murder of his wife, Cyndi, and that's when I'll be leaving. So, you see it all works out in the end. Cosmic justice will prevail after all, even in the face of—"

"It wasn't his fault, Lisa dear," Saundra said, her demeanor taking a 180-degree turn. "He couldn't help himself, for God's sake. He did it because he was abused himself." Saundra covered her face with her hands.

"Oh, please, mother. Trying to justify his abuse of me to the bitter end. It's pathetic and it's not gonna work."

"Why are you bringing this up now?" Tim said, stiffening, staring his mother down. "She's not gonna believe a word of it. Besides, that was so long ago, I don't even remember it."

"See, mother? Even the sick fuck doesn't buy your weak excuse."

"'Weak excuse'? Those motherfucking priests who raped my son completely fucked up his life. Their dirty hush-up money never meant a thing, either. The priests were never punished
but were secretly moved to other parishes where they continued their depraved behavior."

"How convenient to place the blame on the priests rather than on the actual perpetrator. What's next? You're gonna blame the priests for making Tim gay?"

Tim yanked his arm away from Lisa, causing her to stumble backwards. Reaching for her gun, Tim's sweaty hand couldn't get a solid grasp on it, causing him to wobble sideways in the process. Shuffling to her right, Lisa avoided a bum-rushing Saundra, who ended up falling into the waiting arms of Stan Heatherly, who'd just entered the room with his junior partner, Phil Jorgensen.

"What the living hell is going on in here?" Heatherly said, propping up Saundra, who was trying to wriggle out of his grasp.

"Nothing we can't handle ourselves," Saundra said, combing her hair back with her fingertips, her cigarette holder stable between her fore and middle finger.

Seemingly forgotten, silently standing at the rear of his office, Todd had a long-barreled revolver in his hand aimed at Lisa, who had instinctively ducked in time and was now scrambling out of the room.

"What the fuck–" Jorgensen said under his breath, reaching for his Glock, aiming it at Todd, who now had his revolver trained on the detective.

"Drop the gun, sir," Jorgensen said sternly. Getting no immediate reaction or response, and obviously fearing for his life, he shot two successive rounds into Todd's chest.

Saundra screamed while Tim ran to his father's side. Jorgensen stood still, assessing the scene as his partner helplessly watched Lisa slip out of the office. Unable to stop her, Heatherly then hustled over to Todd, who was bleeding profusely from two bullet wounds. As Saundra continued to wail, Jorgensen approached a kneeling Tim, slapping handcuffs on him.

"Timothy Benton, you are under arrest for the murder of your wife, Cynthia Lynn Arrington-Benton," Jorgensen said monotonically, grunting when he uttered the word "arrest," hefting up a non-compliant Tim. "You have the right to remain silent–"

"You shot my dad, you motherfucking pig!" Tim shouted, resisting Jorgensen's strength. "Now he's dead, too. And it's all your fault!"

"You're arresting the wrong person," Saundra cried, throwing herself at Tim. "My son may be guilty of many sordid things, but he's no murderer!"

"Please, ma'am, move out of the way or I'll have to arrest you as well."

"Fuck off pipsqueak, or I'll call in my debts with the LAPD!"

Jorgensen blinked, then said matter-of-factly, "Last warning, ma'am."

Saundra stared Jorgensen down, then complied by moving back to the sofa. Sinking into its plushness, she sucked on her unlit cigarette, sighed and then lamented, "When will this all stop? When will the goddamned Ogilvie curse be lifted?"

CHAPTER 73 FRIDAY EVENING

Relieved to have narrowly escaped the chaos that went down in her father's office, yet still dazed by her parents' reaction to seeing her, Lisa drove back to Elizabeth's place, only vaguely aware of her surroundings. Driving instinctively toward her friend's apartment, she compartmentalized all the events of the previous hours in pursuit of her brother, satisfied but not truly content with the way things came to a conclusion. Satisfied to have closed the door for good on that ugly chapter of her life, Lisa couldn't help but feel a little disquieted with not finishing her brother off herself, as she intended to do from the beginning. Still, she couldn't have planned a more appropriate punishment for Tim had she strategically plotted out the scenario herself. Tim would now go down for the murder of his wife, undoubtedly pleading till the bitter end that he was innocent.

Lisa sighed loudly and grabbed her phone, punching in Elizabeth's number. All she wanted was a bit of normality, an innocent comment from Kendall and a genuine smile from Liz. She could honestly say she was tired of chasing down predators. Exhausted from hunting evil doers with no end in sight. Enough was enough. Her goal had been achieved, albeit not by her hand. All she wanted right now was to hear a sweet voice tell her his day had been fantastic, filled with sweetness and fun and–

"Hi Liz, it's me. What's going on? Can't wait to see you guys. I should be there in a few."

"*We're good, everything's cool, just waiting for you to get here,*" Elizabeth said. "*You sound tired. Beat. Everything good?*"

"Yeah. It's all good. All's well that ends well, as they say."

"Uh, that doesn't sound like the Lisa I know. What's up?"

"Yes, I am beat. I need a hot bath." Lisa got into the left-hand turning lane and waited for two cars to pass before turning. "Is Kendall okay?"

"He's good. The only hitch if you could call it that—"

"'Hitch'? What the hell does that mean?"

"Nothing to worry about, really. Nothing I couldn't handle."

"Speak to me. I don't like your tone."

"It's just that we ran into Kendall's social worker when we were—"

"Are you kidding me? What the fuck? What did she say?"

"Don't worry. We ditched her."

"Yeah, but now she knows he's back in LA and that can only mean one thing."

"What? What does it mean?"

"It means he's gonna be a ward of the state. They'll take him and place him in some godforsaken foster family. That's what they'll do. He'll die there. I will not let that happen."

"What do you mean? What are you going to do with him? You were going to turn him over yourself, you told me so, which will be the same result; foster system."

"No. I can't let it happen. He needs love, not a pretend family that's just doing it for the money they get from the county."

"'Pretend family'?"

"He needs a mother. He needs a mother's love. Someone to care for him and to teach him values and to play basketball with him. Someone to take him to Disneyland and fishing. And someone who'll teach him how to shoot. Well, eventually."

"Lisa? Are you trying to tell me something?"

"Yes, actually I am. I want to adopt Kendall. I want him to be my son."

"Whoa, whoa. What? Wait just a minute. I can't be—"

"Look, Lizzy, I'm just pulling up to your door. I'll be right in."

Elizabeth stared at her phone, watching it fade to black. Shaking her head, she placed the mobile on the kitchen table and strutted down the hall to her bedroom where Kendall was playing.

"Kendall, get your stuff ready, Lisa should be here any minute."

"Okay, Liz. I just need to use the bathroom."

"No problem, sweetie, I'll grab your—"

Distracted by the doorbell chiming, Elizabeth dropped Kendall's bag of toys and scooted toward to the front door, expecting to see the smiling face of her mentor and friend, Lisa. But to her horror, it was the vindictive visage of social worker, Charlene Buzzard-McMuffin, scornfully bearing down on her, nostrils flaring.

"I know Kendall is here, so don't even deny it," the social worker spat out, peeking behind Elizabeth, trying to scan the living room. "Those are his toys, in that bag," Charlene said, jabbing a pointed finger around Elizabeth. "You're not so clever after all, thinking you'd fool me into believing your fairytale."

"You have a lot of nerve coming here, Ms. Lizard-McMuffin, or whatever your name is," Elizabeth said, pushing the older woman backwards. "Kendall is not here and you're trespassing on private property. So, leave before I call the police."

"Get your hands off me before I call the police," Charlene said, wriggling free of Elizabeth. "And I won't just have you charged with assault, but I'll also tell them who you really are."

"You're not only crazy, but you're also delusional."

In an oval mirror hung on the wall to the left of the front door, Elizabeth caught the reflection of Lisa sneaking in through the back of her apartment. Watching Charlene's mouth moving but not hearing a word of what she was saying, Elizabeth tried her best to block the social worker's view of her apartments' interior.

Bobbing and weaving, blocking Charlene from seeing Lisa snatch Kendall from the guest bathroom, Elizabeth spied her friend sneaking down the hall with the kid in tow, entering her bedroom.

"...sure the police would love to know about you..."

She's done it, Elizabeth thought, trying to suppress a smile, watching Lisa rescue Kendall from certain institutionalization. *Lisa is amazing. She's my hero.*

"...murdering your husband."

Elizabeth whipped her head around and glared at Charlene.

"What did you just say?"

"You heard me. Loud and clear. You're a murderer. And I intend to tell the authorities that a felon has kidnapped an underage child whose mother has mysteriously disappeared." Charlene withdrew her mobile phone from her purse, scrolling for a name. "So, I'd say you don't have a leg to stand on."

Elizabeth's eyes widened, suddenly unable to respond, her jaw dropping as if she'd just seen a ghost.

"Hello, is this the Pacific Division?" Charlene spoke deliberately into the phone, staring down Elizabeth. "I want to report a kidnapping...yes, that's right, a child—"

Charlene Mullins-McMillan never knew what hit her, as she crumpled to the ground, her cell phone flying out of her hand, eventually landing on her ample midsection.

Smiling contentedly, Lisa grabbed Kendall by the hand, winked at her protégée and then disappeared into the damp Los Angeles night.

Regarding the knocked-out Charlene Mullins-McMillan straddling her front door jamb, Elizabeth called her shooting instructor, DJ, casually letting him know she needed him to come over right away. She'd have him drive Charlene to a park in downtown LA, leaving her to be found by the local homeless crowd. By the time Charlene Mullins-McMillan woke up from her unexpected nap, she'd have no idea what the hell happened to her.

9 781495 831096